Accidentally
AMISH

Accidentally AMISH

VALLEY OF CHOICE BOOK I

OLIVIA NEWPORT

BARBOUR
PUBLISHING

Dedication

For Caleb and Cana, luminous in my life

Acknowledgments

So many bits and pieces come together to make a novel. Thanks go to Rachelle Gardener, my literary agent, who first pointed out a newspaper article about the Amish settlement near Westcliffe, Colorado.

One of my uncles has spent years on a quest for information about our family history. He was the one who first turned up information about Jakob Beyeler, which made me curious enough to weave a historical thread into the contemporary fabric.

I found Diane Klopp by clicking an Internet link of indeterminate reliability. At the other end of the link, Diane had a copy of a hard-to-find book and gladly supplied missing research details about land grants and property descriptions in Berks County, Pennsylvania. As it turned out, she knew the land well, having grown up on a farm that adjoined the Byler property of my ancestors.

Thanks go to Lorene and Julianna Hochstetler, representing descendants of the Hochstetlers whose family history quite likely intersected the Bylers' in some way. Their comments on an early draft mattered.

And of course thanks go to the Barbour team for seeing what this might be and making it possible for so many to read.

One

$\mathcal{H}$is kiss was firm and lingering as he cradled her head in one broad palm.

"Annie," he murmured as he took in a breath. His hand moved to brush her cheek. He kissed her again.

Annie's stomach churned while her lips went on automatic pilot. Kissing Rick Stebbins was nothing new and, frankly, less exciting every time. But in the moment, it seemed the safest choice among miserable alternatives.

She pictured where her blue Prius was stashed in the parking lot behind the modest glazed-brick office building. A small red duffel lay on the passenger seat and a compact suitcase on the floor. The denim bag she had carried since high school, on the desk she was leaning against, held her laptop in its padded case. Car keys hung from a belt loop on her jeans. Her cell phone was in a back pocket.

Annie Friesen was ready.

Rick would never admit to what she suspected. More than suspected. She was no lawyer, but she knew it would take more evidence to make an accusation stick.

And Rick was a lawyer. *Her* lawyer. Her intellectual property lawyer. If only he had not slipped that extraneous document between the pages of the last contract awaiting her signature in triplicate. Whatever she thought she felt for him dissolved with that test of her attention to detail. He was the one who failed. She would sign nothing more from Rick Stebbins.

Rick took another breath. The air he exhaled on her neck was hot, and his fingers moved down to the front of her neck, toying with the gold chain resting on her collarbone.

I am so out of here, she thought, and ducked her head to avoid further lip contact. She stroked his tie before putting her fingers lightly on his chest and pressing him away gently.

"I have work to do," she said, "a meeting tonight. I told you about it."

"You can be late." Rick put his hands on her elbows.

She had seen him when he did not get his way—the weight of his hand slamming the desk in frustration, the set of his jaw, the frenzy of work that ensued. This time Annie did not plan to be anywhere in sight. He would calm down once he accepted that his plan would never happen. And then they would be over.

Annie shook her head and squirmed out of his grip. "You're the one who said I have to protect my copyright at all costs."

"Isn't that what you pay me to do?" Rick asked. "Are you sure I shouldn't be with you tonight?"

To Annie's relief, he did not move toward her again. "I want to try the civilized approach," she said. "Barrett and I have worked together a long time. Surely we can still talk to each other."

"He's adamant the new program was his idea. He even retained his own counsel." Rick laughed. "I guess he doesn't trust me any more than he trusts you."

"Our relationship has been no secret to anyone working here." Annie picked up the denim bag and slung it casually over one shoulder. *But it's over now. That was your last kiss, buddy.*

"Don't sign anything I wouldn't want you to sign." Rick raised his dark eyebrows at her.

What he wanted her to sign was precisely the problem.

Annie opened her office door, stepped through, and waited for Rick to follow. She locked it behind him and concentrated on breathing evenly. No one would think twice about seeing them together at the end of the day leaving the building that housed Annie and Barrett's small company.

They were more than successful. The first financial security software program Annie wrote, which Barrett marketed, sold rapidly. First, small credit unions bought it, then large ones, then conventional banks. Before long, a firm specializing in serving the financial industry recognized their program for the gem it was and bought them out. Annie was twenty-seven and had more money in her bank account than her parents had seen in all their working lives—or would ever see. She and Barrett decided to open another company and see if they could do it again, this time with a program that used store discount cards to track grocery inventory movement according to customer shopping habits and product placement. They also served a number of local companies with website design and custom software. These clients provided a working lab. Sometimes the problems she solved on a smaller level became just what Annie needed to get past a glitch in the bigger project.

Annie just wanted to write software. She was happy to see Barrett get rich right along with her. He was brilliant with the marketing and sales side and had earned his share of the fortune.

But Barrett wanted it all. He couldn't write software to find his way out of his gym socks, in Annie's opinion, but now that she was on the verge of a breakthrough, he wanted to squeeze her out of the latest deal.

And Rick was helping him. Annie was sure of it. She couldn't prove it, but that didn't mean she was going to lie down and let it happen. She merely needed a few days where she could think clearly and make a plan to fix this mess.

Outside the building, she pushed the button on her clicker,

and the lights on her car flashed.

"Call me later?" Rick's brown eyes glimmered in familiarity and suggestion.

"It might be late." *More like never!*

"It's never too late if it's you."

Aw. He can say the sweetest things. Not.

Annie let him peck her cheek and then walked briskly to her car while he seemed to saunter toward his on the other side of the lot. She navigated out of the maze of look-alike buildings in the complex and pulled out onto Powers Boulevard, a north-south arterial. Early on a mid-July evening, the Colorado Springs sky was still a stunning blue. The rush-hour traffic that glutted Powers in late afternoons had thinned—as much as it ever thinned on Powers—to midweek moviegoers, diners, and chain-store shoppers. Annie whizzed past one shopping center after another, a progression that also thinned and gave way to industrial complexes.

She glanced in her rearview mirror and glimpsed Rick's bronze Jeep two lanes over and six cars back.

Maybe she should hire a private eye. Or another intellectual property attorney. Someone who had a clue what to do. But she could do nothing with Rick Stebbins hovering over her every move, waltzing into the office at his whim, and making plans for them every night. A room in a bed-and-breakfast in Steamboat Springs awaited her, but she had to slip off Rick's radar.

Barrett was waiting—supposedly—and Rick was following. He was not even going to wait for a report from Barrett, apparently. Annie may have been trusting and naive up to this point, but she was not going to walk into a trap now.

Would he hurt her? Annie did not intend to risk finding out.

Heart racing, she turned right just where Rick would expect her to turn and headed west around the south edge of the city. A few seconds later, his Jeep slowly made the same turn. If she deviated from the predicted route too soon, Rick's suspicions would go into high gear. And if she made the wrong turn, she would hit a dead end. Neighborhoods of Colorado Springs were not tidy little squares on a grid. They were full of curves and angles and cutoffs and one-way streets and dead ends. Annie had grown up in this town and had been driving her own car for almost ten years. At the moment, she wanted to slap herself for not being sure where these side streets would take her.

Annie jerked the wheel to the right and swung into a sedate neighborhood of lawns and front porches, as if decades ago builders were determined to recreate the Midwest in the high desert climate. She couldn't squeal her tires without raising attention, but she pushed over the speed limit as much as she dared.

A moment later, Rick's Jeep appeared. Was it her imagination, or was he following more closely?

Annie tapped on the GPS and glanced at the map showing her location. Rick had a system, too. It would take some doing to outsmart him.

She had to try.

Moving generally in the direction Rick would expect, Annie varied her turns, making several maneuvers in quick sequence as if she were knowingly zigzagging across town. The area was coming back to her now. In high school she had a track teammate who lived down this way. Annie used to come down here on weekends after she got her first car, her first real independence.

Think! Where is that place you used to go?

The Jeep narrowed the distance behind her. Annie pounded the steering wheel. Her phone sang Rick's tune, and she ignored it. A moment later, it announced a text message. She refused to look, instead making another sharp turn into a hotel parking lot.

This was it. The hotel had been new when she was in high school. Now it had a ready-for-remodel quality, but it still anchored her geographical bearings.

Another message zoomed in. Again she ignored it. She cruised around the back of the hotel, staying as close to the building as she could. This was not the place where Barrett was waiting, and it was not where Annie had intended to go, but it would have to do. So far the Jeep had not followed her into the lot.

Annie pulled into an empty parking spot in the first row outside a back door of the building. She dropped the keys into her denim bag then pulled its wide strap over her head before picking up the small red duffel that held a change of clothes and a few personal items. This was not exactly going according to plan. The rental car was waiting for her in Castle Rock, where she would have brought the trail of her own car to an end by stashing it in a friend's garage. Now she would have to leave the suitcase and find another way to get there.

A glance over her shoulder reassured her that Rick had not made the same turn into the hotel lot.

Not yet.

She opened the car door, got out, closed the door behind her, and listened to it lock. Behind the hotel, a grove of aspen trees shuddered in the wind, their leaves twinkling in waning sunlight. And beyond that, if it was still there, was a lumber distribution center the local contractors used. Specialty woods. Trims, cabinets, that sort of thing. Annie used to go to the parking lot for purposes she would never have admitted to her parents.

The Jeep's headlights glared just as Annie reached the edge of the grove. She pressed up against a tree, knowing that a slender aspen would never fully hide her form. Golden aspens that were a spectacular sight on a sunny autumn mountain drive were not much use for hiding behind in the summer. Perhaps the growing shadows would disguise her, though, if she kept still.

Rick parked the Jeep. He got out. His dress shoes clicked against the pavement.

Annie wished for someone—anyone—to pull into the lot right then, or come out the back door of the hotel.

He stood at the edge of the grove now. Annie's denim bag bulged on one side of her, and her red duffel on the other.

Way to be inconspicuous.

"Annie, I know you're here." His bass voice resonated confident, calm. "It would seem we understand each other fully now."

Annie held her breath.

Rick advanced into the grove.

Annie suddenly itched at the base of her neck. And her hands. And her twitching nose. She refused to scratch.

"I don't know why you're running, Annie. Nobody wants to hurt you." Rick's silky timbre slithered between the trees. "We just want you to sign some papers and this can all be over. It's sound business."

More sound for him than for her. She had to disappear for the next few days so there could be no question of her signature on any documents.

He was three feet away from her. With one turn of his head, she would be done for.

Annie heaved the red duffel bag and hit her target, thankful for the weight of a hairdryer. Rick stumbled off balance for a split second, tripping over the bag and swearing. Annie ran through the grove. She heard his footsteps behind her, but the voice of her high school track coach rang in her ears, warning her not to turn her head to monitor a competitor's progress. The grove was not deep, and she was soon out of it and in the parking lot of the lumber center. Several trucks of various ages and sizes created a maze in the small lot. The first truck she spied, a red pickup with a long bed, had a tarp folded away from one corner with the back gate down. Annie hurtled herself onto the gate without breaking stride and pulled the tarp over her. Knees pulled against her chest, she wedged in between two neat stacks of lumber at the edge of the bed.

And held her breath again. Her lungs burned in fury.

Rick thudded past. "Annie!"

His volume startled her, but she did not move. Not one millimeter. His steps retraced their route.

Annie heard the shuffle of other footsteps. *Barrett!*

"Can we help you, sir?"

No. Not Barrett.

Rick stopped. "Looks like I need to come back when the place is open," he said amiably.

Annie could picture the grin that surely accompanied the comment. No doubt he had his hands in his pants pockets, looking friendly and harmless.

"They open at seven in the morning," the mystery voice answered. A pause. "Are you a contractor?"

Sure. In the dark-suit attorney's uniform Rick wore.

"I don't want to hold you up," Rick said. "I'll come back another time."

His footsteps tapped away. Annie took a real breath.

"Odd fellow, don't you think?" the voice said. "Dressed funny for this place."

Another man chortled. "You're standing beside a man in homemade clothes, and you want me to agree that a fellow in a suit is odd?"

Both men laughed. One of them yanked on the tarp and secured a corner onto a hook.

"I'm so used to you, Rufus," the first man said. "I don't think of you as odd."

"Well, you're a good friend, Tom. Let's go home."

"Let me just fasten everything down and we'll get on our way."

Go home? Where is home?

Annie winced as the truck's gate slammed shut so close the hair on her arms fluttered. She clutched her denim bag. The man tugged on the far corner of the tarp and hooked it in place. She did not dare reveal herself now. She couldn't be sure where Rick was. How would she explain herself to the truck's driver?

Two doors slammed, the engine turned over, and the truck backed up.

A third text message buzzed in Annie's back pocket. She didn't have room to reach for the phone.

Two

Pinholes in the tarp where the canvas threads were stretched thin suggested the sun soon would be fully set.

Without access to her cell phone, Annie could only guess at how long she had been squatting in the back of the truck between piles of lumber. Ten minutes? Twenty? The driver left behind city streets for a highway. Annie felt the acceleration and merging sensation that forced her body to lean to one side.

I-25.

But which direction? Even in daylight Annie used the view of the mountains to the west of Colorado Springs to orient herself. Under a tarp in a vehicle that made multiple turns, she had long ago lost any sense of direction. If they were on the way to Denver, she would know where she was when the vehicle finally stopped. From there she could go anywhere she wanted or needed to go. If they were headed south, getting out of Pueblo would not be as easy. Walsenburg would be impossible. Annie pictured herself on the side of the interstate with her thumb out.

She still clutched her denim bag to her chest, her arms now wedged in by her own knees. With her phone, she could give herself a hot spot Internet connection and work on her computer anywhere. At the moment, though, not being able to open her laptop meant the new software at the heart of her flight was being tested. If it withstood the hacking attempts Barrett was surely making at that moment, Annie would know it was secure. Barrett would not be happy when he discovered the changes she made a few hours ago—changes that took protecting her creative work into her own hands. How long would it be before she could decipher his efforts and know that her own work had done its job?

Getting her laptop open under these conditions was physically impossible. If she could get to her cell phone, though, she could get online and discern what Barrett was doing. Inch by inch, she twisted an arm away from her chest and down the side of her torso. She just needed to slip her fingers into her back pocket. She tipped her hip up as far as it would go.

No luck. Just wasn't going to happen. All she accomplished was scraping her forearm and making her shoulder sore.

She was cut off. Completely. Indefinitely. This had never happened to her before. In resignation, Annie leaned her head against the wood stacked on one side. Mentally she created a list of the first steps she would take as soon as the pickup stopped.

Wherever it stopped.

Lumber creaked with the sway of the bed. Exhaustion engulfed her.

The truck stopped. Annie bolted awake—with no notion of how long she'd slept.

Please, God, don't let me be in Texas.

A few seconds later, she heard the truck doors open and slam shut again.

"Are you sure you don't want to unload tonight?"

Annie tried to reconcile the voice with the ones she'd heard earlier and the names they exchanged in the parking lot. Rufus was the deeper voice, Tom the pleasant tenor.

"No Rufus, it's ten o'clock. That's late, even for me, and it's the middle of the night for you."

"Tom, I hate to tie up your truck," Rufus said. "I'm sure you have other loads to haul tomorrow."

"I'll meet you at my place first thing," Tom said. "We can go to the job site together. We'll have more help unloading there. It won't take long."

"I hate to say it," Rufus said, "but the load is probably safest at your place for the night."

"I don't understand why Karl Kramer doesn't leave you alone." Tom's voice spat irritation. "You do good work for a fair price."

"He doesn't think it's fair. He thinks I'm underbidding him to force him out of business."

"That's ridiculous."

"Tell that to Karl Kramer." Rufus's rich voice softened.

"I have half a mind to do just that," Tom said. "But I guess it won't be tonight. I'd better get home."

"At least let me get you a glass of lemonade before you get on your way." Rufus perked up again. "It's been a long, hot day."

"I would accept that gladly."

"Maybe some of *Mamm*'s peach pie?"

Tom hesitated. "I'd better not. Tricia has me on some new-fangled diet."

The voices drifted away after that, and Annie couldn't decipher what they said. They were only going for a glass of lemonade. She did not have much time to figure out where she was.

Annie fumbled in the dark for some sort of latch to release the gate. She couldn't find it. Finally, she ran her hand along the edge of the tarp until she found a hook, unfastened it, climbed over the gate, and hooked the tarp back in place. Crouching beside the truck, she took in her surroundings.

A barn. Definitely not Denver. About forty feet off was a sprawling two-story log home with a dim light emanating from one corner of the first floor. Annie didn't see any other lights, though she saw the shadows of what looked like a chicken coop and some sort of workshop.

I am in the boondocks.

After a quick stretch, she reached into her back pocket for her phone. A touch on the screen brought it to life.

10:08.

Strong signal bars.

I must be close to someplace.

A horse neighed behind her, making her jump. Annie's eyes adjusted to the shadows, and the horse nudging the edge of a split-rail fence came into focus.

At least it's not a yelping dog giving me away.

But did she want to stay here? She would have to sit out the night and figure out where *here* was in the morning. Or she could get back in the truck, uncertain where she would end up. Tom's place. Where was that?

The horse neighed again at the same time that Annie heard voices returning.

"What does Dolly want?" Tom asked.

"Once she's in the barn, she'll settle down," Rufus answered. "I'll see you in the morning, Tom. Thanks again for hauling the load."

Annie's decision was made. She had no time to climb back into the bed of the truck. She had to get out of sight—now! She dashed through the shadows to the barn's door, slightly ajar, and slipped inside.

Tom got behind the wheel and started the engine. Rufus slapped the side of the truck as it rolled past him.

"Come on, Dolly," he said. "Time for bed."

Annie glanced around the dark barn. There was not so much as a nightlight. As if in response to her presence, a cow mooed and a second horse snorted. Annie had no idea if a barn had a back door, but she felt her way along the stalls, hoping for one nevertheless. Rufus was sure to notice his animals acting strangely. It was just too dark, though, for her to find an escape. The moon outside was barely a sliver, and the barn's walls were solidly built, admitting no light. The horse snorted again, and a tail swished against a stall wall.

The barn door whined slightly as Rufus opened it wide. Annie froze in place, out of options. With one hand, Rufus led Dolly, and with the other he reached into the darkness. A moment later a gas lantern cracked the shadows. Annie could see now that Rufus would have to walk past her to reach an empty stall.

Dolly pawed the ground with one hoof.

"Come on, girl," Rufus urged. "I'm tired. We have a long day ahead of us tomorrow."

Annie scanned the barn. A buggy. Two buggies, actually. A large black one and a smaller one, more of a cart. They looked just like the pictures in history books illustrating the nineteenth century.

Her head turned toward Rufus now. Violet-blue eyes gleamed in the lantern's light, and brown hair fell across his forehead under a hat. Annie blinked at the straw hat then assessed the rest of his clothing—a plain, collarless, long-sleeved dark blue shirt, sturdy black trousers with suspenders, heavy brown work shoes. Her eyes widened. He was *Amish*!

Rufus stopped his forward progress and stared at her.

"I'm sorry, Rufus," Annie stammered. "I can explain."

He stiffened. "How do you know my name? Did Karl Kramer send you here to cause trouble?"

"No! I don't even know Karl Kramer."

"I don't want to seem inhospitable, but what are you doing in my barn?"

"I need a place to stay for the night." Annie put her hands up, palms out. "I'll get out of your way first thing in the morning."

"How did you get here?"

"It's a long story."

Annie held still under the inspection of his violet-blue eyes. Finally, Rufus led Dolly down the center of the barn and into her stall. Annie held still as man and horse passed. Once the horse was settled, Rufus closed the stall and turned back to Annie.

He crossed his arms across his chest. "I enjoy a good story."

"I didn't say it was a good story, just long." Annie's mind raced with questions of her own. "The truth is, I'm not even sure where I am."

"I can help you with that. You're in the San Luis Valley between the Wet Mountains and the Sangre de Cristos. In the daylight, the view is spectacular."

"I'm sure it is."

Rufus seemed in no hurry to leave. "You never said how you know my name."

"I heard you and Tom talking." Annie exhaled slowly.

"How do you know Tom?"

"I don't."

He pressed his lips together. "Perhaps you can give me the short version of your story."

Annie sighed. "I was. . .in a bit of trouble and had to hide."

"And?"

"I stowed away."

"In Tom's truck?"

She nodded.

"What kind of trouble are you in?"

"I'd rather not say," Annie answered. "If you want me to leave tonight, I will. Right now."

"And go where? How?"

Annie tilted her chin up. "I can take care of myself. I don't want to be trouble."

They stared at each other for a solid thirty seconds.

"I have an empty stall. I'll get you a quilt and some fresh hay," Rufus finally said. "But I'm not going to leave a gas lantern in the barn with an *English* who doesn't know to be careful."

Rufus woke before the sun, as he had since childhood. As always, his mother already stirred in the kitchen downstairs. Even when they had first moved from Pennsylvania five years ago and the early weeks in Colorado were erratic and challenging for all of them, the rhythm that formed her forty-seven years hardly wavered. In a few more minutes, his sisters Sophie and Lydia would be up, along with brothers Joel and Jacob.

He got out of bed and dressed quickly, thinking of the mysterious guest in the barn. She was like Ruth, the same slender build putting skin on fierce determination. Rufus moved into the hallway, cocked his head to listen to the sounds below, and ducked into the small room where his sister used to sleep. On the hook behind the door, he found what he was looking for. He folded a deep purple dress and a white bonnet, then with quiet steps, he descended the stairs and slipped out of the house.

It was silly to think the *English* would want the dress. She wanted to leave, did she not? She had promised she would leave. Whatever happened to her the night before surely rattled her, but he was certain she was not the sort to be frightened in the daylight.

But something had compelled her to trust her welfare to a stranger's truck. He only wanted her to know she was welcome and it was safe to stay if she wanted to.

He did not wake her. She slept on the quilt, her arms around her bag, her hair the same color as the hay behind her head. She was an *English* woman, yet he could not shake the sense that she somehow belonged here in his barn. He watched as her long eyelashes fluttered in resistance to coming wakefulness.

Rufus laid the folded dress next to her hair spilled on the hay then went back to the house for his breakfast.

Annie woke abruptly with the distinct sense that someone had been there. She pushed herself upright and immediately checked her bag for her laptop then patted the bulge in her back pocket. Relief. Everything was right where it should be. Except her. She definitely did not belong here. Annie pulled her phone out and touched the screen. The three text messages she ignored the night before were now seven.

Don't be a fool, Annie.

You're throwing everything away.

This is not over.

She deleted the rest unread then checked her e-mail. Four messages, four taps on the Delete option.

Then she saw the dress. The deepest, richest purple cotton cloth she had ever beheld, the color of an African violet bloom.

She was sure it had not been there the night before. Rufus must have brought it. But why? She reached for it and let the smoothness of its texture slide across her hands.

This time Annie heard the barn door open, and Dolly was nudging the stall door looking for attention. Rufus stood silhouetted in the opening, the rising sun behind his head brushing the sky pink.

Three

Annie lurched to her feet, dropping the folded dress and clumsily brushing hay from her clothing.

Rufus pulled the barn door nearly closed with one arm then moved toward her. "I brought you some breakfast."

"That was kind of you." Annie ran one hand through her hair, dislodging more hay.

Rufus set a tray on a small stool and backed away.

"Thank you." Tentatively, Annie lifted the dish towel that covered the tray and discovered hot buttered biscuits and a bowl of applesauce. "I found the clothes. Thank you for that as well."

He smiled. "You're being polite, but I don't suppose you can really see yourself wearing my sister's dress."

Annie liked the way his cheeks spread when he smiled—then she could not believe the thought had crossed her mind under the circumstances. He was Amish, after all. "That smells good." She picked up a biscuit.

"My mother is a very good cook."

Annie took a hefty bite. She had not eaten since breakfast the previous day, so extenuating circumstances or not, she was ravenous. She swallowed two large bites rapidly.

23

"Um, about the clothes?" she said.

Rufus shrugged. "It was just a thought."

"And thank you so much." She just was not sure what the thought was. "I promised I would leave first thing this morning."

He nodded. "I began to think about what made you run in the first place."

"I can't imagine what you must think of me."

"Maybe you have a good reason to be here. Perhaps it is *Gottes wille*. God's will."

Annie swallowed more of the moist biscuit and scooped a spoon-ful of applesauce. *God's will?* That thought had not occurred to her.

"You don't have to eat so fast," Rufus said. "I did not tell anyone you are here."

Annie forced herself to wait a few seconds before her next bite. "You've had your breakfast, I suppose."

He nodded.

"Are you even supposed to be talking to me?"

"You're in my barn. I'd say that gives me good reason."

"But you didn't have to feed me."

"It's the Christian thing to do."

"Thank you again. I'll get out of your hair in just a moment. How far will I have to walk to find. . ."

"Civilization?"

His arched brow made Annie look away. "I didn't mean anything. I'm sorry if I offended you."

He shook his head. "It takes much more to offend. We're about five miles from Westcliffe. I can take you. I'm going anyway."

"That's right. You're meeting Tom," Annie said.

"Whom you don't know," Rufus reminded her.

"I know he'll be waiting for you to empty his truck." Annie wiped her mouth on a corner of the dishcloth. "I don't want to hold up either of you."

"It's no trouble. I'll get the buggy ready."

Both horses neighed softly, and behind Rufus the barn door cracked opened slowly. A small boy shoved against its weight, gradually widening the gap.

Annie's eyes widened as well. Her gaze went back and forth between Rufus and the boy. The resemblance was remarkable. *His son.* Something in her sank.

Triumphant, the boy brushed the dust off his hands and for the first time looked inside the barn. He wore black pants and a white shirt. From under his straw hat, straight-cut blond hair hung over his forehead. He swirled one bare toe in the dirt of the barn floor and stared at Annie.

"I'm Jacob Beiler," he said. "Who are you?"

Rufus chuckled softly. "Good question."

"I'm Annie. Annalise, actually. It's nice to meet you, Jacob."

"Do you have a last name?"

"Friesen," Annie answered. "I'm Annalise Friesen."

"Are you from Pennsylvania?" Jacob asked, moving to stand next to Rufus. "I'm from Pennsylvania, but I do not remember Pennsylvania."

"I'm from Colorado," Annie said. "I've never been to Pennsylvania."

"Jacob was a baby when we moved here." Rufus rested a hand on Jacob's shoulder. "We've only been here about five years."

"Oh, I see." Annie supposed a wife would be the next character to enter the scene.

Rufus smiled again. "You didn't even know there were Amish people in Colorado, did you?"

"Well no," she admitted. "I don't come this way often."

"So why are you here now?" Jacob asked.

"Don't be nosy, Jacob," Rufus said.

"I'm not nosy," the boy responded. "*Mamm* says I'm just curious about everything."

"*Ya*. But don't be so curious about this. Have you had your breakfast yet?'

25

"I forgot," Jacob said. "The sky called me, and I wanted Dolly to see."

Another form split the glare coming through the open barn door. A woman paused to inspect the scene. "*Guder mariye*."

"*Mamm*, Annalise is here," Jacob announced.

"*Ya*. I see that." The woman's floor-length dress was a deep turquoise under an apron that matched the purple garment still folded at Annie's feet. A white bonnet sat loosely on her head, the ties hanging down her chest. "I'm Franey Beiler. I see you have met two of my sons."

They're brothers! "I'm pleased to meet you as well," Annie said awkwardly. She stooped quickly and picked up her bag. "Perhaps I should leave now."

Franey looked from Rufus to Annie, but her face remained open, even amused. The hard edge Annie expected from an Amish mother who had just found her son in the barn with a strange woman did not appear.

"I'm sure you're wondering why I'm here," Annie said. "Rufus had nothing to do with it. I take full responsibility."

"I raised my son to give a cup of cold water to a traveler in need," Franey said. "Or at least a cup of *kaffi*. Do you like *kaffi*?"

Coffee? "Very much."

"I'm going to take her into town," Rufus said. "I have to meet Tom."

"Tom can wait ten minutes while our guest straightens herself out," Franey said. "Please come to the *haus*, Annalise." She gestured out the wide door toward the house. "Sophie should have been out to milk the cow by now."

Annie felt compelled to accept the invitation and fell into step beside a woman she judged to be about twice her age—or perhaps not quite that old. If Rufus was her son and Jacob was her son, Franey Beiler had spent a lot of years having babies. She must have had a handful by the time she was Annie's age.

In the house, Annie made a couple of false starts with the

water pump at the bathroom sink but finally succeeded at splashing water onto her face. She dug in her bag for something to tie her hair back and stared at her reflection in a small, dull mirror. If she didn't know better, she would not have guessed that the young woman who stared back was a successful software creator who already had made a small fortune.

Yesterday morning she woke in her own paid-for condo and drove to her own office in her own loan-free car. She had known the day would bring upheaval, but she had not expected to end up in the San Luis Valley preparing to ride in an Amish buggy.

Where in the world was Westcliffe, anyway? What would she do when she got there?

Annie didn't have a clue.

Safely behind the closed door, she opened her laptop. She pulled her phone out of her pocket. Within seconds, she found service and used it to give herself a hot spot connection to the Internet. A quick look at Barrett's web activity was all she needed for now. When she got to Westcliffe, she would figure out her next physical move.

She could see that Barrett had tried. Persistently. For a long time. But he had not hacked her system. Annie saw no activity in the last several hours and imagined Barrett and Rick had knocked some furniture around before deciding to sleep a few hours. They would try again. Determination was one of the qualities Annie admired most in Barrett.

Annie couldn't help opening a new search window and typing in the words "Amish bathrooms." She scanned through information that surprised her then laughed softly at herself. She was standing in an Amish bathroom, after all. Other than the lack of mirrors and excess lighting, the basics were there. Annie closed the computer and slipped it back into her bag.

In the hall, she smelled the rich fragrance of serious coffee and followed the waft to its origin. Despite its log exterior, the home was spacious with generous rooms flowing into each other. The simplicity of furnishings slowed her pace with their beauty. An armless rocker beckoned, and Annie let her finger trail along its curved back. She had not sat in a rocker in years. Over the dark, scrubbed hardwood floor, a handcrafted rug warmed the space with its rich hues of browns and blues. Simple maple tables accented the room, each one also clearly serving a purpose, holding a lamp or basket. A German Bible sat on its own stand, the large volume prominently displayed. Annie squeezed her eyes shut, trying to picture the last place she had seen her Bible.

"There you are," Franey said when Annie finally found her way to the kitchen. She handed Annie a steaming mug. "*Kaffi?*"

Annie sipped carefully to test the temperature of the coffee, grateful for the first swallow washing down her throat. Out the kitchen window, she saw a slim girl in a gray dress move toward the barn. She could not have been more than twelve or thirteen— Sophie, she supposed.

"Rufus said you're in trouble," Franey said.

Annie was startled by her directness. "Well, I. . .ran into an unexpected circumstance. I'm not sure it qualifies as trouble. I'll figure it out. I'm good at solving problems."

Franey nodded. "We don't have too many visitors from the outside in our *haus*, but I trust Rufus."

"I got myself into this mess," Annie was quick to say.

"It is not our way to turn our backs on someone who needs help."

"Thank you," Annie said again. She couldn't imagine how an Amish family could help her out of her muddle, but she did appreciate Franey's sincerity.

"The buggy is ready," Rufus said, saving her from having to muster a more complex response.

Annie took a deep swallow of coffee. "So am I."

A few minutes later, Rufus clicked his tongue to get Dolly moving. Annie shared the bench of the small green, cartlike buggy with Rufus. Behind the open-air bench was flatbed cargo space.

It would not accommodate nearly as large a load as Tom's truck, but Annie supposed Rufus used the cart frequently to haul loads of wood for whatever his work was. She pondered the network of leather strapping across Dolly's brown haunches, the animal's swinging white tail, and the smooth shafts of wood that connected the cart to Dolly's shoulders. With no experience to compare to, she had little vocabulary available for what she saw. The wooden wheels cranked in rhythm to the horse's pace. Annie turned her head slightly at the drift of an unpleasant odor.

Annie wondered if it would be polite to ask how long it took a horse and buggy to traverse five miles. Rufus carefully kept the rig to the side of the road, leaving ample room for cars to pass them. She watched the cars, one after another, and could not help noticing the empty passenger seats in most of them. Although Dolly seemed to keep up a brisk trot, to Annie the pace was torturously slow.

"You might as well enjoy the scenery," Rufus said. "I don't imagine you get to see views like this too often."

"Colorado Springs is beautiful, too."

"Somehow I suspect you don't see the views there, either." Rufus lifted one hand from the reins to gesture. "God's beautiful creation."

He was right. Other than glancing at the mountains to remind herself which way was west, she paid little attention to the landmarks of nature. Her eyes were on the road or on her computer screen or on her phone display. Her world spun around clicks and taps and memory and data patterns. Beside her, Rufus took in a deep draft of air, and Annie found herself doing the same.

"Is there a place in Westcliffe to rent a car?" she asked, recovering her purpose.

Rufus laughed. "The population is 417."

"Oh."

"There's always Silver Cliff, next door." He paused. "Population 523."

Annie flushed. She would just have to figure it out when she got there. She turned her head and looked in both directions, understanding she truly was in a rural mountain valley. Changing the topic of conversation seemed prudent.

"What brought your family to Colorado?"

"Look around. Land. Wide-open spaces. Pennsylvania is getting crowded, and land is expensive." Rufus paused for another deep breath. "I decided to try my hand out here, and my parents chose to come, too. I have younger brothers who will one day need land of their own."

"Was it hard to leave?"

He shrugged. "Two of my *brieder* are married and chose to stay in Pennsylvania. I know my mother misses them—and especially the *kinner*. She only hears about her grandchildren in letters. About fifty Amish families are scattered around the valley, so we do have company."

"Beiler." Annie crooked a finger under the gold chain at her neck. "I've heard that name somewhere."

"It's a common Amish name."

She shook her head. "I don't know any Amish people. I heard it somewhere else." She sat up straight. "It's my great-great-grandmother's name. That's what it is. Malinda Byler. I've seen it in the family Bible. She married Jesse Friesen."

"Do you have ancestors from Pennsylvania?"

"I don't know," she said. "I'll have to ask my mother."

He looked at her out of the side of his eyes. "Speaking of your *mudder*, does she know you're in trouble?"

Annie looked away from him. "I'll call her when I get a chance."

"You should go see her. A telephone is useful for business, but it's not a relationship."

"I will. I promise." *He's rather free with advice,* Annie thought.

Rufus turned the buggy on a new road. "We're almost there. If you don't mind, I'll stop by Tom's and let him know I'll be right back."

Annie spotted the red pickup from a hundred yards away.

"Something's wrong," she said. "The truck doesn't look right." It sat too low to the ground.

They both peered down the road. Tom stood outside his truck with a phone to his ear. Rufus urged Dolly to trot faster. Annie leaned forward as Tom turned and waved. He flipped his phone closed just as the buggy came alongside the pickup.

All four tires were slashed.

Four

In one practiced motion, Rufus pulled Dolly to a halt and jumped out of the buggy. Annie took a little longer to climb down with more care. She stood behind Rufus, who squatted beside the left rear tire. She had a clear view of the back of his neck, where brown hair met white collar.

Tucking his phone into his shirt pocket, Tom looked at Annie, questions in his eyes.

"I'm Annie," she said. "It's complicated."

"I would imagine so." Tom glanced at Rufus.

"Do you know when it happened?" Rufus slid a finger along the gap in one tire.

"I didn't hear anything," Tom said.

"They might have parked at a distance and come in on foot. Looks like a big knife to me."

"You're really not going to tell me why you have an *English* woman in your buggy?" Tom asked.

"I found her in the barn."

"Oh. That explains it."

"Before that she was in the back of your truck." Rufus stood up and flipped back the tarp. "My guess is she was wedged into that space right there."

Annie nodded.

Tom's expression hardened. "Who are you? If Karl Kramer put you up to this, you're making a mistake."

"She doesn't know Karl," Rufus said. "She's harmless."

Harmless? Not exactly the word Annie would have chosen. If only Rufus Beiler knew her net worth and what she could do with a computer.

Tom twisted his lips to one side then turned his attention to Rufus. "It's time for you to get the police involved, my friend."

Rufus shook his head and stood up. "I understand if you need to report this because your property was damaged, but it is just not our way to get involved with the *English* courts."

"How many times are you going to let things like this happen?" Tom asked.

"As many as it takes, I suppose."

Takes for what? Annie wondered. "That's what Kramer is counting on," Tom said. "This nonsense is not going to stop as long as he knows that you won't do anything about it. He'll think all he has to do is outlast you, and you'll leave."

"The valley holds plenty of work for both of us. He will figure out I mean him no harm."

"You give him more credit than he deserves." Tom paced slowly around his truck, shaking his head.

"I'm sorry you suffered for your kindness toward me," Rufus said, "and I understand if you don't want to taxi for me anymore."

"Of course I'll taxi for you. I have insurance for stuff like this," Tom said. "But the police are not going to believe this was a random prank. I live too far out of town. It won't take a rocket scientist to trace this to the fact that I was hauling *your* lumber."

"*Es dutt mirr leed.* Again, I'm sorry."

"I'll be fine. It's you they're after."

"Who's after you?" Annie wanted to know. "Who is this Karl Kramer you keep talking about?"

Tom and Rufus stared at her.

"Okay, so I'm sticking my nose in," Annie admitted. "But after all, I'm standing right here. Am I supposed to cover my ears and sing while you have this conversation about an obvious crime?"

Tom glanced at Rufus. "She's got spunk."

If you only knew. Annie dug one heel into the dry soil.

"What would you suggest we do about the load?" Rufus asked Tom. "I was planning to take Annalise to town then come back to ride with you to the job site."

"Go ahead and take her in while I figure something out."

"Hello?" Annie said. "No one answered my question."

"It does not concern you," Rufus said.

"Maybe I can help." Reflexively, she armed herself with her cell phone. "What harm can come from telling me what's going on? I do rather well at getting the results I want."

"Somehow I suspect the result you wanted last night did not involve ending up in my barn," Rufus said.

"Low blow." Tom kicked a slashed tire, hiding a smile.

Annie was unfazed. "You have no idea what result I was seeking. I assure you I fully met my business objective last night and have ample resources at my disposal for my next steps. On the other hand, your business seems in peril, not to mention your friend Tom."

Tom extended a hand toward Annie. "We seem to agree on that point."

Annie shook Tom's hand. "I don't know all the background, but I agree that Rufus should talk to the police. Clearly this is not the first incident of this kind."

"Karl Kramer thinks he runs the county's construction industry," Tom said. "He is convinced he is losing business to Rufus's considerable woodworking skills."

"And he's not happy about it," Annie said, "so he misses no opportunity to let Rufus know how he feels."

"That about sums it up."

"Can these incidents be documented for legal action?"

"If Rufus would cooperate, they could be," Tom said. "But he says that is not the Amish way."

"It's not," Rufus reiterated.

"Tom, is this the first time you've been a target?" Annie asked.

"Other than the libelous muck that spews out of Karl's mouth, yes."

"Then perhaps we can capitalize on the fact that Karl crossed a line."

"We?" Rufus tilted his head at her. "I was under the impression you were leaving town."

Annie shrugged. "We can build a case against Karl that doesn't have to involve Rufus directly."

"I won't be a witness in court to anything," Rufus said.

"If Karl keeps this up, you won't have to be."

"I like this girl," Tom said.

"I promised to take you into town." Rufus ignored Tom's comment. "So I'm going to do just that." He gestured toward the buggy.

"You might as well go on to the job site after you drop her off," Tom said. "I've already spoken to my insurance agent, and they need an official report, so I have to call the police. I'm not sure when I can get your load out to you."

"Don't worry about it," Rufus said. "And I'll cover any costs your insurance doesn't pay for."

Rufus was tempted to urge Dolly to a faster pace to make up for lost time. His crew would be idle and expect to be paid for showing up on time.

"I think it's better if you don't involve yourself with the trouble here," he said to Annalise. "I may know someone in town who can help you get back to Colorado Springs today."

"What if I don't want to go back?"

He looked at her out of the side of his eye. "Are you running from something?"

"Of course not."

"Yet you felt compelled to take refuge in Tom's truck and my barn."

"It's not what you think."

"That depends on what you think I think."

"Don't play word games with me," Annalise warned. "I'm very good at them."

"You seem to be very good at a lot of things."

"I don't like to brag."

"You're definitely not Amish." Rufus chuckled. "May I speak plainly?"

"By all means."

"If you set aside your pride, you'll admit you were frightened last night. You're used to solving problems, but you're in a predicament you don't know how to get out of."

"No I'm not." *I know exactly what I'm doing.*

"Do you make a habit of jumping into strange trucks?"

"Of course not."

"So what happened?"

"It's complicated."

"So you've said."

"Well, it is."

"Fair enough." Rufus could not help noticing the way her gray eyes reflected the colors of the scene around them. "I can respect your privacy. Just do not feel you must solve my problems."

"You made your point, all right?" Annalise turned slightly away from him and gripped her phone in front of her.

"Good." He watched her for a moment. Thin strands of hair worked loose from the blue cloth tie and floated against her smooth white neck, intermittently airborne in the breeze the buggy's motion created. The gold chain around her neck glistened in the sun.

Rufus turned his eyes to the road, his blood pumping hard because of her presence. His life was predictable. Calm. Ordered. This outsider would never understand his way of living, no matter how much she poked her nose into his business. The best thing he could do for both of them was find her a ride back to where she came from.

Westcliffe still lay two miles ahead of them. Mentally Rufus inventoried the tasks and supplies available at the job site at the far edge of town. *Crew* was an overstatement for the two Amish teenagers who worked for him. He had hoped to frame in a new rank of cabinets in the family room of the private home he had helped to build, but he needed the long pieces in the back of Tom's truck. His mind wandered to cabinets ready to hang in other parts of the house and the sanding and staining still to be done on the downstairs mantel.

Beside him on the bench, Annalise cradled her cell phone in one hand and rapidly jabbed at it with the forefinger of the other. Her motions were too erratic to be dialing a phone number. She was going straight to the Internet, no doubt intending to become an expert in something or other in the next few minutes. During his *rumschpringe*, when he tried out some of the *English* ways of living before he was baptized, Rufus dabbled with the Internet. He knew how easy it was to get information quickly. Perhaps she was researching her options for getting out of Westcliffe and would know more than he did by the time they got to town.

Rufus wished he did not care that she was leaving so soon. But Tom was right. Annalise Friesen had spunk, something that compelled him to turn his head and look at her again.

"How much farther?" Annie raised her eyes to the road before them and shoved her phone into her back pocket.

"About two miles," Rufus said.

"Is it straight down this road?"

He nodded.

"You were right this morning," she said, inhaling. "I forget to look at the view."

"Sit back and enjoy."

"Actually, I'm wondering if I should walk the rest of the way." She met his gaze and saw for the first time the violet-blue dance of his eyes. "I just follow the road, right?"

"That's right. It would be hard to get lost at this point."

"Then if you don't mind, I think I'd like to walk." Annie tightened her grip on her bag and breathed in the mingled scents of roadside vegetation.

Rufus pulled on the reins, and Dolly slowed. "Are you sure about this?"

Annie nodded.

"It feels strange to just leave you on the side of the road."

Annie shrugged. "It's a beautiful day and a simple walk."

"You won't know where to go when you get there."

"They speak English in Westcliffe, don't they?"

"Of course."

"I'll be fine. I can take care of myself."

His Adam's apple bobbed up and then down as he swallowed his reply.

"I know you think I can't look after myself or else I would not be here," Annie said, "but I assure you, I'm fine. Thank you for the accommodations last night, and I hope Mr. Kramer comes to his senses soon."

"Thank you," Rufus said.

"Please thank your mother for me as well."

"I will. If you're ever down this way again, I'm sure she would enjoy seeing you. I know Jacob would."

The buggy stopped, and Annie climbed down. To be polite, she looked at Rufus, but she tried not to really see him, lest she decide to get back in the buggy just because he was there. The sensation shivered out of her.

"Look for Mrs. Weichert's shop on Main Street," Rufus said. "She sells some of my mother's preserves. Sometimes her daughter has business in Pueblo. She might give you a ride."

"I'll be fine."

Annie stood still and watched Rufus ease the buggy back onto the highway. Then with her bag slung over one shoulder, she progressed toward town in no particular hurry. Hues of green and brown and red she had never before noticed passed imperceptibly from one to the other. A breeze stirred in a pristine Colorado blue sky and ruffled her hair with a tender touch.

She was free.

She wasn't suspecting Barrett. She wasn't dodging Rick. She wasn't juggling three calls on her phone. She wasn't reading between the lines of a contract. And while it was not impossible for Rick to discover where she was—he could pull strings and find a way to track her—it was unlikely he was anywhere nearby.

Free. *Please, God, let it be so.*

Another mile down the road, a blue-and-red sign announced the presence of a roadside motel. Annie's eyes followed the direction of the arrow and saw the humble structure set back from the road and up a steep slope. The building was not large—perhaps twenty rooms—and the outdoor green-and-purple color scheme was hideous. Nevertheless, the place whispered her name. Giving into whimsy, Annie turned her steps toward the motel.

Her phone buzzed in her pocket. She paused with one hand ready to extract it.

Five

The screen announced, Mom/Dad. Annie answered the call.

"Where in the world are you?" Myra Friesen demanded. "I just want a peaceful cup of coffee with the newspaper, and the phone won't stop ringing."

"I'm sorry," Annie said. "I'm fine. No one needs to worry. Who called?"

"The police called about your car."

Annie grimaced. "What happened?"

"That's what they want to know. It was parked in front of a hotel but not registered to any known guest. So it got towed. Imagine my surprise when I sit down with my morning coffee and get that phone call. I had no idea you still had your car registered at our address."

"I've been meaning to change that," Annie said. "What did they do with it?"

"The towing company has it. They'll charge you for storage, you know, if you don't go get it."

"I don't think I can get it today." She could afford to store the vehicle indefinitely. At least Rick did not have his grubby hands on it.

40

"Where are you, Annie?" Myra asked again. "You sound like you're outside."

"I am." Annie licked her lips. "I had to go out of town for business reasons, but I'm enjoying the beautiful day."

"Your assistant called, too. She didn't say anything about a business trip."

"I didn't have a chance to tell Jamie before I left. I'll catch her up soon. Go back to your coffee."

"What about Rick?"

"What about him?"

"When he called, he seemed quite concerned that he did not know where you are. Considering how close you two have been, it was odd that he thought I would know your whereabouts when he doesn't."

Annie sighed. "Rick and I are not close now, Mom. I don't tell him everything."

"When I told him about the car, he was concerned something happened to you."

Yeah, right. He wishes.

"I'm fine," Annie said. "I just need to take care of a few things before I come home."

"You still haven't said where you are."

"It's better if you don't know, Mom. Trust me."

"That sounds ominous. Are you going to have to break my kneecaps?"

"Maybe. You know, the usual top secret stuff with a tech company in the cutthroat modern business world."

Myra laughed. "Next you're going to tell me not to bother my pretty little head about it."

"Something like that."

"I don't understand most of your techno-garble anyway. Do you want me to get your car out of hock? I could go to your condo for the extra keys."

"Don't bother. E-mail me the name of the tow company, and

I'll deal with it." After a pause, she added, "Use the private family e-mail address."

They were quiet for a beat, then Myra spoke, "Honey, are you really all right?"

"Fine, Mom. I'm fine."

"I love you."

"I love you, too."

After the call disconnected, Annie considered her phone. For years she literally never powered her phone off. Perhaps the moment had come. It might at least slow down Rick's search. With no doubt in her mind that it was only a matter of time before he wore down his contact in the police department and triangulated her location, she powered off and stuck the phone back in her pocket.

Her attention reverted to the motel before her. She had not stayed anywhere but a five-star resort in years. Her business dealings required a certain image of success. But this place was a portal to another world. No one would think to look for her here.

Rufus Beiler assumed she wanted to leave as soon as possible. Annie certainly had led him to that conclusion. But a nondescript motel in a place she had never been before might be exactly where she belonged now. The Steamboat Springs reservation had already gone to waste. Westcliffe might be just the place to set up a temporary headquarters and try to thwart the alliance that Barrett and Rick had formed.

Instinctively, she reached for her phone to log on and see if the two men she had trusted most—until a few days ago—had managed to do any damage in the last two hours. The black screen reminded her she had taken step one in cutting herself off from them.

Annie decided. Ten minutes later, she put seventy dollars cash on the counter in the motel's small lobby.

"We do take credit cards." The middle-aged woman behind the counter tended toward plump and battled gray. "Debit also."

"Cash is more convenient for me." Annie could not afford to

reveal any movement on her financial accounts right now. Rick knew too much about them, and Barrett could get into anything he decided to get into.

Except my program, she thought, *at least so far.*

"My name's Mo," the woman said. "Let me know if you need anything. Breakfast runs from seven to nine."

The room was modest and in need of fresh paint, but the owner clearly wanted to bill the place as belonging in the twenty-first century. The television was small, but it was a flat screen with basic cable channels. The high-speed Internet access would let her use her computer without turning on her phone. Annie plugged in both laptop and cell phone to juice them up.

Next she spent a few minutes scrambling the passwords of every online account she could think of, even minor sites she had no reason to believe Rick would be interested in tracking. She checked on the secure server that backed up her software program and breathed relief when she saw no evidence Barrett had hacked his way in, though she saw several new attempts that morning. Annie puzzled over what else she could do to ensure he would never succeed and clicked her way around the keys for another half hour. Then she stretched out on the bed and turned on the television to pass the time until computer and phone were fully powered. Idly, she searched "Amish in Colorado" and read several newspaper reports of the group's migration west. Every few minutes she glanced at the charging icons to monitor progress.

When she slammed Rick's head with the duffel back in the aspen grove, Annie surrendered personal items that would have kept her going for a few days. At minimum, she was going to need a fresh shirt and perhaps a baggy T-shirt to sleep in. Annie pulled up Google Maps and looked at the route between the motel and Westcliffe shops.

The walk to Westcliffe's quaint Main Street was an easy mile with the placid mystery of the Sangre de Cristo Mountains unfolding in constant view. Annie followed the gray highway across ground growth rolling in yellowish stripes before giving way to an irrigated green that signaled a town. A hazy memory niggled at her of a family trip to the Great Sand Dunes when she was small. Her intuition told her she was not far from where she played in a flowing creek with her sister while her mother sat in an orange lawn chair with her feet in the water on a beastly hot day. Other than that, Annie could not recollect being in this part of the state. Now the beauty crooked a finger at her, and she did not reach for the phone in her pocket even once.

Annie's pace slowed as she came into town and guessed at the ages of the stone and brick buildings that anchored it. A gabled church bell tower thrust a cross into the air, and Annie's feet turned in that direction without explanation. At the sight of it, a hundred years of history shivered through her, and she wondered if the residents who built the church could have imagined what she did for a living. The simple old-fashioned church stirred in her an impression of a place to belong. Before it became historic, this was simply a church where the community gathered.

The twentieth century had rumbled through the region, leaving in its wake signs that lit up and blinked, vehicles of various eras, practical business shelters, rehabbed houses, and ATMs. Yet the town stood poised in the past, weighing its future.

The ATM outside a stately bank gave her pause. How long could she stay afloat without resorting to a traceable electronic transfer of funds? She could not afford to lose herself in daydreams of scenery and history. She had a business to protect, and neither Rick nor Barrett would give up just because she managed to give them the slip. There was always her retirement fund. Rick might not think to track an IRA that she opened before she met him. The tax hit would be worth it if it meant she could halt Rick's aggression.

On Main Street, Annie found a couple of promising shops and rummaged for essentials. Surely it was only a matter of a couple of days, a week at the most, before she could safely return home. She would hire someone to help her, and in a few days she would stop

Rick and Barrett's attempt at legal thievery of her creative work.

Annie thought of Rufus. The offense against him was plain to see, and now it was spreading to his friend. Yet he refused to take action.

I've got too much invested, she thought. *I'm not giving up without a fight.*

She stood in the bright afternoon sunlight, unsure what to do next. Find food, she supposed. She could have a meal now and take something back to the motel for later.

A passing patch of purple made Annie lift her eyes from the sidewalk. Two Amish women, one middle-aged and one younger, exited a furniture store. Annie considered the sign that hung over the door and surmised it was an Amish business. The women smiled at her as they passed on the sidewalk then entered the same discount store Annie had just come out of. Annie watched their long skirts and sturdy shoes disappear from view—then chided herself for staring. No one else seemed to find the women's movements noteworthy.

An image of herself in the dress Rufus had left in the barn flashed through Annie's mind. It hardly seemed possible that only that morning she had woken to his peculiar offering.

Annie glanced around the street, stuffed her purchases in her shoulder bag, and scouted the environs for any sort of restaurant. She ate quickly at a sandwich shop, promising herself that when she was not under pressure to save her business, she would return to explore Westcliffe. On the way out of town, she noted the gas station with a couple of cars for sale and idly wondered how she could buy one without leaving a trail.

She shook the thought out of her head. *I have a perfectly good car. I just have to clean up this mess, and I can go get it.*

An hour later, Annie was showered and wearing her jeans with a fresh forest green T-shirt. A front porch ran across the length of the motel with Adirondack chairs scattered at irregular intervals. Annie settled into one with her laptop. The vista was nearly irresistible, but she forced herself to focus, compromising by working where the sun warmed her skin. If she could sort out a plan for dealing with Rick and Barrett, she would have plenty of time to relish the views.

Rufus spent the day sanding and staining detail pieces for woodwork around the house under construction and satisfying himself that the mantel was perfect. Tom showed up in the midafternoon with the new load, and the crew started on framing in the family room cabinetry. On his way out of town, Rufus took the buggy to an office building where the owners were dabbling with the idea of renovating and wanted him to quote on the job. He collected measurements, asked a few questions, and promised to make a formal bid. Perhaps if he focused more on remodeling rather than new construction, Karl Kramer would stop harassing him.

It was almost six o'clock when he let Dolly move at her own pace down the road toward home. His mind wandered to what awaited him at the farm.

Jacob could be a daydreamer. No one doubted the little boy's good intentions when he headed out for his chores, but often it fell to Rufus to double-check and make sure the animals had hay and fresh water and to look for eggs Jacob missed. His sisters, twelve and fourteen years old, were more dependable about milking the family's only cow and keeping up with churning butter and making cheese. *Daed* would have been in the alfalfa fields all day with sixteen-year-old Joel and no doubt would be soaking his sore feet by the time Rufus came through the door. *Mamm* would put down her sewing and check on the chicken potpie in the oven.

A mile out of town, Rufus happened to glance up from the road. Even from a distance he was sure of the slender form stretched out in the Adirondack chair, her hay-colored hair hanging loose as she hunched over a computer.

What was she still doing there?

Six

Annie rubbed her eyes and glanced up just in time to see Dolly *clip-clop* past. Was it her imagination, or was Rufus Beiler looking at her just before the buggy moved out of sight behind a tower of blue spruce?

Rufus Beiler.

Annie's hand moved to the phone in her back pocket. When she had spoken to her mother, she missed her chance to ask about the Byler name in her own family history. She hesitated over turning the phone on, but curiosity mounted, and she hit the speed dial number for her parents' house.

"Mom, it's me."

"Are you all right?"

"Fine, Mom. Relax. I just remembered a question I wanted to ask."

"What's that, honey?"

"I met someone named Beiler today, and that got me thinking about Daddy's grandparents. Wasn't there a name like Beiler in the family?"

"It rings a bell, but I'm not the best at keeping track of your father's side of the family tree."

"I suppose I could ask Daddy, but I don't think he keeps track, either."

"His grandparents died when he was a little boy. He never talks about them."

"But I saw the name somewhere. Malinda Byler." Annie spelled the name. "I think it was a maiden name. Are you sure you don't know anything?"

"Aunt Lennie gave us a book years ago," Myra said. "A genealogy mishmash that some distant cousin put together."

"That's it!" Annie said. "It had a black comb binding and a pink cover. I remember looking at it in high school."

"It must still be around here somewhere. You can look in the basement the next time you come."

Annie groaned. "Half the boxes down there don't have labels."

"Then you'd better hope the one you're looking for does," Myra said. "I don't have time to go digging, but if I think of it, I'll ask your father."

"Thanks."

"Still don't know when you're coming home?"

"Nope." Annie paused. "Mom, I may not be able to have my phone on much. Don't freak out if you can't get me. If something's important, just use the family e-mail."

"I worry about you, Annie."

"No need."

Annie ended the call then turned off her phone. She opened her laptop again and considered the screen. What were the odds of finding a competent and available intellectual property attorney in the San Luis Valley? She did not want glitz. Rick was well connected, so Annie wanted someone who was *not*, someone Rick would look right past. But this someone needed the guts to go up against Richard D. Stebbins and get the job done.

Cañon City, Walsenburg, Alamosa. How hard would it be to find a bus or catch a ride to one of those cities? Surely once she got there, she could rent a car and operate independently but still stay under Rick's radar. Annie looked through the Yellow Pages listings and clicked through to one link after another to study the scope and experience of each attorney. The list narrowed to three. It was too late in the day to phone an office number and expect someone would answer, but first thing in the morning, Annie would make the calls. In the meantime, she had to think through how to tell her story succinctly and with enough urgency to persuade an attorney to drop other work and jump on her case.

Annie clicked over to her e-mail, which she had not looked at all day.

Four frantic messages from Jamie, her assistant, time stamped at two-hour intervals throughout the day.

Fourteen messages of varying importance from clients with complex business needs for whom she did custom website work.

One message from a corporate partnership she did not recognize, making her heart lurch with dread that Rick was bringing in reinforcements. What was Liam-Ryder Industries, and what did they want?

Twenty-three Facebook notifications.

One terse message from Barrett underscoring that their business success was primarily due to his efforts.

She did not check Twitter.

Nothing from Rick. Annie was not sure if that was good or bad.

Annie answered one message from Jamie, assuring her that she was simply taking care of unexpected business, and gave instructions for responding to the more high-maintenance clients. She promised to be in touch soon. She ignored Barrett and did not even open the message from the unfamiliar corporation.

Somewhere behind her a cell phone rang. When she heard a man's vociferous swearing, Annie nearly jumped out of her chair. A door slammed, and a man in jeans and a blue work shirt stomped out of the room next to hers, a hammer in his hand. He brushed past her on the long porch. At the far end, near the lobby, Mo stepped outside.

"Hurry up, Jack," Mo said.

"I'm coming." His statement of the obvious weighed heavy with irritation.

"It's going to fall down! I told you hours ago I was getting nervous."

"I said I'm coming!"

Annie could not help watching the interchange. Jack made no effort to hurry his pace in response to Mo's agitated movements—which only made her more visibly disconcerted. When the crash came, Jack rolled his eyes and entered the lobby. Mo squeezed her head with both hands and moved down the porch toward Annie.

"He'll pitch a fit if I stand in there and watch what he's doing," Mo muttered.

Annie wondered if a response was required and finally said, "I hope everything is okay."

"He's just aggravated he had to pull the sink out of the room next to yours. I trust he's not disturbing you."

"I didn't even know he was there until he came out."

"He's the most cantankerous handyman I've ever had." Mo sighed. "I arranged for a carpenter to come tomorrow. I knew those shelves in the lobby needed work, but I didn't think they were going to fall apart today. I doubt Jack can do anything now but clean up the mess."

Annie nodded. "I hope it works out." She went back to inspecting her e-mail.

"Don't forget, continental breakfast from seven to nine every morning."

"Did Annalise sleep in the barn again?" Jacob Beiler asked in the morning over his bowl of oatmeal.

"No, Jacob," Rufus answered, "Annalise was our guest for only one night."

"If she was our guest, why did we make her sleep in the

barn?" Jacob waved his oatmeal-laden spoon precariously. "I don't understand why she was here."

"She just needed a place to stay for the one night."

"She's pretty."

The image of Annalise Friesen sitting on the porch in front of the motel lingered. Rufus wondered if she was still there. He would find out soon enough, he supposed. But he could not allow the lithe *English* woman to absorb his attention.

"Are you thinking about Tom's truck?" Franey ladled oatmeal into a bowl and handed it to her daughter Sophie, who passed it on to Lydia. Franey filled another.

"He had new tires on by the afternoon," Rufus said, "but it pains me that he suffered for helping me. I'm not sure I should ask him again."

"Don't you need his help?" Sophie asked.

"Yes I do," Rufus said. "I just don't want him to get hurt again."

"You pay him to taxi you, don't you?" Sophie said.

"Yes, of course."

"Then if you don't ask him to drive you, you won't be paying him, and you'll hurt his business."

Rufus tilted his head. "Maybe it's better if he only taxis for us when we have appointments, and he should not carry my lumber."

"That's up to him to decide," Lydia said.

"If you don't ask him, you'll have to find someone else," Sophie said. "And who will want to taxi for you if they think it's dangerous?"

Rufus looked from one sister to the other. "When did you two get so smart?"

"What is the dress for?" Jacob asked before shoveling more oatmeal into his mouth.

"What dress?" Franey asked.

"The pupel um," Jacob mumbled.

"Don't talk with your mouth full."

Jacob swallowed dramatically. "The purple one. I saw it in the barn this morning when I watered the animals."

Rufus blanched.

"What is he talking about?" Franey asked her eldest son.

"*Verhuddelt.*" A mix-up. Rufus pushed his chair back from the table. "I'll see."

He was out the back door before his mother or sisters could say more. Offering Ruth's dress to Annalise had been a silly gesture in the first place, but leaving the garment in the barn was sheer foolishness. Rufus went directly to the empty stall and picked it up, still neatly folded.

Rufus blew out his breath. *Hochmut.* His own pride would not let him walk through the house with the dress now and stir up another round of questions. In fact, he did not want to go back inside the house at all, preferring to let the incident fade from notice. Instead, he laid the dress between two buggy blankets on a shelf just inside the entrance to the barn.

Out of sight, out of mind, he told himself as he turned to take Dolly's bridle off the hook. He had work to do.

Annie squinted at the digital readout on the clock next to the bed. 8:36. She sat up immediately. The business day was well under way, and she was losing time with sleep. As she swung her feet over the side of the bed and raked fingers through her loose hair, a rumbling stomach reminded her that breakfast would end in less than a half hour. If she missed the motel's fare, she would lose even more time walking to town in search of food.

Annie pulled on the jeans and T-shirt from the day before, splashed water onto her face, ran a brush through her hair, and went in search of food, which theoretically would be available for another seventeen minutes.

Annie closed the door behind her, not bothering to lock it since she left nothing of value. She kept her shoulder bag with her at all times. Paranoid or not, she was not going to leave her computer unattended. She moved down the porch toward the lobby, unsure what to expect after yesterday's crash. Pieces of shelves lay stacked in one corner, and assorted tools suggested a carpenter was already on-site. Annie moved through the lobby toward the small dining room where she presumed breakfast awaited. Despite the noises in her stomach, food held little appeal, but when would she have another opportunity to eat? That depended on the result of phone calls she had yet to make and e-mails she had yet to read. The attorneys on her list were now ranked in order of preference. If she could get hold of them, she would interview all three by phone before making a decision, but she was determined to have someone on her side before the end of the day.

A few motel guests sat at small tables under the wall-mounted television, which was blaring morning news. A small girl played under a table, humming as she bounced a rubber ball. The food counter looked picked over, but the coffee's fragrance was robust. She drifted toward the dated fifty-four-cup urn just like the ones she used to see at church. She found a large Styrofoam cup with a plastic lid and instantly made the decision to take food back to the room. Eating between business actions was a familiar habit. A whole-wheat bagel smeared with cream cheese and a banana would round out a breakfast she was certain she could carry. At the last minute, she also dropped an apple into her bag for later. With the bag over her shoulder, coffee in one hand, and the bagel and banana in the other, Annie smiled absently at her fellow guests and headed back through the lobby.

When she saw Rufus Beiler line up his measuring tape on the wall, Annie's brain flashed the command to back out the other direction, and in that instant of hesitation, a rubber ball rolled from the dining room and under Annie's foot.

When her feet went out from under her, instinctively she let go of her breakfast and clutched her bag, making sure her computer would not take the first hit of the fall. Her head slammed the door frame between dining room and lobby, and when she hit the floor, she was flat on her back. Her first thought was whether she had smashed her phone. The next was that manufacturers of Styrofoam cups should make lids that stayed on during perilous descent.

"Ow! That's hot!" she screamed into Rufus Beiler's face as he kneeled over her. And then she understood why the old cartoons showed characters seeing stars when they hit their heads.

Seven

September 1737

She never imagined such a wicked wind, nor the number of times they would huddle in it, hardly able to breathe for its force and feeling as though their knees would buckle.

Verona Beyeler put one hand to her mouth and extended the other to touch her husband's elbow. She meant to hide both her horror at the sight and the nausea that hit whenever she came up on deck, as she steadied herself against Jakob's solid form. The ship rolled on the rhythmic, swishing swells of the North Atlantic, its sails strung at carefully calculated heights and angles. Verona avoided looking up at the towering masts for fear that dizziness would toss her over the railing. The day had been bright. Only in the last thirty minutes did the dismal overcast fittingly claim the horizon.

A gust snatched the corner of Verona's shawl, sending it flapping, and instinctively she let go of Jakob to retrieve it and clench it back into place. Jakob's head turned for a moment at her gesture, and then his eyes returned to the small shrouded bundle on the board. Verona tugged the strings of her prayer *kapp* to be sure it could not come loose as well.

Not another child. She did not know this child's mother

well, and for the moment she did not let herself feel the woman's heartache. As they stood among the dark-clad mourners, about a dozen, she felt the weight of the group. Sorrow turned to numbness rapidly on these occasions, which were far too frequent.

A man's voice droned words Verona did not want to hear. The wind swallowed most of them, for which Verona was grateful. The children began dying before the ship even left Rotterdam, starting with Hans Kauffmann's little girl. Five more died during the nine days in port at Plymouth. Now they were in the middle of the ocean, and the dying continued. The youngest children seemed the most vulnerable. Already more than twenty children had succumbed to measles and smallpox. Adults who would not forsake caring for their children fell as well. Hans Zimmerman's son-in-law died, depriving him not only of a beloved family member but a practical laborer with whom to homestead. Jakob and Hans were already conniving to claim land next to each other—now with one less man to work the acres.

According to Charles Stedman, captain of the *Charming Nancy*, land was still at least two weeks away, perhaps three. Verona's own five children occupied her hands almost constantly, but her mind was free to fill with dread.

The child on the board now could not be more than two years old. Lisbetli's age. If Verona had seen the bundle lying idly on the deck, she might have mistaken it for tightly wadded bedding waiting for the wash.

Two men picked up the board, balancing one end on the deck's railing. Fathers put on their hardened faces, and mothers pulled scarves up to hide quivering lips. The droning man pronounced his final words, and the two attending the board gently tipped the end up to an acute angle. The bundle lost grip and slid. A few seconds later came the slight splash, barely noticeable in the wake of the ship.

The mother's wail rent the air but was soon stifled.

Verona turned and once again reached for Jakob, this time

with a gasp. Behind them stood two of their daughters. At eleven, Anna was a help with the younger children, but at five, Maria demanded unceasing attention.

"How long have they been there?" Jakob asked softly.

Verona shook her head. Unless the girls could not see past the mourners, they would have seen the body go into the sea, not a memory she wished for them.

"The sickness is not a secret," Jakob murmured. "Anna is old enough to know what happens, and Maria will probably forget what she saw."

Verona was not so sure. As the funeral onlookers dispersed, she stepped across the deck as steadily as she could manage and reached her daughters.

"What are you two doing up here?" she asked.

"Maria got away," Anna explained. "Maria always gets away. She was halfway up the ladder before I saw her."

Verona planted a kiss on the top of Maria's head. "Go back below. It's cold up here, and the sun has gone away." She would not ask what they saw and make them unnecessarily curious.

"Can we come back later?" Maria asked.

"Maybe. If the sun comes out. Now go down to our berths." Verona touched both girls at the shoulders to turn them around and sent them back to where they had come from. "See if Barbara needs help with Christian and Lisbetli. *Daed* and I will be down in a few minutes."

She felt Jakob's presence behind her and turned to meet his gray eyes. "Tomorrow it could be Christian bundled up on a board."

"It won't be," Jakob said.

"You can't promise me that. He's been sick for two weeks."

"He's getting better or you would not have left him alone with Barbara," Jakob pointed out.

"If we had stayed in the Palatinate, he would not be sick."

"You don't know that," Jakob said. "The first children who got sick were probably infected before we boarded in Rotterdam. You know I'm right."

"But at least the children would have had fresh air and some decent food. That might have kept him well. Maybe it was a mistake to come."

Jakob took Verona's face in his hands and captured her violet eyes. "It was no mistake. We made this decision together. We cannot practice our faith in Europe without putting ourselves in danger. Christian would grow up to be drafted into one war or another, and I can't take that chance. We barely have enough money to make a fresh start now. If we had waited any longer, I hate to think what we would have faced."

Verona said nothing, her eyes no longer meeting his.

"William Penn's sons offer us a new life," Jakob continued. "The process takes time, but it is fairly straightforward. We can afford more land than we could ever hope for in Europe, even if others would have left us alone and let us believe what the Bible says."

"I have heard stories of people waking up in their berths to find someone dead beside them." Even thinking about it, Verona felt the feverish heat of Christian's skin as he lay next to her during her nightly vigil to assure herself he had not gone cold.

With one hand, Jakob gestured widely to the open sea. "There is no turning back, Verona. We have to see this through."

"At any cost?"

"Leaving Switzerland was the best choice for us. You know it was. Anywhere in Europe, life for true believers is unbearable. The Romans and the Lutherans will never accept the Anabaptists."

"We were both baptized when we were babies," Verona said. "Are you sure we had to be baptized again? Are you sure we have to separate from the world?"

"Why all these sudden doubts?" Jakob tugged at the strings of her *kapp*. "Have I ever asked you to believe something you did not know in your heart to be true?"

Verona shook her head. The bun of brown hair at the base of her neck wobbled.

"We chose this together," Jakob said. "We chose our faith. We joined the church because we wanted to. We chose this new life."

"I did not know it would be this hard." Verona's voice cracked. "And we are not even there yet." The dreary horizon now carried rain. She could feel it spattered in the wind.

"We will have *land*, Verona," Jakob said. "I will build you a beautiful home. I will open a tanyard. We will grow acres and acres of food for the children. William Penn's vision was for a place where people could come to live peaceably and worship according to their conscience. We will have a good life."

Verona swallowed hard. "If Christian dies—"

He put a finger to her lips and shook his head. "He won't. He will clear fields at my side. He will grow up to inherit our land and have a good life. Perhaps he will become the first Amish bishop to come of age in the English colonies!"

Verona smiled at the thought.

Jakob gently nudged her out of the path of two families approaching on deck.

"Even the Mennonites do not speak to us," Verona whispered.

"It's just as well. We separated from them for good reasons. What do we have to say to each other?"

Verona knew Mennonites slid their children into the sea just as the Amish did. Mennonite stomachs rumbled from hunger just as loudly as Amish stomachs. Mennonite babies whimpered just the same as Amish babies. She squelched her doubt about whether the separation had been for good reason and watched the progress of the Mennonite mothers, knowing they must share her fear.

None of the adults among the passing Mennonites turned their heads toward Verona and Jakob, and when one of their children smiled at her, a hand reached out and redirected his gaze.

Verona sighed. Perhaps Jakob was right. Perhaps it was just

as well. Twenty-one Amish families boarded the *Charming Nancy* along with the Mennonites. It was enough of a burden to bear the loss of Amish passengers. She was not sure she had room in her heart for the others. She supposed that not speaking to each other was one way of living peaceably together, at least for the weeks on the ocean.

"I'd better go check on Christian," Verona said, "and Lisbetli should be waking from her nap."

Jakob nodded. "I see Hans Zimmerman at the end of the deck. I want to speak to him. I'll be down in a few minutes."

Verona watched her husband stroll across the deck, his dark red hair showing the extra inches of the journey. She would have to trim it soon. When he greeted his friend, she turned her attention to the immediate task. Glancing into the opening she had sent her daughters down a few minutes ago, she gathered her dark skirt in one hand. With the other she gripped the railing that would guide her way down the ladder.

Though the Beyelers were a family of seven, they had only two berths, meant to hold a total of four people. Other families did the same. Some of the children were still small, so Verona wasted little energy feeling sorry for their lack of space. What meager belongings not in barrels in the cargo hold were crammed under the bottom berth—clothing, a few eating utensils, cloths for washing up in scarce freshwater.

Jakob was right, as he always was. The life that lay ahead held so much more potential than what they had left behind. They would miss their families, of course, but no one had suggested they should not go to Pennsylvania, a land of wide-open opportunity for anyone willing to work hard. She would be glad to be in the new Amish settlement, away from the threats that pursued the true believers in Europe.

At least their berths were curtained off with quilts, reminders of their families. The quilts offered some sense of privacy, though the makeshift separations did little to muffle the moaning of the sick or the impatient speech of a weary parent. Neither did they disguise the smells of hundreds of passengers packed into close quarters.

Verona brushed the heads of Anna and Maria, who sat on the floor with a handful of pebbles their only toys. Their prayer *kapps* were missing—again. She cringed at the thought of the scum beneath her daughters and promised herself she would sweep the floor around the family's bunks again before the day was over. Pushing aside the quilt hanging on the upper berth, she found Barbara, fourteen, sitting cross-legged at one end of the compartment, while Christian, eight, sprawled across most of the space.

His eyes were open, which made Verona's mouth drop open in relief.

"He's been talking a little bit." Barbara twisted the ties of her *kapp* in the fingers of one hand. "I gave him a few sips of water. I don't think he's as hot as he was."

Verona laid a hand against her only son's cheek and agreed with her eldest daughter's assessment. "Maybe we'll try a little broth for supper," she said, searching Christian's face for further confirmation of his recovery. He nodded just enough to give encouragement.

Lisbetli squawked from the lower berth. Anna jumped up from the floor and peeked behind the quilt. "She's awake."

Verona hoped Lisbetli would celebrate her second birthday on their new homestead. She smiled at the toddler, who should have been scooting across the berth determined to get down but was instead lying listless, glistening. Verona scooped her up and kissed her ruddy cheek. Was it warm, or was it her imagination?

Maria popped up and tickled the baby's feet. "*Mamm*, what are these red spots on Lisbetli's belly?"

Eight

Violet-blue eyes stared down at her. Annie stared back. Footsteps drummed across the brown-tile floor.

"Is she all right?" Mo knelt beside Rufus.

"My head." Annie gasped in pain.

"Don't move!" Rufus and Mo said in unison.

"She needs a hospital," Mo said.

"I'm fine," Annie insisted, unsure which hurt more—her back or her head.

"I'll call right now." Mo moved to the phone on the desk. "But it takes forever to get an ambulance out here."

"Who needs a hospital?" Annie said.

"Quite possibly, you." Rufus glanced in the direction she had come from. "I don't see what you tripped on. I was careful to keep my tools out of the way."

"It wasn't your tools," she said. *It was seeing you.* "I've been known to be clumsy at various points in my life. This confirms the theory."

Rufus plucked the rubber ball from behind Annie's knee. "Here's the culprit."

Annie moistened her lips and turned her head toward the

dining room, where forks, momentarily frozen in air, now resumed their purpose in the hands of hotel guests. Rufus rolled the ball back toward the little girl who stood staring at the scene.

"I'm calling an ambulance." Mo picked up the phone.

"No!" Annie said, surprising even herself with her volume. "Just give me a few minutes." Gingerly she tested one leg and then the other. Both bent at appropriate angles.

"There's an urgent care center much closer than the hospital," Rufus said. "Let me take you there. My little brother fell out of a tree once and needed an X-ray. They were very thorough."

"With all due respect, Rufus, the buggy is too slow," Mo said, "and you'll bounce her around like a broken bedspring. I'll take her in my car."

Annie pressed one forearm against the floor and shifted her weight to it, rolling to one side as she began to stand up. Her bag suddenly felt like a hundred-pound weight. As if reading her mind, Rufus slipped the strap over her head and off her shoulder then offered himself for support while Annie painfully sat upright.

"I'll bring the car around." Mo disappeared before Annie could protest further.

"You should let her take you," Rufus said. "Let *der Dokder* look."

Annie had to admit she had taken a solid smack. Pain radiated out from her spine in at least three places, and already the back of her head was tender.

"No more arguments," Annie said. "But I hope it doesn't take long. I have a lot to do today."

"First make sure you're all right."

"You don't understand."

"Considering how you ended up in my barn the other night, perhaps I understand more than you realize," he said, "but you need medical attention."

"I thought you people didn't believe in modern medicine." Annie lay back down on the floor with her head turned to one side. Lying flat was less painful than propping herself up.

"Who told you that?"

She tried to shrug and winced instead. "I don't know. Isn't electricity against your religion?"

"It is not that simple."

"You'll have to explain it sometime."

"Gladly. But right now you're going to a doctor."

Mo honked then jumped out of the green sedan parked outside the glass lobby door.

"I'm going to pick you up," Rufus said softly. "Very slowly. You tell me if it hurts too much."

She nodded as his arms slid under her knees and behind her shoulders. She looped her arms around his neck. Once upright, he took a few test steps toward the door.

"You okay?" he asked.

Annie nodded and leaned her head toward his chest for balance, her cheek brushing the soft black fabric of his shirt. He smelled faintly of sawdust and hay, but she was afraid a deep breath would stab her rib cage.

A cell phone rang, and Mo dug in her purse for it. "I can't talk now," Mo barked into the device.

Then she froze and listened. She held up her free hand, and Rufus halted.

Mo snapped the phone shut. "My mother is having some kind of crisis. I'm sorry, but I think I need to head over there right away."

"We'll take the buggy, then." Rufus resumed his careful pace but changed the direction slightly. "I've got you, Annalise."

She nodded against his chest and took a deep breath, not caring about the pain it caused. *I've got you, Annalise.*

Rufus stepped easily up into his cart as if he routinely carried around an extra hundred and fifteen pounds. "I'm sorry. This is not as comfortable as a car."

Annie winced as he set her in the seat. "My bag," she grunted.

"I have it."

The room was cold, and Annie was not fond of the beige printed cotton examination gown. *Some things are stereotypes because they are true,* she thought.

She had not persuaded Rufus to go home. Annie had imagined she could call a cab to get back to her room at the motel. Then she reminded herself where she was and that cabs might not be as plentiful as she presumed. Besides, she had to admit that moving any of her limbs involved pain. *"Accepting a little help is not a sign of failure."* Her mother said that all the time. Annie seldom acted like she believed it, but the fall left her with little choice. She pictured Rufus in the waiting room, guarding her denim bag. At least she had her phone, which she had taken custody of when a nurse helped her out of her coffee-sodden jeans. She searched "Amish medical care."

Rufus sat in the waiting room, sharing a vinyl seat with Annalise's bag. He felt the hard form of her laptop pressing against his hip. Rufus considered using a computer a couple of times in a public library to look up specific information but resorted instead to asking a librarian to help him find books he could carry home. It seemed so much simpler than learning how to communicate fluidly with a machine. He spoke English, High German, and Pennsylvania Dutch, but learning the language necessary to think like a computer did not appeal. What could possibly be on Annalise's computer to make her so attached to it when a live, wild, vibrant world was right before her eyes?

Still, the computer mattered to her, so Rufus would put it in her hands personally. He stood up to approach the reception desk cautiously.

"Excuse me, but can you tell me if Annalise Friesen is all right?"

The gray-haired receptionist glanced up at him. "Is she your wife?"

OLIVIA NEWPORT

"No! She's. . .a friend who was injured. I brought her in. I just want to know how she is."

The receptionist glanced at her computer screen and hit several keys. "The doctor is getting ready to discharge her."

"When she comes out, she will come this way, *ya*?"

"Yes." The woman softened slightly. "I'll see if she'd like you to wait with her."

She was gone before Rufus could object, and when she returned a moment later to lead him to Annalise's room, he no longer wanted to object. When a nurse pushed the door open, Rufus hesitated in the door frame.

"You can come in," Annalise said. "They're about to spring me, but they say I can't go unless I have a ride. I guess that's you."

"I guess so." She was dressed in her own shirt and oversized pink sweatpants that made her appear frail. Though he had only known her a day, already Rufus knew Annalise did not tolerate frailty.

The nurse held a clipboard and flipped through forms. "Sorry about the wardrobe. It was the best we could do. Nothing is broken, but she may have a mild concussion. She might be a little sleepy and confused for a while, and it's better if someone is with her. The doctor says three days of rest. We've given her something for the pain."

Rufus nodded.

"Expect considerable bruising and tenderness." The nurse stuck the clipboard in front of Annalise. "Patient signs here."

"I feel loopy," Annalise said, though she signed the form as directed.

"That's why you need your friend." Now the clipboard was in front of Rufus. "Driver signs here," the nurse said. She reached over to a side counter and picked up a plastic bag to push into Rufus's arms. "Here are her personal items."

"Can she walk?" Rufus asked.

"I've got a wheelchair ready." The nurse stepped into the hall

66

and returned in a few seconds with the wheelchair.

Annalise was going to need looking after. She could not go back to Colorado Springs in this condition, and Mo was running a motel, not an infirmary.

He would take her home, Rufus decided. He would not take no for an answer.

"She can stay in Ruth's old room," Rufus told his mother. "I know I am asking a lot, but I will try to be home more the next couple of days to help."

Annie listened in a vague, medicated haze. She did not recall agreeing to this arrangement and was not entirely sure who Ruth was or why her room was available, but she liked the idea of lying in a bed at that moment. She was on a sofa in the Beiler house and had a fleeting thought that she could no longer understand the conversation. It was as if Rufus and Franey had switched to another language. If she could just rest a few minutes, she could muster the strength to call the attorneys.

The conversation went mute.

When she woke, the sparse bedroom was dim, the only light coming in from the hall through the open door. The shadows formed themselves into Rufus's shape sitting in a straight-backed chair just outside the door, and gradually Annie's brain made the necessary neurological connections. This was Ruth's room at the Beiler house, and she had dozed the day away in the fog of painkillers.

"Rufus," she said. He was instantly on his feet. "Why am I here?"

"Because you need to be." He stood tentatively in the doorway.

"I. . .have business matters. . . ." She sighed, which hurt.

"You are in no condition."

She lifted a lightweight quilt and saw that she was wearing a nightgown.

"Do not worry," he said, "my sisters helped you change. Then they washed your things and put them over there." He pointed to a neat stack on top of a dresser. "I will go back to the motel tomorrow to get whatever you left."

"It's not much," she said.

"Yes, as I recall, you had little with you."

"I really do need to check on some things," Annie pushed herself to a half-sitting position. "Where's my bag?"

Rufus pointed toward the foot of the bed.

Annie winced as she leaned forward to reach her bag.

"You should rest."

"Fortunately, in my business I can work and rest at the same time."

"Does your line of work have something to do with why you ended up in the back of Tom's truck?"

"That has more to do with the people I chose to work with," she said, "and less with the business itself." Slowly, she managed to fish her phone from the bag.

"Must you do this now?"

"Let me just check my e-mail on my phone." She ignored Rufus's scowl. "You can come in."

Rufus stepped tentatively into the room.

Three messages from Jamie reporting on client actions.

Thirteen Facebook notifications.

Six client questions.

One from Barrett.

I am not a mobster, Annie. Let's sit down and talk this through. We've worked together too long for it to end this way.

Annie opened the site her family used for messages and found one from her mother.

You were right. Daddy says Jakob Byler came from

Switzerland in the 1700s. He doesn't remember much else.
We'll find the book the next time you're here. Maybe Aunt
Lennie knows more.

Love,
Mom

"Rufus," Annie said, "did your ancestors come from Switzerland?"

"Nearly three hundred years ago. That is a strange question to ask at the moment, *ya*?"

"I told you I had a Byler great-great-grandmother. Her ancestors came from Switzerland, too."

"I suppose it was a common name then, just as it is now." Rufus moved closer to the bed, glancing at the open door. "I'll get one of my sisters to help you."

"I don't need help. Tell me about your ancestors before I get loopy again."

"Our roots go back to Christian Beyeler, who was a child when he came with his parents to Pennsylvania. He grew up to be prominent among the early Amish in Lancaster County."

"I'll have to find out more," Annie said. "Meeting your family has made me curious. But first I have to deal with some pressing matters."

"Can I help you with any of these pressing matters?"

She lifted one shoulder and let it drop—and regretted the motion. "I doubt it. I run a tech company. Some personnel matters are heating up right now."

"Well, the company will have to run itself for a couple more days." Rufus took the phone from her loose grip. "Are you ready to try to eat something with your medication?"

Nine

October 1737

*C*hristian Beyeler opened his mouth and sucked in a long, slow breath, filling his lungs with fresh air until he thought they might pop. Only that morning had he convinced his mother he was truly well and would not collapse if she allowed him to go up on deck without Barbara standing guard. He did not care that she only relented today because she was absorbed with baby Elisabetha. The little girl's spots disappeared at last, and the fever broke, but she was not taking water very well and was far from the cheerful, curious Lisbetli who entertained the family. His mother was up most of the night with the fussy child, trying to soothe every sound before it emerged to awaken other passengers. Christian closed his eyes and breathed a prayer for his baby sister.

The saltiness that hung heavy in the air across the Atlantic thinned now as the *Charming Nancy* navigated the channel into Philadelphia. The ship had entered Delaware Bay two days ago and was fighting the winds the last miles of the journey. Christian hoped for an early glimpse of Philadelphia. So far he had not seen more than lanterns along the shoreline.

Now the sun was shrugging away from the horizon and pinking up the eastern sky. Christian kept to the starboard side so he could watch dawn's hues meld into the waiting day. He moved toward the bow, determined to be the first one in his family to see Philadelphia.

His parents were doing a brave thing. Of that Christian was sure. Europeans had been moving to the Americas in fits and dribbles for two hundred years because they believed enormous profit lay in the new land, but Christian's father had explained that no one had attempted anything like William Penn's holy experiment. Christian's eight years were pockmarked by sores of exclusion because of what his parents believed. But in Pennsylvania, belief would be as free and abundant as air. He was as sure of that as anything he had ever known.

Jakob watched his second daughter climb the ladder from the third-class passenger quarters to the deck. Barbara had gone up ahead. He glanced over his shoulder at Verona, who sat on their lower berth with Lisbetli limply on her lap and Maria leaning into her shoulder. He had promised he would go up and check on Christian. Once Anna clambered through the opening at the top of the ladder, Jakob began his ascent.

In the time it took him to emerge on deck, the girls had wandered in separate directions. Jakob caught a glimpse of Anna going toward the bow and Barbara toward the stern. Christian was nowhere in sight. Jakob's instinct told him to chase the younger daughter. Anna always had a nose for where her only brother would show up. Barbara was fourteen, practically grown. She would know to return to their berths when the time came.

Jakob had to move quickly to keep up with Anna, dodging rigging, barrels, mops, and idle planks. He breathed a prayer of thanksgiving that the scourge that sent passengers into the sea had calmed. Verona thought the baby was still fragile, but Jakob believed that if she had survived this long, they were unlikely to lose her now. They were so close to Philadelphia. By the end of the day they should be on solid ground and out of the cramped quarters where disease thrived. Perhaps Verona would start to believe again that a better life lay ahead, not behind.

"Anna," he called, "wait for me." He recognized the posture of her reluctance, but she did stop and turn toward him.

"I see Christian." She pointed. "He's right up there, close to the bow."

Jakob followed the line of her finger and saw his towheaded son transfixed as he watched the Pennsylvania coastline with its evidence of settlements and promise of civilization. The boy looked thin, he realized. All the children did. Jakob was suddenly alarmed by his own acquiescence to what the journey had done to his family. Clothing hung on all their frames as if it were made for husky strangers rather than stitched by Verona's fingers for their familiar frames.

But it was over. They had survived. All of them. Many families around them bore sickness compounded by death, but the Beyelers were whole and present. Moving to a new life was not for the fainthearted. If they could survive the journey, they could survive homesteading their own land and living in the freedom of their own beliefs.

"Are we going to have real beds in Philadelphia?" Anna wanted to know.

Jakob stroked the back of her head. "You'll still have to sleep with your sisters, but at least the bed won't be riding the waves of the sea."

"Good."

They reached Christian. The three of them stood, wordless in a sacred moment, peering ahead and scrutinizing the view for any sign of the port city.

"Are we going to have a garden in Philadelphia?" Anna asked.

"No, not in Philadelphia," Jakob answered. "We will only stay there to get the papers we need. Then we will go to our own land. *Die Bauerei.* The farm."

"Will we have a big house?"

"Not at first. But someday, if God blesses us. We will be with other Amish families, and we will be grateful for whatever God gives us."

"Will Lisbetli have to be baptized?" Anna asked. "Will I?"

"Not until you are all grown up and decide to join the church."

"I'm going to join the church as soon as I can," Christian announced. "I already believe in my heart."

"I'm glad to hear that."

"There's Barbara." Anna pointed.

The ship listed to one side as it turned. Anna slid toward Jakob, but it was Christian who caught her.

Verona rubbed circles in the center of Lisbetli's back, a touch that had soothed the little girl since she was a newborn. With her other hand, Verona coaxed the baby to sip water from one of the three tin cups the family shared. Lisbetli had little weight to spare.

At her mother's knee, Maria picked up the loose nail she had gripped every day of this journey. Near the base of the berth's wooden frame, she scratched a mark into the wood.

"How many is that, *Mamm*?" Maria asked.

Verona did not have to think to answer. She had counted every day on the sea, too. "Eighty-three."

"That's a lot, isn't it?"

Verona nodded. "We're almost there. Try some letters now."

Maria put the nail down and poised her finger over the coating of dirt on the floor. "Sing, *Mamm*."

Verona began to hum a quiet hymn, adjusting first her *kapp*, then Maria's. The little girl made four tedious strokes until she formed an *M*. The truth was Verona recognized only the most basic words and could barely spell her own name. She would have to depend on the schooling of the older children to help Maria.

"I'm hungry, *Mamm*."

Verona had little food to offer. She unwrapped a napkin and

handed Maria the last piece of salted pork. The ship's rations had been far from adequate, and Verona early had formed the habit of saving some of her own meals for the inevitable request from one of her children.

"Let's go find *Daed*." The distraction might keep Maria from saying she was hungry again. Verona took her warmest wrap, and the three of them stepped over the baggage and personal belongings of other passengers to get to the ladder.

Maria had learned to do well on the ladder, but for Verona climbing with Lisbetli was always challenging. On deck, Verona squinted as her eyes adjusted to the growing light. She settled Lisbetli on one hip and took Maria's hand as they walked the deck scouting for the rest of the family. Even after eighty-three days on ship, Verona's legs were unsteady. This should be the last day, Jakob had told her. Verona hoped he was right.

Lisbetli seemed to perk up in the daylight, lifting her head off her mother's shoulder. Verona dared to hope that the baby would find her cheerful disposition once again.

Verona supposed she was one of the last to come above. It was not hard to decide where to go stand. The Mennonites were portside, and the Amish had gathered starboard. Her son would be on the bow. If Captain Stedman would let him, Christian would steer the boat.

When Jakob saw her, he opened one arm wide, and she stepped into its arc.

"I knew Christian would be at the front of the boat," Verona said.

"That is because he is looking forward and not back," Jakob said. "He is a wise little boy."

"Like his *daed*." Verona leaned her head against her husband's shoulder for a fraction of a second.

"How is the baby?" Jakob asked.

Lisbetli squirmed and reached for her father. Jakob took her in his arms.

"Does that answer your question?" Verona asked.

"This little one won't remember Europe," Jakob said. "She has only hope to look forward to."

They stood a long time on the deck. As the channel narrowed even further, Verona tried to remember the map Jakob once showed her and the slender, crooked finger of water that led from the Atlantic Ocean, through the Delaware Bay and to Philadelphia. Parents stood more erect, their countenances brightening. Children took their cues from the adults and began to point and squirm with increasing frequency.

"Is that it?" they asked again and again. "Is that Philadelphia? Is that where we're going?"

Christian kept his face forward, his features raised in determination to the breeze. His feet were planted squarely, shoulder width apart. He had no need of the rail. His body adjusted immediately to every shift in the ship's motion. Jakob took delight in his four daughters, but Christian, his only son, lit his face with a color that he did not reproduce for any other occasion.

We are humble people, Verona thought, *but surely it is not a sin to feel this way about your own child. Surely God knows the joy of an only son.* Her son was well. Her baby was well. In a few hours they would be in a city with markets and merchants and an October harvest of vegetables. Her tongue salivated at the thought of food not dried in salt, food that came directly from the ground and not through a barrel.

No one in the crowd wanted to surrender a position with a view of the approaching city. There would be plenty of time to go down and collect belongings later. After almost three months on the ocean, the families on board had eyes only for their new home, their new future.

Verona sighed and put a hand to her forehead to shield her eyes from the sun. Looking after five children and keeping their living area from becoming squalor, Verona had spent much of the journey below deck.

She turned her head and coughed once, a motion that sliced through her head. Determined not to pass out, she gripped the rail. *I'm just not used to the light,* she told herself when the throbbing behind her eyes made her want to empty her stomach. *The important thing is we're almost there.*

Ten

"No more lollygagging," Annie said to the empty room. She was stiff, sore, and slow moving, but she pulled on her jeans and T-shirt and sat up at a small table in the room, rather than on the bed.

She needed a phone—her own phone, preferably. It had been turned off for most of two days, but in the middle of her haze, Annie's systematic brain determined that if she disabled the global positioning feature on her phone, anyone trying to track it would face frustration. Triangulation with wi-fi alone would be a lot harder. She turned the phone on, tapped her way through several screens, and turned off the GPS. Annie let out a slow, controlled breath. At least she could use her phone freely.

Two days of dozing in concussive haze carried consequences. E-mails stacked up to the point it could take Annie hours to sort out the technical issues and respond to her regular clients. Jamie forwarded several inquiries from potential clients. Jamie also reported that Barrett was not spending much time at the office, and the marketing assistant was floundering for direction. The bank was calling with questions the bookkeeper could not answer. Three software writers who worked for the company were nervous.

Where are you? was the clear message. *What's going on?*

But Annie could not lose time dealing with the details when the entire company was at stake.

What would Barrett and Rick be trying to do now? That was the question. Jamie's report that the bank was calling the office suggested they were trying to move funds. Calmly, she logged onto the company's primary bank account and inspected recent transactions. So far everything looked routine. Her personal accounts seemed secure as well. So what were the questions?

Barrett and Rick couldn't turn back now. They were in too deep not to win.

The attorneys. Annie brought the list up on her laptop and dialed the first number on her phone. While she listened to the ring, she checked the charge indicators on both devices. Within a few hours, she would need a place to plug in, and she was pretty sure it was not going to be at Rufus's house.

An answering service responded for the first lawyer on her list and she left a message with basic information. She dialed the second number, and then the third. She got live voices on the line, but the attorneys themselves were unavailable. More messages.

Annie stared at the phone in her hand. Once the lawyers got her voice mails, they could play phone tag for days. She had to leave the phone powered on.

Other than the bathroom across the hall, Annie had not been out of Ruth's bedroom since she arrived. Her head turned toward the footsteps she heard in the hall now and saw the girl who had gone out to milk the cow.

She dug in her bruised brain for the name of Rufus's sister. Sally? Linda?

"I'm Sophie," the girl said softly.

That's right. Sophie and Lydia. "Thank you for all the help you've been the last few days."

"You're welcome. Rufus made me promise to check on you."

"I'm much better." Annie tugged her shirt straight and wondered what her hair looked like compared to Sophie's careful braids and pins. Wincing, she stood and began to pull the bedding into a semblance of order.

"I can do that." Sophie stepped swiftly to the bed and took control of the sheets.

Annie's hands rested on the quilt, pieces of blue and purple and green forming cubes that seemed to tumble over each other. The pattern made her slightly dizzy. She supposed it had a name. Later, when she had sufficient power, she would do an Internet search on "Amish quilts."

"*Mamm* will want to know you're up." Sophie smoothed the quilt into place. "I will walk downstairs with you."

Annie nodded. She stuffed her phone into her back pocket and hung her bag over one shoulder. Every step was pain. She couldn't drive a car even if she had one. But electricity was out there, just beyond the Beiler property.

Franey Beiler met her at the bottom of the stairs. "Annalise! I didn't know you were up. Would you like something to eat?"

"I don't want to be any trouble for you." Annie swallowed the urge to add that she needed electricity more than food right now.

"Go out on the porch," Franey said. "It's a beautiful day. I'll bring you a sandwich and a glass of tea."

"Thank you."

Sophie held open the screen door. "Please excuse me. I need to weed in the garden."

Sophie's soft words drifted with her gaze as she stepped outside. Annie watched Sophie join another girl—it must be Lydia, Annie realized—squatting in the garden. Standing still, Annie thought of her own sister, Penny, and a fragment of memory about digging in the backyard. For a few minutes, Penny had persuaded Annie that they could dig to China.

On the porch, Annie found a two-seater swing, its pine slats sanded smooth along the perfect curve of the back and seat. She had to admit it was still difficult to move around. If her mind were not on an impending need for battery power, she could have surrendered to the unobstructed view of the Sangre de Cristo Mountains and her own recuperation. Instead, the mountains reminded her of her remote location. The late-afternoon sun layered the view with shifting shadows, and Annie wondered anew what she had gotten herself into. Yes, the setting was bucolic. Yes, the mountains were stunning. Yes, the air was unsullied and the land animated in ways the city could never match.

But she had no place to plug in a power cord. And without a place to plug in, the rest of it did not matter.

Annie put the swing into tentative, gentle motion.

Sangre de Cristo. Spanish for the "Blood of Christ." It struck her as interesting that a religious group like the Amish would choose to settle in the shadow of such a religious-sounding name. Was that on purpose or just coincidence?

Was anything on purpose, she wondered, or was everything just coincidence?

Coincidence that Tom's truck was in the parking lot that night.

Coincidence that she got in it.

Coincidence that she ended up here. On Amish land.

Coincidence that Barrett was stabbing her in the back.

Coincidence that Rick chose Barrett and not Annie.

Coincidence that a fall cost her two days of fighting back.

Coincidence that her great-great-grandmother's name was Byler.

Annie typed "Jakob Byler" into the search screen on her phone.

Cemetery listings, genealogy forums, Amish settlements. Annie could not waste battery power clicking through the links right now. She could not even be sure this was the Jakob Byler she was descended from, but she was curious. She put the phone in her pocket, but the Amish settlement link lurked in her mind. What if this were the right Jakob Byler from her family line? Had he been Amish? Was he related to Christian Byler, Rufus's ancestor?

Franey came through the door just then with a plate and a glass. She set them down on a small table next to the swing.

Annie had to admit the sandwich—ham and cheese stacked on whole-wheat bread she was sure Franey had baked herself—enticed her. For that matter, Franey had probably made the cheese and smoked the ham.

"Thank you." Annie reached for half of the sandwich.

"I hope you'll eat more than you have the last few days." Franey sat in the swing next to Annie. "I was beginning to worry about you."

"I feel much better," Annie said.

"*Gut.* Now you can discover God's purpose in bringing you to our home."

Had Franey been reading her mind? Annie glanced at the view again, almost ready to believe she was here for a reason. But the reason would have to wait. She could not afford to be Rick's doormat.

"I have my own business, but I can work anywhere if I have a computer and a phone." Annie bit into the sandwich and discovered how hungry she was.

"Then no doubt you'll need electricity soon."

"Yes I will." Annie watched the girls in the garden. "You have lovely daughters. Do they always work so hard?"

"They are good daughters." Franey leaned back in the swing and smiled. "Your *mudder* must be worried about you."

"I spoke to my mother." Technically this was true, though Annie had spared her mother the details of her dilemma and had not mentioned her injury.

"Here comes Rufus."

Rufus turned into the long driveway from the main road. Annie watched as Dolly pulled the buggy to the habitual spot outside the barn and stopped. Rufus lowered himself from the bench and walked toward the front porch.

Annie flushed when she saw him looking at her.

"I'm glad to see you up." Rufus did not smile, but he caught her eyes with an ease she did not expect.

81

"What's that in your hand?" Franey asked.

"It used to be my favorite saw." Rufus sank onto a porch step below the swing and stared out at the mountains. "Someone snapped it in half today."

"Oh Rufus, I'm sorry," Franey said. "I hate that these things keep happening to you."

"I just left it for a few minutes." He examined the broken pieces. "I guess it doesn't take long for someone to step on the end and yank the handle up."

"Someone is watching you," Annie said. "Someone saw an opportunity and took it. It's a message."

Rufus sighed. "I try to be mindful about who is around when I'm working, but I cannot see everyone."

"What about your crew?" Annie asked.

"My crew? A couple of Amish boys. I can't see what they would have to gain from breaking my tools."

"You never know," Annie said. "Sometimes the people closest to you are the ones you have to worry about."

Rufus turned his head toward Annie. "Be careful, Annalise. You might be giving me a clue about why you're here."

At that moment, Annie's phone rang in her pocket. She sprang off the swing—then winced in pain. Looking at the incoming number, she said, "I have to take this." With one hand holding the phone to her ear and the other supporting a sore spot in her back, she went down the steps and toward the barn for some privacy.

No matter how far she wandered, Annie felt Rufus's eyes on her while she spoke to attorney number two. Franey got up and went into the house, but Rufus sprawled statue-like on the porch steps, his elbows propped two steps behind him. In one hand, the metal of the broken saw glinted in the sun. The slump in his shoulders distracted her enough that she had to turn away from him to explain her legal challenge to the attorney. A few minutes later, she breathed a sigh of relief and started back toward the porch. Rufus had not moved.

"Would you be able to give me a ride into town tomorrow?" she asked. "I just arranged a meeting."

"I leave pretty early," Rufus reminded her.

"I'll be ready." Annie sat next to Rufus on the step.

"Are you sure you're well enough for this?"

"I have no choice."

"You always have a choice," he said.

Annie raised her eyes to the view. "It doesn't seem that way in this situation. It's complicated."

"So you've said."

"Can I ride with you or not?" Annie tightened her grip on the phone in her hand.

"Of course."

"Perhaps it's better if I move back to the motel anyway."

"You're welcome here."

"Thank you. Your family has been lovely and accommodating, but I think I should go."

"To the land of electricity."

"Well, yes. Electricity connects me to my life, after all."

"Or cuts you off from it, depending on how you look at it."

Annie did not respond. She fixed her eyes on the Sangre de Cristos. As remote as the Beiler house felt from her real life, the mountains beckoned into deeper mystery.

"The tea your mother brought me had ice cubes," Annie said, "and the lettuce on the sandwich was crisp and cool. How. . ."

"Propane gas refrigerator," Rufus said. "We heat water with propane, too."

"And the lamps are all propane?" Annie mentally pictured the lamps in Ruth's bedroom.

Rufus nodded. "The wringer washing machine runs off a gas engine. In Pennsylvania, my mother had a blender that ran off of compressed air. We use generators. And you'd be amazed what we can do with a few car batteries if we really want to."

"But no electricity." Annie's fingers itched to type "Amish

electricity" into a search window.

"We don't connect to the electrical grid," Rufus said. "Too much of modern life comes too fast when you do that."

"I can only imagine what you must think of my life."

"I know very little about your life," Rufus said, "but it got you here. You have to wonder about that."

"Believe me, I do," Annie said. "I'm meeting with a lawyer tomorrow. I hope to sort things out soon."

"I hope you get what you want."

"Maybe he could help you, too," Annie said. "Surely what you're experiencing constitutes harassment."

"Talking to a lawyer will not get me what I want."

"If this Karl Kramer would leave you alone, you could get on with your life," Annie said.

"I'll get on with my life either way."

He turned his head to look at her. His wide violet-blue eyes sparkled in the sunlight. Annie's breath caught.

"What is it?" Rufus asked. "Pain?"

She shook her head. "Your eyes. I suppose you know how striking they are."

He tilted his head. "I'm told they are my grandmother's eyes, and her grandmother before that."

She felt his eyes on her then, considering her.

"It's good you're staying another night," he said. "How about if I take you to town tomorrow, you have your meeting and your electricity, and then you come back here for one more night? Just to be sure."

Annie nodded, transfixed. As much as she needed a dose of electricity, she wanted to return to this peacefulness.

He leaned forward and prepared to stand. "I'd better round up Jacob and check on the animals."

"Can I come?"

Eleven

$\mathcal{D}$olly crunched the apple while Rufus stroked the spot between her eyes the next morning. He had hitched the larger buggy. It would be more comfortable for Annalise. Rufus still wished he could talk her into resting one more day. What was so important that it could not wait for her to be stronger tomorrow?

The sound of giggling made him lift his hand from Dolly's face and turn toward the barn. Jacob shot out of the structure with a grin on his ruddy face.

"Annalise doesn't know how to milk a cow." Jacob raised a hand to smother his laughter.

Annalise emerged from the barn, flanked by Sophie and Lydia. "I'm afraid it's true. I haven't been near a cow for twenty years—until now."

"I'm going to teach her," Sophie said. "You'll be back in time for the evening milking, won't you?"

Rufus raised his eyebrows. "I believe so."

"Let's start with just *touching* a cow, all right?" Annalise smiled. "I'm not making any promises."

She was at ease with his siblings, which brought unexpected

relief to Rufus. Her ponytail bounced in the morning light, and Rufus could hardly tear his gaze away. "We should be going."

Annalise took the hand Rufus offered, and he helped her up and onto the buggy bench. Having her there, beside him, as he took Dolly onto the road, made him grasp for conversation. He hoped for something they might find in common, but nothing took solid shape. Instead, he remembered her form in his arms as he carried her to the buggy outside the motel, and later up the stairs to Ruth's bedroom, her face close to his.

Rufus glanced at Annalise, and she smiled awkwardly, as if she were reading his mind. Both of them looked away.

He had to speak. "This meeting will solve your troubles, *ya*?"

She tilted her head. "I hope at least to have an ally by the time it's over."

"Then there is to be a battle?"

"Perhaps *confrontation* is a better word. It's complicated."

"Yes, I remember." She did not believe he could understand her business troubles. Perhaps she was right. "At least the cow will be waiting for you when this day is behind you."

She laughed. "That's bound to be a confrontation of a different sort."

"The *English* have farms," he said. "Surely you have some experience."

"I went to a dairy farm on a school field trip once. Six hundred cows. Machines everywhere."

"Perhaps your visit here gives you a different perspective of the quiet life." Rufus turned her head to see her face.

Annalise met his gaze with a smile. "It's quite tempting to consider that—on many levels. I will know more after this meeting."

The front left buggy wheel hit a hole in the pavement, and Annalise winced at the sudden dip.

"You are still sore," Rufus said.

"Yes, but clear of mind."

Annie chose a table in the coffee shop away from the commotion at the counter and sat in a chair facing the door. The power cord ran from her laptop into the outlet beneath the table. She eyed with satisfaction the icon on her screen that assured her juice was flowing. Her meeting with the attorney was not for two hours, but she had plenty of work to catch up on. She had not said much to Lee Solano on the phone the day before and was leery that someone immediately available and willing to meet her in a small-town coffee shop rather than his own office was desperate for work. What did that say about his practice? But the others had not returned her inquiry calls, making him her only option.

Housed in a beige brick building, the imitation Starbucks coffee and tea shop could have been anywhere in the country with roots from two centuries earlier. With a tall caramel latte within reach, Annie attacked her e-mail backlog. Scanning, she could tell which ones would be simple to answer. A good number she could easily redirect to her software writers. A few were starting to sound snippy about her lack of a timely response. One by one she placated the clients who depended on her technical services.

The company's ongoing bread-and-butter work was writing custom programs with focused objectives that clients identified for themselves. The solutions she found, however, eventually became joints and tendons of the consumer patterns software she now had stashed on a secure server.

On a typical day in the office, Annie would dispense with administrative tasks fairly quickly, motivated by the anticipation of working on the new project as many hours of the day as possible. Barrett would be in his office next door. He did less and less programming and more and more marketing and seemed happy with the arrangement.

Until a few weeks ago. The morning banter ceased. When Barrett refilled his coffee mug, he passed by her open door without a greeting. At the end of the day, he was out the door without stopping in to say good night. It was true he had a wife and baby at home, but that had never gnawed into his extroverted socializing before.

Annie missed the old Barrett.

The string of e-mail messages from Jamie, her assistant, kept Annie informed of routine matters. Jamie was a solid anchor whenever Annie traveled. This absence was no different. Some messages, however, carried an undertone that said, *Please call me.*

Annie wrapped her fingers around her cell phone, which had been turned off most of the time for days. As little as she knew about the Amish, she knew a phone ringing as constantly as hers did would be unwelcome. Now she turned it on. To no surprise, the voice-mail box was full and text messages nearly cascaded off the screen to the floor. Annie ignored them all and dialed Jamie's number.

"Friesen-Paige Solutions," Jamie said.

"Don't let on, but it's me," Annie said.

"How may I help you?" Jamie said evenly.

"Go next door to the doughnut shop. Call me from there."

Annie put the phone down on the table and stared at it, mentally picturing Jamie casually stepping out from behind her desk and leaving the suite then the redbrick building. It was nothing unusual for Jamie to make a doughnut run.

The phone rang, and Annie snatched it up. "Jamie?"

"Annie, what's going on? I opened an envelope from the lawyers today, expecting something routine. But you're named as a defendant in a suit, and Barrett is the plaintiff. Is this some kind of joke?"

Annie's shoulders slumped. "I wish."

"Did you and Barrett have a fight?"

"Not exactly," Annie said.

"Rick drew up these papers," Jamie said. "I thought you and Rick—"

"Not anymore. That's over."

"Oh. Sorry."

"Don't be. Listen, Jamie, I don't know when I'll be back to the office. I'm going to work from where I am for a while."

"And where are you?" Jamie asked.

"That doesn't matter." It was better if Jamie did not know. "I promise to stay in touch. Do me a favor and watch for any funny business on my credit cards or debit card."

"This all sounds very cloak and dagger," Jamie said.

"I'm just being careful."

"What should I do about the papers Rick sent over?"

"Scan them and e-mail them to me. Can you do that in the next few minutes?"

"Yes, of course."

"I've been through my e-mail. Any other fires I should know about?"

They talked for a few more minutes about routine matters. Barrett was staying away from the office, Annie was glad to hear.

"Thanks, Jamie," Annie said. "Don't forget to take doughnuts back to the office with you."

Annie ended the call. A lawsuit. So that is what it had come to. Barrett stopped talking to her, and Rick—who supposedly loved her—chose sides and cast her away.

Why would Barrett do this? He knew they had a good thing going. They were both making great money. He never once hinted that anything was wrong.

Perhaps Rick had been planning this for months. Their first date, the sweetness of their first kiss, the hunger in the ones that followed—maybe it was all about the company. And when Rick saw that she was too savvy to do anything careless—such as sign a document she had not read carefully—he turned to Barrett. With his affable, trusting nature, Barrett was an easy target. Any number of arguments coming from the mouth of the firm's legal representation could persuade Barrett to hack into Annie's work.

Annie steamed. To think that she had ever trusted Rick Stebbins, and even let herself care about him. Poor Barrett. No matter how Rick had lured him in, Barrett's pride would not let him back out now.

The main door to the coffee shop opened and a man in a gray suit entered. Annie stood and fixed her eyes on him. It wasn't a very good suit and did not fit well. The man pushed sunglasses off his face to the top of his balding head. In a few seconds, he figured out who his client was. They introduced themselves with a handshake, and Lee Solano went to the counter to buy the socially obligatory coffee that would entitle him to conduct business on the premises.

Annie had asked questions about his practice and experience the day before on the phone. Now she probed further. She had to be as sure as possible that Lee Solano was outside Rick's sphere of influence, and she had to feel confident he understood what was at stake in an intellectual property matter—now a lawsuit. When she was as satisfied as she could be under the circumstances, Annie blew out her breath and began her story. Lee Solano dutifully took notes with a cheap pen on a classic yellow legal pad. Just as she finished, a new e-mail dinged in. Jamie had sent the attachment.

Annie opened it and turned her screen toward Lee. "Can they do this?"

Lee squinted as he scrolled through the document.

"What does he want?" Annie asked.

"Everything," Lee answered quickly. "You must have some serious work going on. This Barrett fellow claims his creative contribution was the impetus leading to the work, and that without it the work would not exist. On that basis, he wants your name separated from the work, leaving him free to pursue legal agreements involving the work without requiring your permission."

"I don't understand. We're partners. We run a company together."

"He's making the claim that this particular work does not

fall within the boundaries established by your partnership. I would have to see your partnership incorporation documents to comment on that."

"But that's ridiculous." Annie took a gulp of coffee. "Barrett and I have worked together for years. We have different strengths, but we share the profit equally."

Lee shrugged. "Existing intellectual property laws were developed decades ago without any glimmer of application to software. Intellectual property used to be about words and music and art. Entries like software take some thrashing out in the courts. I'm afraid we're a long way from having clear application of the law under either copyright or patents."

"Where does that leave me?" Annie swallowed hard.

"We'll start with a countersuit," Lee said, "and I'll bury Mr. Stebbins in paperwork. But our best bet is to find some way to keep this from going to court. Don't worry, Miss Friesen. You've got someone on your side now."

Rufus spent the morning making sure the custom cabinets installed throughout the house under construction were exactly as ordered and that no damage had occurred to the black oak panels. A flooring company from Walsenburg was in the midst of installing carpets and hardwoods. It would not be long now before the family could move in.

Rufus collected his tools and laid them carefully in the back of the buggy. The two teenagers who worked for him were gone for the day. Rufus had a few fix-it jobs around town, and the Amish families in the valley always seemed to require a carpenter, but he needed another big job. Under his father's skill and Joel's help, the farm was doing as well as could be expected in the arid Colorado climate but not turning much of a profit. Coaxing growth from seeds in the ground seemed to require a different set of farming habits than in Pennsylvania. The dry air and soil left a lot for the

Beilers to learn about farming in the West, rather than in the long-tested soil of Lancaster County, Pennsylvania. Land might be cheaper in Colorado, but it was also more stubborn.

He was not unhappy with his business prospects, but lately they had grown thinner, making Rufus wonder what Karl Kramer was telling people about him. The Amish community was still small. Rufus needed jobs from the *English* to build a profitable business.

Rufus swung up onto the bench, picked up the reins, and directed Dolly into town. For a few minutes, he sat in the buggy in front of the coffee shop. He had heard of people who spent hours in coffee shops and could well imagine Annalise as one of them. After securing Dolly to a signpost cemented into the sidewalk, he reached under the seat for an item then pulled open the shop door.

She looked up almost immediately. And smiled.

Rufus pulled out the chair across from her and sat down. In his hand was his cell phone and the power cord. Behind a sober face, he gave in to amusement at her wide eyes.

"You're using a phone *and* electricity?"

"I promised to tell you our views on electricity."

"By using it in a public place?"

"Electricity is a useful form of power. We recognize that. We simply do not want electricity to become the focus of our lives by bringing it into our homes. That is the place of our families."

"And the phone?"

"Our district has a generous position on phones because we are so widely scattered. We are permitted to use phones for business and safety."

"But not convenience?"

"Convenience is for the individual. For us, the community comes first. If electricity or a phone carries us away from community, it also carries us away from God."

"I never thought of it like that." Annalise fidgeted with a pen on the table.

"You can ask any questions you wish."

"Thank you. Maybe when I don't have so much on my mind. . ."

"Of course. How did your business meeting go?"

She laid her head to one side, and her loose hair danced in the light as it fell away from her face. If he never married, he would never see a woman's hair fall away from her ear in just that way and be able to reach out and catch it.

"It went well," she said. "We have a plan of action." As if she could read his thoughts—for the second time that day—she smoothed her hair close to her head and tucked it behind her ear.

"And will this plan of action carry you home—to your own community?"

She pressed her lips together. "I hope so."

Annalise did not quite meet his eyes this time. "I promised Mo I would stop by the motel," he said, "but I can enjoy a cup of *kaffi* first."

They did not leave the coffee shop for another hour. When they reached the motel, Rufus helped Annalise down once again. Her pale complexion told him she was more tired than she would admit.

The door of the motel lobby swung open, and Mo emerged. "Well, if it isn't our star guest. How are you?"

Annalise managed a smile, Rufus was glad to see.

"How is your mother?" Annalise asked.

"Cranky as ever, but the crisis is averted for now." Mo turned to Rufus. "Just the man I want to see. I've had a vision of remodeling the lobby, and you're just the person for the job."

In the lobby, Annalise stood to one side and held her computer to her chest, glancing at him from time to time as Mo gestured and explained. Rufus hardly heard a word Mo said about the work.

"Do it!" Jacob urged.

Annalise grimaced. Rufus spread hay.

"*Die Kuh*," the little boy said, "and it's a very nice cow." He leaned his head into the side of the cow, next to where Sophie sat on a three-legged stool.

"Her face is pretty," Annalise said. Both of the animal's pink ears stood up straight. Between her eyes a white stripe divided a mass of brown.

"Touch her nose," Jacob said. "She likes that."

"Jacob," Rufus said softly, "if Annalise does not want to touch the cow, she does not have to." It was, after all, a texture bearing no resemblance to her sleek laptop keys.

"It's not that I don't want to," Annalise said. "It's just not as simple as it sounds."

"I must start milking soon," Sophie said. "Please don't startle her."

Annalise's hand moved, slowly, toward the white stripe. When the cow moaned, she flinched but immediately resumed her purpose.

Rufus smiled and tossed a pitchfork of hay into Dolly's stall, glad to see Annalise's determined spirit on display in a cow stall as well as a coffee shop.

Two slender fingers made contact in the space between the cow's eyes and nose, and a moment later, a full hand began a soothing stroking motion.

"It feels harder than I thought it would," Annalise said.

His sisters were giggling, and Annalise's laugh blended with the sound.

She relaxed. He saw it. Rufus leaned on his pitchfork and savored this image of Annalise Friesen in his barn with members of his family. Even the denim bag slid off her shoulder and nested in the hay as she now rubbed the sides of the cow's face with both hands.

Twelve

Annie wrestled dreams that night and woke more than once hoping for daylight to creep through the curtains in Ruth's bedroom. Finally, she sat up and turned on the propane bedside lamp. She was beginning to miss the pillow-topped mattress in her condo, surrounded by familiar possessions.

She had spotted three thrift stores in Westcliffe—which she found curious given the insignificant size of the town—so she had some options to find more clothing. It looked as if she would be here another few days while Lee Solano conjured whatever kind of magic he had in his power. For now, his instructions were for Annie to lie low and not show any response to Rick's legal maneuvers. Returning to Mo's motel would at least put electricity on her side. She was taking a break, she told herself, a short break that would save her business.

She threw back the quilt and stepped to the desk four feet away to power up her laptop. For now she ignored her e-mail, but she could not resist checking her secure server. It looked as if Barrett had been knocking around the edges of the project but had not gotten through the barricades she had in place.

Annie smiled. All this time and he wasn't making a dent. She touched a hand to her neck to finger the gold chain—and felt nothing but skin.

Panicked, Annie opened every drawer in the room and unfolded her paltry wardrobe. She dumped her denim bag onto the bed and separated the contents for inspection. Not finding the gold chain, she bolted to the bathroom across the hall, trying to remember everything she had touched in the last few days. Annie could not even remember the last time she had been sure the chain was around her neck.

She sank into the bed to wait for first light.

Rufus moved the envelope aside as he had done dozens of times already and rummaged for a pencil in his toolbox. The letter had arrived five days ago. Rufus was not sure he wanted to know what it said. Ruth repeatedly wrote to him in care of Tom and Tricia, so he could only conclude she did not want their parents to know of the letters.

What happened was between Ruth and *Daed* and *Mamm*. Rufus did not want to find himself in the middle. And he did not think it was a good idea to involve Tom and Tricia even just to deliver a letter that arrived at their home.

Ruth had taken almost nothing with her that day. Rufus was never sure if it was because she did not truly intend to go or because she did not want to be beholden to anyone, not even for a change of clothes.

Rufus missed her. Ruth was the sister nearest to him in age, though two married brothers filled the span between them. When he raised the question of moving to Colorado, Ruth was the first to say she wanted to go. His married brothers thought Rufus ought to at least find a wife before heading out for a new settlement. When his parents decided they were in favor of the move because it could mean land for their younger sons, Rufus's determination set in.

In Colorado, the chances of finding a wife among the Amish—
the only wife Rufus could accept—were far from encouraging. He
was already twenty-eight and was still required to keep his face
clean shaven and sit in church with the younger unmarried men.
If it was God's will for Rufus to be alone, so be it. He would still
work hard for the sake of his family.

Mo made it clear the previous afternoon that she was not
looking for bids on the work she had in mind. She wanted Rufus.
He had done enough odd jobs to prove he was dependable and
honest, she said, and she had seen his cabinetry craftsmanship in
the home of a friend. Mo was finished repairing falling shelves.
She wanted new ones. A new reception desk. New cubbies behind
the desk. Perhaps a new look for the small lobby that would appeal
to more upscale customers.

In his workshop across the yard from the barn, Rufus sketched
the lobby from memory before breakfast. A vision emerged as his
pencil skittered across the page, shading in cabinetry and a desk
with rounded, welcoming edges. The day before, Mo gestured widely
with her own ideas, but they were vague. Rufus's sketch would
accomplish her objectives and improve the traffic flow through the
lobby as well.

Engrossed in the task of putting his vision on paper, Rufus did
not hear Annalise approach the open door of his workshop.

"Hi, Rufus."

He turned toward her approaching brightness as he ripped the
page from the pad in satisfaction. "*Guder mariye*, Annalise. Are
you hungry for breakfast?"

"Famished," Annalise said. She looked around. "So, this is
where you work?"

Her shoulders and back looked less tentative. Her hair hung
loose, cradling her face in softness before draping her shoulders
with its sheen. Rufus turned his gaze away, abruptly aware of the
effect she was having on him.

"I am a simple cabinetmaker and carpenter."

She touched a small chest awaiting its lid. "It's beautiful."

Suddenly he wanted to give it to her, but he had promised it to Sophie.

"I'm missing the gold chain I always wear," Annalise said, her hand at her unadorned neck. "I wonder if you've seen it."

Rufus slapped his own head. "It's not lost. They removed it at the clinic when they were doing X-rays. Sophie found it in the bag when she washed your things. She was afraid of losing it, so she brought to me." Rufus suppressed the warmth that came with thinking about holding the chain in his hand.

"You have my chain?"

"It's in the buggy," Rufus said, "in a box under the bench. It did not seem right to have it in the house. Our women do not wear jewelry. I'm sorry I forgot about it."

"Can I go get it?"

"I will get it. Just wait here."

Rufus dropped his pencil and sketch into his toolbox and disappeared out the front of the building, leaving Annie standing alone in the workshop. She buzzed her lips and looked around for a place to sit down, settling on a low, rugged bench beside the door.

Curious, Annie tilted her head to try to look at Rufus's sketch, but he had laid it facedown. All she could see were the impressions of the heaviest lines making slight ridges in the back of the paper. An envelope obscured the bottom of the page. Annie did not have to look too hard to read the writing on the sealed message. The top left corner clearly said "Ruth Beiler" with an address in Colorado Springs. Annie recognized the street name. It was just off a major intersection she drove through several times a week.

Rufus came through the door. Annie stood and moved toward him. He opened a small plastic envelope and poured the gold chain into her open hand. She closed her fist around the gold, brushing his fingers in the process. Was it her imagination, or did his hand quiver just once?

"Thank you!" She opened the clasp and raised the chain to her neck. Her hands met at the back of her neck and buoyed her hair for a moment while she fastened the clasp.

"You're welcome." Rufus closed his own hand over the small plastic bag, now empty. "I'm sorry I didn't remember sooner. It seems to mean something to you."

"It's twenty-four-karat gold. I bought it when—" Annie stopped herself. Rufus would not be interested in how she celebrated making her fortune. "Never mind. Just thank you."

"We should go have breakfast."

"Yes." Annie paused. "I do have one question, though."

"Of course."

"Why haven't you opened that letter from your sister?"

Ruth Beiler flipped back to the beginning of the chapter in her textbook. After reading for forty minutes, she would be hard pressed to write a paragraph identifying the chapter's main themes. In four hours she had to be in class ready to take a quiz. Starting over was the obvious choice.

Thinking coffee might help her concentrate, she rose from the chair and moved to the wide ledge under the window that held a small coffeemaker and an electric kettle. Ruth's dorm room was compact, but it was private. When she first arrived, she tried living with a roommate, with disastrous results. The young woman assigned to share a room with her did not know what to make of someone with such conservative views and habits. Though they were both nursing students at the University of Colorado, they found little common ground.

In those days Ruth still wore her *kapp*. Now it hung on a hook by the door, and she had traded in her aproned dress for simple long skirts and high-necked solid-colored tops. Her hair was still in braids coiled against the back of her head. She stood out when she walked across campus or boarded a bus to go to her job at the nursing home, but becoming modern had never been Ruth's intention when she left Westcliffe.

Ruth scooped coffee into a fresh filter and poured water through the small coffeemaker. In a few seconds, the familiar dripping began. She absently tapped the top of the pot while she pondered what really kept her from studying.

If Rufus had read her letter and answered it right away, she would have heard from him by now.

And what if he never read it?

Ruth wasn't sorry. Her choice was not without consequence. She regretted the pain she caused. But she would choose the same again.

It was an impulse on his part to invite her, Annie was sure. And it was an impulse on her part to accept. Perhaps he regretted it. She would not blame him. Spiritual devotion had little to do with why she accepted, and neither did curiosity.

Little Jacob was glad to see her when Rufus brought the small buggy to pick her up on Sunday morning. The rest of the family would come in the larger buggy pulled by Brownie, the second Beiler horse. Jacob chattered away the miles between the motel and the farm where a cluster of six or eight Amish families would gather to worship.

Church, Amish-style.

Annie's Protestant upbringing included more or less weekly church attendance. She carried fond memories of going to church and the people who cared for her there. In high school, though, training for track competitions dominated her schedule, and then she went away to college. As an adult, her churchgoing habit was a long way from regular. A few months earlier, though, she had attended a friend's baptism. In her teen years, Annie always intended to be baptized, but the timing never seemed right.

She believed. Certainly she never decided *not* to believe. But getting an education and launching a career—and starting two companies—required focus. Time. Energy. Now she wondered if she had moved too far away from God for it to matter that she had not been baptized.

Supposing that God still spoke English, Annie decided to pray. After all, she was in church. *Please, God, make this mean something.*

Annie now sat on a bench in the back on the women's side of the room. Rufus gave her enough notice that she was able to rustle up a modest skirt among her thrift-store finds. People around her spoke German, including Rufus's mother and two younger sisters. The idea of going to church with Rufus should have made her think twice. If she had known the service would be in German and she would not even be sitting with Rufus, she might have thought three times.

Sophie leaned over and whispered into Annie's ear. Annie quickly tucked her gold chain under the top of her blouse. She had a lot to learn about Amish worship.

The women faced the men. Annie wanted to shift to one side and look for Rufus among the unmarried men—all of them younger than he was. Perhaps she could catch his eye. But she knew better than to wiggle in church. Rufus mentioned that the services tended to be long, but Annie never imagined he meant three hours and two sermons.

With no hint of modernity in the service, Annie supposed the Amish had always worshiped this way, even in the days of the first settlers to land in Pennsylvania. She made a mental note to do a fresh Internet search on "early Amish worship" as soon as it was appropriate to use her phone.

At last the final hymn began with a single male voice. Others gradually joined. Sophie shared a battered hymnal with Annie, but the page held only German words that meant nothing to Annie. Everyone seemed to know the tune.

Annie filed outside with the other women. It wasn't long before the transformation was under way to accommodate a meal for sixty people. Annie just tried to stay out of the way as men rearranged benches and women arranged dishes on three serving tables. Sophie and Lydia greeted friends they only saw every two weeks at church before being prodded to help with the food. Annie watched the constant movement, but she was at a loss for how to step in and help. Instead, she wandered farther away, past the row where the horses were tied and out to a fence around a field. In a brief episode of English, someone had mentioned that the host family grew barley.

In the middle of the commotion, Annie was relieved to find Rufus walking toward her.

"You might have prepared me a bit more," she said playfully.

"Would you have come if I had?" He looked over his shoulder, and she followed his eye toward men standing in a group.

She shrugged. "Now we'll never know."

"Was it torture?"

"Let's just say my High German is not any better than my Pennsylvania Dutch."

"When you learn one, you will no doubt learn the other."

When. He said "when." Annie soaked up his countenance. These were his people. This was his life. And he had honored her by inviting her to share it for these few hours.

"Are you hungry?" His face crinkled.

"Let me guess," Annie said. "Men eat separately from women."

"You are learning our ways well."

"The ways are new to me, but I have a feeling they are very old."

Rufus adjusted his black felt hat. "We do not rush into change."

"But you do change, don't you?" Annie gestured toward the house. "Lights, hot running water. This is not exactly camping out."

"We consider our choices carefully. Are they good for the family? For the community? Our old ways remind us that we live apart, separate from the ways of the world."

Annie resisted the impulse to raise her fingers to her gold chain. "Yet when I blundered in bringing the twenty-first century with me, you welcomed me."

"We welcome anyone who seeks truth."

Annie's reply caught in her throat. Perhaps he was right. Perhaps she wanted more from Westcliffe than a place to hide from Rick Stebbins. She could have gone somewhere else when she had the chance. And yet she was here.

"Maybe after lunch you could give me the abbreviated English version of the sermon."

"Which one?" He grinned.

"The one you think would do me the most good."

A voice boomed from beyond them. The only word Annie could pick out was Rufus's name.

"They need my help," he said.

She nodded, and he walked backward away from her, smiling. She again watched the activity, mesmerized by how little it must have changed in the last couple of hundred years.

Thirteen

October 8, 1737

"I want to go right now." Maria pulled on her brother's hand.

Christian held his position solidly. "We can't. We just have to wait a little while longer."

"No more waiting!" Maria hollered.

Christian clamped a hand over her mouth and turned her around to face him. "Maria Beyeler, you hush," he hissed. "This is important."

This was no time for child's play. While he knew Maria was too young to appreciate the solemnity, Christian did not intend to miss the moment. The ship's deck was at capacity with families ready to debark after one last formality.

Captain Stedman lined up the men, sixteen years or older, and prepared them to march off the ship.

"Why can't we go?" Maria wanted to know.

"It's the law," Christian said. "First *Daed* has to promise to be a good subject to the king of England. We have to wait for him to come back."

"I'm tired of waiting." Maria stomped away, and Christian let her. He could see she was headed for their mother, standing only a few yards away. He was tired of waiting, too.

When the men began filing off the ship, the officials watched them carefully. Small boys were another matter, Christian realized. At the moment, no one cared what he did. His heart pounding in triumph, he found himself on the pier a few minutes later. He could see his father's height among the throng of men and ran sideways to keep up with the march yet not lose sight of his *daed*. The words the men spoke would mark their decisions to settle in the New World, and Christian wanted to see his father's face when he took the oath.

Christian felt his feet lift from the ground as his shirt tangled around his neck. "*Daed!*" he screamed.

A gruff, middle-aged man picked Christian up and set him atop a barrel on the pier. His red face spouted angry English words, and he shook his finger in the boy's face, but all Christian could do was shrug.

"*Daed!*" Christian screamed again before the man clamped his hand on Christian's mouth.

The man pointed toward what looked like a market to Christian—but they were selling people. Christian remembered his parents had said they were fortunate to have funds to pay for their passage, while others crossed the ocean as redemptioners who would work for years to redeem the price of their journey. Panicking, he struggled against the man's grip.

Christian managed to free his face. "Amish!" he shouted, "Amish!"

The man stepped back to look at him more closely.

And then Jakob was there, scooping up his son. He rattled at the man in German. The man screeched at him in English. Christian clung to his father, and Jakob hustled to rejoin the march before anyone could stop them.

"What were you thinking?" Jakob had a firm grip on the back of Christian's shirt.

"I just wanted to see you take the oath," Christian said.

"You almost got yourself sold as an indentured servant," Jakob said. "I'm sure he thought you stowed away on the ship. The men who run these shipping lines are not known for their mercy toward boys who are able-bodied workers."

"*Es dutt mirr leed*," Christian said. Triumph dissipated into shame. "I'm sorry. Please forgive me."

"I do forgive you." Jakob did not break stride. "But you must be more careful."

There was no going back now. Shamed or not, Christian would see his father swear allegiance to King George. The oath would be in English, which amused Christian, because his father knew only about two dozen words of the language, which he had picked up from the crew of the *Charming Nancy*.

At the courthouse, an official with a sheet of paper for reference began to call out phrases, which the men, whether Amish or Mennonite, in a collective rich bass, echoed.

We subscribers, natives and the late inhabitants of the Palatinate upon the Rhine and places adjacent, having transported ourselves and families into the Province of Pennsylvania, a Colony subject to the Crown of Great Britain, in hopes and expectation of finding a retreat and peaceable Settlement therein, do solemnly promise and engage that we will be faithful and bear true allegiance to his present majesty King George the Second and his successors, kings of Great Britain, and will be faithful to the proprietor of this province and that we will demean ourselves peaceably to all his said majesty's subjects and strictly observe and conform to the laws of England and of this province to the utmost of our power and best of our understanding.

A thunderous cheer rose from the men, Christian's voice among them. He caught his father's eye and grinned.

Verona was frantic when she discovered Christian gone, but Jakob managed to calm her when he returned to the ship with their son. Now the family stood in line to debark. As they inched forward, Jakob shoved the heavier barrel and the older children managed the lighter one together. Verona cradled the subdued Lisbetli and gripped Maria's hand as much as she could. In addition to the barrels, they had three small trunks that Jakob hefted easily one at a time and bundles the children carried.

This was what it came down to. Fifteen years of marriage, five children, a life of being ostracized for daring to stand by their beliefs, and what she had to show for it was right before her eyes in shades of gray and brown crammed into barrels and bundles. Everything she had for setting up housekeeping in a wilderness was within her reach.

On the ship, Verona had traded away a few items for things that seemed more pressing at the time. When Christian wanted a book of botany descriptions that no longer amused the Stutzman boy, Verona parted with a tin platter. When Maria fell in love with a small bucket, Verona parted with two wooden spoons. She could do so little to give her children pleasure during the months at sea. Trades among passengers seemed to provide diversion that made the journey less tedious. Jakob assured her they could find what they needed in Philadelphia. Ships came in every week bearing goods from Europe and the Caribbean, and he had budgeted funds for bedding and a few simple pieces of furniture.

Verona absently let go of Maria and put her hand to her own forehead, not sure whether it was her hand or her face that was clammy. The headache that began several hours ago had not abated, but the demands of getting the family ready to leave the ship left her no time to indulge in rest.

"Maria, come back here," Barbara called. "We have to wait in line."

Verona snapped to attention, only now realizing that Maria had left her sight.

"No more waiting!" Maria pouted. But to Verona's relief, she returned.

One by one the passengers filed past a makeshift table where their names were checked off lists. Jakob gave the sonorous announcement of his name and the names of everyone in the family. Barbara stood at his side, her eyes flicking from one set of papers to another and watching pens scratch and spill ink. Finally, Jakob turned and grinned at Verona, signaling their freedom.

"*Daed*," Barbara said, "they didn't spell our names right."

"What does it matter?" Jakob said. "We know our names."

"But the ship's list says *Biler*. And I saw a man write *Byler*." She spelled the difference aloud.

Jakob chuckled. "They've made us sound properly English."

It was not easy getting their meager belongings lowered to the dock. At one point, Verona handed the baby to Barbara because her own arms were too unsteady to carry her, much less help hoist the barrels and bundles. She wanted only to close her eyes and lie down. As soon as the first crate was upright on the dock, Verona sat on it and settled Lisbetli in her lap once again.

As anxious as everyone had been to get off the boat, now they looked lost. Verona's ears were unaccustomed to the sound of English coming from wharf workers, and her head hurt too much to try to make sense of the strange words. Passengers huddled with their earthly possessions and spoke their comfortable German. A few experimented with walking on solid ground again, while others sat on their trunks and looked around, trying to get their bearings. Verona sat with her back to the ship with its masts and sails and rigging. She was not sure what she expected of Philadelphia, but not this. Dozens of piers protruded into the Delaware River. Each was a hive of activity. Sailors roamed while stevedores moved goods off and on ships. Laborers pushed carts laden with goods. Horses pulled against the weight of wagons.

Beyond the docks, brick and clapboard structures looked solid, for which Verona was grateful, but also they were also foreign and unfamiliar.

Two mothers clutched each other in a moment of grief. Verona recognized them. Between them they had lost a husband and four children during the journey. Gratitude for the safety of her family stabbed her heart. Was it selfish to be glad her husband and children were walking around on the dock when so many had been lost? She squeezed Lisbetli tighter.

Jakob paused to catch his breath. Two barrels, three trunks, assorted bundles. Everything seemed accounted for. Around them, families gradually made their way off the dock at various paces. It was time for him to sort out his own family's next move.

"Where will we go now, *Daed*?" Anna asked.

"I have an address," Jakob answered. "An English Quaker family rents out houses to Germans and Swiss. We will be comfortable waiting there."

"No more waiting!" Maria stomped her foot. "I want to go to the new farm right now."

"Shhh." Verona beckoned the protesting child to her side.

Jakob tilted his head and considered his wife. He had expected her to be more animated upon arrival. She sat on the top of the barrel, gripping Lisbetli, staring without focus.

"We have to wait, Maria." Christian's voice carried an authority Jakob had not heard before. "It takes time to get the papers for the farm."

"How much time?" Maria wanted to know.

"That's hard to say," Jakob said. "First I have to apply for a land grant, and then we'll have to wait for a survey."

"I want to grow beets."

"I'm afraid you'll have to wait until spring to plant your beets."

"How long until spring?" Maria stamped her foot.

"About six months."

"I don't want to wait."

"You have no choice," Christian said. "*Daed*, we need to hire a wagon, don't we? Someone who can take us to the address?"

Jakob nodded. "It's a German part of town. Some of our families from the ship will be nearby."

"I'll go up to the road and find a wagon," Christian said.

"We'll go together," Jakob said. He was not about to let his only son run off unattended again. "Perhaps we can share a wagon with the Zimmermans."

Jakob hoped the information he received was reliable. If it was not, he would not know where to go. Although they came from England and not the Continent, the Quaker owners of the house had some sympathy for another religious group that simply sought freedom. Jakob carried a letter of reference from their sponsoring family in Rotterdam to ease introductions in the new land. The immediate challenge was to negotiate with a wagon driver. Jakob listened for every snatch of German around him.

Maria and Anna were stomping on the dock in glee, as if testing to see if it would remain solid. Jakob laughed, happy to let them dispel their excitement before corralling them into a wagon. Lisbetli began to whimper in her mother's arms, and Jakob reached for the baby.

"She's taking too long to get well," Verona said softly.

"She'll be fine." Jakob laid his cheek against the baby's head. "We're here now. Everybody is going to be fine."

"Maria, come back," Anna's voice called after her restless little sister, who had darted into the throng making their way up the dock. Anna turned to her parents. "I can't see her anymore!"

Jakob glanced at Verona, as if to ask which of them would chase Maria.

Verona paled and slumped. A second later, she slid off the crate, unconscious.

Fourteen

No matter how early Annie walked through the foyer to the dining room for breakfast, Rufus was already at work. He measured and calculated and sketched and spread wood samples around, evaluating the natural light.

Eight days.

Eight days since she fled the threat to her livelihood. Eight days since meeting the Beiler family and wondering about her own Byler family history. Eight days since she looked into those violet-blue eyes for the first time. Annie shook off the sensation that came with that memory. She had moved back to the motel, where Rufus had begun the remodeling project with steadfast attention to detail.

Lee Solano had hurled a wall of paperwork against Richard D. Stebbins and successfully postponed the court date assigned to the suit Rick filed. This gave Annie time to build a case to strike back. Rick stopped trying to contact her, and Barrett seemed to have ceased trying to hack her system. Annie breathed easier and had begun to use her credit card when she ventured into town.

Today Rufus was on his knees inspecting the back of the reception desk when Annie approached the lobby with her bag over her shoulder. She slowed her steps for a moment and watched him, wishing that she could see him in his workshop crafting form and function together.

"Good morning, Rufus," Annie said.

He nearly bumped his head getting himself turned around to greet her. "*Guder mariye.*" He gestured toward the desk. "It will take three men to get the desk out."

"Are you at that stage already?"

"No. I just like to be prepared when it's time."

"How is your family?" Annie asked.

"They are well, thank you. Jacob asks about you every day."

"He's a sweet boy. Give him my best greetings."

"Perhaps you would like to do that yourself tonight at supper." He tilted his head. "It would make Jacob happy."

"Then by all means." Annie would have accepted the invitation on any excuse. Was it possible that she missed the farm?

"We will go together from here at six o'clock."

Annie nodded. "That's fine."

Rufus turned back to the dilemma of how to remove the desk, and Annie went into the dining room to pick up an apple and a blueberry muffin to eat while she walked to town. Meaning no offense to Mo, who made passable coffee at the motel, Annie was holding out for the more robust offering of the coffee shop. In only a few days, she had formed the habit of spending her mornings there with her laptop.

Annie settled in with a mocha caramel grande nonfat latte and flipped open her computer. In a few seconds the Internet connection icon went solid and she was online, scrolling through her e-mail looking for messages from Jamie or Lee Solano. A grunt at the next table seemed just purposeful enough to make her look up.

"You have a cool computer." A teenage boy slouched in his chair, his knees sticks poking out of baggy green shorts.

"Thank you," Annie said, unsure if she wanted to encourage conversation. He looked to be about fourteen with a stereotypical adolescent chip on his shoulder.

"I really need a computer," the boy said, "but my parents say we can't afford it."

"Don't you have any computer at home?"

"Just a stupid desktop that's like, ancient. It's almost three years old. My dad says it's good enough for homework and he doesn't have money to throw around on a computer every time something new and better comes along."

Annie twisted her lips to one side. "I guess it can get expensive."

"No kidding. I've tried to find a job, but there aren't any around here. I'm not old enough anyway."

"Maybe something will turn up."

"I have two sisters. They spend more time on the computer than they do in the bathroom. I never get a chance."

"That doesn't seem fair." Annie sipped her coffee, her eyes on her screen.

"I know. My dad just says, 'Life's not fair.' Like that solves anything." He stood up. "Hey, can you watch my bag for a minute? I need a bagel."

Annie glanced at the backpack the boy left behind. An ID tag hung from the strap with a name and address in clear block letters. She did not even have to get up to see it.

She turned back to her laptop. A few clicks later, she smiled smugly to herself. One teenage boy was going to be very happy in about three days. What was the point of having money if she could not be spontaneous with it?

Rufus helped Annalise into the buggy promptly at six o'clock. She had changed into the same full skirt she had worn to church a few days earlier and a simple blouse. Rufus appreciated her attempt to be respectful of their lifestyle, but it would have been more convincing if her denim bag did not hang from her shoulder. His mother and sisters carried purses—sometimes backpacks—so the bag itself was nothing unusual. But anyone could tell it held her laptop. Why was she loath to leave it behind? Her cell phone was no doubt silenced but in her skirt pocket as if it were a third hand.

"What's the matter?" Annalise asked. "You're scowling."

"It's nothing."

"It's something."

He hesitated then said, "Your computer. You never go anywhere without it."

"I can't be sure it's safe if I don't have it with me," Annalise said. "Don't worry, I'm not going to sneak off to use it in the middle of dinner."

Was he wrong to wish she would confide in him?

"If I ask you about it," Rufus said, "you'll tell me it's complicated, right?"

"It *is* complicated."

They rode in silence for more than a mile. Then Rufus spoke, "It seems to me it takes a great deal of energy to grasp at the air as much as you do."

"What is that supposed to mean?"

"I'm sorry. I should not have said that." Rufus sighed. He felt the wall rise between them and changed the subject. "Jacob will be so glad to see you. It's a surprise."

"Tell me you told your mother you were bringing me home for dinner."

"How could I? I haven't seen her since breakfast."

"You have a cell phone."

"I only use that for business or emergencies."

"That doesn't sound very convenient to me," Annalise said. "What if it's a not a good evening for having a guest?"

Rufus laughed. "I know my mother well. And you have a lot to learn about our ways."

Annalise raised one hand to check the hair she had pinned down in a severe manner. Annalise was trying too hard to respect their ways. With a pang, he wished she would remove the pins and let her hair fall around her face. It would be beautiful in the afternoon light.

And immediately he felt guilty. To have such thoughts about any woman—if it was God's will for him to be alone, he could not have such thoughts.

"I hope you will enjoy a good home-cooked meal," Rufus said. "I imagine you have exhausted the restaurants in Westcliffe by now."

"Twice and three times over." Annalise laughed. "But I'm used to eating out. I'm afraid I'm not much of a foodie."

"A foodie?"

"I'm not much use in the kitchen."

"I see." He paused. "Would you like to be?"

"Useful in the kitchen?" She turned toward him and twisted up a lip. "I would need a committed teacher."

"Amish women are determined. My mother would teach you." He had gone too far, but he did not want to take back the words.

They rode another mile. This time Annalise broke the silence.

"Can I ask you a question?" she said.

"Of course."

"I thought Amish people didn't have anything to do with outsiders. I mean, I understand you can build cabinets for them to make a living. But why. . .I mean. . .me? Taking me in when I fell. Church. And now dinner with your family?"

Rufus swallowed. "People sometimes want to visit our church, and I've invited you to share a meal to make a little boy happy."

"Aren't you encouraging Jacob to get a taste of the big, bad world or something? Face it. I'm a technology addict. I'm the ultimate un-Amish. What must your family think about the last week?"

"I can see that you are in trouble," Rufus said. "You hide away in Tom's truck. You hire a lawyer. You do not let your computer out of your sight, and you jump if your cell phone rings. I may not live in the way of the *English*, but I can see what is plain before my eyes. The Good Samaritan could not walk past what was plain before his eyes."

"Well," Annalise said, "Thank you for your concern, but I'm managing quite well under the circumstances."

"Managing? You're hiding. How is that the same thing?"

Her face blanched, but he was not sorry he challenged her. She did not know her own value. Three cars whizzed by them on the highway, leaving the buggy to quake in their wind.

"Those people should slow down," Annalise said.

Yes. And they are not the only ones.

Eli Beiler read from a German *Biewel* while food steamed on the table. The aroma of Dutch-spiced pot roast made Annie suddenly ravenous. Her eyes feasted on the beans and carrots from the garden, rich in color. The family bowed for silent prayers. When at last Eli said, "*Aemen*," Pennsylvania Dutch flew around the table with the passing dishes. Annie filled her plate and smiled.

"We have a guest," Eli reminded everyone. "We will speak English."

"My brothers in Pennsylvania have sent letters," Rufus explained quietly to Annie.

The conversation switched to English.

"Daniel says the new *boppli* looks just like our little Jacob at his age." Franey heaped mashed potatoes onto her plate.

"What did I look like when I was a *boppli*?" Jacob wanted to know.

"You were round and bald and slobbery," Sophie said, ignoring Lydia's elbow in her side.

"Matthew says the farm is doing well this year. He bought a new plow." Franey's face lit with a sheen Annie had not seen before. "And he and Martha want to come to visit. I wonder if Tom would be willing to drive all the way to Denver to get them from the train."

"We can ask," Rufus said.

Serving dishes clinked around the table, and Annie's plate filled rapidly. Although she could not understand the family jokes, clearly Sophie and Lydia were teasing each other, and Joel was quick to add to the banter. Jacob, sitting between Annie and Rufus, wove between speaking English to Annie and Pennsylvania Dutch to the family. Every few minutes, Annie was caught off guard when someone addressed her and anticipated a response.

"Annalise is interested in our family history," Rufus explained unexpectedly. "Her grandmother's name was Byler. Maybe there is a connection."

"Perhaps," Eli said. "We have a book you are welcome to look at."

"What sort of book?" Annie asked.

"Genealogy of our family name," Eli said. "Beiler is a common Amish name spelled several ways, but we suspect all the spellings go back to Pioneer Jakob Beyeler who came from Switzerland."

"I would love to see the book." Annie leaned forward to see Eli at the end of the table.

"Then you shall. I'm afraid the print is small and hard to read. You are welcome to take it with you and study it as much as you like."

"Thank you! I'll be careful with it."

"Let us know what you find," Franey said. "I don't think anyone here has ever looked at that old book."

Jacob wiped his face with his cloth napkin in dramatic fashion. "I don't understand what you're talking about. It's time for my chores in the barn, anyway. Can Annalise come with me?"

Faces around the table turned to Annie.

"I would love to." She looked over Jacob's head to catch Rufus's eye.

"It won't take long," Rufus assured her. "He just needs to check on water for the horses and the cow, and sweep the work area."

"Sounds great," Annie said.

Rufus shook a finger at Jacob. "I left my toolbox in the barn.

You stay out of it."

Jacob took Annie's hand and led her out the back door and down a path past the garden to the barn. Refusing her help, he pushed the wide door open by himself.

"This is where we found you," he said.

Annie smiled. "Yes it is."

"You were like a present for Rufus."

Annie felt the blush rise in her face and was glad Rufus was not in the barn. "Your brother was kind to me."

"Don't tell Joel, but Rufus is my favorite *bruder*. Matthew and Daniel don't count. They live too far away, and I don't remember them."

"You have a wonderful family, Jacob."

"I'm blessed," he announced as he reached for a broom.

"Yes you are," she agreed.

Behind them, a cell phone rang. Rufus's toolbox sat right inside the door on a low shelf. Jacob looked at the phone and twisted his lips. "It says, Ruth. She taught me how to read her name before she left." He turned away from the phone and began to sweep.

The phone rang several times then stopped. A moment later, it rang again, and again the caller ID announced, Ruth. Annie moved toward the phone.

"We're not supposed to answer it," Jacob warned. "She left."

"Left for where?" Annie asked. The phone rang again, and the sound seemed to send a neurological signal compelling her to answer.

"I'm not sure. But she's gone. We can't answer." Jacob moved deeper into the barn as the phone's insistence grated on Annie.

She snatched it out of the toolbox and flipped it open. "Hello?"

"Uh-oh," Jacob said, dropping his broom and running out of the barn.

"I'm sorry. I must have the wrong number," a voice said softly into Annie's ear."

"Hello, Ruth," Annie said. "You have the right number. I'll be happy to give your brother a message."

"Who is this?"

"My name is Annie. I met Rufus recently."

"Are you. . . Is your family one of the new families to come?"

"No, I'm not Amish," Annie said. "What would you like me to tell Rufus?"

"Tell him. . .tell him. . .just ask him to please read my letter. It's important."

"I'll make sure he gets the message. Hopefully you'll hear from him soon."

"*Danke*. Thank you. For answering. And taking a message. It's probably the best I could hope for."

Annie wanted to ask so many questions, but she squashed them. Before she could think of anything more to say, the call ended. Annie replaced the phone in the toolbox and sat alone in the barn. If Rufus could be such a Good Samaritan to her, then why couldn't he read his own sister's letter?

A moment later, Rufus stood in the doorway. "Jacob said you answered my phone."

"It was Ruth. She wants you to—"

"You should not have done that."

His voice had an edge she did not recognize. He was close enough that she could have reached out to touch him, but she stilled the impulse. Something clouded his eyes. Anger? Pain?

"She's your sister. She sounds. . .lonely or something." The tips of two fingers brushed back and forth along the gold links at her neck.

"She knows better than to call that number for anything other than business or an emergency." His tone was unbending. "I'm sorry you felt you should answer it."

"Don't you even want to hear what she said?" Annie pressed, frustration welling.

"As you like to say, it's complicated." He averted his eyes. "I should take you back to the motel now."

Fifteen

Rufus tugged on the reins to make Dolly turn into Tom's long driveway. That the red truck was parked outside the garage attached to the house told him he had not missed Tom. He watched the front door as Dolly ambled down the gentle slope. Rufus took Dolly and the buggy to the side of the driveway where Dolly could nuzzle the ground and waited. A moment of Tom's time was all Rufus needed, and if Tom's daily habits could be trusted, he would emerge from the house at any moment ready to begin his work-day. When Rufus met Tom five years ago, he had run a hardware store in town—one where Rufus spent money on a regular basis. More and more, he left the hardware store in the hands of his capable staff and filled large blocks of time taxiing for Amish families and hauling assorted supplies for contractors. Rufus only wanted to be sure he was on Tom's schedule for tomorrow.

In the back of Rufus's buggy was a sample cabinet for Mo's approval. If she liked it—and Rufus was sure she would—he would need supplies from the lumberyard in Colorado Springs to build the rest. The owners were particular about their wood to a degree that Rufus appreciated, but it was worth traversing the distance to choose his boards from their lot.

Between a couple of odd jobs, building a sample cabinet for Mo, and updating his oversized accounts book, Rufus had not been at the motel for four days. He wondered now if Annalise was still staying there. The truth was he wondered about her more than once while he sanded white oak, mitered precise corners, and calculated income and expenses. Would she come through looking for breakfast just as he unwrapped the cabinet for Mo's inspection? Would her gold necklace lie against her skin under a T-shirt, or would a blouse open at the neck let the chain catch the light?

Dolly nickered, and Rufus shook the thought away. *What nonsense. I am spending far too much time with the* English. *If I'm not careful, I'll have something to confess to the whole church.* A silly ornamentation. That was all the chain was.

The front door opened, and Tom stormed out of the house.

Rufus jumped down from his buggy. "Tom, do you have a moment?"

Tom stomped toward his truck, a cardboard box under his arm. "Sorry, not now, Rufus."

Rufus strode alongside the truck as Tom opened the driver's door and nearly threw the box onto the passenger seat. "I just want to confirm the trip to Colorado Springs tomorrow."

"Yeah, yeah, we're good. I'll pick you up at seven." Tom sat in the driver's seat and fumbled his keys.

"What is it?" Rufus asked. "Is it Karl again?"

"Worse." Tom slammed the door.

Rufus jumped back when the engine roared. A few seconds later, a screech and a cloud of dust bore witness to Tom's fury as he pulled out onto the highway.

Annie did not have to order at the coffee shop anymore. The baristas saw her coming through the door and had a mocha caramel grande nonfat latte in process by the time Annie reached the counter to pay for it. She tipped generously and settled in at her favorite table to wait for someone to bring the completed concoction to her.

Annie punched the speed dial for Jamie.

"Friesen-Page Solutions."

"It's me," Annie said.

They ran through a few routine matters.

"I'll take care of things," Jamie said, "but I'm not sure I understand why you don't come home. Barrett is making himself scarce; you have a lawyer on your side. We haven't had so much as an invoice from Rick in a week. Why aren't you here?"

Annie sighed. The question was legitimate. "Things are working this way, aren't they? The work is getting done. I talk to clients every afternoon."

"You haven't talked to Liam-Ryder Industries," Jamie pointed out. "Shouldn't we at least find out what they want?"

"First, we should find out who they are," Annie said. "Have you got time for a little research?"

"Of course."

"Make sure they're not a legal firm in disguise."

"Okay. When can I tell people to expect you back in the office?"

"I don't know. Soon."

Jamie was right. Lee Solano had quelled the legal crisis for the time being. Barrett was behaving himself and leaving her system alone—no doubt trying to play the good guy who would appear sympathetic to a judge. Whatever his reasons, it did seem that matters were calm enough for Annie to show her face at the office. Yet she felt no particular urge to go home. Living in a low-level motel room with a wardrobe that quickly became redundant was not so bad, even without a car. She got plenty of exercise walking into town, cultivated a striking tan, and gaped every day at the Sangre de Cristos so close she could almost feel their ridged rocks and cushioning trees.

And Rufus Beiler was here. Annie would never say that to

Jamie, and of course it was a fantasy to think there could be something between them. Answering his phone had made that clear. But Rufus stood for something, and Annie was not finished finding out what it was.

Annie looked up at the duo bursting through the shop's door. "Jamie, I have to go. I'll talk to you later."

"That's the one," a teenage boy said, pointing. "She's the lady I talked to."

Annie had only seen Tom a couple of times, but she would not have pegged him for someone infused with rage. Behind him was the boy she had spoken to four days earlier. She wanted to smile, thinking of him getting the package, but the color of Tom's face suggested she temper her enthusiasm.

"Sorry," the boy muttered. "He found the box this morning and came and got me from my friend's house. I had to show him the laptop."

"You did this?" Tom said.

He set the cardboard box on the table hard enough to make Annie wince, considering the contents.

"I talked to this boy, yes," she said.

"This boy is my son, Carter Reynolds."

"I didn't know."

"Would it have mattered?"

"I'm not sure," she admitted.

"Annie, right?" Tom asked. His face flashed through six moods in a second but remained stern.

She nodded.

"You sent my son a computer? A strange boy you met in a coffee shop?"

"It sounded like it would be a help to the whole family to have another computer in the house," she answered evenly.

"This is a small town. Maybe we do things differently than a place like Colorado Springs, but around here we think it's odd for a complete stranger to take up with a child and give extravagant gifts."

"I didn't think of it that way." Annie blanched. "Everybody can use a computer. I didn't mean anything. . .predatory."

"Now that I see it's you, I believe that. But parents make decisions for their own kids."

"Of course." She glanced at Carter, who stood with his hands jammed into plaid shorts pockets, his shoulders folded forward.

"Not that it's any of your business," Tom said, "but we have our reasons for restricting Carter's computer access."

"I overstepped. I'm sorry." Annie met Tom's stare.

"Carter can't keep it." Tom nudged the box an inch toward Annie. "You may have innocent intentions, but we are trying to accomplish something else with our son. It does not include giving him an electronic appendage."

"I'm sorry. I don't know what else to say."

Tom's shoulders loosened. "I hope you can return it."

"It's no problem."

Tom turned toward his slumping son. "Come on, Carter. I'll take you home. Then I have work to do."

"I'm sorry for the inconvenience," Annie said.

Tom and Carter strode out of the shop, and Annie resisted the eyes of any spectators. Suddenly working outside on the motel's porch appealed.

Rufus saw Annalise coming with her arms full and stepped across the lobby to open the door.

"Thank you," she said.

She huffed through the door and unloaded her arms onto the reception desk next to the sample cabinet. Her eyes barely lifted from the box. Her fingers rested on one edge of it. "The cupboard is beautiful."

"You didn't even look at it," Rufus pointed out.

"I'm sure everything you do is gorgeous." She glanced at his workmanship. "Mo must love it."

"She seemed happy." He nodded at the box. "Is that something special?"

"It's a mistake, that's all."

Rufus had never seen that particular slant in Annalise's shoulders, a slope of surrender. "Annalise, what happened?"

He listened to her cryptic explanation of meeting Carter and impulsively giving him a computer. Rufus picked up a rag and needlessly brushed at absent dust on the sample cabinet.

"I'm sorry for how you must feel, but surely you understand Tom's point." He hoped his tone found the right balance of sympathy and realism.

"Yes, I understand Tom's point." Annalise spun to face him.

"You're bringing your ways into new territory," Rufus said. "Answering my phone. Pressing questions about my sister. Giving Carter a computer just because you can."

"You've made your point once again." Annalise rested both elbows on the desk behind her and glared. "I'm an idiot city girl bumbling around a small town—with Amish to boot."

Her phone rang before Rufus could respond.

Annie rolled her eyes as she answered the phone. How much worse could this day get?

"I hit pay dirt," Lee Solano said.

"What do you mean?"

"You're going to want to write this down."

"Just a minute. I'll put you on speaker and find a pen."

Glancing at Rufus, who discreetly stepped away when her phone rang, Annie pushed a button that brought Lee's voice into the lobby. She rummaged around the reception desk for a pen and flipped a registration card to its blank back.

"Take this number," Lee said.

Annie jotted down the digits then repeated them back to Lee.

"If you have any questions about what I'm going to tell you, call that number and ask for Jeannette. She'll tell you."

"Tell me what?" Annie asked.

"Where did Barrett go to college?"

"University of Northern Colorado, in Greeley." Annie wondered how that was relevant to the current crisis.

"That's what you think. That's what everyone thinks. The truth is he only attended two semesters."

"But—"

"It gets better." Lee's pitch rose. "He was expelled for plagiarism."

"What?"

"This should be enough to stop the suit." Lee spoke with pure triumph. "We just let Barrett know we have this, and he'll pull out of the suit."

"Wait. That would ruin him. It would throw doubt on everything he's accomplished."

"Isn't that the point?" Lee said. "He's the one who started playing hardball. Now you've got a fast pitch of your own."

"What if I don't want to throw it?" Annie thought of Barrett's wife and infant daughter. More futures were at stake than just Barrett's.

"You hired me to make this mess go away," Lee said. "This will do it."

"Yes, I suppose it would. But it seems. . .extreme." She was expecting legal proceedings, not extortion.

Lee laughed. "Don't you consider what he's done so far to be extreme? Quid pro quo."

"Can I think about it?" Annie tucked the phone number into her bag. "The court date is not for a month. What difference will a couple days make now?"

"There doesn't have to be a court date," Lee emphasized. "Not only do we make the suit go away, but we get Barrett to sign over his interest in the company. Whatever you want."

"I need some time." Annie's head spun with the implications of what Lee suggested. "I'll call you in a few days."

"I'm ready to jump as soon as you give the signal."

The call ended, and Annie looked up at Rufus leaning against the door frame. "I suppose you heard all that."

He nodded.

"It sounds pretty terrible, doesn't it?"

He folded a sheet of paper with deliberation. "Complicated, as you said."

"I didn't agree to anything." Annie adjusted the bag hanging from her shoulder.

"You're thinking about it. Is that not enough?"

"This is not the same as you and Karl Kramer." The trembling almost got the best of Annie as she returned her phone to a pocket. "You have no idea what's at stake."

"Don't I?" He let the silence dangle between them.

Annie picked up the box. "I should go to my room. I have work to do."

"Annalise." Rufus put a hand on the box to stop her. "I'm sure I sounded harsh earlier. I am not trying to be rude or to hurt you. But I think it is time for you to go home."

"I'm happy here. For now, at least."

"You're hiding here." He took his hand from the box and let it glide over the sample cabinet. "You're pretending at the small-town life and flirting with the Amish ways because of some possible connection three hundred years ago. You look things up on the Internet instead of living them. You can't be accidentally Amish. It's time to go home and figure out what you want from your life."

"I'll think about it."

"This gentleman is pushing you into an uncomfortable corner. Is this really what you want?"

"Maybe. Maybe not."

"Tom is taking me to Colorado Springs in the morning." Rufus picked up his toolbox. "I'm sure there's room for you in the truck."

Sixteen

Annie sat squished between Tom and Rufus on Colorado State Route 96, heading east. The urge to defy Rufus and insist she would go home on her own terms—and was perfectly capable of finding her own transportation, thank you very much—lasted about as long as an untied balloon let loose. The air went out of her, and she knew he was right. Jamie was right. Her mother was right. It was time.

Lee's voice ringing in her ears was the last push. She should try to talk to Barrett one last time. What Lee proposed was beyond anything Annie imagined when she hired an attorney. Annie wanted to stop Barrett—and Rick—but not shame him for the rest of his career.

Conversation on the drive was sparse. Annie wondered if it was always this way or if her presence between the two men muted them. She would have preferred to sit in the rear seat, but Tom had boxes stacked there, along with the battered suitcase Mo had given Annie to hold her thrift-store wardrobe. The denim bag also was in the back, along with the second computer, which Tom was gracious enough not to mention. Annie's phone was in her pocket. It was all she could do not to get it out and pull up a map of where they were going to track their progress. They rode for miles between signs of any businesses, following fence lines and warning signs about curves in the road. Clearly they were in ranching territory, though what the ranches produced was not immediately evident to Annie. Horses? Cattle? All she saw was hardscrabble for miles on end, pocked with random bundles of brush and patches of scrub oak.

A tree bent by lightning. A religious billboard. Crumbling log cabins. A boxcar parked miles from any track. No doubt Tom and Rufus knew these landmarks well. Then the road cut through the rock of the gently sloped Wet Mountains in the San Isabel National Forest. Her ears responded to the shifts in elevation with increasing pressure, but she was determined not to widen her mouth to make them pop. Ponderosas grew out of crags in a straight line toward the sun.

"It's a little different than your view of the trip in," Tom said.

Annie refused to blush. If she were not so beholden to Tom, she would have let him know she could hold her own in taunting banter. And Rufus had practically ordered her to go home. She said nothing.

"Well, enjoy the view," Tom finally said. "It certainly helps give a person perspective on what's important in life."

"My perspective on life is just fine." She couldn't help herself. "It may be a different life than yours, but it's a good life."

Rufus leaned ever so slightly into her shoulder. "Don't take everything personally. He only means to admire God's handiwork."

Another thirty miles passed in silence.

Signs for Colorado Springs popped up on the route, heartening Annie.

"Where did you say your car was?" Tom asked.

She gave him directions over the next half hour. When they pulled into the tow company's lot and Annie saw her Prius, relief she had not expected wrung through her. As much as she might try to convince herself she did not miss driving, the sight of her car, unharmed, made her adrenaline surge. A life she knew was within sight.

Except without Rick Stebbins. Definitely.

And without Barrett Paige. Probably. That part hurt.

Rufus got out of the truck to let Annie out then opened the rear door and removed her belongings.

"Are you sure you want us to leave you here?" He glanced around the lot. "You are not *naerfich*? Nervous?"

"I'm fine." She put her head through the strap of her denim bag and took the suitcase. "The office is right over there"—she pointed—"and I can see my car from here."

Rufus nodded. "Well, all right, then. It was a pleasure to know you."

The past tense stabbed. But he was right, as usual. She was not sure he would shake her hand, but she extended it anyway. "Likewise. I'm sorry I didn't get to say good-bye to Jacob."

"I'll tell him. He'll understand." He covered her hand with his, infusing sensation up her arm and straight to her heart.

She shrugged and took her hand back. "Yeah. It's not like I was going to move to Westcliffe or anything. Thank your mother for me. She was very kind. Your whole family, actually." She fingered the gold chain at her neck.

"Go see your own mother," Rufus said. "She must miss you after all this time."

"I will."

"I pray things become less complicated for you."

Annie moistened her lips. "I don't pray as much as you do, but I will try."

He got back in the truck. Tom waved and put the vehicle into gear. A moment later, Annie stood alone in the garage's lot.

She missed Rufus already.

Which was about the silliest thing ever to happen to her. *Please, God, give me my senses back.*

Annie drove straight to her office.

Jamie gasped when she saw her. "You didn't say you were coming!"

"It was a last-minute decision," Annie said. "Get everybody in here. I'll talk to all of you at the same time."

Annie took her usual spot at the head of the conference table in her office and waited for the others. Jamie returned with the three software writers, the marketing assistant, and the bookkeeper.

"So you all want to know what's going on." Annie folded her hands in front of her on the table. It was the only way they would stay still. "We're facing some changes. I doubt Barrett will be back, so I'll need to hire someone to fill his spot on the marketing side."

"What happened to Barrett?" Ryan, the marketing assistant, asked the question on all their minds.

"I wish Barrett well." Annie chose words carefully and with sincerity. "But he has different ideas about the business than I do, and it's almost certainly an irreconcilable situation. I intend to continue to grow the products and services we offer, and your creative contributions mean a lot to me."

"What about Rick Stebbins?" Paul asked.

Paul was the best software writer Annie had ever hired. "Mr. Stebbins and I no longer have an association of any sort," she said. "I have engaged other counsel from out of town for the time being, though I imagine I will look for a local firm when the dust settles."

As Annie talked, the sensation was as if she were telling one of those peculiar stories of people who claim a near-death experience on the operating table. She was talking. The voice was hers. The words were hers. She calmly answered questions with as much transparency as she deemed appropriate. But this was someone else's story.

Jamie, the last to leave Annie's office, closed the door behind her. The entire afternoon stretched ahead. She would be back in a few minutes with a turkey avocado sandwich and coffee, and Annie would dig in.

This was Annie's real life.

She knew right where Rufus was, at the lumberyard where this out-of-body experience began. He was selecting the wood that would become the front desk and cabinetry of a little motel outside of Westcliffe. She could see his hand brush along the grain of the wood as if to test it. He would get out his little notebook and short pencil and make calculations, and he would have his order ready to load when Tom returned from his own errands.

And somewhere in town was Rufus's sister Ruth. Based on the address Annie had seen, brother and sister were probably not more than five miles apart. The only difference was Rufus knew where Ruth was. Ruth had no idea her brother was so near.

Ruth Beiler hefted her backpack and was among the last to leave the lecture hall at the university. She could hear her mother's voice telling her to stop dawdling. Her small dorm room was a ten-minute walk, and already she dreaded the heat that would slam her as soon as she left the air-conditioned brick building. She missed the cooler mountain air of home, two thousand feet higher than Colorado Springs.

Home.

Where she could never belong.

If only Rufus would read her letter—and answer it. If only she had some news of her sisters and Joel and little Jacob. Sophie was the spunkiest of the bunch, but even she would not dare to send a letter behind their mother's back.

Ruth had not expected to be this lonely, certainly not after eighteen months. It was not as if she had time to sit around feeling sorry for herself. She carried a full course load even in the summer months and rode the bus to a nursing home, where she spent another twenty or more hours a week as a certified nursing assistant. She could talk to as many people as she wanted to during the day. And while many people looked at her oddly because of her conservative dress and the way she kept her hair fastened closely to her head, in some settings she found fragments of friendship. In a laboratory session, all that mattered was helping each other see what they were supposed to see on a microscope slide. At the nursing home, she worked regular shifts and saw the same people routinely. Occasionally in the break room, conversation that started over patient care shifted to personal plans. On Sundays she went up the road to the modern Mennonite church, and sometimes she managed to attend a young adult Bible study. Ruth forced herself to be more outgoing than her natural inclination and usually succeeded.

But it was not family. It was not home.

She was not baptized. She had not broken any promises. *Ordnung* did not demand that her family shun her. It was the way she left. She knew she hurt them, especially her mother. But did not *Ordnung* require them to forgive?

Out of long habit, Annie tossed her keys in the tray by the door and flipped on the lights.

Her condo was just as she had left it nearly two weeks ago. Well, not exactly. The cleaning service had been in for their regularly scheduled visit, so everything looked plumped up and squeaky clean. The rooms were cool. Annie had not changed the timer on the thermostat before she left. She winced at the wasted electricity but was glad for the relief from the heat now. She went straight into the bedroom to release her load onto the bed. She opened the small suitcase and gripped the paltry stack of clothes in both hands. They had come from a thrift store and were likely headed to another one. For now they would go on a shelf in her walk-in closet. She turned the light on in the closet and found a niche for them. For two weeks, she got by with a handful of clothing items. Now she stood amid racks of clothes she had not worn in a year or more. She had everything, from silk suits to little black dresses to workout clothes and jeans and sweaters.

Exhaustion closed in on her. Annie went into the bathroom, easily four times the size of the one at the motel, and turned on the shower with the custom showerhead she spent three days selecting. She peeled off her clothes and dropped them in the hamper then stepped into the steam.

She was out only a few minutes later. A luxurious hot shower failed to deliver the satisfaction she expected. Wrapped in a towel, she went back to the bedroom and found her oldest, softest pair of pajamas. She stared at the flat screen television mounted on the wall but had no urge to turn it on. An even bigger screen hung in the living room, but Annie didn't want to go there, either. She just wanted to get in bed.

The shabby suitcase still lay open on the bed. Planning to slide it under the bed, Annie moved to close it.

The book.

The genealogy book Eli Beiler loaned her lay in the suitcase. She should not have brought that home with her. What was she thinking? She supposed she could mail it back.

But she might as well finish exploring it. Annie removed the book, closed the suitcase, and slid it under the bed. Then she climbed under the bedspread and opened the book.

Lists. Dates. Random anecdotal recollections. The name of a ship, the *Charming Nancy*, thought to have carried the family of pioneer Jakob Beyeler to the new world.

Annie grabbed her laptop. With a few clicks, she had the ship's passenger list. There they were: Jakob and Verona, with Barbara, Anna, Christian, Maria, and Elisabetha. Real people who crossed the ocean in 1737. What circumstances greeted them when they got off the *Charming Nancy*? Annie sank into her pillows, thirsting for details she would likely never discover, but her imagination was already at work.

Seventeen

October 1737

She slept—too much, Jakob thought. Verona barely had been awake since they arrived in Philadelphia three days ago. When she woke, she insisted she was fine, just overwhelmed by the journey. Her smile did not quite persuade when she assured him she was glad to finally be in Pennsylvania after a year of planning and sailing. And then she dropped off to sleep again. Each conversation varied the theme only slightly. Jakob hardly dared to leave but at minimum had to find food, candles, and coal. Fortunately, their accommodations among German-speaking merchants made basic purchases far simpler than he had feared.

The house belonged to Quakers who once lived in it themselves before building a larger permanent home. Now it served as the entry point for one German-speaking immigrant family after another. The owners left several publications about William Penn and Pennsylvania in the house, and Christian already had spent hours poring over them, sounding out English words and trying to decipher from diagrams what the words might mean.

They occupied two small rooms, one for sleeping and one for cooking over the fire and sitting on crates to eat. The sleeping room had two narrow beds and assorted pallets on the floor. To let Verona rest, Jakob kept the children out of this room except at night. Near the fire in the front room, Jakob had pried open the barrel containing kitchen supplies, and Barbara had done her best to arrange them. She knew without being asked that she must try to produce meals at reasonable intervals and keep Maria and Lisbetli quiet. Jakob ventured out for a few minutes at a time to buy whatever they required for the next few hours.

Barbara took the other girls on walks three times a day. Lisbetli needed the fresh air, and Maria needed the physical activity. Anna was oddly quiet about the whole experience of arriving in Philadelphia and awaiting the next step, but she did what Barbara asked her to do to help. The girls were gone now, and Christian was reading again in the other room while Jakob watched Verona sleep.

She stirred. "Jakob?"

"I'm here."

She exhaled. "I should get up."

"You don't have to."

"I thought you would be gone."

"Where would I go?"

"To the land office. Last night you said you wanted to make your application today."

"I don't have to go today."

"Yes you do." Verona pushed herself up on one elbow. Slowly she raised her torso and swung her feet over the side of the bed. "I'm sorry I haven't been much help."

Jakob moved to the bed and sat beside her. "Don't talk nonsense. You're ill."

"I'm better now. Really. You have to go make the application."

"It can wait." He kissed the top of her head.

"There's no point waiting. The sooner you apply, the sooner we get land."

He couldn't argue with that. "I'll make you some tea. Perhaps by then Barbara will be back."

"You can take Christian with you. He's tying himself in knots waiting to see the city. He thinks I don't know, but I hear the way he talks."

An hour later, with Christian at his side and Barbara sitting with Verona, Jakob set out, expecting to find the land office easily. Most of the public buildings were on the main square on High Street at the center of the city.

As they walked, Christian tilted his head to listen. "How many languages do you think there are in Philadelphia?"

"At least Dutch, Swedish, English, French, and German," Jakob answered. "Probably a lot more. Settlers have been coming for a hundred years."

As they approached the square, Christian cut away from his father abruptly and stopped in front of a muscled gray horse. Jakob followed, patting the horse's neck and wishing he had an apple for her. If he had an apple, though, he would cut it up for his children.

"We're going to need horses, aren't we, *Daed*?" Christian asked.

"Yes we will."

"I want to help you choose them."

"When the time comes," Jakob said, though he knew the time would be soon.

"She's for sale," a voice said in German.

Jakob turned toward the man who emerged from a dim shop. He tried to make sense of the English words on the shop's sign.

"We have everything you need," the man said.

The words were German, but the accent was English.

"Horses, plows, barrels, ropes, beds, salt, flour, jerky. You are homesteading, yes?" the man said.

Jakob nodded. Was it that obvious? He put a hand on his son's shoulder, though Christian was well mannered and would not intrude on an adult conversation. Maria was the one who could never be quiet.

The man continued listing the items he had for sale, and Jakob understood. Homesteaders flowed through Philadelphia like a river. There was money to be made in supplying what they needed.

"I can get anything you need," the man said. "Just give me a list."

"Perhaps I will," Jakob answered. "But I don't even have land yet."

"Don't wait too long," the man cautioned. "The Penns are efficient. You might as well be ready when the warrant comes through."

Jakob patted the gray animal again and said, "Perhaps we will talk in a few days."

Jakob nudged Christian's shoulder, and they continued on their quest.

"Can we buy that horse?" Christian asked when they were out of the man's earshot.

"Buying a horse is an important decision," Jakob said. "We can't just buy the first one we see."

"She looks like a good horse to me."

"Yes she does," Jakob agreed. "I have a feeling we'll meet other men with similar businesses. You can help me find the best one to work with."

"Can I go with you to find the land?" Christian asked. "I promise I won't be any trouble."

Jakob shook his head. Christian had big ideas, but he was still just an eight-year-old boy. "I think it's better if you stay with your mother. We can't leave the womenfolk on their own, after all."

They found the land office, and Jakob realized how strategically the outfitting business was located. No doubt the pace of business in the center square swelled when ships disgorged immigrants and quieted in the weeks between arrivals. Jakob had spoken with Hans Zimmerman, the Stutzmans, and other Amish families from the *Charming Nancy* who had been to the land office already. A couple of families immediately succumbed to offers in the street. Though they were now well outfitted for the wilderness, they had very little means to sustain themselves for the weeks of waiting in Philadelphia. Jakob was keeping a tight mental inventory of every expense. He knew exactly how much money he had, but he was not sure how long it would have to last.

Hans Zimmerman was getting impatient. He wanted Jakob to ride with him to scout land as soon as the necessary permissions came through. Many of the settlers walked into the wilderness, but Hans was determined to take a horse. Jakob was going to need a horse as well, or at least a mule to carry gear.

The land office throbbed with activity. Jakob recognized families from the ship as he waited his turn for a haggard gray-haired clerk behind a desk to fire a series of questions.

"I am Jakob Byler, and I wish to apply for a land grant." Jakob spoke German.

Immediately the clerk raised an arm and signaled to a young man, who crossed the room to the desk. "German," the clerk said, pointing at Jakob.

"I will translate," the young man said in German. "We do this often."

Jakob nodded in relief.

While Jakob answered questions, Christian found pamphlets and picked out English words he had begun to recognize. When they left, Jakob felt confident he had satisfied the requirements of William Penn's sons, Richard and Thomas. The warrant would come through soon enough.

Verona was still sitting up when he returned to her after an absence of several hours, which encouraged him. When Jakob entered the room, Verona lifted her flushed face and smiled. Lisbetli sat on the bed with her, playfully tickling her mother's neck and giggling. Verona tickled in response, which sent Lisbetli into spasms of laughter.

"Mrs. Zimmerman was here," Verona said. "Hans has information on some land he wants to look at when you go."

"In Northkill?" Jakob asked.

"Irish Creek."

"The name certainly sounds more peaceable than Northkill."

Jakob examined his wife's face. Was she really better, or had she forced herself to stay awake because Mrs. Zimmerman visited?

"It's very close to Northkill," Verona said. "We would be near other Amish families."

Jakob nodded. "The Siebers are on Irish Creek. They came last year."

"I remember them," Verona said. "I always liked Mrs. Sieber."

"Perhaps someday we will have a real congregation," Jakob said. "Even a bishop." He paused. "I don't know how long I'll be gone. I hate to go off into the wilderness and leave you still in bed."

"I won't be in bed," Verona said quickly. "I'm so much better. Besides, we both know you have to go."

"I don't have to go right now with Hans."

"But you should. It's what you've planned all along."

"Winter is coming."

"All the more reason to go soon. Choose your land and be ready. When the papers come, you can engage a surveyor right away."

"And we pray that winter holds off long enough to get the survey done. Then we could move at the first spring thaw."

"So we will spend the winter here, then." Verona looked around the room. "I will make a home for us."

"When you are well, I will look for work," Jakob said. "Surely Philadelphia has tanyards."

"Not an Amish tanyard. Would you work for an outsider?" Verona asked.

"Will I have a choice? I must provide for my family. I'm only interested in honest work."

"Any tanner would be blessed to have you."

Jakob began to believe he could leave Verona safely. If she napped with the baby, she managed to be wakeful for most of the day. The Penn brothers approved his application for a land grant. By the time the papers were complete, she had organized the cooking and laid in food supplies. He and Christian chose a sure-footed horse with a mellow temperament and loaded leather satchels with bedding, warm clothing, and food. Hans Zimmerman did the same. Jakob and Hans consulted their maps and planned their foray into the thick forest northwest of Philadelphia.

They followed the Schuykill River as it meandered generally north, and turned west in the shadow of the Blue Mountains. When they could, they rode the horses. When the path grew steep or hidden, they walked laboriously. Hans constantly checked his compass, and in the end they did find Northkill Creek and several Amish families who had taken this sojourn the previous year. The Detweiler and Sieber families lived in cabins with stone chimneys and the evidence that their gardens had yielded well that year and stocked the root cellar.

When Hans and Jakob arrived, Mrs. Sieber did not hesitate to twist the neck of one of the chickens strutting in back of the house and prepare it for the pot. The eldest Sieber boy went to a makeshift smokehouse and came back with a skinned rabbit and squirrel. Jakob winced slightly at the offering, supposing the families did not enjoy meat every day, much less three varieties. He spied two rifles leaning up against the Sieber fireplace.

"Is the hunting good?" he asked.

"The boys do pretty well with Melchior Detweiler's boys," Sieber said. "They take down the occasional deer or elk, which feeds us a long time. Even a bear now and then. And they seem to get all the rabbit, grouse, and turkey we could ask for."

Jakob nodded, encouraged. He would have to teach Christian to hunt. First, he would need a gun.

By noon the following day, Jakob stood on land at the far west end of Irish Creek and knew he wanted to own it. He leaned against a black oak, feeling drenched in good fortune.

"Let's use this oak to mark our land," Hans said. "Our farms will join at this tree. Our families will join here as well."

Jakob nodded, smiling. Verona would love this view. The Blue Mountains sloped on the western horizon over woods that rose thickly from rich soil. They would have all the timber they needed. The creek would provide smooth stones to spark Verona's pleasure in the fireplace that would someday warm the home they would someday inhabit. A vision of a free life colored the expanse before him with one hint of shadow.

Jakob gestured toward the mountains. "Indian territory is on the other side of that ridge."

"I know," Hans answered. "But William Penn took great pains to build friendly relations. He paid the tribes for the land."

"William Penn has been dead for nearly twenty years. Things change."

Hans went silent.

Jakob continued, "Considering the threats we left in Switzerland and what we survived on the ship, I don't intend to lose anybody I love now."

"We must be careful and watch out for each other."

Jakob thumped the tree. "This black oak will remind us that this is no time to give way to fear." He once again scanned the view of his land then pointed toward a small natural clearing close to the creek. "There! Verona will want the house there!"

Eighteen

Barrett agreed to meet her. Annie had not been sure he would even answer her phone call, but he sounded amicable. Even wistful.

Annie pondered three outfits laid out on her bed. The goal was businesslike but friendly. Warm but firm. Finally, she put on a dark print skirt cut straight with a sassy flair at the hemline and a short-sleeved summer sweater in a shade of blue she knew Barrett was partial to. Her gold chain followed the neckline of the sweater in a perfect parallel curve. She would use a real briefcase today.

Annie closed her eyes, inhaled, then exhaled slowly. "Please, God, help me figure this out." She wanted to do the right thing— if only she knew what the right thing was.

In the middle of the morning, small clusters of people in business attire dotted the restaurant. In another couple of hours, the lunch crowd would surge through, but for now it was a quiet place to talk. Cutlery clinked occasionally, and voices ebbed and flowed with pleasant laughter and the buzz of getting down to business. Annie just wanted to hear straight from Barrett's mouth what he wanted out of their partnership. Sitting down together in a public place—without lawyers—might stir enough friendship to come to an agreement without going to court. And she would not have to ruin Barrett's future.

"I'm meeting a friend," Annie told the hostess. "His name is Barrett Paige. I don't see him."

The hostess checked the note on the seating chart. "Yes, he's here. He specifically asked for the back room."

She followed the hostess through the main dining room, breathing in the aroma of omelets and coffee and waffles and bacon.

Something was not right. Annie slowed her steps and sniffed. Aftershave.

Rick's aftershave. She had spent enough time close to him to recognize it.

Annie paused at a table and set her briefcase in a chair. "Excuse me," she said to the hostess. "Would you please tell my friend I'd like to eat out here?"

"It's no trouble to put you in the back. We've already set up."

"I prefer this spot." She pulled out a chair and sat down.

The hostess shrugged. "I'll tell him."

The scent grew stronger, and a moment later Rick Stebbins stood across from Annie, his fingers splayed on the back of a chair.

"Well, well, Annie Friesen." He leaned toward her. "Imagine running into you here."

Annie picked up her briefcase and moved it to her lap. "What are you doing here, Rick?"

"It's a popular place for business meetings."

"Barrett told you, didn't he?"

"Told me what?"

"Don't play games." Annie's pulse pumped harder.

Rick crossed his arms over his chest. "This is a public place. How was I supposed to know you would be here?"

"That's pretty thin, Rick." She met his flaunting gaze with a scowl. What had she ever seen in him?

"I just came over to borrow a chair." He rolled one out from the table and tilted his head toward another table. Two men in suits looked in his direction. "Meeting with new clients."

"How convenient."

"I believe you know how to reach me when you're ready to sign the papers Barrett asked me to prepare."

"Not gonna happen."

"I think you'll find your meeting has been canceled." Rick smiled as he rolled the chair toward the other table.

The hostess reappeared. "I'm sorry, miss. Your party seems to have left."

So this was how it was going to be.

Rufus looked up and raised an eyebrow. Karl Kramer sauntered from his car toward the motel and casually opened the lobby door. Rufus dipped the brim of his hat about an inch but held his pose in a straight-backed chair.

"I saw your buggy." Karl's hands were in the pockets of his blue work pants. "I heard you got some work going here."

"Yes, Mo asked for some cabinetry."

"Probably a new desk." Karl ran one hand along the nicked and notched front edge of the desk. "This one's been here about a hundred years."

"Yes, a new desk as well."

Karl glanced around. "I don't see tools or a crew."

"I am drawing up some final plans." Rufus looked past Karl Kramer to where he had left Dolly and the buggy. The horse seemed unperturbed, and the buggy was upright.

"When do you plan to install?"

"Mr. Kramer, with all due respect, I don't believe that's your business," Rufus said.

"I suppose it takes time to build. Handcrafted and all. You must take great pride in your work."

"We are humble people." Rufus spoke politely. "*Demut*. We do not seek pride. I find satisfaction in my craft and hope it reflects the beauty of the Creator." Where was Mo? She had said she had the original blueprints of the building and dashed off to find them before Rufus could tell her he did not really need them. His own drawings were accurate, checked and measured three times. He just wanted her signature on his final quote. Then he would buy the remaining wood and start crafting cabinets in his workshop.

Karl thumped the desk. "It would be a shame if something happened. After all your hard work, I mean."

Rufus eyed Karl, his heart beating a little faster. "Why would something happen?"

"You just never know."

Mo entered the lobby just then and took up her position behind the desk. "You need something, Karl?"

"Just dropped in to chat with Rufus here."

"Rufus is busy." She held the blueprints out toward Rufus. "I'm ready to look at your numbers now."

Karl spoke. "Let me have a look at the blueprints. I can have a bid for you by the end of the day. We will install next week."

"Rufus and I have already come to an agreement, Karl. If you're trying to drum up business, this is the wrong place."

"Perhaps I'll drop by again after the work is done." Karl ambled toward the door.

Mo and Rufus said nothing more until Karl was out of the building.

"Is he threatening you?" Mo asked sharply.

"Not directly."

"Everybody in town knows Karl Kramer is gunning for you. I'll call the police."

"No," Rufus said. "That is not the way to solve our differences."

"He'd better not step foot in my motel ever again."

Annie sat in her office with the door closed, the phone in her hand. Lee Solano was on speed dial. Number nine.

On the phone just a few hours ago, Barrett sounded sincere. He wanted to talk. He didn't want to go to court. The whole mess was out of hand.

And now this.

It was all show. Barrett must have called Rick as soon as he hung up. Or perhaps Rick was in the room and heard the whole conversation. They probably had a good laugh.

"I'm being stupid," Annie announced to the empty room. "It's clear where Barrett's loyalty lies."

One little phone call to Lee. Not more than fifteen seconds. Everything would change.

The phone in her hand rang, startling her. Annie looked at caller ID.

"Hi, Mom."

"Hi, yourself. You haven't called for a week."

"Sorry."

"Where are you?"

"Back in town. Back at work."

"I'm glad to hear that. Everything okay?"

"It will be. I just need to make a phone call."

"Then I won't keep you. I've been thinking about that gene-alogy book you asked about. My brain is zoning in on where it might be. I wonder if you want to come over and help me move boxes around and find it."

"Sure, Mom. How about tomorrow afternoon?"

"After three. Stay for supper."

"I'll be there."

"You sound preoccupied."

"Just trying to find my stride again now that I'm back."

"You'll find it. You always do. I'll see you tomorrow."

Annie ended the call. She really did want to see the genealogy book. Though Annie had never heard of anyone in her family being Amish, she felt compelled to follow the trail of the Byler name.

She exhaled heavily, the phone still in her hand. She could almost see the scowl on Rufus's face at what she was about to do.

She had to.

She tried the peaceable route and it didn't work.

She had no choice.

Annie punched 9 on her phone, and an instant later Lee Solano came on.

"This is Annie Friesen," she said. "Do it."

"You're sure?"

"Yes." *No!*

She clicked off.

Nineteen

November 1737

The temperature took a distinct downturn by the time Jakob returned to Philadelphia ten days later. The sky looked as if a worn gray sheet containing the inevitable snow had unfurled behind the city.

Jakob was anxious to get back to his family with good news, but he was unprepared for what he found.

"*Daed* is home!" Maria squealed when Jakob opened the door. She jumped into his arms. His eyes scanned the room as he kissed the top of her head.

The bread on the table was hardened, and the fire in the hearth was dangerously close to going out. The flour bin was empty and the coal bin as well. The water bucket was depleted. Dishes on the rugged table looked as if they had not been scraped in three days. A rat feasted on food spilled in one corner.

"Maria, where is everybody?" Jakob worked to keep his voice calm.

"Bar-bar is sleeping. Anna takes care of Lisbetli now."

"Who takes care of you?" Jakob set Maria on her feet again.

"I'm big. I take care of myself."

Jakob tousled the girl's hair and led her into the bedroom.

Barbara was indeed in one of the beds, sound asleep. Anna sat on a pallet on the floor with Lisbetli, who was taking great delight in sweeping an area of the floor with a few pieces of straw tied together.

"*Daed*!" Anna hurtled at him.

Lisbetli stood and toddled toward him, and Jakob took her in his arms. He sat on the empty bed and motioned for Anna to join him.

"Tell me what happened, Anna. Where is *Mamm*?"

"It was time for Mrs. Habbecker's baby," Anna explained. "Mrs. Zimmerman said *Mamm* had to go and help because it was going to be a hard birth."

"But your *mudder* has been sick."

"She said that she is strong now, but I do not think she is. She sleeps too much."

"When did she leave?"

"On Thursday. In the morning."

Panic welled in Jakob. "But today is Saturday!" He glanced over at Barbara. "Is Bar-bar all right?"

Anna nodded. "She is sleeping. Lisbetli has been crying for *Mamm*. She does not sleep at night, and she will not let anyone hold her but Bar-bar. I try to cook, but I keep spilling things."

"And Christian?" Jakob asked.

"He just left to look for coal, but I don't think he remembers where you showed him to buy it."

"We must find your brother and your mother." Jakob stood. "Help your sisters get into something warm, please, and we'll go out together."

If Anna's account was accurate, Verona had been gone for two days. What would possess her to do that? Jakob racked his brain to remember where the Habbeckers had found accommodations. All he remembered was that it had not seemed near when he first heard of the place.

Jakob moved to the bed where Barbara lay and jiggled her

shoulder. He needed to see for himself that she was simply sleeping. She roused easily enough and sat up straight when she saw him. He let out his breath in relief.

"*Daed*! I'm sorry. I fell asleep." Barbara wiped one hand across her face and glanced at the waning light coming through the window. "I did not mean to sleep so long. Lisbetli—"

"Anna told me. Thank you for taking care of the baby, but I'm worried about your mother."

"Mrs. Habbecker—"

"She can't still be birthing two days later. I'm going to go look for *Mamm* and take the girls. Will you wait for Christian?"

Barbara nodded.

"I will get some water before I go."

The nearest Amish neighbors Jakob could think of were the Stutzmans, so he went there first. They sent him to Wengars, who knew how to find the Habbeckers. As he moved through the streets, his eyes scanned for Christian. Though Christian might return without coal, he had too fine a sense of direction to get lost. It was Verona Jakob was frightened for. Two days.

Verona dried her hands, unsure whether to surrender to grief or embarrassment. Either way, tears weighed in her eyes. The birth had not gone well. By the end of the first day, she was certain the child would not survive. Mrs. Habbecker was so spent she had stopped screaming with the pains, as if she also realized that her labor was in vain.

And then Verona collapsed. Caring for her own family exhausted her every day. Waiting more than twenty-four hours for a baby to be born without breath ultimately was beyond her. When she came to, having been tucked into a strange bed, another Amish wife was at her vigil post, and Mrs. Habbecker was pushing in grievous silence. Moments later, someone wrapped the baby and took him away, confirming Verona's fear.

Where? Verona wondered. He could be buried, at least. This child did not have to be put into the sea, leaving no trace of his existence. His grave marker might be small, but it would be more than the children who died in the crossing had.

Her own heart heaved in anguish for the Habbeckers even as shame washed over her for failing them at a crucial moment. Now two days had passed since she had seen her own children, and she finally found the strength to get on her feet again and help clean up after the birth before excusing herself as gently as she could. She did not even try to form words to speak to the Habbeckers. What could anyone say that would be of comfort?

Verona was settling her shawl around her shoulders when the knock came. She opened the door.

"Jakob!"

He stood in the door frame with two little girls, his face in question pose.

This was no place for the girls. Gathering the front of her shawl in one hand, Verona said a hasty good-bye to Mr. Habbecker and stepped outside.

"I was worried, Verona. The girls said you have been gone two days. The baby—"

She shook her head, and Jakob stopped. He understood.

"Can we see the baby?" Maria asked.

Verona hesitated. "Not right now." She reached out for Lisbetli, who let go of Jakob's neck and latched on to her mother's. Verona breathed in the scent of her child, her baby who was safe in her arms.

"You must be exhausted."

"I just wish I could have done something to help."

"You helped."

"I mean—"

"I know," Jakob said softly, "but that is in God's hands. You did what you could. God's will. . ."

Verona exhaled deeply. "I'm sorry for you to come home to this. But I am very glad to see you."

In that moment, she knew she might have accounted for the last few hours—her own unconsciousness. But she did not. And she would not. She saw the relief in his face that she was all right and imagined the possible explanations that must have run through his head when he discovered her gone for two days. She was fine. Jakob was home. They would go on from there.

Jakob filed a description of the land he wanted to claim at the first opportunity, as did Hans Zimmerman, and they began the next season of waiting. Jakob got rid of the rats that had taken shelter in their rooms against the deepening cold outside, and Verona determined to keep a spotless house and not give rodents further reason to seek sustenance there. Christian learned where to buy coal and where to draw water, and Barbara and Anna became as adept as their parents at striking bargains with the local merchants. Jakob found a place to board the horse—they had no grazing land or shelter for it beside the narrow house in a row of narrow houses—and set about finding work in a tanyard. Jakob located an outfitter he trusted and began to collect supplies they would need for homesteading, beginning with a wagon.

One by one the Amish families received their land grants and surveys. Some left for Northkill, believing they still had time to erect a shelter that could withstand the winter. Some hoped to form settlements in other counties.

The Stutzmans hosted a shared meal to bid the Buerkis farewell. Verona cooked that day to contribute to the meal but declined to go with the rest of the family.

"Are you all right?" Jakob probed.

Verona put a hand on his arm. "It's been a very busy time, and I'm tired. I don't know the Buerkis well, and I could use a couple of hours of quiet."

She felt the scrutiny in his eyes but remained firm, determined to give him no reason to think her choice to stay home was anything more than fatigue.

"All right," he said. "I will take the children so you can rest."

Jakob was amused by the way Christian hung on him all evening. After the meal, while the women cleared dishes and leftover food, the men spread their maps on the table. With candles positioned to light every corner, they took turns pointing to places where they had applied for land and calculating the distance between points. Most of them would be two miles or more from the nearest neighbor. Christian had been paying close attention to conversations over the last few weeks. He soaked up information about soil quality and tree density and water supply and wildlife and crop potential. Jakob smiled in pleasure when grown men began to ask his son, just turned nine, what he knew about the various locations where Amish families intended to settle. Christian even calculated with surprising accuracy how long each step in the land grant process took based on the experience of each of the settlers so far. Hans Zimmerman's survey was already under way. By Christian's estimation, his father should receive news any day now that his own application was moving to the survey step.

Jakob glanced across the room at his four daughters. Barbara soon would be fifteen. Before long he would have to entertain the thought of finding her a husband. In Europe she had gone further in school than any of his children could expect to go in this new world. In the last few weeks, he saw that Barbara was becoming competent both to keep a house and care for small children with attention and patience. Fleetingly he wondered if she would prefer to remain in Philadelphia. She was near enough to being grown that she could decide what she wanted. But he was not going to raise the question. He wanted her with him. He had not come this far to begin separating his family, and her best chance of finding a husband was among the sons of the Amish families moving to Northkill. More would come in the next few years. His daughters could marry men of their own people.

Verona stirred up the fire in the hearth to ensure it would be burning when Jakob returned with the children. Lisbetli was probably already asleep in someone's arms.

Verona had spoken the truth when she told Jakob she was tired. Her deceit was only in disguising the depth of her exhaustion and the frequency of the headaches that sliced through her eyes. The illness she carried from the ship had never fully left her.

And it would not.

She knew that as surely as she knew Mrs. Habbecker's baby would not draw breath. The vistas of the homestead on Irish Creek were not for her eyes, but she would not stand in the way of Jakob's future there with the children. The authorization to make the legal survey of the land would come any day, and she would make sure Jakob mounted his horse and rode off to meet the surveyor. Every detail of the survey must be accurate. There must be no question of the land Jakob was investing his life in, so he would want to be present to verify each measurement. Already Christian loved the land without even seeing it, and Maria was determined to plant beets. The Bylers would have their fresh, free life. But without Verona.

Verona carried her candle to the bedroom, where she undressed and got into bed. Tomorrow she would make Jakob ready to ride before the week's end.

Twenty

Annie stood at the bottom of the basement stairs and turned to her mother with widened eyes.

"Are you in a contest, Mom? She who has the most boxes wins?"

Myra slapped Annie on the arm. "Half of this stuff is yours."

"Is not."

"Is too. You never had room at the apartment. But now your condo has lots of space. You should take it."

"What if I don't want it?" Annie poked at a box with her name on it.

"Then why would I want it?"

"Well, I'm not here to go through my childhood mementos," Annie said. "Where do you think the book is?"

Myra led the way. "There's a pile of boxes in the back corner that came from Grandma Friesen's house."

"That stuff is still here?"

"It just never seems urgent to go through." Myra shrugged. "Speaking of mementos, did you bring any back with you?"

"Back with me?"

"From wherever you were. You never said where you were.

On your covert operation."

"It was just business, Mom." Annie turned her gaze to a tower of cardboard. "Not the kind of place you pick up souvenirs."

"You start with this one." Myra shoved a box toward Annie. "Can't you tell me now where you were?"

"Westcliffe. I was in Westcliffe."

Myra plunged a hand into a box. "As in speck-on-a-map Westcliffe?"

"That would be it."

Myra sucked in air. "You met somebody! You finally broke up with Rick."

Annie riffled through a box of her deceased grandmother's dresses. "Mom, why do you have Grandma's clothes?"

"Think vintage. And stay on topic."

Annie folded the box flaps down. "Rick and I didn't exactly break up, but the result is the same. He's history."

"And who is the future?"

"No one." Annie reached for another box. "You were right about Rick all along, that's all."

"Is he still your lawyer?"

"Nope."

"And you didn't meet someone else?"

Annie was slower to answer. "No."

"Annalise Friesen, you tell me the truth."

"I. . .met a family. They. . .befriended me."

"And?"

"And nothing."

"You're not telling me everything."

"Okay." Annie lifted her eyes to her mother's. "They are Amish."

"Amish!"

"They're not freaks, Mom. They just have their own way of living and believing."

"Of course. I'm just not sure what you would have in common with them."

"Circumstances sort of threw us together. I told you I met someone named Beiler." She paused to spell the name. "It was the Amish family." *It was the Amish family's son.*

"So you think those Beilers and our Bylers might be connected," Myra said.

"It just got me going down an interesting trail. There was a guy in 1737 named *Jakob Beyeler.*" She paused again to spell the name. "It looks like the Beilers are related to him. Maybe we are, too."

"Was he Amish?"

"Quite likely." Annie opened another box. "I'm sorting that out still."

"I've never heard any stories about any Amish ancestors. But you know who might know? Your great-aunt Lennie."

"But she lives in Vermont, and she can't hear on the telephone."

"You're in luck. If you hadn't stayed incognito for so long, you might have heard the family news. She's coming for a visit. She'll be here in a few days, and then she's off to California to see her new great-grandchild."

Rufus cleared the large worktable and wiped wood shavings away before laying out the carefully cut panels. He welcomed a few days in the workshop instead of on a job site. In the morning, his two sometime employees would arrive to help sand and assemble. They had talent—one more than the other—but would require close supervision. At odd moments, he wondered if it was worthwhile to pay for their help at this stage, but how else would they learn?

Beside Rufus, Jacob perched on a stool with his elbows on the edge of the worktable. "Am I going to be a cabinetmaker when I grow up?"

"Would you like to be?" Rufus flicked his eyes at his little brother.

"You make pretty cabinets. It might be too hard for me."

"It might be hard now, but I'll teach you."

"Who taught you?"

"*Daed*. And his *daed* taught him."

"When can I learn?"

"I'll tell you what," Rufus said. "I have some scraps from this project. I'll help you make a little box for *Mamm*'s birthday. Would you like that?"

Jacob sat up straight. "*Ya!* When is *Mamm*'s birthday?"

"In two months. We should have plenty of time."

The little boy stilled, his shoulders limp. "I wish Ruth could come for *Mamm*'s birthday."

"You miss Ruth, don't you?"

"Don't you?"

"Yes I do," Rufus answered quietly. "Every day."

"I know *Mamm* misses her."

"I'm sure she does."

"Do you think Ruth misses us?"

"Of course."

"Then why can't we see her? If I ask *Mamm*, she cries. No one will tell me."

Rufus put a man's long arm around a boy's small shoulders. "Do you remember when Ruth left?"

"A little bit. But *Mamm* told me to go to bed, and in the morning Ruth did not come down to breakfast."

"Ruth wanted to go, and *Mamm* wanted her to stay. That's why *Mamm* cries."

Jacob looked up at Rufus. "That's not the real story. But I guess I'm too little to hear the real story."

"It's real enough."

"Is it against *Ordnung* for me to still love Ruth?"

Rufus shook his head. "I don't think so."

"Is it against *Ordnung* for me to love Annalise, even though she's *English*?"

"Well, God tells us to love everyone."

"That sounds hard. But I do love Annalise. I guess she won't come back, either."

"No, I don't think so." Rufus was not going to lie to the boy.

"I wish I knew how to write better. I would write a letter to Ruth, and I would write a letter to Annalise. And I would tell them I love them just like God told me to in the *Biewel*."

Rufus was silent. The chance that Jacob would be allowed to mail such letters was almost nothing. But the moment seemed too tender to offer the boy an explanation that would not satisfy either one of them.

"It's almost time for supper," Rufus finally said. "Why don't you go see if *Mamm* needs some help?"

Rufus watched Jacob scamper across the yard and up the steps to the front porch. His thin form disappeared into the house. That little boy could be the closest thing Rufus ever had to a son of his own.

Rufus had filled his mind with Annalise, and his mind's eye saw her again, standing alone in a parking lot, armed with the contents of her denim bag. He said a prayer for her then for himself.

He turned back to his panels, the sound of Karl Kramer's steps across the motel lobby reviving in his ears. He almost wished he had a lock on the workshop door.

Annie's phone buzzed in her back pocket, and she took her hands out of a box of hand-tatted table linens. She recognized the calling number. Lee Solano.

"Hello."

"I went straight to your man Barrett."

"And?" Annie glanced at her mother and shifted to wander to another corner of the basement. Even there, she would be careful about her end of this conversation.

"He's backing down. Withdrawing the suit. Your genius is safe."

"Did he ask for something?"

"He still holds a financial stake in the company. He wants you to buy him out."

"That seems reasonable." Speaking calmly, Annie caught her mother's eye briefly. Her heart pounded.

"I recommend you sue for damages to reduce the amount."

"Oh, I don't think that's necessary." Annie smiled at her mother. "The matter seems to be equitably resolved."

"Don't you want to make him sweat a little more?"

"Has his representation spoken to the matter?"

"You mean Mr. Stebbins? I'm sure we'll hear about it when he finds out."

"Thanks for the update," Annie said lightly. "I'll speak to you soon."

Okay, God, why don't I feel better about this?

She shuffled back to her mother, who was still sifting through boxes. "Sorry. Business."

"Do you ever get to take time off?" Myra asked. "Were you working the whole time you were gone?"

"I'm running a company, Mom. That's a full-time commitment."

"But you have a partner. Can't he carry some of the load?"

Annie sighed. She would have to tell her parents sooner or later. "Barrett has decided to leave the company." That much was true. "I'm going to buy him out." Also true. "And Rick is going to represent Barrett while we sort it out." Probably true.

"Wow." Myra's countenance sagged. "I thought you and Barrett were getting along great."

"We had a good run. I guess he's ready for something new."

"You need some time off, honey."

"Maybe when this all gets sorted out." Annie ran her hands over a pile of old magazines. "Maybe I'll go back to Westcliffe. Find a front porch. Sit and look at the mountains."

"I knew it. You *did* meet someone in Westcliffe."

"No, Mom." Annie flipped open a random *National Geographic* from 1992.

"I haven't seen your face turn that color since the tenth grade." Myra grinned. "You didn't know that I knew Travis Carlton kissed you."

"Well, nobody has kissed me this time. Can we just look for the book?" Her phone buzzed again. "It's Jamie. I'd better take it."

"A courier just brought a package," Jamie said when Annie answered. "More legal papers."

Rick.

"Can you tell what it's about?"

"Let's see," Jamie said. "Something about a patent. In *his* name, in connection with. . .it's all mumbo jumbo."

"Thanks, Jamie." Annie felt her mother's unspoken questions even as she reassured Jamie.

"Aren't you worried?"

"I'll take care of it."

Annie ended the call and smiled at her mother. "I need to make a quick call. I don't want to bore you. Maybe I'll just run upstairs while I do it."

"If you don't come right back, I'm quitting," Myra said. "You're the one who wants the book."

"I'll be right back." Annie had already punched 9. By the time she got to the top of the stairs, Lee answered.

"It's bogus," Lee said after Annie explained what little she knew. "He can't patent something he had no part in creating. He's trying to edge in before your partnership legally dissolves so he can have a piece of the action."

"So he can't do this?" Annie paced across her mother's kitchen, where she used to sit and do homework.

"I'll have to see the papers, of course, but it sounds like a sneaky maneuver to me."

"Sneaky doesn't mean unsuccessful," Annie pointed out. "That's what lawyers do. No offense."

"I'm on your side, Annie. I'll do my best."

"How could he have these papers ready so fast?"

"Because they were already sitting on the corner of his desk. He's two steps ahead. Does he play chess?"

Annie groaned and put her face in one hand. "I never once could beat him."

"Well, I will. Just get me the papers."

"I'll take care of it right now."

She clicked off.

"Honey, are you all right?"

Annie spun to face her mother. "Just. . .a complication I didn't foresee. But my new lawyer is not worried."

Myra held up a spiral-bound book with a pink cover. "I found it."

"Oh, thank you!" Annie took the book in her hands and flipped to random pages. List after list of names, single spaced, filled a hundred pages.

"I'd better get supper going." Myra turned to the sink behind her, lifted the faucet handle, and ran water over her hands. "Pork chops in applesauce just the way you like them."

Annie grimaced. "I don't think I can stay after all, Mom. I need to run back to the office." She held the book against her chest. "Let me know when Aunt Lennie gets here. I promise to come to dinner."

Twenty-One

January 1738

"You must go," Verona insisted.

"We've only had the warrant two days," Jakob countered. "There's plenty of time for the survey."

"The weather is clear *now*." Verona would not give up easily. "Surveyors will be eager for winter work. If you do the survey now, we'll have no trouble with the papers come spring."

"You can always smell spring in the air."

"I don't smell spring, but I smell enough clear weather for the survey. It is the first day of a new year, Jakob. Celebrate by engaging a surveyor."

When Verona's deep violet eyes lit up in that particular shade, Jakob knew not to argue further.

So he found a surveyor well recommended for his efficiency and mounted his horse in the middle of winter to visit the land he had already come to think of as his own.

The next week, the surveyor did his work with Jakob pointing and describing and gesturing. They started at the black oak Jakob and Hans Zimmerman had leaned against together, and the surveyor marked three other trees as well. Jakob's land had corners now. Assured that the legal description would be filed as soon as possible, Jakob shook the surveyor's hand and watched the man pack away his brass and oak instruments, mount his horse, and head in the general direction of Philadelphia.

Jakob decided to stay another day and make his own sketches. The Siebers offered night shelter in their barn, but Jakob spent the daylight hours on his own land along Irish Creek. In winter sun, he dipped a quill and drew ink across thick paper. A great stone fireplace would anchor the house. He would carve the mantel out of black oak—plentiful on the land—with a table to match, both of them sanded and polished to a sheen. He sketched paths to the smokehouse, the icehouse, the barn, the stables. Pastures, crops, orchards, and gardens took form in black on white. Jakob drew a little square and wrote in it, "Maria's Beets." The creek bubbled through his drawing in the shade of black and Spanish oaks. A tanyard, farthest from the house in its own clearing, would supplement his income. If he could clear fifty acres of the 168 the surveyor had measured, the family would do well.

At first light the next day, Jakob closed the Siebers' barn door behind him and mounted his horse for the ride to Philadelphia. Verona had been right to insist he come, he reflected. Perhaps in as little as two months they would all come back together to Irish Creek.

"If my calculations are correct," Christian announced to his sisters, "*Daed* should be back in no more than two days."

Verona smiled as she stirred the stew in the pot hanging in the fireplace. She loved the feeling of having her children gathered in the warm room. Only three of them could sit on crates at the small table at one time, but they had acquired a couple of rickety chairs, and Lisbetli never stayed in one place very long anyway. Christian was rarely without a map anymore. Even Hans Zimmerman said that Christian knew distances and terrain better than most of the men. He had begun marking his maps with the names of

Amish families to indicate their future homesteads. To keep up with Christian, Maria was taking more interest in learning to read. Verona was pleased that Barbara, who had more schooling than anyone else in the family, made up lessons for the other children.

Verona gasped when the pain burst behind her eyes again. The ladle clattered to the floor as she put both hands to her temples. Though she closed her eyes, she felt Barbara and Anna lurch in her direction. Anna picked up the ladle, and Barbara caught her mother's elbows.

"I'm fine." Verona waved her daughters away. "It will pass in a moment."

"It's happening more often." Barbara did not let go of her grip. "Go lie down."

"Supper is almost ready." Verona reached toward the pot.

Barbara stopped her. "I will feed the children. Please, *Mamm*, lie down."

Verona feared that if she put her head to the pillow, she might never get up again. She would never get to tell Jakob about the new baby. Perhaps it would be better if he did not know.

Until the moment the horse buckled under him, Jakob had let his mind wander, dreaming of the homestead and fields rich with buckwheat, rye, and vegetables. By bedtime he would be sharing his sketches with Verona.

Suddenly his feet left the stirrups and his hands lost their loose touch on the saddle horn as his body flew off the mount. He landed on his back, inches from a tree trunk that could have cracked his skull. The breath went out of him, and for a moment he lay on the ground unsure whether he was capable of inhaling. Eight feet away, the horse neighed in protest and struggled to regain posture. To Jakob's relief, she did. He could see now the hole she must have stepped in with her left front leg, the soft depression camouflaged with wet leaves and broken branches. The horse limped in a small circle, and Jakob, still flattened, felt a swell of panic. If the horse's leg was broken, he did not even have a rifle to put her out of her misery. This was not a hunting trip, after all, and he had no other use to carry a gun through the wilderness. He would never shoot anyone, not even natives on the attack. And he didn't know how he would pay for another horse if this one turned up lame.

The immediate question was whether Jakob himself could stand. Pushing up on one elbow, he regretted the decision to take a deep breath. His hand went immediately to his rib cage. Once, years ago, he had broken three ribs. Instantly, he remembered the injury. With his fingers, he gently probed his side. If he was lucky, this time only two had cracked. Controlling his breathing, he managed to sit up and lean against the tree trunk he had come so close to striking. With quick, jagged breaths, he watched the horse.

Jakob clicked his tongue to call the horse to him, and she came. At first, he limited his evaluation to visual inspection of the fetlock in question. No bone protruded. Mindful of his precarious position, within easy kicking range and barely able to move, Jakob slowly reached for the animal's leg and ran his hand gently down the line of the bone. He felt no break. She seemed to favor the leg less with each step.

With a few minutes' rest, the horse would be fine. Jakob, on the other hand, winced at the thought of trying to mount in his present condition, never mind withstand the motion of riding. He studied the sky. Light would fail soon, and the temperature would plummet. Scanning the immediate vicinity, Jakob determined he could support a fire with deadwood for several hours if only he could manage to strike his flint hard enough to create the required spark.

Mrs. Zimmerman shook her head. "How long has she been like this?" She touched Verona's cheek.

"She only went to bed a few hours ago." Anna's face scrunched anxiously. "We asked if she wanted some stew, but she wouldn't wake up."

"She has been ill much longer than a few hours," Mrs. Zimmerman said.

"Since the boat." Christian stood in the doorway watching his mother sleep.

"She gets tired." Barbara choked on her words. "I try to help as much as I can so she can rest. Christian should not have bothered you."

"She is burning up with fever." Mrs. Zimmerman dipped a cloth in a bucket of water once again and turned to the boy. "Christian did the right thing to come and get me. Now he must go find my husband."

"What can Mr. Zimmerman do?" Anna asked.

"He knows the road your father would take back from Irish Creek."

Lisbetli wailed from the other room.

The fire burned low. Jakob examined the eastern sky for any hint of pink before deciding to put on more wood. His sense of time was gone, swallowed by catnaps he jerked out of without knowing whether he slept two minutes or twenty. Most of the night he was awake, partly in pain and partly on alert for the sounds of the forest around him. A squirrel's scamper, a twig's snap, the fluttering wings of a bird—it all made Jakob twitch. In the dark, he parsed every sound, making sure it belonged.

At the sound of hooves approaching, Jakob straightened his back with a silent wince.

A lone horse.

It could carry a single Indian.

The rhythm he heard was too rapid for the dark and getting louder.

Jakob slithered into the woods behind him. There was no time to kick dirt on the fire or untie the horse.

The hooves stopped. Someone dismounted and moved around the campsite.

"Jakob?" a voice called.

Jakob looked out from behind a tree to see Hans Zimmerman patting his horse's neck on the other side of the fire.

"Jakob? Are you here?"

"Yes!" Jakob called back. "I'm here!" With an arm cradling his ribs, he moved into Hans's view.

"What happened?" Hans rushed forward to catch Jakob's weight.

Jakob shook his head. "First, you tell me why you're looking for me in the middle of the night."

"Do you think you can ride?" Hans asked. "We have no time to spare."

"What happened, Hans?"

"It is Verona."

"*Daed*! What's wrong?" Anna cried when she saw her father.

Jakob, clutching his ribs, waved her off. "How is your mother?"

"She is not talking."

Maria threw herself at Jakob's legs. "Are you going to make *Mamm* better?"

Lisbetli screwed up her face and wailed. Christian handed her a wooden spoon, which she threw down, petulant.

"She wants *Mamm*," Anna said.

"I want *Mamm*, too," Maria said.

Hans, coming in behind Jakob, peeled Maria off of Jakob's legs and tipped his head toward the bedroom. "Go see her."

Jakob opened the door that had shielded the younger children from the sight of their mother. Closed off from the fire, the room was cold. Barbara sat on the edge of Verona's bed, and as Jakob entered, she pulled a cloth out of a bucket of water, wrung it slightly, and laid it across her mother's forehead. Then she moved out of the way, and Jakob took his daughter's vigil post.

"Verona, my love." He spoke into her ear.

Just when he thought she would not respond, she turned her head slightly, without opening her eyes. "Jakob?"

"Yes, I'm here."

The effort of trying to speak consumed her breathing. "Survey?"

"It's finished," he said. "We'll have the papers soon."

"Sorry." Her eyes opened to slits. She swallowed.

Jakob moved the damp cloth to her chapped lips for a moment. "Shh. Just rest."

"I cannot go." Her chest rose and fell in shallow rolls. "Promise me you will."

"We will wait till you are well."

She shook her head. "No. This is the end for me."

"Don't say that, Verona." Jakob laid his hand along her burning cheek.

"Love again, my love." Her eyes closed. "Don't be alone." Her chest fell and did not rise.

When he sketched his dream, it never occurred to Jakob to include a cemetery.

Jakob hired a wagon and, with Hans Zimmerman's help, took the pine box to Irish Creek. He would be gone at least five days, but Mrs. Zimmerman knew his heart and took the children home with her. Jakob could not bring himself to leave Verona in Philadelphia behind a church whose teachings she did not believe. He would tend a fire as long as it took to thaw the land enough to dig. She must be buried on Amish land.

Their land. The survey was a formality. It was only a matter of time before he could move his family to the home Verona wanted for them.

By the time Jakob returned to Philadelphia, Lisbetli had been inconsolable for a week, her usual compliant disposition shattered by the absence of her mother. She clung to her father's neck constantly, unwilling even to go to Barbara's arms. The little girl slept only when exhaustion overwhelmed and never for long. Jakob slipped out in the mornings—sometimes to Lisbetli's screams—to work at the tanyard, only to come home every night to a distraught toddler and a teenager with the face of a woman who knew pain. In a few days, Barbara would be fifteen. How could he ask her to mother her siblings? But how could he manage without her?

Jakob knew what the coming weeks would bring. For a while, Amish families would stop by with food or an invitation for one child or another to play with their children. But they were all marking time, and there were not many families from their ship left in Philadelphia. The true goal was to leave the city, to claim their land, to forge settlements where they could live apart and unencumbered by conflict over their beliefs. Wasn't that why they had come to the New World?

The survey came in. Jakob breathed relief that the choice to bury Verona on Irish Creek was without regret.

Love again, my love.

Twenty-Two

"I'm sorry, Mr. Beiler, but the bank officers have determined it's necessary to discontinue your line of credit."

Rufus squinted under his straw hat. This made no sense. "I wonder if there has been a mistake. Perhaps some confusion with another account."

The woman at the desk tossed her wavy black hair over one shoulder and made faces at her computer screen. "No, I'm sure it's the correct account. Would you like to set up a payment schedule for the outstanding balance?"

Rufus looked at her in confusion. He had opened his business account five years earlier when the Beilers first arrived in Colorado. A few months later, the bank extended him a small line of credit, and gradually over the years it grew with his business. Why would they suddenly withdraw it?

"We can convert the balance to an unsecured signature loan for a term of forty-eight or sixty months."

"I'm sorry." Rufus shook his head. "I don't understand. Is there some concern about my payment history?"

She pushed out her bottom lip and studied the screen again then clicked a couple of times on her keyboard. "The only information

I have is that the line of credit is discontinued. You'll have to talk to a bank officer if you want to know more."

"I do want to know more, please." Rufus fixed his eyes on the back of the computer monitor that seemed to determine the woman's statements.

"Please have a seat." She gestured to an imitation leather loveseat. "I'll see who is available."

Rufus sat, stunned. This had to be a mistake. Without a business line of credit, he would not be able to pay his employees—or himself—between payments from clients on bigger jobs. He would not be able to bid on any jobs that required more cash up front than he had in the bank. The new housing development north of town would be off-limits to him. The happy owners of the home where he installed custom cabinetry had given his name to two friends building in the new construction area. Both wanted bids, but already they were anxious to work with Rufus. Both—especially in combination—would require considerable cash outlay up front. The most he could ask from the customers was half of what he needed for supplies. Without a line of credit, it would be impossible.

Karl Kramer.

It was no surprise when the woman returned and reported that no officers were available, and perhaps he would like to come back next Wednesday to discuss his options.

No, he would not like to come back next Wednesday.

Rufus stepped out into the harsh end-of-July sun and wiped sweat from the hairline against his hat. In the heat, the weight of Karl's scheme fell against him, making Rufus anxious for the shade of the buggy. He barely even patted Dolly's face before taking his seat and picking up the reins. On the bench, though, he sat still, his chest heaving. "*Demut,*" he muttered. "*Demut.*"

Lord, this is impossible. Not my will, but Yours.

Ruth put her slight weight on the pad that automatically opened the sliding doors at Vista Valley Nursing Home. Every time she entered, she found the name of her place of employment ironic, and perhaps a contributing factor to her ongoing homesickness. Though she lived and worked and went to school snug against the foothills to the Rockies, she longed for the wide vistas of the San Luis Valley. Someday she would go back. That had been her plan all along.

Ruth walked briskly down the hall then took the corridor to the left, the one with the teal green stripe on the floor to direct visitors in and out of the wing where she spent twenty-five hours a week.

The nurse at the desk greeted her. "Ruth! Good. Mrs. Watson has been asking for you."

"Thanks, Angela," Ruth said. "Let me clock in, and I'll go see her."

In the break room, Ruth spun the dial on a padlock and opened her locker. She laid her purse on a shelf and picked up the comfortable white shoes she always left there. In a moment, she had changed her footwear and pulled on a smock. The other staff wore scrubs, but Ruth couldn't quite allow herself to don them and was grateful that—so far—the administration was sensitive to her religious leanings. Her skirts were simple and easy to move in, and the name tag on her smock clearly identified her as an employee.

When she was ready to go out on the floor, she slid her time card into the machine and awaited verification that it registered properly. It was precisely 6:00 p.m. Her shoes squeaked as she padded down the hall to Mrs. Watson's room.

The resident, sitting in a wheelchair, lit up as soon as she saw Ruth. "My favorite person in the whole place!"

"You're sweet, Mrs. Watson. I could probably squeeze in ten minutes of reading to you now, if you like, then more a little later."

"I know they don't pay you to read to me."

"They pay me to care for you, and reading does that. Besides,

I would come even if they didn't pay me."

"Now you're the one being sweet," the old woman said. "I was just thinking today about how long we've known each other."

"More than a year," Ruth supplied.

"That's how I reckon it, too. And in all that time I don't ever remember you taking a week off."

"No, I guess I haven't." Ruth picked up a couple of magazines from the end table. Mrs. Watson had particular reading tastes. "Do you want *BBC History* or the *Smithsonian*?"

"You don't have to read to me now, dear. I'm talking about a vacation for you."

"I'm fine, Mrs. Watson. I go to school year-round. There's not much time for a vacation."

"But you haven't been home in all this time."

"No," Ruth said quietly, "I haven't."

"Won't you have a break between terms at the end of the summer? If you request the time off now, surely they'll grant it."

"It can be hard to find a sub." Ruth flipped a few magazine pages.

"Nonsense. People take vacation days all the time. Don't you want to go home?"

"Very much."

"Then you should go."

Ruth smiled as she laid the magazines back on the table. "I have a few things to do. I should be back in about an hour to help you get ready for bed."

She slipped out of the room and leaned against the pale pink wall in the corridor. How could she explain to a sweet old lady like Mrs. Watson that she was fairly certain her mother did not want her to come home? Not after the way she left. Not after her *mamm* found her hiding and waiting for a ride on that day of all days. Her departure had wrenched an enormous wound through both mother and daughter. Ruth was not sure it could ever heal enough for her to be welcome on the farm again.

The roast beef was juiced to perfection. The sweet potatoes were mashed and baked with a golden brown-sugar crust. Garden-picked green beans and fresh red pepper slices splashed color across the table. Annie had lifted the buttermilk whole-wheat loaf from the bread machine herself not twenty minutes ago.

Even without the vegetables, Aunt Lennie would have added all the color the table needed. At seventy-nine, she moved more slowly than Annie remembered, but her determination faltered no more than it had twenty years ago. She made Annie smile every time she blew through town. A comfortable, sprawling two-story home in Vermont was home base, but Lennie always seemed to be on the way to somewhere, and Annie couldn't help but admire that.

After her father gave thanks for the food, Annie lifted the bowl and offered a spinach and strawberry salad to Aunt Lennie.

"Aunt Lennie," Myra said as she moved a generous portion of sweet potatoes to her plate, "Annie is doing some family research. We thought you might fill in some of the blanks."

Brad Friesen transferred a slice of meat to his plate. "I confess I don't know too much about the family history, other than what I remember about my parents—and you, of course."

"Most of what I know can't be proven." Lennie winked at Annie. "But I've stored away a tidbit or two. What would you like to know?"

"It's about your grandmother Byler." Annie smeared butter on still-warm bread. "Do you know anything about the Byler name further back?"

"Oh, there was an Abraham Byler and a string of Jacobs. Abraham was a sheriff, I believe. Malinda's father. Shot in the line of duty. But the Jacobs? I can't tell you too much."

"If Abraham was a sheriff, then I guess he wasn't Amish."

"Hardly. Why would you think that?"

"I didn't really." Annie stabbed three green beans. "It's just similar to the name of some people I met recently."

"Amish?"

Annie nodded.

"In Colorado?" Lennie clanked her fork and sat up straight. "Well, I'll be!"

"It's a fairly new settlement. Only a few families."

"So they're trying again." Lennie scratched an ear.

Annie perked up. "What do you mean?"

"Now, I told you, I can't prove any of this. Family lore says the Amish came to Ordway around 1910. A Byler cousin fell in love with an Amish girl and joined up. He got baptized and everything. He was going to live off the land and make a bunch of babies."

"You mean we really have an Amish relative?" Annie picked up a bite of roast on her fork but did not raise it to her mouth.

"Don't get ahead of me." Lennie put one finger on her chin as she thought. "Story has it that those poor folks never could get any irrigation out to their farms. After a few years, they packed up and went back to Pennsylvania. All except our cousin. Harold, I think his name was. Turns out he didn't believe all that much, and when the babies didn't come along, maybe he didn't love all that much, either."

"What happened?" Annie asked. Around the table, eating had stopped as everyone waited for the story. Lennie was the only one who systematically moved food from plate to mouth.

"Pennsylvania was the last straw," Lennie said between two bites of sweet potatoes. "What was left of the community was giving up and going home. Except Pennsylvania wasn't home for Harold. He disappeared the night before they were supposed to leave."

"What happened?" Annie pulled her phone out and started making notes.

"He turned up in California a few weeks later and never did come back to Colorado." Lennie tore a piece of bread in half.

"I haven't thought of that story for years."

"What about the Amish girl—his wife?"

Lennie shrugged. "Don't know."

Annie now had names to look for in her books. She tapped them into her phone. Abraham Byler. Harold Byler.

"What do you remember about your grandmother?" Annie asked, poised to enter more information into her phone.

"Malinda Byler? Not too much. Your grandma Eliza and I were little girls when she died. I remember she told us Bible stories on Sunday afternoons, and she could twist a chicken's neck faster than anyone I ever knew in all the years since." Lennie paused. "Of course, I don't see too many people twisting chicken necks these days. It's a dying skill." She laughed at her own pun.

Annie shook her head with a smile. Aunt Lennie was always the same.

"Her son Randolph was your father, right?" Annie asked, picturing the family tree she had sketched.

"Right. But she had other children. Most of them moved back to Arkansas at some point, but Daddy always liked the wide-open spaces of Colorado. I never thought I'd leave, either, until your Uncle Ted used his wiles to lure me to Vermont."

"It's amazing how geography brings an end to the story so fast," Annie mused. "Especially a hundred years ago."

"This is all fascinating," Brad Friesen said, cutting into his meat. "I should have paid attention long ago. But, Annie, why are you so interested now?"

Annie shrugged. "I just am. I've been so focused on getting where I'm going that I never thought much about where I came from."

"The Bylers are good stock." Lennie nodded emphatically. "Except perhaps for that character Harold. When you make a promise, you ought to stick to it, not run the other direction."

"Thank you, Aunt Lennie," Annie said. "You've told me things I might never have known."

"Yes," Brad agreed. "I'm glad you put us on your route west."

Annie picked up a red pepper slice and bit into its crispness. Moments divided families for generations. She had the urge to call her sister in Seattle for a long chat. And she had the urge to track down Ruth Beiler, no matter what Rufus thought. She was never going to see him again anyway, so why did it matter?

Twenty-Three

March 1738

Jakob tapped the paper twice and looked at his daughter sternly. "You must practice your letters, Maria."

Maria twiddled the quill between her thumb and forefinger. "I don't want to. I can't do it without *Mamm's* songs."

Jakob had barely cleaned up from his half day at the tannery before Lisbetli latched onto him as she did every day. He shifted her now from one arm to the other. The toddler's head remained tucked under his chin during the whole maneuver. "*Mamm* would want you to do your letters, Maria. How else will you learn to read?"

"I don't care about any stupid books!" Maria threw the quill down, spilling the inkwell in the process.

"Maria!" Jakob righted the inkwell then lurched for a rag. The sudden motion made Lisbetli clutch his neck all the tighter and add a whimper to the commotion. Ink already soaked through the sheets of paper stacked on the table and dribbled off the edge before Jakob could slap the rag in place.

Maria leaped away from the table. "It's going to ruin my dress."

Jakob sighed and sat in a chair to sop up the mess.

"No. No down," Lisbetli protested, her predictable response

to the possibility that he might want to put her down for a few minutes.

Christian was gone to the livery to check on the horse, and the other girls were shopping for vegetables for the evening meal. Even if Barbara was home, Lisbetli would not release her father. She had been clinging to him for weeks, as if she was afraid he would disappear the way her mother had.

Jakob reached out a hand toward Maria. "Get your capes. We will go for a walk. It's not too cold out today. There is even a bit of sun."

"Where will we go?"

Jakob shrugged. "It does not matter. But I am going to need some new ink."

Maria hung her head. "I'm sorry about the ink."

Jakob tipped Maria's chin up and looked in her blue eyes. "I know you miss your mother. We all do."

They walked toward Market Street. Jakob scanned the pedestrian traffic every few yards, wondering if they would see the other girls. If Barbara managed to find beets, Maria's mood was sure to improve. Maria walked ahead of Jakob for the most part, and he let her wander at will. Occasionally Lisbetli would lift her head and point at something, but by and large she was content to mold herself to her father's chest as she had for the last two months.

The stationer's shop caught his eye, and he wondered why he had never noticed it before. It was in a row of narrow shops at the base of a three-story brick building close to the center square of town. He must have walked past it dozens of times. It was the laugh that caught his attention this time. The shop's door was propped open to welcome the springlike weather—though the danger of frost was not over—and as he walked past, a woman's lilting laughter lit the air.

"Maria," Jakob called as he slowed his steps and angled his head to look in the shop. Maria retraced a few steps and stood beside him.

Jakob watched a young woman behind the oak counter use a large sheet of plain brown paper to wrap a purchase for a well-dressed gentleman. The laughter drifted off, but a broad grin still cracked her face. Her chatter bore the familiar accent of Jakob's own birthplace in Bern, Switzerland. The customer seemed pleased with whatever he had said to elicit her convivial response as he tucked his package under his arm. Outside the shop, Jakob stepped clear of the doorway to allow him to pass.

"Are we going in?" Maria asked.

"Yes we are," Jakob answered, though he had not known until that moment.

Inside, the shop carried an assortment of writing papers, envelopes, inks, quills, and a few books.

"May I help you?" the young woman asked.

"I require a small packet of black ink powder, please." Jakob shifted Lisbetli in his arms.

"Your daughters are beautiful." The young woman pulled a jar of ink powder from a low shelf and laid out a sheet of paper to fold into a packet.

"This one is a little worn out these days." Jakob stroked Lisbetli's head.

The woman reached toward Lisbetli with curled fingers. To Jakob's shock, the little girl reached back, gripping the woman's hand.

"This is Lisbetli," Jakob said.

"So her given name must be Elizabeth." The woman smiled at the toddler. "My name is Elizabeth, too. Elizabeth Kallen."

"She is Elisabetha," Jakob said.

"Very similar." She reached across the counter and touched Lisbetli's cheek. "Hello, Lisbetli."

"I am Jakob Byler."

"It's a pleasure to meet you, Mr. Byler."

Lisbetli twisted in Jakob's arms and reached toward Elizabeth Kallen with both arms.

"Would you mind?" Elizabeth reached now with both of her own arms.

Jakob gladly surrendered the child across the counter. Elizabeth Kallen propped Lisbetli on one hip and tickled her with a finger under the chin.

"Do you have any books for children?" Jakob was not at all sure that the coins in his pocket would cover both the ink and a book—not to mention replacing the ruined paper still on the table beside the fireplace. Christian would not be happy to discover what his sister had done. Perhaps some of the sheets could be salvaged.

"I believe we have some illustrated folktales and a primer or two."

"Perhaps we'll look at a primer. Would you like that, Maria?" Jakob glanced up at Miss Kallen. "She is just learning her letters."

"Our books are all used," Miss Kallen explained, "so I believe you will find the prices reasonable."

She carried Lisbetli around the end of the counter and led Maria to the bottom shelf of a rack on the back wall of the shop. Jakob stayed where he was, watching his daughters. Maria apparently had forgotten that she did not want to learn her letters and held a slim German primer as if it were gold. Lisbetli had a thumb in her mouth and looked thoroughly comfortable in Miss Kallen's arms. Other than when Barbara twisted her baby sister from their father's arms so he could go to work, this was the furthest Lisbetli had been from Jakob since Verona's passing. Jakob used the moment to count his coins.

When he heard the baby's laughter, his eyes misted. Lisbetli hadn't giggled in so long. She popped her thumb from her mouth and grinned at Miss Kallen.

"We are moving to Irish Creek," he heard Maria announce. "There is no school there, and my mother died."

"I'm sorry about your mother," Miss Kallen said softly.

Maria's thin shoulders lifted and fell a few times before she continued, "I have to learn my lessons from my brother and sisters."

"I think you're probably a very good student."

"My brother especially likes maps. Do you have maps?"

"We get one every now and then."

"Try to find one with colors on it," Maria said. "Christian loves the ones with colors."

"Perhaps I will set aside the next one I see for your brother. You can remind your father to stop in again." Elizabeth Kallen glanced in Jakob's direction, and he couldn't subdue the upturn in his lips. Her tenderness with his children moved him more than he would have imagined.

And then he took back the smile. He had no business smiling at a young woman in a shop.

"We should go, Maria," he said. "Your sisters will be wondering where we are. We will take the primer home with us." He stepped toward Miss Kallen and reached for Lisbetli, freeing the woman's hands to seal the packet of ink.

When Jakob pushed open the door to their two small rooms, he found Barbara chopping onions and potatoes on one end of the table, and Christian scowling and scrubbing at ink stains at the other end. Anna sat on an upturned barrel near a window, staring out. Jakob supposed it did not much matter what was beyond the pane. These days she just stared for long stretches.

"I copied over the list, *Daed*," Christian said. "The old one was getting too hard to read. But the ink is nearly gone."

"You're an organized young man." Jakob reached into his pocket for the powder and dropped it on the table. Christian would know what to do with it. Lisbetli was stuck to him again, but he carried the hope that she would recover her childhood in the kindnesses of people like Elizabeth Kallen.

"I have three columns," Christian continued. "One column tells us the supplies we already have, like axes and hammers and pots. The second column is a list of things we absolutely need before we go. I put the bellows there. We can't go without those."

"When I get my wages next week, we'll go see the blacksmith," Jakob said.

"And the third column are things we can get when we can afford them."

Jakob leaned over the table and glanced at his son's lists, surprisingly neat and straight. The boy took the planning tasks so seriously that Jakob sometimes had to remind himself he was only nine.

A knock made all their heads turn. Christian hopped off his stool and opened the door. Hans Zimmerman stepped inside. The two men exchanged a greeting by lifting their chins toward each other.

"We're almost ready." Hans straightened his hat. "We'll be leaving in a few days."

Christian's eyes moved to his father and widened. Jakob nodded. His son was full of questions, but he knew better than to enter the conversation uninvited.

"There might yet be a blizzard." Jakob laid a hand on the top of Lisbetli's head.

"As the Lord wills," Hans replied, "but the Siebers have offered us shelter for the last of the winter. When the weather allows, we will begin clearing. We might still get a late spring garden in."

"I don't suppose we'll be far behind you. By Christian's reckoning, we will soon be outfitted ourselves."

"Would you like some coffee, Mr. Zimmerman?" Barbara asked. "It's fresh."

Zimmerman nodded. Jakob offered the best chair in the room to his friend and sat on a crate with Lisbetli in his lap.

"Christian, what news do you have?" Zimmerman asked as Barbara handed him coffee.

This was all the invitation Christian needed. He pulled his stack of papers out of his lap and reviewed the Byler progress in collecting homesteading supplies. Their wagon was stored with the man who kept their horse, and as they acquired items, Christian and Jakob secured them in the wagon. Christian had drawn his own scaled sketch of the farms emerging along Irish Creek: The Stehleys had arrived a few weeks ago and immediately claimed land west of the Bylers. Hans Sieber was to the south, and Hans Zimmerman to the west, beyond the black oak. Kauffmanns, Buerkis, Masts, and other familiar names had sprouted on Christian's map.

Jakob listened absently as Christian prattled on and Barbara cooked. The Amish community already on their farms would make sure each family had shelter as they arrived. Barns would go up quickly, followed by cabins. Although winter weather was still possible, more likely conditions would shift radically any day now. He should be excited to go—as excited as Christian. Jakob did look forward to being near Verona, but it would not be the same as being *with* her.

Love again, my love.

He was nearly fifty years old and moving to the wilderness with five children and a few other families. *Where would I find another wife?* he asked himself.

Jakob struck a deal with the blacksmith for hoes and tongs and an anvil. From the dry goods store, he bought yards of ticking and hired a seamstress to sew it into mattress covers. Verona would have wanted to do it herself, but it was too much to ask of Barbara and Anna. They labored enough by candlelight over their own clothing, simple dark dresses and practical aprons. He consulted his daughters about supplies for the kitchen and slowly but surely put checkmarks next to each item on Christian's list of essentials. Working less at the tannery, Jakob put his energy into filling the wagon and finding a second horse to help pull it over rugged terrain.

And he did much of this with his youngest daughter's arms around his thick neck. She seemed most soothed when he walked, so Jakob began to stroll in the late afternoons in weather that crept more certainly toward spring each day. Lisbetli would find enough solace to eat a good meal before falling onto her pallet exhausted. Unconsciously, his route settled into one that took him past the stationer's, and he found his steps slowing on that block.

One afternoon he heard the laughter again.

Lisbetli lifted her head. Before Jakob realized what she intended, the little girl wriggled out of his arms and slid down his legs to the ground.

She ran to Elizabeth Kallen, who squatted and opened her arms to receive the tiny, hurtling form.

Jakob followed his daughter.

Elizabeth smoothed loose hair and stood up with Lisbetli. "I was hoping you would come by."

Jakob's heart sped up. She wanted to see him?

"I have a map for your son," she said.

A map. For Christian. "How thoughtful of you."

"I understand it's very similar to one that William Penn used," Elizabeth explained. "I thought it might be of particular interest."

Jakob nodded. "I'm sure Christian will find it invaluable."

"I hope you will accept it as my gift." She held out the map.

Jakob's fingers closed around the map, brushing hers. "I should not infringe on your profit."

She shook her head. "It is torn on one end. We would not be able to sell it, so I thought your son might as well have it."

Lisbetli laid a hand on Elizabeth's face, and Elizabeth instinctively turned toward it and kissed the little palm.

Jakob's heart cracked open.

Jakob smoothed the quilt, one of Verona's last, at the front of the wagon right behind the driver's bench. He patted the pile. "Hop in, girls." Christian would ride at his side, and the girls would have their comfortable corner, where Lisbetli and Maria could enjoy a small space to wiggle. Tied to the back of the wagon, a cow nosed around in vain for a patch of grass. With the children in the wagon, Jakob took one last look around the two rooms, making sure they left nothing behind that belonged to them and took nothing that belonged to the Quaker owners. Traveling with a loaded wagon and leading a cow would require several days to reach Irish Creek. Gear to make camp each night hung from the rim of the wagon.

Jakob heaved himself onto the driver's bench and took the reins from Christian. "Ready to see Irish Creek?"

Christian nodded, his eyes wide in anticipation.

A slender form appeared at the side of the road, and Jakob blinked twice before he believed his eyes. "Miss Kallen! What are you doing here?"

"I suspected you were leaving today. I have something for Lisbetli." She held out a small, soft doll with a carefully cross-stitched face.

"You are too kind."

"May I give it to her?"

"Of course."

Elizabeth approached and leaned over the side of the wagon. Lisbetli popped her thumb out of her mouth and wiggled her fingers in a wave. When Elizabeth placed the doll in her hands, Lisbetli giggled shyly and held it tightly.

"Thank you, Miss Kallen."

"You're most welcome, Mr. Byler."

Maria leaned over and inspected the doll. "But it has a face, *Daed*! Our dolls don't have faces. It's a graven image."

"I hope I have not caused offense." Elizabeth laid one hand over her heart.

"Of course not." Jakob dared not offend her, either. "It is not our usual way for a doll to have a face, but Lisbetli loves it already."

Elizabeth looked crestfallen. "I have a lot to learn about the Amish ways."

"Christian," Jakob said, "why don't you thank Miss Kallen for the map she found for you?"

188

"It is a wonderful map." Christian bobbed his head sincerely. "*Danke.* Thank you very much for thinking of me."

"It was my pleasure." She looked from son to father. "May your journey be safe, Mr. Byler. You have my prayers."

"Thank you, Miss Kallen."

Elizabeth stepped back, and Jakob nudged the horses forward. He wanted to go, but she made him want to stay.

Twenty-Four

On Saturday morning, Annie sat cross-legged on her bed with a genealogy book on each side and her laptop straight in front of her. She looked from page to screen to page. Each source revealed twists on the spelling of family names and slightly different lists of descendants, but it all added up the same.

Jakob Beyeler arrived in Philadelphia with an Amish wife and five children.

His wife died.

He married again and had five more children, but no records indicated that this second wife was Amish.

Annie sank back against a stack of pillows. What a wrenching choice Jakob must have made. But somehow his older children remained Amish.

As she traced through the generations in the book Franey and Eli had loaned her, Annie found their names. At the time the book was assembled, they had one child. Rufus. A descendant of Jakob's first son, Christian Byler.

And she found her own name easily enough in the book her mother unearthed from the basement. A descendant of Jakob's second son, born to his second wife.

Beyeler. Byler. Beiler. Biler. Even Boiler. No matter how the name was spelled, the dates and random bits of information matched. It was all one family line that traced back to Switzerland in the eighteenth century and a countercultural religious group who simply wanted to live in peace.

Annie put her finger on Rufus's name and imagined the line completed with the siblings who followed. Daniel. Matthew. Ruth. Joel. Lydia. Sophia. Jacob.

She riffled the leaves of the bound book. Pages and pages of names and birth dates and death dates, each one a story. Most of them were gone from memory, but thick paper between plain brown covers collected the evidence of their existence. The pink-covered, spiral-bound book in which her own name appeared overlapped in the beginning with the record in the brown book. Quickly it diverged into a family line absorbed in mainstream culture and left behind increasingly distant relatives faithful to the Amish life.

Jakob's choice spawned two sets of descendants who would be hard pressed to find common ground three hundred years later. *Had he chosen for love?* Annie wondered. *Or necessity? How dearly had he paid for his choice?*

Annie's mind wandered to Ruth Beiler. Why had she left her family? What was really going on?

"Only one way to find out," Annie said aloud. She closed both books and moved them to the nightstand.

In her back pocket, her phone buzzed. Annie saw the caller ID: Lee Solano.

What now?

"Did you get your bid in?" Tom asked Rufus. "The town council just gave the green light for remodeling the visitor's center."

Rufus hesitated and glanced around the house where he was installing a set of built-in bookcases with Tom's help. "I have some matters to work out."

"It's not a big job, but it seems like a good opportunity for you."

"It would be," Rufus agreed.

"Then why don't you bid on it?"

"It might not be the right time for me." Rufus dropped his hammer into the toolbox. "I've got the motel project and custom built-ins for two of the new homes. That will keep the crew busy."

"You can always take on more help."

Not if I can't pay them. "Tom," Rufus said, "do you know any banks you like in Colorado Springs?

"A few. Why?"

"I need to try a new place. Can we go next week?"

"Sure. Bidding is open for another three weeks."

Annie drove north on Rangewood toward the subdivision dominated by townhomes where Barrett lived with his wife, Lindsay, and their infant daughter. She slowed as she approached his street and eventually parked three doors down. Maybe he was home. Maybe if she did not make arrangements ahead of time, Rick would not be able to foil their meeting.

Annie had just about persuaded herself to present herself at Barrett's home when his garage door went up. A few seconds later, his green Subaru backed out. The car was filthy, which made Annie's stomach shoot acid up her throat. Something was not right. Barrett kept his car in impeccable condition. Had Rick done this to him?

If Barrett saw Annie's idling car, he gave no indication. He put the car in gear and roared forward, away from her.

Behind her steering wheel, Annie sighed. She glanced at the clock then put her own car in gear. One more stop might yet answer some questions.

Ruth turned a page in the textbook and encountered yet another list she would likely have to memorize and reproduce on a quiz. Music blared from the room on one side of her. Ruth could not identify the artist, and she did not care. It all sounded the same to her—deafening, bleating, clamoring. And constant. How did Amanda, the student in that room, find space for a thought? On the other side, through thin walls, Ruth heard dribbles of Tasha's phone conversation that landed in random intervals during slight lulls of the music. Every time she caught a snippet, she was surprised anyone could *still* be on the phone for that length of time.

Ruth called it artificial noise—sounds people chose to fill tender spaces but, as far as she could see, brought them no joy.

She began to hum one of the slow, soulful tunes from the *Aumsbund*, the music of her childhood, and simultaneously transferred the list in the textbook to an index card she could carry around and study.

The music went off abruptly, and Ruth heard footsteps in the hall that joined the five rooms of the dormitory suite. A sharp knock startled her.

"Somebody here for you, Ruth."

She scooted her desk chair back and went to the door. Opening it, she saw a woman a few years older than she was with blond hair and gray eyes. Jeans fitted her hips in smooth perfection. A white eyelet shirt with a slight suggestion of sleeves hung loosely above the jeans, revealing tanned arms. Ruth pulled on the cuffs of her own long-sleeved blouse.

"Ruth Beiler?" the woman asked.

Ruth nodded, straightening the plain blue skirt that fell nearly to the floor.

"I'm Annie. We spoke on the phone last week."

Now the voice registered for Ruth. A voice of compassion. "You answered my brother's phone."

Annie nodded.

"Please come in." Ruth stood back from the door. "I don't have much to offer, but I can make tea." The music cranked up again next door. Ruth gestured with one hand. "And entertainment, of course."

"Is it always like this?" Annie asked.

"Only when Amanda's here." Ruth moved to the counter that served as her kitchen to make tea. Stilling the tremble in her hands that came with her visitor's presence required great focus. "How did you find me?"

"Your letter. I saw the return address on the envelope."

Ruth looked hopefully at Annie.

Annie shook her head. "No. Rufus has not read the letter."

Ruth's shoulders lost their ridge. "It's not the first letter. At least he doesn't send them back. So there's hope." She moved quickly to the bed and smoothed the woven cotton blanket. If only she had thought to take a quilt when she left home—not that there had been any time to think that night. "*Sie so gut.* Please. Sit down. I'm afraid I am out of practice at being a good hostess."

Annie sat down on the end of the twin bed. "Do you mind that I've come?"

Ruth shook her head and swallowed. "Not at all. But I don't understand who you are or why you've come." All she knew was that this stranger had seen her brother—perhaps her whole family—just days ago. Whoever she was, she was a welcome guest.

The music shut off, and a door slammed.

Ruth caught Annie's eye, and they both sighed relief.

"How do you know Rufus?" Ruth asked.

"I met him accidentally a couple of weeks ago." Annie let her bag slide off her shoulder and set it on the floor next to the door. "Then I got hurt, and he took me to your family's home for a few days. He was very kind—except when I said something about a letter he carries around."

"He carries it around?" Hope flowed in Ruth's veins.

"In his toolbox. I got the feeling he wanted it close."

"He was probably angry that I called his cell phone."

"I'm not sure Rufus gets angry." Annie twisted her mouth on one side. "But when he's disappointed, it comes through loud and clear."

"You seem to understand him well for. . .an *English*. Forgive me, but I can't help wondering about your friendship with my *bruder*. It's not like him."

"I know. It's odd. And 'friendship' may be too strong a word. Circumstances threw us together briefly. I don't expect to see Rufus again." Annie pressed her lips together momentarily. "On the other hand, I get the feeling you would like to."

Ruth's eyes filled, and the tremble rose afresh. She would not be able to withstand long.

"Ruth?" Annie's voice was barely audible.

"Why are they punishing me?" Ruth burst into tears. "I made a choice. It's a good choice. An honorable choice. I'm going to be a nurse and help people. Why can't they understand?"

Annie was on her feet now and wrapped her arms around Ruth.

"*Es dutt mirr leed*," Ruth muttered. "I'm sorry."

"We all make choices every day." Annie stroked Ruth's back, stilled the tremble. "You have to do what's right for you."

"That is not the Amish way." Ruth spoke into Annie's shoulder. "When you're Amish, choices have deeper meaning. You can't imagine what it's like."

"Help me imagine, then." Annie held her tighter. "I know I'm an outsider, but I do care."

"Most people just want to gawk at us." Ruth breathed in the unfamiliar scent of this stranger who had been with her family, hoping for the fragrance of home.

"I hope that's not what I'm doing. At least not anymore. Not after meeting your brother and seeing what matters to him."

Ruth pulled back from their embrace. "Are you sure there's not something between you and Rufus?"

"How can there be? I'm not Amish." Annie waved both hands

in front of her. "I was in a jam. He helped me, and I'm grateful. That's all."

Ruth dragged fingers across both eyes. She did not quite believe her guest. "Then why did you want to find me, Annie Friesen?"

Why indeed?

Annie lifted one shoulder and let it drop. "I don't understand what happened in your family, but I want to help." Ruth's resemblance to Rufus was strong—the same brown hair and violet-blue eyes and a more feminine version of his facial structure. Annie saw bits of Lydia and Sophia in Ruth's expressions, too.

"How?" Ruth turned to fiddle with mugs awaiting the boiling water.

"Well, I haven't figured that part out yet."

"Rufus would say you're interfering."

Annie nodded. "He made that clear."

"Still, you are here."

"I am. I'm used to getting what I want."

Ruth put a tea bag in each mug and poured water. "For some people, just wanting what they get would be enough. My life would have been easier if I were one of them."

"But you're not." Annie stood up straight for emphasis. "If I could make Rufus read your letter, I would. Jacob misses you, if that's any consolation."

Ruth smiled and handed Annie a mug. "I miss him back. He must have changed in all this time. Taller, I suppose. Reading."

"He read your name on the caller ID and was afraid."

Ruth sat in her desk chair, and Annie perched on the end of the bed again.

"I don't want Jacob to be afraid of my name," Ruth said, her shoulders hunched.

"Then we have to fix this."

"It's not so simple. What I did—"

"You made a hard choice, that's all," Annie said. "Something tells me you never meant to hurt anyone."

"I didn't!"

"I believe you." Annie saw Ruth's tears threatening another assault. "I know how important family is to all of you. I don't accept that whatever is between you and your mother must always be painful for you both."

"I did something awful." Ruth's words were a hoarse whisper.

"I'm good at solving problems. If you'll let me, I'll find a way to help you."

Ruth gulped tea, and then slowly she nodded.

"We'll make a plan," Annie said, "and go one step at a time. But first, I want to tell you something I learned because I met your family."

"What's that?"

"My family line traces back to the original Jakob Byler."

Ruth sat up straight. "So we're related?"

"Like ten generations ago and six times removed." Annie grinned. "But we might have a marker or two in our DNA to connect us."

"I can think of worse people to be related to. *Danke*." Self-conscious, Ruth looked in her mug. "I need more tea. Can you stay for another cup?"

In the middle of the second cup, Ruth said, "I am trying to obey God. *Glassenheit*. Submission. That is our way."

"But if you submit to God by staying in school, you are not submitting to your parents or to the church."

"You understand." Hope caught Ruth's breath.

Annie shook her head. "Not really. It's hard for me to understand why other people get to make choices for you."

Ruth sighed. "The *English* think we spurn their ways. The truth is we are simply trying to choose God's way. That's all I'm doing."

"Even if it takes you away from your family?"

The pressure in Ruth's chest forced its way out through her

throat. "I don't like to choose between God and. . .those I love. But it seems to be the only way."

"I don't accept that." Annie shook her head widely from side to side. "I'm not as close to God as you are—at least not yet—but this doesn't seem right."

"Is it true what you said—that you're good at fixing things?"

"Absolutely. I'm going to help you."

Ruth closed her eyes and breathed out. "You are an answer to my prayer."

They drank three cups of tea. When Annie left and Ruth was cleaning up, for the first time in eighteen months, she did not feel alone. And an *English* was the reason.

By the time Annie turned the key in the lock at her condo, she wanted to see Ruth again. She wanted to see Ruth standing between her brothers or in the embrace of her mother.

She had to go back to Westcliffe. It was the only way to fix this.

Twenty-Five

June 1738

Jakob used both hands to grip the shovel's handle and send the implement's sharp edge into stubborn earth. Again. Again. Little by little the ground gave way. This day was like every other day in the nine weeks since they arrived on Irish Creek.

The land was dense with trees. They had their pick of fir and pine and spruce. The barn went up in a day with the help of the Siebers, Zimmermans, and Stehleys, all on adjoining Irish Creek land, and the Detweilers and others from Northkill. Then came the cabin, which was not large, because Jakob still dreamed of the real house he would have given Verona. But with a loft for sleeping, the family had more space than in the two rooms in Philadelphia. Even with no furniture to speak of, the determined older girls spread their mother's quilts around so the inside would feel like a home. As soon as Jakob and Christian cleared and turned enough land, the garden went in, and it was beginning to show promise that it would yield. Maria planted a square of beets and refused to let anyone else tend that section of the garden.

Jakob taught Christian to hold a rifle and aim steady enough to drop a deer. The animals browsed the black oak all over their land, so it was surprisingly easy to sight them. After a few sudden movements that sent the wildlife scurrying before Jakob could lift a rifle, Christian learned to move with stealth through the woods. So far they had a bounty of meat—deer, rabbit, squirrel, wild turkey—but Jakob was looking forward to some vegetables.

They had cut dozens of trees already, some of them as tall as seventy-five feet. Oak and elm, sycamore and walnut stacked up to be crafted into furniture, planed for floor planks in the permanent house, or cut to warm his children at the hearth when winter raged anew.

For now Jakob did not want to think about winter. Early June sun gave lengthy light for felling and hauling logs, and the days would grow even longer through the summer. Soon he would yoke the horses and begin wrenching out the stumps scattered across the property. Then they could plow. Then they could plant more than a vegetable garden.

Whether he swung an ax, notched a log, joined a corner, or tucked Lisbetli into bed, Elizabeth Kallen hovered in Jakob's moments. He raised his face to the sun, closing his eyes to see her once more standing in the road while the wagon rolled past.

The flicker in the flame told Jakob he needed to seal yet another draft above the small window. The children were asleep in the loft, but Jakob had abandoned his bed in favor of these quiet moments alone with a pen in his hand.

Dear Miss Kallen,

For a long time, he got no further.

I have been remiss not to thank you more promptly for your final kindness toward Lisbetli.

But he had thanked her at the time. And it was only a rag doll.

*How could you have known she would become as attached
to the doll as she has?*

What he wondered most was how she had known where to
find them. And why she had come.

*Christian has plotted the homesteads on his map and
refers to it often. Maria's progress in the primer is gratifying,
and she writes her letters on a slate each afternoon. How
thoughtful of you to suggest the perfect items for both of them.
I admire your tender heart.*

The last sentence was far too forward.

~~*I admire your tender heart.*~~

Now he would have to copy the letter onto fresh paper. That
being the case, Jakob supposed he might as well try out other
phrases he feared to breathe.

I find myself thinking of you often.
*I trust this finds you well. I would hate to think you are
distressed.*
*Would you extend your kindness to an old man by
allowing him to call on you?*
I know you are not of the Amish, yet your heart touches mine.

He couldn't say any of those things. He drew lines of ink
through the words.

Jakob laid his pen down and stood up, rubbing his shoulder.
He took three steps back. *What am I thinking? She does not believe.
This cannot be.*

Jakob moved to the fireplace and examined the embers. He
had to leave enough burning to be able to stir up a cooking fire in

the morning. Barbara had used the last log for supper. Jakob went to the door, intending to bring in enough wood for the day that would arrive in a few short hours.

When he came back through the door, he stopped in his tracks.

"Barbara, what are you doing up?"

She turned to him from the table, a page in her trembling fingers.

"*Daed*, why are you writing this?"

Jakob took a breath and stepped toward the fireplace, where he deposited his load as quietly as possible. No other children need wake and hear this conversation. "That is a private letter, Barbara."

"I can see that."

"Then I ask you to respect my privacy."

"But you are writing to a woman. Are you going to marry her?"

"It is only a letter. She was kind to us."

"*Daed*, I understand if you want to marry again. Many of our people marry again quickly. But you have written right here that she is not of the Amish. How can you consider this?"

Jakob strode across the room and took the page from her hand. "Someday you will want to marry, Bar-bar. You will understand certain. . .feelings."

"Are you *in lieb*? Do you love her?"

Jakob did not respond.

"We suffered so much in Switzerland and Germany because of our faith. We came to this place—we watched *Mamm* die. For this?" She snatched the paper back and threw it down. "No, *Daed*."

Barbara turned and climbed the ladder to the loft without looking back.

Jakob blew out the candle but lay wakeful for long hours.

It was no surprise when Barbara disappeared with Lisbetli for a long time after breakfast. It was no surprise when Hans Zimmerman's horse maneuvered between black oak stumps and came to a stop where Jakob and Christian worked.

Jakob pulled out a handkerchief and wiped his forehead.

"Christian, go to the creek and bring us a jar of water."

"But we still have—"

"Just go, Christian."

The boy dropped his hoe, picked up the half-full water jar, and reluctantly turned his feet toward the creek.

When his son was out of hearing distance, Jakob spoke. "So Barbara has confided in your wife, and she is duly appalled at my behavior."

Hans slid off his horse. "We just want to understand, Jakob. Barbara believes you have intentions."

"How can I have intentions? I barely know Miss Kallen."

"You know we are meant to live apart, Jakob. 'Wherefore come out from among them, and be ye separate, saith the Lord.' Second Corinthians, the sixth chapter and verse seventeen."

"Separate from what, Hans? Am I to live separate from affection? Separate from a mother for a two-year-old who doesn't understand? Separate from someone who might free Barbara to consider her own future?"

"You know the community will care for your family," Hans said. "That is our way."

"You have a wife, and your children have their mother," Jakob countered. "The question has become far more complicated for me."

"You cannot go against *Ordnung*." Hans's jaw set firmly. "If you marry this woman, your life will change. Think of your children."

"I *am* thinking of them."

"Has the community failed you? Have we failed to encourage you in God's will? If we have, we will repent and help you to do the same."

"Elizabeth Kallen has the heart of God in her. I can see it in her eyes. Lisbetli knows this, too."

Hans scoffed. "Lisbetli is hardly more than a babe. But you have been baptized into the church. You cannot consider this step frivolously."

"I assure you that I do not," Jakob said. "But the fact remains that the number of our people is small. I am unlikely to find a wife among the Amish settlers here. Am I to grow still older while I hope that the next ship brings me a desperate woman widowed on the journey? Miss Kallen is a capable woman who would appreciate the challenges of homesteading and care for my children as her own."

"But would she join the church?" Hans challenged.

Jakob leveraged his shovel under a large stone, hefted it, and moved toward a pile of stones. "The stones here are smooth and well shaped. They will make a beautiful fireplace someday."

"Jakob, this is a serious question. Would she join the church?"

Jakob scraped at dirt. "I don't know."

"Would you ask her to?"

"I don't know."

"I don't think you've thought this through, my friend."

"I quite agree," Jakob answered. "Perhaps that is what I was trying to do last night when I wrote a *private* letter."

"She must join the church, Jakob."

Jakob plunged his shovel into the dirt until it stood upright. He turned to look his friend in the eye. "Must she? If I were to wed a woman like Elizabeth Kallen and give my children a mother in the middle of the wilderness, might I be answering a higher calling than the call to join the church?"

Christian returned with the jar of water. Jakob took a deep, cool draft. And Hans mounted his horse.

"Mr. Sieber is leaving tomorrow for Philadelphia to get supplies," Christian said a few days later over lunch. "We should give him a list."

Jakob nodded. "*Gut.* Make a list. I will take it to him this afternoon."

Barbara popped off the crate she sat on. "But we are supposed to go to the Stehleys' to welcome the latest families. Mr. Zimmerman offered to pick us up in his wagon since he comes right through our land."

"You take the children and go with him. I will meet you later."

Anna spoke up. "Is it true that you are going to marry the lady from Philadelphia?"

Jakob stiffened and glanced at Barbara.

"I'm sorry, *Daed*," Barbara said. "I thought Christian and Anna should know. They are old enough. They are not *boppli*."

He turned both hands palms up. "There is nothing to know."

"There might be." His eldest daughter clearly had her mother's stubbornness.

"I'm not going to give up the true faith." Anna was resolute.

"I would never ask you to," Jakob told her. "Your mother and I taught you to do the right thing. You must make the decisions of your own conscience."

Hans Sieber looked dubious when he saw how Jakob's letter was addressed.

"She is at the stationer's shop off High Street," Jakob said firmly.

"Should not the letter be addressed to the owner of the shop?"

"I do not wish to correspond with the owner."

Sieber raised his eyebrows.

"If you don't wish to take the letter," Jakob said, "I will ask someone else."

"We have been friends a long time, Jakob."

"This is why I trust you." Jakob met his friend's gaze.

Sieber nodded and added the letter to his satchel, along with Jakob's supply list.

Riding to the Stehleys' land, Jakob pondered how many days he should give Elizabeth to consider his carefully crafted words and planned his own departure for Philadelphia accordingly. The children could stay with the Zimmermans.

Twenty-Six

I've got to get to the bank," Annie told Jamie. "They're expecting me promptly at ten."

"You can go just as soon as you sign this letter." Jamie laid a single sheet of paper in front of her.

Annie scanned the page. "This should do it. We're officially severing the company's relationship with Richard D. Stebbins, attorney at law."

"I can send it by courier, and he'll have it inside twenty minutes." Jamie tapped the paper on the desk with a triumphant index finger.

"Handy having a courier service across the street, eh?"

"Then sign the stinkin' page and make it official."

Annie picked up a black pen, with the thin rolling point she favored, and signed her name with flourish.

"Careful there." Jamie wagged a finger in warning. "The signature has to look right enough to be legal."

Annie laughed. "We're done with Mr. Stebbins. After I sign the documents to buy Barrett out, we can focus on moving forward."

Jamie picked up the signed letter and creased it in neat thirds before sliding it into an envelope. "I miss Barrett. It's not like him to just up and leave this way."

"I miss him, too," Annie said. And she did. Annie had withheld most of the story from her staff. Let them remember Barrett with fondness, she figured, even if they thought he lost his marbles for leaving. "I don't think I'll be long at the bank. The new attorney assures me he has arranged for the papers to be ready for signature when I get there."

"When you get back, I'll get Liam-Ryder Industries on the line."

Annie nodded. Liam-Ryder Industries had been patient for two weeks. She couldn't keep ignoring a prospective client with the deep pockets this company seemed to have.

"I'm calling the courier right now." Jamie stepped out of Annie's office to her own desk and picked up the phone.

Annie checked the list on her phone to see what else she had to do before she could go to Westcliffe sometime in the next few days. Eli's brown book was already on the front seat of her car.

Tom steered the red truck into the parking lot, pulled up in front of the building, and shifted into Park. "Are you sure about this?"

Beside him, Rufus nodded. "It seems the most peaceable thing to do."

"It's a lot of nuisance for you to bank all the way over here. People would come to your aid if they knew Karl somehow got his fingers into the bank decisions. Give them a chance to help."

Rufus shook his head. "I am not trying to cause harm to Karl Kramer. I simply want to earn a living."

"I could come in with you."

Rufus smiled. "You're a good friend even if you are *English*. But I will be fine. I have my tax returns showing my business history and value. I can put up my share of the family land if I have to."

"Okay, then." Tom straightened behind the steering wheel. "I figure it will take about two hours to go see my mother. If you need a place to wait, there's a little garden area behind the bank. I'll look for you and honk."

Holding a soft, deerskin satchel, Rufus got out of the car and watched Tom's truck merge into the unforgiving traffic of Powers Boulevard, eight lanes across. He could not imagine driving a buggy in this town. All Rufus needed in Colorado Springs was a bank manager with a fair-minded sense of business practices. He stepped onto the sidewalk and paced over to the front door.

It was not far to the bank. Still, ever since Rick beat her to the restaurant where she was supposed to meet Barrett, Annie scanned the road whenever she drove. Rick could still try to interfere with signing papers. His grill could show up in her rearview mirror any moment.

But nothing was there. A bedraggled soccer mom in a white minivan. Businessmen with Bluetooth headsets in their ears and miniature offices spread across the front seats of the vehicles. Teens in aging hand-me-down cars heading for the movies. No bronze Jeep. No Rick.

Rufus entered the bank and asked to speak to a loan officer. He ignored the strange looks he always garnered when he came to town. Black suspenders pressed tracks into his white cotton shirt. Today he wore a black felt hat instead of his usual straw hat. Everybody who saw him did a double take and then politely acted as if it were perfectly normal to see an Amish man standing in the bank waiting patiently to apply for a business line of credit in Colorado Springs. Rufus was used to it.

"Mr. Endicott will see you now." Rufus was glad to duck into one of the offices and out of sight of the customers traipsing in and out of the lobby.

Barrett opted to sign the agreement in advance, so Annie knew she would not see him. She was just as relieved as he was to avoid a face-to-face meeting at this point. *What would he do now?* she wondered. He would have money, at least. But knowing Barrett, money was not the real question. He loved the frenzied din of a challenge. Lee Solano insisted on a thorough noncompete clause in the documents that dissolved the partnership, but Barrett could take off with his own ideas and build another company.

The branch manager was waiting for her when Annie entered the bank, and led her past a row of small offices with closed doors flanked by tall, narrow windows. The manager's office was larger and less cell-like. He slid a packet of papers across a smooth, uncluttered, glass-topped desk.

"Three copies of everything," he said. "Please sign all three, and I'll assemble one set for you."

Knowing she would sign in his absence, Lee had prepared Annie well for what the papers would be. Annie scanned each one to make sure it corresponded to what Lee directed and signed all three sets. In a matter of minutes, she had a manila envelope of documents in her hand and watched while the bank manager transferred funds as Barrett had previously directed. The company account showed considerably fewer assets, but Annie now held 100 percent of the company and anything it might create. She stood and shook hands with the bank manager, tucked her manila envelope under one arm, and left the bank.

He was waiting for her when she turned the corner on the sidewalk.

Rick Stebbins backed her up against the brick and crunched a piece of paper in her face. "How quaint. Sending a letter by courier. This means nothing."

"It means you have nothing to do with me," Annie answered evenly.

Rick pulled the envelope out from under her arm. "Is this what I think it is?"

"It's no business of yours." She smelled onion on his breath and knew where he had eaten his morning omelet.

Rick lifted the envelope flap and pulled the papers up a few inches. "So it's done, then. You and Barrett are no more."

Annie said nothing. His breath hovered over her face. She fought to keep her own breathing from turning ragged.

"You can't think it would be over that easily." Rick's brooding eyes held Annie's in a vise now. "Barrett was never the goal."

Annie felt his breath. He had never leaned in so close except to kiss her.

Rufus left the bank encouraged. He would have to wait for a letter confirming the line of credit, but the loan officer saw no reason not to think it would be approved. It was too early to expect Tom would be waiting. Rufus opted to wander behind the bank.

He stopped in his tracks. A man in a dark suit leaned against the brick with one arm, his face close to a woman's. At first Rufus thought he would disturb a romantic moment if he kept walking. *English* would kiss anywhere, after all. It did not matter who was watching.

The man's arm blocked the woman's face, but the color of her hair made Rufus suck his breath in. His eyes moved from her hair to assess her height and form.

Annalise. In trouble.

Rufus said nothing, just stepped right up to the pair and stared into the man's eyes.

The man jerked away from the brick. "What are you looking at?"

Rufus turned his eyes to Annalise. "Is everything all right, Annalise?"

"You know this guy?" Rick asked.

"None of your business," Annalise answered.

"Perhaps you should be on your way." Rufus spoke calmly and firmly to the man.

The man slapped an envelope against Annalise's chest. "I'm very good at what I do."

"So am I." Annalise pushed on the man's chest with one hand and gripped the envelope with the other.

The man glared at Rufus and got into a bronze vehicle and roared away.

Annalise was trembling now. Rufus wished he could gather her into his arms the way he had when she fell at the motel.

"What in the world are you doing here?" she said.

"It's good I came, *ya*?"

"*Ya*," she answered then laughed at herself. "He wouldn't have done anything. He just tries to throw me off balance."

"He does a good job." Rufus glanced in the direction the man had driven. "I assume he is what you mean when you say, 'It's complicated.'"

She nodded. "Part of it. Most of it."

Rufus tipped his hat toward the garden behind the bank. "Let's sit down and watch something grow."

Annie let Rufus steer her to a bench positioned for admiring a bed of irises and daylilies. The irises had finished blooming weeks ago, but strong stalks almost as tall as Annie still foisted deep orange daylily blossoms upward. Annie thought absently that the flowers were the same kind her mother cultivated.

She sat next to Rufus on the bench, and though he kept a careful distance, his nearness overwhelmed her. If he held his arms open to her, she would fall into them gladly, hear his heart beating, savor the pressure of his embrace.

"Annalise, you're in trouble." Rufus planted his hands on his knees and leaned forward.

Annie shook her head. "No. Most of it is sorted out already. I have a lawyer. I just signed papers. That man is angry that he did not get his way." Annie tried to restore order to the documents still sprouting from the envelope in several directions. She put the tidied papers on the bench between them. "How do you do it, Rufus? How do you keep from striking back? I'm not trying to take advantage of anyone. I'm just fighting to protect what's mine."

"What does fighting solve?" Rufus leaned back. "Is what you call your own any safer now?"

Annie sighed. "You make it sound so simple."

"It is far from simple. But it is a choice to trust God's will."

He stretched one arm across the back of the bench, his fingertips now a mere inch from her shoulder. She ached for his hand to rest on there.

"I saved my company—for now—but I lost a friend in the process." Annie picked up the envelope, put the prongs through the hole, and fastened it shut. "I really tried to be peaceable, but he left me no choice."

"You always have a choice. The trouble comes when you judge the consequences and find some of them too high a price to pay."

His fingertips found their way to her shoulder, brushing up and down once and settling. She shivered in the heat.

"You don't even know what I chose, what I did." How could she expect Rufus to understand?

"I can see that what you chose did not make you happy. Or safe."

"Maybe you're right." The space between them called for closing. Annie inched over, laying the envelope on the other side of her. His hand rested firmly on her shoulder now. If he kissed her, she would let him. Even encourage him. "You know, in the *English* world, this is where you would kiss me."

"But that is not my world." Despite his words, he held his position.

He wasn't going to. She would have to do it.

Annie leaned into Rufus, one hand on his chest, and still he did not move. She found his mouth, and he did not move. She pressed into the softness, and he did not move, except to press back against her lips. Or was that her imagination? Warmth oozed through her as she waited for him to break the kiss. But he did not.

Her phone rang, and she jumped back to snatch it out of her pocket. Lee Solano.

"Hi." Intuitively, she strayed from the bench and turned her back to Rufus.

"Everything go okay?"

She ran her tongue over her lips, still tasting Rufus. "The papers are signed. It's done."

"No sign of Stebbins?"

"Well, he did show up, but I handled it."

"Harassment. Find a witness," Lee said. "We'll get a restraining order."

"Oh, I have a witness." Annie turned back to the bench.

But Rufus was gone.

A horn honked, and Annie raised her eyes to the red truck in the bank parking lot. Rufus pulled open the passenger door and got in.

Tom would carry Rufus back to Westcliffe. She had not even mentioned seeing Ruth or thought to return Eli's book. All she had wanted was that kiss, no matter what.

Annie sighed and pulled out her phone to look at her schedule. She was having dinner with her parents the next night and a meeting with Lee the day after that. Then came a day of client meetings. Something had to give.

Maybe Rufus would not even want to see her. Maybe he would not listen once she spoke Ruth's name.

Twenty-Seven

July 1738

Elizabeth Kallen yanked on a crowbar to pry the crate open.

"And what did this week's shipment bring us?" Rachel Treadway, whose husband owned the shop and provided Elizabeth with a small room at the back of his house as most of her compensation, barely lifted her head from her accounts.

Elizabeth grunted and wrenched on the crowbar one more time. The lid came free.

When Elizabeth moved in with the Treadways nine years ago, she did not expect to stay more than a few months. As the years passed, though, she thought less and less about living anywhere else.

Until recently.

Elizabeth reached into the crate and pulled out a tightly wrapped bundle of rose-colored paper in half-sheet size.

"It is a new color. There must be matching envelopes." Elizabeth carefully laid the paper on the counter and turned back to the crate. "Yes, here they are. The usual yellow and blue are here as well."

"Any ink?"

Elizabeth moved crumpled paper around the crate. "Blue and black."

Rachel groaned. "The artist over in Elfreth's Alley has been begging for purple and green for his drawings."

Elizabeth shrugged. "Only ordinary paper and ink today."

"We get more and more people asking us for books." Rachel waved the feather of her pen against her chin. "I wonder if I should speak to Mr. Treadway about adding a few more racks."

Elizabeth couldn't imagine where more racks could go in the narrow space of the shop.

"I heard that the Helton girl is finally getting married." Rachel spread several receipts on her desk. "She's nearly thirty. I know for a fact her mother had given up hope she would ever marry."

"Love has no timetable." As Elizabeth turned away, a bead of perspiration formed at the back of her neck and began its slow descent between her shoulders. "I'm thirty-two."

"Oh, but you're different. You have spunk. You came from Switzerland all by yourself when you were twenty-three, and things have worked out well, haven't they?"

Elizabeth nodded. "Well enough."

"We think of you as our own, you know."

"You've been very kind."

Elizabeth had not sailed from Europe to be a shopgirl, however. She was supposed to marry Dirk, who had moved to the New World two years ahead of her. He died in a lumber accident the day her ship left Rotterdam. But how could she have known? She spent two months at sea dreaming of a life that would never be.

She could have married, she supposed. It was not as if she never had another opportunity. But the Treadways, friends of her parents, had sheltered her in the first raw weeks of grief, and Elizabeth had not felt any urgency to move past her lost love.

And then she approached thirty, and passed thirty. Wives her age had five or six children. She had become an old maid who worked in a stationer's shop. After all these years, Robert Treadway trusted her to run the shop with Rachel while he devoted his own time to more lucrative business interests. She rather enjoyed chatting with customers, and she was free to spend her evenings quietly surrounded by books in her small room. On Sundays she went to church and dined with friends. It was not a bad life. If someone had asked, she would have said she was happy.

Until the day Lisbetli Byler reached across the counter and Elizabeth lifted her eyes to the face of the child's father.

Jakob stopped just short of the shop's door. The solid curve of the cobblestone beneath his feet reminded him he had come from a rough-hewn cabin to ask a woman he barely knew if she might leave the comforts of Philadelphia.

The letter had been delivered three weeks ago now. Had he allowed her enough time to consider?

With his eyes focused on where he was putting his feet, Jakob walked past the shop's open door. He would go see the cooper first for two new barrels to keep their foodstuffs in. Then perhaps he would go to the dry goods.

He stopped once again and looked back at the shop, its door propped open in case a breeze might stir in the street. On the farm, he would remove his jacket and work in shirtsleeves. But he could not call upon Elizabeth Kallen in his shirtsleeves.

He did not even know where she lived to make a proper call. He knew her only from the shop. Though he did not marry Verona until he was thirty-five, Jakob had little experience with these matters. His parents had joined the Amish when Jakob was ten. Since that time, he had barely even spoken to a woman who was not part of the church except to make simple purchases of items the Amish did not provide among their own.

He took a deep breath and stepped into the shop, certain that if she were horrified at the sight of him, he would know immediately and retreat without speaking. He would never trouble her again.

"Mr. Byler!" Sitting on a stool behind the counter, her face brightened with welcome. "What a pleasant surprise."

"I hope you are well, Miss Kallen."

"I am quite well, thank you. How is our little Lisbetli?"

Our little Lisbetli. Jakob couldn't help a smile. "She carries the doll with her everywhere she goes."

"I'm so glad. And Maria? And Christian?"

"Maria has learned to read quite a few words, and Christian is a great help with the work." He had written these things in the letter, but he would gladly say them again.

"I suppose you have come to town for supplies." Elizabeth stood. "What kind of paper and ink do you require?"

He had come all the way to Philadelphia to have this conversation, but this was not how he expected it to begin. Jakob's mind spun, confused. Had his letter not made it clear that his interest went beyond paper and ink? He had chosen his words so carefully. How could she not know?

Sieber. His neighbor might well have changed his mind about delivering the letter.

He blinked his eyes rapidly, feeling light-headed.

"Mr. Byler?" Elizabeth leaned across the counter. "Are you all right?"

The color drained from his face before Elizabeth's eyes.

"I wonder if you received my letter."

Elizabeth shook her head. "No, I don't believe we did. Were you trying to order a particular item?"

He looked as if he might stop breathing. Elizabeth grabbed her stool and ran around the end of the counter to offer it to him.

"Please sit down." She put a hand on his shoulder to urge him. "I will get you a cup of water."

Almost afraid to leave him unattended, Elizabeth pushed through the green velvet curtain that separated the main shop from the cramped space she and Rachel used as an office. Still hunched over accounts, Rachel sat at her small desk with a pen in her hand.

"Mr. Byler is here." Elizabeth took a tin cup off the shelf above the water barrel. "Apparently he sent a letter that did not reach us."

"Byler?" Rachel sat alert. "Isn't he one of those Amish people?"

"Yes, I suppose he is. But he's a paying customer."

"I think you should steer clear of him."

"I don't believe you've even met him." Elizabeth gestured to the main shop. "The poor man is out there having some sort of spell because we did not get his letter."

Rachel sighed. "We got the letter." She reached under her stack of accounts.

Elizabeth's eyes widened as she took the envelope. "This is addressed to me, but it is open."

"It might have been an order. But something about the handwriting made me uneasy. It is just not right."

"What is not right?"

"The things he says. He has no business making such a proposition."

Elizabeth lifted the flap of the envelope and slid the paper out.

Twenty-Eight

Two days later, Annie was in her Prius with an iPod full of her favorite bands cranking through the sound system. In comfortable navy slacks and a purple cotton shirt, she was ready to get down to business.

She liked Lee, and he had done a good job of dispatching her legal issues. She also liked the idea of throwing corporate work toward an independent attorney rather than a large firm. But his office was an hour away, and she was used to an attorney virtually around the corner. They would have to figure out how they were going to have a satisfactory professional relationship at a distance.

Annie parked outside Lee's unpretentious office in Cañon City, a second-floor suite in a corner building that likely did not exist three years ago. An hour later, she emerged into the sunlight, having agreed to a three-month trial of full corporate representation by Lee Solano. August had just begun. The searing heat of summer would persist for another six weeks. Wincing at the blast of heat that came from opening the car door, Annie sank into the seat and put the cooling system on maximum.

Lee had suggested she lie low for a few days. She persisted in her opinion that Rick would not hurt her physically, but Lee countered with the wisdom of not taking any chances while he sorted out the legal ground. Work from home. Stay away from the gym. Change where she shopped. Eat at someplace new. Use an uncommon route to everywhere.

An uncommon route to everywhere. That's what Lee said.

She was halfway to Westcliffe already. What was more uncommon than that? At least in Westcliffe she could step into the sunlight without expecting to see Rick Stebbins around every corner.

At least she hoped so.

Annie sat with the air, now hinting at turning cool, blowing in her face, and surveyed the environs of the office building and parking lot. She put the car into gear and rolled out of the lot and onto the street, where she made a complete turn around the block. Then she went to the next block and toured around a slightly wider radius in full alert, looking for any sign of a bronze Jeep with a small dent in the left front bumper.

No sign of Rick. He did have a law practice to run, after all. He could not spend all his time following Annie.

She exhaled with slow control. It was the middle of the week already. A couple of workdays—and then the weekend—in Westcliffe might be just what she needed to wait out Rick's fury. Her gym bag, tossed in the backseat, held workout clothes and two clean outfits. This time she would have a car in Westcliffe. Annie pulled over in a residential area, took out her phone, and shot a quick e-mail to Jamie with instructions to distribute her client meetings among the software writers and to set up the second phone conference with Liam-Ryder Industries for the following week. Then she let her mother know where she was going.

Besides, when Lee had found out she knew the name of the witness who had seen Rick confront her, he had prodded her to ask the person to stand by ready to recount what he saw. She neglected to mention the witness was Amish and lived in Westcliffe. Why should that matter? It only meant that her best chance of getting Rufus to agree to the plan was to go see him in person. She punched some information into her navigational system and hoped some of the scenery would look familiar.

An hour later, Annie slowed into the long Beiler driveway. The barn and the chicken coop were on the right, Rufus's workshop on the left, and the house straight ahead. It was a simple and efficient layout in the daylight, far from her first late-evening arrival. The view was comforting to Annie, and she thought of Ruth and what it would mean to her to see this place again. To be welcomed here.

She still did not know the whole story. Even after three cups of tea with Ruth, Annie knew the young woman was holding something back.

Annie shut off the engine, dreading the scorching instant that would come with opening her car door to the outside air. She looked at her denim bag on the seat beside her. It held her laptop, an e-reader, and several folders of legal papers. A fleeting impulse to grab Eli's book and leave the bag on the seat passed, and she reached to sling the bag over her shoulder and grabbed her iPod out of its slot at the same time. She couldn't leave valuable electronics in the car on a hot day like this.

When she cracked the door, Annie was surprised at the flutter of wind against her face. A couple of thousand feet in elevation made a difference. The day was warm, but the mountain air moved steadily. Still, she kept the bag on her shoulder and stepped out of the car.

"What am I doing?" she said under her breath. *Especially after that kiss.*

Shot through with doubt, Annie set her sights on the front porch. She went up the three wide steps and paused a moment at the swing where she had sat during recovery from her fall, where Franey Beiler tried to make her feel welcome, where Rufus sat with his broken saw, refusing to retaliate.

Sucking in a big breath, Annie knocked on the front door.

"Annalise!" Franey pushed the screen door open. "What brings you here?"

Annie held out the book. "I should have returned this before I left."

"Come inside," Franey urged. "I'll make some cold tea."

Annie shook her head. "Thank you, but I need to speak to Rufus. Do you know where he's working?

"He's in his workshop. He's been working constantly on those cabinets."

"For the motel?"

"Yes. He's almost finished."

"Is it all right if I go find him?" Annie glanced in the direction of the workshop.

"Let me walk you out there." Franey fell in step with Annie on the path to the workshop. "Do you have business with Rufus?"

"Not exactly." Annie was not sure what she would say to Rufus. "I need to ask a question. A favor."

"I see. You are welcome here, Annalise," Franey said softly, "but I hope you don't have expectations about Rufus. He is a baptized Amish man. It is unusual for an *English* woman to take such an interest."

"I like to think of Rufus as a friend." Annie's heart rate surged. Had Rufus told his mother, of all people, about the kiss? "He showed me kindness more than once."

"I'm glad to hear you speak well of him, and our family enjoys you. But even an Amish mother recognizes a certain look in her grown children. Be careful."

Annie did not want to meet Franey's eye at that moment. She swallowed hard. "It's not like that."

"Isn't it?"

They were at the workshop. Franey pushed the door open, greeted her son, and revealed Annie's presence.

His shirt was open halfway down his chest, and both sleeves were rolled up to the elbow. Annie hesitated, embarrassed. The sight of him in that moment moved her more than all the shirtless men she had ever seen.

Rufus immediately dropped his awl and reached to adjust his shirt.

"I cannot get involved," Rufus said, after Franey left them and Annalise explained that he might help by giving testimony about what he saw. She had flustered him when she arrived, but not enough to make him do what she asked.

"But you saw him." Annalise leaned on his worktable with both hands. "He was right in my face. He's trying to ruin my business."

"He knows I saw him. I made sure of that." Rufus picked up a plane, though he was not sure what he meant to do with it.

"Right! So you could identify him if need be."

"I only meant to deter him from harming you. I cannot get involved with an *English* court case. How does that serve the cause of peace?"

"What about justice?" Annalise's face reddened. "Do you think I should let Rick Stebbins walk all over me the way you let Karl Kramer walk all over you?"

"Is that what it looks like to you?" Rufus carefully set down his plane and swiped his hands together to shake loose the sawdust trapped in the crevices of his skin.

"Well yes."

"Then I have failed." As much as it made sense to deny it, Rufus wanted Annalise to understand his ways in a way most *English* did not. She was so smart. Why could she not grasp this?

"What is it supposed to look like?"

"Jesus," he said softly. "It's supposed to look like Jesus turning the other cheek. Jesus loving His enemy."

"And if the enemy wins? If the enemy gets everything and you are left with nothing?"

"God will provide." If Annalise could understand this one truth, so many more of their ways would follow.

"That doesn't mean God does not expect us to work hard. You

work hard to make a living."

"God provides through the blessing of work. That is not the same as court battles and lawyers." Rufus picked up a rag and ran it across the worktable, knocking sawdust and bits of wood to the floor while Annalise was quiet. His words were soaking in, it seemed.

"Well, I didn't think you would testify, but my lawyer wanted me to ask."

Annalise leaned against a post at the end of the workbench. She had not expected to persuade him. Right next to her stood a stack of cabinets. She raised one hand to lightly follow the curved edge in the front design. "These are exquisite."

"Thank you." The moment he had hoped for was gone, but perhaps it would come again.

"Mo must be excited," Annalise said. "When will you install them?"

"I'll take them over tomorrow afternoon, and we'll begin installing the day after that. My crew is busy with something else right now."

He waited for her to bring up the subject they were avoiding, and after a couple more minutes of small talk, she did.

"I suppose we should talk about what happened the other day." She stopped fidgeting with the cabinets. "After. . .on the bench. I'm sorry."

She was five feet away from him, and still he could feel the warmth of her against his chest as he had on the bench. He wanted to put his arms around her then, and he wanted to now.

"Don't be. I'm not."

"You're not?"

He smiled at her surprise. "No." He occupied himself with hanging his tools in their respective spots.

"But—"

"Yes, but. I am an Amish man who wants to live simply, and you are an *English* woman whose life is *complicated*. I let myself feel my own loneliness for a moment."

"That's all it was? Loneliness?"

"That's all it can be, Annalise. I am not going to stop being Amish, and you cannot stop being *English*."

They stared at each other. Rufus knew she would have no words to raise against the simple truth he had spoken.

The door opened, and Jacob burst in. "Annalise! *Mamm* told me you were here. She says you can stay for supper if you want to. Please want to!"

Annalise looked from Jacob to Rufus, and Rufus nodded. He heard the choke in her voice when she answered, "I want to, Jacob."

"Do you like beets?"

She scrunched up her face. "Not very much."

"Good. Then I don't have to dig more." Jacob scampered off. Annalise laughed.

"I'm glad you're staying," Rufus said.

She nodded. "Me, too."

Annie had a "regular" chair at the Beiler table now. In addition to the beets, Franey Beiler served a ham-and-potato casserole and a salad of fresh garden greens. Rain pattered during the main meal, eventually rising to a steady sleepy rhythm.

"I hope it keeps raining all night," Lydia said.

"You just don't want to water the garden," Sophie said.

"It takes too many buckets. We need more rain."

"For the fields, too." Joel reached for the plate of bread. "Are you sure you cannot hire me, Rufus?"

"You have work on the farm," Rufus answered.

Eli cleared his throat, and Joel grimaced. "I love the alfalfa fields, *Daed*. But it might be nice to have a bit of real money now and then."

"God will provide," Eli said.

There it was again. Annie looked from Eli to Joel, two generations of Beilers sorting out what those three words meant.

Occasionally Jacob leaned in close to Annie to interpret what the family was saying in Pennsylvania Dutch. Jacob's English was very good for a small child who did not see all that much of the *English*. Rufus did not catch Annie's eye.

By the time Lydia and Sophie carried twin peach pies to the table for dessert, thunder jolted them all. The rain was a lashing whip now.

"Annalise," Franey said as she handed the visitor a slice of pie, "perhaps you should plan to spend the night."

"I thought I would see if Mo had a room at the motel," Annie said. "I plan to stay a few days."

"No point in going out in the storm. Ruth's room is just as you left it. You may stay as long as you like."

Now Annie did look at Rufus to catch his eye. He gave a nod. *Yes, stay the night,* it seemed to say.

"I'd love to," Annie said. "Let me help you do the dishes."

In the morning, Annie made a point to be up in plenty of time for breakfast. The last thing she wanted was Franey Beiler thinking she was a lollygagging guest. When Franey knocked on her door, Annie was already dressed and straightening the quilt, made of deep purple, blue, and green.

"Did you sleep?" Franey asked.

"Very well." Annie stroked the quilt, wondering how many years Ruth had slept under it. "The quilt is beautiful."

"It was Ruth's favorite," Franey said quietly. "My mother made it forty years ago. I used to keep it in the cupboard, but Ruth nagged and nagged for me to let her use it. I finally gave in, and then she was gone."

Annie swallowed hard. Would her next words bring comfort or sorrow? "I saw Ruth last weekend."

Franey's breath stopped as her eyes widened. "My Ruth?"

Annie nodded.

A second quilt hung over the foot of the satin black wrought-iron bedstead. Franey lifted it now and refolded it for no good reason. Annie hadn't even used it. "How is she?"

"She misses you."

"She knows where to find us."

"Would you like for her to visit?"

"I would like for her to come home. That's not the same thing, though, is it?"

Annie shook her head and held her tongue.

"It must seem to you that we are harsh toward Ruth."

"I don't know what happened," Annie said. "I only know she loves you."

Franey hung the quilt on the bedstead again with finality. "You're right. You don't know what happened."

Twenty-Nine

Jacob gave her an I'm-going-to-be-mad-if-you-leave look, but after a breakfast full of chatter, Annie gathered her bag and headed into town. In her car, compared to the buggy rides of her last visit, the five miles zipped by. She parked on Main Street in front of an antiques shop. The sign on the door read, BACK IN 30 MINUTES, which amused Annie both because in Colorado Springs no business would risk missing a customer by closing in the middle of the day, and because the sign did not indicate when the thirty minutes began.

She waved her phone around in the air to catch a signal then checked her e-mail while she walked slowly.

"What are you doing?" Annie winced at her mother's typed words. *"What is this fixation you have with Westcliffe? Call me so I can talk some sense into you."*

Jamie had a list of questions. Annie considered walking three blocks down to the coffee shop to sit down and answer them. Would the barista still remember her beverage of choice, or had she already fallen out of favor?

And then she saw it.

She wondered why she had not seen it three weeks ago.

228

Perhaps it had not been there.

The FOR SALE sign pointed down the side street, directing her to the narrow green house toward the end of the block. She turned the corner, paced past three houses, and stood across the street. The house was two stories but barely wide enough for a decent living room. Probably a living room at the front, with an eating space and something that passed as a kitchen at the back, with perhaps two small bedrooms and a bath upstairs. Annie could not immediately detect where the stairs were, but she had a couple of guesses.

She doubted the whole house was more than eight hundred square feet of usable space. Her condo was three times that big.

This place was waiting for the big bad wolf to breathe too hard and blow it down. Her condo was brand new.

This would be Annie's idea of camping out, while her condo had every modern convenience.

The garage here looked like it was built to house a couple of bicycles. The condo had a reserved underground extrawide parking space.

Annie dialed the number on the sign and spoke to a real estate agent who assured her she could just go on in and look around. The back door was unlocked. The half-acre pasture behind the house was part of the property being offered. Water came from a well beneath the pasture. The realty office was at the other end of Main Street. Call if she had questions.

Annie's heart rate sped up as she strode down the driveway and found the three cement steps up to the back door. A wooden railing she was afraid to lean on enclosed the tiny porch. She paused to glance at the fenced-in pasture. "Horse property," they would call this on the outskirts of Colorado Springs.

The knob turned easily, and Annie stepped into the kitchen— she was right about the downstairs layout—and could see straight through the house to the place where she had stood on the street. The stairs, narrow and steep, rose from one side of the dining room. Downstairs, the walls were a cheery pale yellow. Though the place was empty, someone had obviously cleaned thoroughly and painted in hopes of persuading a buyer of the home's worthiness.

It was working.

Annie climbed the steps, almost afraid to hope for what she would find upstairs. A larger bedroom at the front of the house mirrored the dimensions of the living room, and a smaller one—about the size of her closet at the condo—sat over the kitchen. Neither one of them had a real closet, but the previous owner had left tall wardrobes probably deemed too difficult to bother moving. In the back bedroom, Annie pulled the latch of the wardrobe and imagined it filled with clothes from the condo.

Off the hall in between the bedrooms—papered in green and yellow stripes—was a bathroom with a claw-foot tub.

A claw-foot tub.

Annie had always wanted a claw-foot tub.

Gingerly she reached for the sink's faucet and turned a knob. The pipes rattled but produced clear water.

Rapidly, the picture began filling in. A copper pipe rose from the tub to a shower head. Annie would install a fixture from the ceiling to hang a shower curtain that enclosed the tub. She would do the bathroom in silver and pale pink. Eventually. Of course, the first job would be to make everything functional.

She was going to buy the place, not imagining there would be much competition if she offered just under the asking price. It was only two hours from the condo—a great weekend place. Something to fix up. A hobby. She needed a hobby. Everyone said she worked too hard, especially her mother.

Everyone. Who was everyone? Annie's work habits had cut her off from most of her friends a long time ago. Barrett was her buddy, and now he was gone from her life, taking with him his outgoing wife with whom Annie had always enjoyed spending time.

Annie stood in the upstairs hall, a whisper blowing through

her. She was meant to find this house on this day.

God's will. This house would be more than a hobby. She blinked against the picture taking form in her mind.

She walked through again, testing light switches and faucets. What she presumed was a broom closet off the kitchen opened to stone steps leading to a basement. Down the creaky stairs she found an ancient furnace and hot water heater. On the way back up, she noticed the shelf of cherry preserves and canned green beans. How long had they been there?

Yes, she was definitely going to buy the house. She would wait to tell anyone until her offer was accepted in writing. A cash offer would help speed the sale.

God's will.

Tires screeched through her dreams, but it was the pounding that made Annie throw back Ruth's quilt and leap out of bed. She was sleeping in her workout clothes. All the Beilers were in the upstairs hall at two in the morning, as Eli and Rufus scrambled down the stairs. Wearing shorts and a tee, Annie stood in the midst of the family waiting on the landing. When Rufus opened the front door, Tom's flashlight lit his face.

"It's your cabinets, Rufus," Tom said. "Karl got to them. Mo already called the police."

"I'm coming with you." Annie pushed past Sophie.

"Oh Annie," Tom said. "Do you have your car? Can you bring Rufus? I promised Mo I'd come right back."

"Absolutely."

Rufus was already on his way up the stairs to exchange a robe for real clothes. Annie ducked back into Ruth's room for jeans, shoes, and a sweater. Seven minutes later, they were in the Prius.

"This sounds really bad, Rufus." Annie backed up the car to turn around. "You just took those cabinets over there yesterday."

"Let's wait and see what happened."

"The police are going to be involved."

"That's Mo's decision, not mine."

"They're your cabinets. Your hard work."

Annie turned into the lane leading to the motel. Lights blazed across the scene. She spotted Tom's truck and two squad cars labeled CUSTER COUNTY SHERIFF. The other vehicles were unfamiliar—likely guests at the motel but perhaps also gawkers. She parked as close to the lobby entrance as she could.

Rufus was silent as he got out of the car and walked past a couple of women in shorts and sweatshirts. Annie followed closely, scanning for Mo.

An officer greeted Rufus. "I understand you are the carpenter doing the work here."

Rufus nodded, his eyes looking past the officer with the clipboard to the cabinets. Twelve hours ago, he left them stacked neatly in a suggestion of their final arrangement. Then he had covered them with pads and tarps. Now the pads and tarps were bunched in one corner, and blue and green spray paint splattered and squiggled across the exposed panels.

Annie squatted beside Rufus as he ran his fingers though the paint, barely dry. "Will it come off?"

"It should, but I'll have to sand and finish everything again."

"What about this?" Annie stuck a finger in a hole at the bottom of one front panel. Rufus's shoulders sagged.

"They used an auger," he said on a sigh. "Took a plug right out."

"Clearly it's premeditated." Annie pushed to a standing position, huffing in fury. "This is not the work of bored teenagers."

Rufus stood up. "See how many holes you find. I'd better check the desk."

Annie carefully examined all eight cabinets and found three more auger holes and one deep scratch, the kind a key made in the grip of determination. Rufus threw back the tarp from the new reception desk and found a long gouge across the top.

One officer was absorbed with taking Mo's report. Annie

listened in. Mo was asleep in her apartment behind the lobby. The lobby door was locked. Guests accessed their rooms from the outside. New guests arriving at odd hours could ring a doorbell that woke her, but it was uncommon for anyone to arrive past midnight. Mo heard nothing until an engine gunned. She called Tom, then the sheriff's office.

"This is the work of Karl Kramer," Tom insisted to the officer.

The officer turned his hands palm up. "Innocent until proven guilty. We'll investigate, but we can't arrest a person without something that smells like evidence just because you say he has a grudge."

The second officer questioned people standing in the parking lot, who turned out to be three motel guests and Tom's wife, Tricia. Nobody saw anything. One of them, who had been watching television, said she might have heard a truck, but she wasn't sure.

"We have breaking and entering, and we have vandalizing," the first officer said. "Mo, we'll do the paperwork in the morning. You can come by and make sure it's right."

"What about Rufus?" Mo turned toward Rufus, who was silent. "The ruined cabinets and the desk are his work."

"They were on your premises," the officer responded. "Check with your insurance agent."

Annie spoke up. "Someone drilled holes in the cabinet, someone who wanted to hurt Rufus. Not just anyone would have an auger lying around."

"You'd be surprised in these parts, ma'am."

"They didn't touch anything else," Annie persisted. "Not a drop of paint on the floor, not a scratch in any other furniture. Only Rufus's work."

"Annalise." Rufus voice came softly. "This is not necessary."

"Yes it is." Annie looked to Mo for support. "Whoever did this was not out to hurt Mo. They wanted to set Rufus back. They want him to bear the cost of righting this."

"Annalise, please," Rufus said.

The officer shrugged. "I'll make note that Mr. Beiler is a possible witness if we make it to court. And I'll have a conversation with Karl Kramer, see if he has an alibi that checks out."

"He wouldn't be stupid enough to do it himself." Annie balled her hands at her sides. "He'll say he was home in bed."

"I know you're frustrated, ma'am, but right now we don't have enough to charge anyone."

The officers left. The guests went back to bed. Tom and Tricia went home.

"I'll put on coffee. We'll sort out what's next." Mo disappeared into the motel's dining room.

"It's not fair!" Annie sank into a small armchair.

Rufus sat on the floor across from her and held one hand up tenderly on an unscarred side surface of a cabinet. "The damage is only on the surfaces that show."

"See! Karl thought this through."

"We don't know it was Karl."

"Don't we?" Annie sat forward, her back straight. "I bet you could tell me exactly what kind of auger makes that kind of hole, and I bet Karl has one."

"You have not even met Karl Kramer," Rufus reminded her. "I barely know him myself."

"If the police won't do anything, we have to take the matter into our own hands. We have to find proof."

"You know I'm not going to do that." Rufus did not move off the floor. "Anger will not rebuild the ruined cabinets."

Annie huffed. Rufus was nothing if not consistent.

It was well after three in the morning by then. Mo returned with steaming mugs of coffee.

The buggies began arriving at four.

Eli and Franey Beiler were the first. By six in the morning, eight buggies lined the lane, with horses nosing around for grass to nibble. When the day cracked open with light, Amish neighbors buzzed around the motel. Sawhorses and plywood planks created worktables. Tools and cleaning supplies emerged. Women put out food bright with color and wafting scents. Men carried the defaced cabinets out of the lobby and spread them on the makeshift workbenches, where they patiently awaited Rufus's discernment about which pieces of craftsmanship could be redeemed and which would be recreated. A group of teenagers, both boys and girls, eyed each other wistfully over the tops of their brooms as they restored order to the lobby.

Annie watched, flabbergasted. When she bought her condo, she couldn't even get anyone to help her move. But here, for Rufus, a couple of dozen people—no doubt with ample obligations of their own—rearranged their day to help one cabinetmaker keep his business on track. Inspired, she did what she could to contribute. Mo put on two large canisters of coffee to perk, and Annie rounded up mugs and arranged them on a rolling cart. Mo produced a tub of lemonade mix with a half dozen pitchers, and Annie went to work. For a good part of the morning, Annie kept the beverages flowing as sandpaper and skirts swished around her.

Around eleven o'clock, she leaned against a broad elm and slid down until she sat on its protruding roots. Wet blotches smeared her cheeks, tears leaking from her eyes against her will. *Please, God, make me understand what I'm seeing.*

"Annalise, what's wrong?" Rufus squatted beside her.

She startled, surprised he was so near. "It's beautiful. I can't believe what they're doing."

"This is our way. When one suffers, we all suffer. It's better together than alone. That is the body of Christ."

"I can see that. I just don't have anything like that in my life. I mean, I have my parents. But all these people dropped whatever they planned for today and came to help you. How did they even find out so fast?"

"They have phones. Someone decided this was an emergency." Rufus let his weight down on the ground and stretched out his long legs beside her.

They leaned against the tree trunk without words for several minutes, their eyes on the bustle of work. Perspiration gathered along her hairline. Annie ran her hands through her hair, wishing she had thought to grab something to draw it off her neck when she hastily dressed in the middle of the night. She swept her hair off her neck with both hands and held it up. The next instant, she felt Rufus's eyes on her. On her neck. She dropped her hands immediately, and her hair tumbled back around her shoulders and face. Annie scooped it behind her ears.

Beneath his hat and under his long sleeves, Rufus perspired as well. Annie breathed the scent willingly—the scent of honest work. She sat beside a man of trust and integrity.

Annie turned her head toward him. "Rufus, can I tell you something you will think is wildly ridiculous?"

Rufus half smiled and cocked his head at her. "What is that?"

"I bought a house yesterday. Here in Westcliffe."

He lifted an eyebrow. "That does seem out of character."

"There's something here that gives me a piece of my life I'm missing." Her eyes lifted above the Amish crowd to the mountain sheen.

"Knowing you're missing something is the first step toward filling the hole."

"So you don't think it's ridiculous?"

"That depends. I haven't seen the house yet." Rufus wiped his sleeve across his dripping forehead.

Annie laughed. "There's just something about being here. . . about you and your family and your people. You once said I was grasping at air. Seeing all this generosity makes me think I'm holding on too tight."

"You won't know if you don't let go."

"I'm not sure I can."

"If you are grasping at air, what are you really holding?'

"I haven't begun to tell you what I do for a living. I'm successful, Rufus. Wealthy, even." Annie turned to look at Rufus.

He raised a hand and drew his fingers across her damp cheek. "Have you heard the story of the rich young man in the Bible who came to Jesus?"

Annie's brain clicked through the stories she had learned as a child. "Jesus told him to sell everything and give the money to the poor."

"That's right. But he could not do it, not even for eternal life."

"People depend on me for their jobs, Rufus. Am I supposed to walk away from my own talent? From responsibility?"

"What does Jesus ask you to give up, Annalise? And what will you gain?"

Annie swallowed. "You always give me something to think about."

Rufus glanced up the lane. "We may be in the way of Mo's business. Here's a customer now."

Annie followed his gaze toward the woman sauntering toward the commotion. She jumped to her feet.

"Mom! What are you doing here?"

Thirty

Myra Friesen scanned the scene. "Annie, what exactly are you involved with?"

"Isn't it beautiful?" Annie turned toward Rufus only to find he had stepped away, though he glanced over his shoulder to catch her eye.

"I had no idea your Amish fixation had gone this far." Myra planted her hands on her hips. "Is this some sort of barn raising?"

"Kind of. Vandals made a mess last night, and these people are all here to clean things up. What they're doing is amazing."

"Well, it's touching, I'm sure, but you're my concern. I'm worried about you, Annie. You've been vague about why you came to Westcliffe in the first place—I don't buy the line about business. What business could you have in a town this size? Why did you leave without your car? And now you're back here, apparently tangling with vandals."

"I'm fine, Mom. Can I introduce you to some people?"

"I stick out like a sore thumb." Myra wiped one hand along the thigh of her blue capris. "And so do you."

"You'll get used to it. And you don't have to meet everyone. Just a few people." Annie waved a hand toward the workers. "Just the Beilers, the people I've stayed with."

"Oh. That's what this is all about. I suppose you found them in the books."

"As a matter of fact, I did. And I found Dad, too. And you and Penny and me."

Annie steered her mother to where Franey and Eli stood sharing a paper cup of lemonade at the end of one workbench. Eli had nearly finished scrubbing the paint off a panel and was getting ready to sand.

"Mom, I would like you to meet Franey and Eli Beiler." She gestured from the Beilers to her mother. "This is Myra Friesen, my mother."

Franey smiled pleasantly, and Eli nodded.

"It's nice to meet you." Myra awkwardly extended a hand in an indefinite direction.

"And you, too." Franey corralled Myra's hand and shook it, then guided it toward Eli's. "Perhaps I'll get to see how your daughter comes to be so spirited."

Myra looked around. "She has always had a mind of her own. I am trying to understand just where her spirit has taken her."

"She turned up in our barn in a most curious way," Franey said. "Our youngest was smitten immediately, so of course we took her in when she was injured."

"Barn?" Myra pivoted toward Annie. "Injured? Why do I think I'm not getting the whole story?"

"Mom, I'm fine."

Myra furrowed her forehead and glanced at Franey. "She's behaving in such an unusual manner lately."

"Daughters do that sometimes." Franey's voice instantly dropped to a murmur.

"Do you have daughters?"

"Three." Franey's response was barely above a whisper.

Eli offered the lemonade cup, and Franey took it—a little too eagerly, Annie thought. Before she could sort out what to say,

Rufus joined them then, sandpaper in one hand and soft cotton cloths in another.

"Everything all right?" he asked.

"Perfectly fine," Annie said. "This is my mother, Myra Friesen. Mom, this is Rufus Beiler."

"Hello, Rufus." Myra ran her eyes up and down his height. "I've just learned you have three sisters."

"And four brothers."

"Oh my. That's a houseful."

"Not everyone lives here." To Annie's relief, Eli spoke up. "Two of our sons are married in Pennsylvania. Our eldest daughter is also. . .away."

"Oh, then you can understand that I wanted to see where my daughter had taken herself off to without explanation."

Annie saw the color shift in Franey's face. "Mom, how about some lemonade? You've had a long drive."

"I could do with a bit of refreshment."

"I'll get you something," Rufus offered.

"No thanks." Annie avoided his eyes. The last thing she needed was for her mother to see how she looked at Rufus. "I'll get it. We should get out of the sun anyway."

Annie led her mother inside the lobby, which had been stripped bare, to where the rolling cart held half-empty pitchers of lemonade. She filled a paper cup, handed it to Myra, and proceeded to the empty dining room, where they sat at the end of a table.

"They seem friendly enough." Myra poured liquid down her throat.

"For Amish people, you mean?"

"For any people," Myra said flatly. "Must you think the worst of me?"

"I'm sorry." And she was. What was the phrase the Amish used? *Es dutt mirr leed.*

"You have to admit it's odd that you should take such an interest in them."

"Perhaps. But if the genealogy books are right, I very nearly could have been one of them."

"But you're not."

"No. Not by birth." Annie quickly gauged how far to push this conversation. "But what's wrong with being interested in learning about their way of life?"

"Nothing, I guess." Myra set her empty cup down a little too firmly. "Isn't it unusual that they should take you in? What was that business about being injured?"

"I fell and hit my head. I stayed in their home while I recovered. I'm staying there again now."

"Well, that's handy, what with how you feel about Rufus."

Annie's head snapped around to meet her mother's eye. "What do you mean?"

"I wasn't born yesterday. It's hardly your first observable crush."

Annie rotated her cup in her hands. "There's nothing between us."

"No, I don't suppose there could be. But when you look at him, I see more in your eyes than you ever showed for Rick Stebbins."

"I think we've established that you were right about Rick." Annie pinched a piece of wax-covered paper from the rim of her cup. "And you're right again. How could there be anything between me and Rufus Beiler? We come from different worlds." Even as she heard her own words, Annie did not believe them.

"I'm just looking after you." Myra patted Annie's twitching hand. "You're my baby girl."

Annie rolled her eyes. "I can look after myself, Mom."

"You've done very well for yourself. No one can argue with that. But in the last few weeks, you broke up with your boyfriend, dissolved your business partnership, and went incognito. A mother worries about these things."

If only her mother knew the extent of recent events. Rick Stebbins always one step ahead of her. Barrett's embarrassing secret. Kissing an Amish man in the park behind the bank. The narrow green house just off Main Street that would be hers in a matter of days. Yes, her mother would have plenty to freak out about if she only knew.

"As long as I'm here," Myra said, "you might as well show me around town."

"That will take about ten minutes." Annie stood up, grateful for the distraction.

They retraced their steps through the barren lobby and the bustling work zone and got into Annie's Prius. She backed up and did a three-point turn, watching the horses and buggies carefully. A couple of minutes later, they pulled out onto the highway.

"Who was that man in the gray Windbreaker?" Myra asked. "He didn't look Amish."

It was a warm day for a Windbreaker. "Fiftyish and balding?" Annie thought of Tom, the only *English* man at work on the cabinet panels.

"No." Myra shook her head. "Thirtyish and skulking. He got in that tan sedan that pulled out ahead of us. I noticed him when I arrived, but he didn't seem to be working. He stayed on the fringe of things."

Annie had not noticed. But she had a good guess. She squinted into the sunlight and reached for the dark glasses she always stored on the dash. In a moment, the tan sedan came into focus. She did not recognize it, but she closed the gap slightly and paced her speed to maintain an even distance. The turn onto Main Street and downtown Westcliffe came up on the right, but Annie continued past the intersection, keeping the sedan in sight.

"That looked like town to me." Myra craned her head to the right and back.

"Blink and you miss it." Annie pressed her lips together. "There's some new construction up this way that might give you an idea of the town's potential. People are building some nice homes. Rufus has a couple of custom cabinetry jobs there. His work is art."

They went past a sprawl of new homes and into a stretch of active construction. The tan sedan slowed, and Annie let off the accelerator slightly. When it turned into a construction zone, Annie drove past.

"There's not much more up here. We'll go back to Main Street." Annie pulled to the shoulder, waited for a minivan to pass, and swung the Prius around to head back toward town. As she passed the tan sedan, she looked carefully at the sign on the site.

Kramer Construction. Just what she thought.

"Mrs. Weichert runs an antiques store in town," Annie said. "Well, antiques and miscellaneous items of interest. We can stop if you like."

"No time. May Levering is expecting me for tennis this afternoon, and then there's some dreary fund-raising dinner that your father says I must attend."

Annie turned down Main Street and slowed. "Welcome to Westcliffe, Colorado. The signs tell you when it changes from Westcliffe to Silver Cliff, but it's not much." Annie pointed out the coffee shop, a thrift store, and the local newspaper office, then swung down a side street. Within four minutes, they hit the old schoolhouse, the historic Lutheran church, and a railroad museum. "That's about it." Annie turned again to head back to the highway. *Except the house I bought.* They were headed west toward the shimmering Sangre de Cristos now. "You can't beat the view."

"It's spectacular—I give you that." Myra twisted slightly in her seat belt to look at her daughter. "But somehow I still think it's not the view that pulls you here."

Thirty-One

Annie drove by the construction site two more times later in the afternoon. All she wanted to know was if the man she saw was Karl Kramer himself or someone who worked for him. Either way it was suspicious for him to leave a car up by the highway and take refuge in the trees while a couple of dozen people worked—and then drive to a place with a Kramer Construction sign. Once, she pulled over to the side of the road to take out her phone and do an Internet search on images of augers.

She seethed just thinking about it. Rufus would tell her to let it go. But Annie had some choice words spinning in her head that she would love to spit out at a prime suspect.

The day was over. Rufus would have to recraft four face panels, but the sides and top of the framing to hold the cabinets were salvaged. Patient volunteer scrubbing, sanding, and refinishing had cabinet surfaces looking as they were meant to be, saving him days of labor. Rufus was confident he had sufficient wood left to create the new front panels and the top of the desk. Mo fussed about how long the delay would take before Rufus could attempt installation again, but eventually she accepted the answer he gave.

Annie pulled her car into the long Beiler driveway. She turned in the gravel alongside the barn and negotiated her car to the back, where the structure provided a path of shade during the hottest part of the day.

As Annie walked around the barn, voices—in Pennsylvania Dutch—drew her inside. Rufus stood feeding an apple to Dolly while Lydia and Sophie gathered garden tools. They were all laughing about something. Annie hoped it wasn't her. When she stood in the open doorway, conversation switched to English.

"We should be able to pull the carrots soon," Lydia said.

"The beans just keep coming," Sophie said.

Somehow Annie thought the conversation must have been less mundane before she arrived.

"Do you want to help us in the garden?" Lydia said. "We're just doing a little weeding and looking for what needs picking."

"I don't know anything about gardens or how to tell if something is ready to pick." Annie took a step backward.

"We'll show you what to do." Sophie reached for her arm and pulled her deeper into the barn.

"Okay, then," Annie said. "Annalise Friesen at your service."

Jacob burst into the barn breathing fast. "A man is at the house looking for Annalise. *Mamm* said to see if she was here."

Annie saw Rufus stiffen. She sucked in her breath.

"What does he look like?" Rufus glanced at Annie and then back at Jacob.

"He's *English*. He's wearing a suit, and his shoes are really shiny. He came in a car that looks gold and brown at the same time."

"Bronze." Annie stepped even farther into the barn.

"Is he on the porch?" Rufus calmly fed the last bit of apple to Dolly.

The little boy nodded.

"Jacob," Rufus said, "I want you to walk slowly—don't run—back to the porch and ask the man if he would like to talk to me."

"Shouldn't I tell him Annalise is here?"

"Just ask him to talk to me. Do you understand?"

The little boy nodded.

Rufus turned Jacob's shoulders back toward the house. "Remember, slowly."

Jacob nodded. Annie watched the boy concentrate on moving slowly, his stride like that of a toddler.

Rufus, on the other hand, spun around. "Quick. In the dress." He turned to the shelves that held blankets the family used in the buggies in the winter and pulled out the dress he had left there weeks ago.

"That's Ruth's dress," Sophie said.

"Just help Annalise get it on." Rufus thrust the dress at Annie. "Get her hair up under the *kapp*."

Annie felt like a fashion model with a crew transforming her. Lydia dropped the dress over her head and rapidly pinned the front closure. Sophie removed Annie's shoes, rolled up her jeans, then grabbed Annie's hair—painfully—and punched it under the white *kapp*. With no hairpins to hold the hair in place, Lydia tied the *kapp* under Annie's chin

"To the garden, all of you." Rufus shoved a rake into Annie's hands.

By the time Jacob returned to the barn with the stranger, three young Amish women were working barefoot in the garden sixty feet away. One of them, in a deep purple dress, kneeled to pull weeds by hand, her back to the barn. Rufus assessed the man. Yes, this was the man from behind the bank. Rufus met him at the barn's doorway, leaning on a pitchfork.

"Can I help you?" Rufus crossed his arms.

The man laid his head to one side. "I'm looking for Annie Friesen."

"Her name is Annalise," Jacob said.

"Jacob," Rufus said calmly. "Thank you for showing our guest the way. You can go back to helping *Mamm* now."

"But—"

"Jacob, you must go."

"Yes sir." The boy turned to go, disappointed.

"Just a minute." The stranger glanced across the yard to the garden. "How many sisters do you have?"

"Three," Jacob said simply.

Rufus almost smiled at the perfection of it all. "*Mamm* is waiting for you, Jacob."

"I'm going, I'm going."

The two men stared at each other.

"I don't believe I got your name the last time we met." Rufus set his feet solidly shoulder width apart.

"Names don't matter." Rick's friendly veneer proved thin. "How quaint. Did she find you charming at the bank as well?"

Rufus shoved the pitchfork more firmly into earth. "Why have you come here?"

"I wanted to talk to Annie. I was told she might be at the Beiler place. I had no idea I would find you."

"Who did you speak to?" Rufus wanted to know.

"The woman at the motel." Rick waved a hand casually. "She's a little frazzled about something, but she said Annie was staying here."

"How did you find the motel?" Rufus asked.

Rick exhaled. "I'm not going to play twenty questions with you, whoever you are. I just want to talk to Annie. She is my fiancée. I'm worried about her."

"It did not appear that way to me the last time we met."

"Mind your own business. Isn't that what you people do?"

"Of course. But I would have to say that an *English* man standing outside my barn making demands is my business."

"Just show me where she is."

Rufus opened his arms wide. "Do you see her?"

Rick leaned to one side to peer into the barn. "Must be a dozen places to hide in there."

"You are free to inspect the barn," Rufus said. "Many people are curious about Amish ways."

Rick rolled his eyes. "Look, I'm not here for some lame tour."

"Then perhaps our business is concluded." Rufus met Rick's eyes. "In fact, I'm quite sure it is."

Rick pivoted and walked to his Jeep. On the way, he glanced around the property again. Rufus followed a few steps behind, smiling blandly until Rick got in his vehicle and turned the ignition. Rick reversed, turned around, and churned up clouds of dirt on his way to the main road. Rufus did not move until the car was out of sight.

When he turned around, Annalise had grabbed fistfuls of the purple dress and was hurtling toward him. Rufus pointed to the barn. Better to be out of sight, just in case.

She threw her arms around him the minute they were inside. "Thank you!"

"You're welcome." The weight of her against his chest. Her blond hair escaping the *kapp*. The sight of her in an Amish dress. Suddenly he wanted nothing more than to kiss her. Gently, he stepped out of her embrace before he could not stop himself.

"He must have followed my mother."

"Have you explained to her what is going on?"

"Not. . .every detail. I suppose I'll have to tell her something now." She paused, looked him in the eye. "Why did you hide me?"

Why indeed? "Was I supposed to hand you over to someone I know means you harm?"

"I'll call my attorney. He'll do something. I don't know what. But something." Annalise patted the dress fabric, no doubt looking for a pocket where her cell phone should be.

"You look stunning," he said softly. "I always knew you would. I guess that's why I brought you the dress in the first place."

Annalise's motion shifted to smoothing down the full skirt. Then one hand went to the *kapp*. "Am I doing this right? I notice your sisters leave their ties loose."

"Because their hair is braided and pinned up," he said. "It stays put."

"I'll have to learn to do that." She tugged, and the knot gave easily. With the *kapp* loosened, her hair tumbled around her shoulders.

A woman's hair. Who would have thought it could move him so?

"The dress fits." He soaked in the beauty of her. Her gold chain had worked its way over the round neckline. "I imagine it feels strange to you."

Her answer was slow. "Not as strange as you might suppose." She ran a tongue along her lips then pressed them together, holding her breath.

His own breath ran shallow. "In the *English* world, I suppose this is where I would kiss you."

"And in your world?" She stepped toward him and tilted her head up. Her *kapp* slipped off her head and hesitated at her shoulder before falling. Neither of them moved to stop it from hitting the ground.

"In my world, I very much want to," Rufus finally said.

Annalise laid a hand on his upper arm, sending him spinning. Her face was right there, and upturned.

Rufus stepped back, and Annie moaned, a sound she did not intend to release. He was not going to kiss her.

Rufus sighed heavily. "It would be wrong, Annalise."

"Would it? Maybe there could be something between us, after all, if we explore the possibility."

He shook his head. "That's not our way. The sight of you in Ruth's dress took me away for a moment. It gave me a picture of something that is not real."

Annie knew when a man wanted to kiss her. That part was real. A man's self-restraint at the moment of opportunity was unfamiliar, though. She took a step toward him. "I like the dress."

"You're playing dress up," Rufus said. "It's not you."

"Maybe it could be." Annie wanted to believe the words coming out of her own mouth.

"You don't know what you're saying." Rufus stepped back from her. "You've had a few Amish meals, been to church, admired some quilts. But you have no idea what it means to be Amish."

"I could learn."

"You would never choose it." Rufus looked away now. "It's not you."

"You don't know what I could choose." Her voice rose. "That's for me to decide."

"First, you have to understand what you are choosing between."

Annie bent over and snatched up the *kapp*. "Am I wearing Ruth's dress because she chose between? Even she couldn't choose your way."

Rufus exhaled. "She understood the seriousness of her choice."

"Then why must she be punished for it?"

"No one is punishing her."

"No one is speaking to her. No one even speaks *about* her. Is she being shunned?"

"Of course not. She's not baptized and has done nothing to deserve shunning."

"She believes she is following God's will. She misses you all so much."

He caught her eyes and held them. "You've seen Ruth, haven't you?"

"Yes. I can't believe you go to Colorado Springs as often as you do and you haven't seen her yourself."

"When she left, something broke," Rufus said. "My mother has never been quite the same. No one knew she was leaving. No one else was there when the moment came except my mother, and she won't talk about it."

"So you don't want to get in the middle of it? Is that it?"

"It's not my place."

"You've gotten in the middle of my problems several times now." Rufus sucked in his lips.

Annie took a deep breath before speaking. "What if I arranged for you to see Ruth? Would you do it?"

"Did you promise her already?"

"She doesn't know anything about it."

"I can't ask Tom to wait on me while I go off visiting. He's running a taxi service, and I pay for his time."

"I'll bring her to you," Annie said. "You name the place."

He turned away slightly and straightened some tools hanging on the wall. "I'm taking several pieces to the Amish furniture store on the north end of town next Thursday."

"I know where it is. What time?" Eagerness flushed through Annie at the thought of what this meeting would mean to Ruth.

"Three o'clock. I won't be able to wait past three thirty."

"You won't have to. I'll have her there at three." She could not fix whatever was broken between Ruth and Franey, but perhaps she could give Ruth her brother back.

"I can't promise, you understand," he said. "Some of this depends on Tom."

"You could call me."

"I only use my phone for business."

"She's your sister, Rufus. She needs you. At least read her letters."

"I'll try." He moved toward the door. "Be careful with the pins when you take the dress off."

She was alone in the barn then, wearing Ruth's dress. Slowly she felt for the pins Lydia had placed in the fabric and began pulling them out.

Thirty-Two

Ruth Beiler pushed the cart of empty food trays to the end of the hall where someone from the food services team would collect it. She was free to go on her own meal break, which meant she had a few minutes to study the posted schedule for next week.

When Annie called, Ruth immediately agreed to go with her to the furniture store on Thursday afternoon. But her normal shift at the nursing home began at three in the afternoon. She had to figure out which other morning CNA would be willing to stay late and cover the time Ruth needed. If she could just have an extra hour before she had to clock in, she could manage.

In the break room, in front of the posted schedule, Ruth filled a mug with coffee and lifted it to her lips while she mused the options. She raised a finger to Thursday's grid. Laura was out. She only worked during school hours and never stayed a minute past two thirty. Elisa was blacked out for the whole week on vacation. Heather wouldn't have child care for her two-year-old if she stayed past three.

"What's up?" Erin breezed in with the high-speed motion that carried her everywhere. Even when Ruth worked her hardest and fastest, she still felt like she didn't keep up with Erin, who now picked up a stack of magazines and grabbed a paper towel to wipe off the counter, all in one smooth motion.

"I have a schedule conflict," Ruth said. "I need to come in late on Thursday. I thought I'd just ask someone on the early shift to stay late."

"Naw. No one likes to do that. But I'll work the late shift if you'll work my early shift on Thursday."

Ruth nodded. "That would be fine. Thank you, Erin."

"You'd better go see Mrs. Watson. At least stick your head in before your break is over. She keeps track of these things."

Ruth laughed.

"And we have a new patient, Mrs. Renaldi." Erin set the magazines on the counter in perfect alignment. "She was in the rehab wing after a fall. She graduated out of there, but they're not sure she'll be able to live alone. The family wants to see how she'll do here first."

Ruth nodded, already feeling sad for a woman she had not met. Though she worked in a nursing home, she never quite adjusted to how easily families agreed it was the best place for their loved one. Growing up among the Amish, she never saw elderly family members living anywhere but with their families.

With ten minutes left on her meal break, Ruth padded down to Mrs. Watson's room and knocked lightly. "It's me, Ruth."

"It's about time." Mrs. Watson sat up in the armchair.

Ruth smiled.

"You're happy about something. I can tell," Mrs. Watson said.

"I'm happy to see you, as always." Ruth folded back the covers on the bed. Before long, it would be time for her to get Mrs. Watson ready for the night.

"No, it's something else. News from home, perhaps."

Ruth plumped a pillow and laid it in place. "Perhaps."

"Do tell."

"I'm going to see my brother on Thursday," Ruth said.

"Little Jacob?" Mrs. Watson asked.

"No. I wish he could come, too. But it will just be Rufus."

"The one you've been writing to?"

"That's right. A friend has arranged a meeting when he comes into town on business. It will just be a few minutes."

"It's a place to start."

"Yes, a place to start," Ruth echoed. And perhaps a place to finish.

Annie planned a long lunch break away from the office, figuring it would take about a hundred years to break even on all the days she worked through lunch. She snagged a primo parking spot outside the mall and entered the maze of shops through the chain bookstore, stopping to buy a coffee to carry with her. The usual department stores anchored the mall, and a couple of other furniture places had sprung up. She told herself she was just looking for ideas. After all, the purchase of the Westcliffe house had not even closed yet. Buying furniture to be delivered there would be jumping the gun. Still, what harm was there in looking?

By the time the tall, disposable coffee cup was empty, Annie's stomach gurgled, prompting her to think about eating. There was always the food court or the small café on the mall's upper level for something approximating real food. Annie's thoughts arced to her sister. Three years older than Annie, she had exactly the same face, everyone said, but Annie's eyes were gray and Penny's shimmered green. Most of Colorado Springs considered the café a decent place to grab a meal, but Penny always turned her nose up at it. Penny was a foodie who wanted to know that the cows she was eating had lived a good life. She would have known what exactly was growing in the Beiler garden with just a glance. Not like Annie.

Annie talked about taking time off to fly out and see Penny in Washington, but somehow it never happened. Penny breezed into town for two or three days at Christmas and then went back to her own life, with an occasional e-mail or phone call aimed at her family.

Annie laughed at herself when she thought of digging in the garden as if she knew what she was doing while Rufus fended off Rick Stebbins. She did call Lee Solano about the event. He pledged to choke Stebbins in legal actions. Annie was beginning to think Lee might actually get Rick off her back, though of course she would pay for it.

Sadness sluiced through Annie. She missed her sister. Penny was scrappy. She would have taken protecting her little sister into her own hands if she knew any of what was going on. Annie smiled at the thought.

They had not had a traumatic rupture in their relationship, but the truth was that Annie didn't speak to her sister much more than Rufus spoke to Ruth. Life diverged, and they let it. She put her hand on her phone, wondering what Penny would do if she called her in the middle of the day for absolutely no reason.

"Annie? Is that you?"

Annie blinked at the young woman beside her. "Lindsay!" She glanced at the stroller. "And the baby. How is she?"

Barrett's wife. Barrett's baby. In the mall.

"She's fine." Lindsay moved the blanket to allow Annie to see the baby's face. "She loves sleeping in the stroller, so I come here to walk. I have to do something about my baby fat."

"You look great." Annie took a breath. One of them would have to ask the obvious questions. "How's Barrett?"

Lindsay pushed the stroller back and forth with one hand. Then she broke into tears.

Annie's breath stuck for a moment. She was calculating how to get past the questions looming over them, and suddenly a sobbing new mother stood between her and the furniture stores.

"Lindsay?" Annie put a hand on Lindsay's quaking shoulder.

"He doesn't talk to me," Lindsay blubbered. "He says he made a lot of money when you bought him out, so we don't have anything to worry about. But I still don't understand why he wanted to sell his half when he was so happy working with you all these years."

Annie could not think of a thing to say.

"He says he's going to find something else to be passionate about, but he just sits in the house." Lindsay swayed at the hips with the motion of the stroller. "He hardly pays any attention to the baby, and I'm lucky if he says six words to me all day."

Annie gulped. "I'm sorry. I didn't know."

Lindsay stopped pushing on the stroller and dug in the diaper bag for a tissue. "I shouldn't dump on you in the middle of the mall. But I don't understand what happened. Barrett left the company, and then Rick didn't want to hang out with him, either."

"Rick doesn't want to hang out with him?" Annie tried to make sense of the statement.

"Barrett doesn't do anything he used to love," Lindsay said, "and I don't know what to do."

"I wish I knew what to tell you."

"You could tell me what happened. Why did it all fall apart?"

Annie's phone rang, and the baby squawked at the same time.

"It's the office," Annie said. "I'd better take it."

"Never mind. If I don't keep going, she won't go back to sleep."

"It was nice to see you." Annie spoke to Lindsay's back as she raised the phone to her ear. "Jamie, what's up?"

"The assistant of that guy at Liam-Ryder Industries has called three times." Annoyance rang in Jamie's voice. "He's in town just for the day before he flies out of Denver tonight, and he really wants a meeting."

"Tell them two o'clock," Annie said. "Let's just find out what they want once and for all."

By four o'clock, a plan formed in Annie's mind. She sat at the conference table in her own office and listened to the groaning tectonic shifts in her life. Jumping from one plate to the other was still possible, before they separated too far.

Lee Solano would have to be present at the next meeting with Liam-Ryder Industries. That much was clear.

This could happen fast.

And it could be good in so many ways. For so many people.

As the visitors left her office, Annie let her mind drift to a choice made three hundred years ago that ultimately brought her to this moment.

Thirty-Three

July 1738

They sat in Rachel Treadway's parlor, Jakob on a cushionless straight-back chair and Elizabeth across from him on a stuffed velvet settee.

"I'm so pleased you found time to visit Philadelphia again." Elizabeth's hands were crossed neatly in her lap. They spoke the familiar German of their childhoods.

This was Jakob's second visit in just a few weeks, leaving his farm and children in the care of others for days at a time. His choice to see her came at a high price. "We have much to discuss together," he said.

"Yes, I agree." *Ask me. I'll say yes.*

"The cabin is well stocked now. The children don't like to leave it."

She heard the nerves etched through Jakob's voice. "I would love to see your children."

"Especially Lisbetli?"

"Especially Lisbetli." *I would go back with you now. Ask.*

Jakob nodded. "That would make her very happy."

Elizabeth leaned forward, poured a cup of tea, and handed it to Jakob. "And your friends? Do they ask you to get their supplies also when you come?"

"I bring a list. It must be worthwhile to bring two horses and a wagon." He sipped his tea.

Elizabeth poured her own tea. "I see much to admire in the Amish."

He looked up. "Do you?"

I admire you most of all. "Yes." She added sugar and stirred her tea. Why did he not just say what was on his mind?

"We live plain and apart, you know."

Her heart bursting, she barely heard his voice. "Yes, I know. But you are strong people. Even when I was a child in Switzerland I could tell."

"Some would find our ways difficult."

"I suppose so." *Sip.* "Do any of your people ever choose to live otherwise?"

"It is very hard to do," he said. "It would be seen as a loss of faith."

"And would it be?"

"For some."

"And for you, Mr. Byler?"

"I am not as sure as I once was on that point." His teacup rattled, and he set it down.

"Do you think you will always live apart?"

She watched him swallow hard.

"I have been examining my faith for some time now. God works in mysterious ways."

"I have seen this to be true in my own life as well." Elizabeth hoped they were talking about the same thing.

"If God revealed His will, I would obey."

"As would I." Elizabeth sipped her tea. *I will say yes!*

"I have prayed that God would show His will."

"As have I."

"Very good."

Ask, she thought, *just ask.*

Jakob was silent. He picked up his teacup again. He took one delicate sip and carefully replaced the cup and saucer on the low table. "It is kind of the Treadways to provide for you as they have, but I wonder if you have thought of having a home of your own."

Finally. "Of late I have considered the matter with increasing frequency."

"And you are disposed to have your own home, Miss Kallen?"

She felt the hope in his words and answered quickly. "I am quite keenly so disposed, Mr. Byler."

"Ah. I am glad to hear this."

Jakob went silent again. Elizabeth poured another splash of tea into her own cup.

"I wonder if a particular religious atmosphere would make you uncomfortable," Jakob said.

Elizabeth chose her words carefully, mindful of what it was costing Jakob to have this conversation. "I believe each person must follow conscience, Mr. Byler. My faith means a great deal to me. I do not presume to judge another person. Only God sees the heart."

"I see. And do you have any particular aspirations for your home?"

"English." Her answer was firm. "I want my children to learn to speak English."

Jakob blushed. "Perhaps you would teach me as well."

"I would be happy to."

Jakob blew out his breath and dared to smile. "Perhaps you will speak to your minister, then. I wonder how much time you require to be ready."

Elizabeth nodded. "I will speak to the Treadways immediately so they can find someone else for the shop. I have very few possessions of my own."

"Thank you, Miss Kallen. You do me a great honor."

She smiled at his blush.

"You married Miss Kallen?" Maria's pitch rose with the realization. Her face broke into a grin as she looked at her siblings gathered around the table.

"*Daed*, no, you can't do this." Barbara stood up and moved to the hearth, where she gripped a blackened pot in both hands.

"It's done." Jakob glanced through the tiny window in the front of the cabin. "She's outside, anxious to see all of you. I expect you to make her welcome."

"She's a nice lady." Maria took Lisbetli's hands and clapped them together.

"Is she going to join the church?" Barbara asked accusingly, pot in hand.

"I don't know what she might decide to do in the future." Jakob knew this was not the last time he would hear this question. "I have not asked her to join."

"Then you're going to leave the church. You did not even wait for the bishop to marry you." Christian straightened in his seat. "You can't be Amish if your wife is not Amish. You're defying *Ordnung*."

"I don't want to stop being Amish." Anna's violet eyes—Verona's eyes—widened.

"I won't ask you to." Jakob touched Anna's trembling hand. "Neither will Elizabeth."

"Why did you marry an outsider?" Christian asked. "Don't you believe in our ways anymore?"

"The questions are not that simple, Christian." Jakob's eyes moved among the faces of all his children. "Elizabeth is eager to help us make a home."

"*I'm* making a home." Barbara set the pot on the table with a thud. "I'm cooking. I'm looking after the children. I'm mending your shirts. I never complain."

"You're doing a wonderful job, Bar-bar. But someday—soon—you will want to do those things for your own husband."

Anna scraped her chair back and began to pace around the room.

"I still don't understand." Christian leaned forward on the

table, his chin in his hands. "Do you not believe we must follow *Ordnung?*"

"I believe God has brought us to a new land for a purpose." Jakob leaned over and picked up Lisbetli from the crate she balanced on. "God has given us great opportunity. It is hard for all of us without your mother. God sent us Elizabeth to make it easier."

"But we keep separate from outsiders." Christian pushed back from the table. "How can we have an outsider living with us?"

"I hope she won't feel like an outsider." Jakob kissed the top of Lisbetli's head.

A gust of wind blew through the cabin. Jakob turned his head to see the front door standing wide open. He got up to close it. As he leaned against it to be sure it latched, he realized with a lurch how the door had come to be open.

"Where's Anna?" He spun around and pulled the door open again.

At the edge of the clearing, he saw Anna's dark apron disappear from sight into the black oaks. Elizabeth was already running after her.

Thirty-Four

Annie's laptop was open on the conference table on Thursday afternoon. In an open electronic document, presumably she was taking notes on the meeting with representatives of Liam-Ryder Industries and corporate attorneys. However, she spent more time glancing at the digital time display on the upper right corner of the screen than she did typing. If the meeting did not wrap up soon, she would have to leave anyway.

Twenty minutes. Fifteen. Twelve. Ten. Eight. Five. Three. One. She snapped the laptop closed and stood up.

"Gentlemen, I'm sorry, but I have another appointment, and it's impossible to reschedule." Annie scooped a stack of papers off the table and stuffed them into her bag. "I'm glad we've come to general agreement. Please feel free to use my office as long as you like to hash out the details of what we've been talking about. Jamie will assist you with anything you need."

"Excuse me, gentlemen." Lee Solano jumped up from the table and followed Annie out. She pulled the door closed behind them and looked at him expectantly.

"Are you sure about this?" Lee asked.

"I've never been more sure."

"But Barrett? I don't get it. We went to a lot of trouble to take him out of action."

"I know. At the time it seemed liked the thing to do."

"And now?"

"And now it seems like the time to make things right. I'm sorry for my mistaken judgment. Barrett was never the enemy. I should have known better than to think Barrett would try to steal my work. That was Rick."

"Don't forget the college plagiarism," Lee said.

"Which may or may not be true." Annie slung her bag over her shoulder. "I'm inclined to think somebody got the best of him then as well."

"You can't be sure."

"How can we ever be sure of what is in someone else's mind and heart? Maybe Barrett was already a victim, and we made it worse. If you could turn up that information, anyone could."

"Like Rick?"

"We broke Barrett's spirit," Annie said softly. "Now I want to put the pieces back together. I want to do the right thing."

"And Rick?"

She shrugged. "He doesn't figure into this new deal and hopefully never will. Barrett won't own the company. He'll just run it as a division of LRI. Rick will have nothing to gain by going after him again."

"This is happening fast." Lee drew a hand across his forehead. "I want to ask for some time to do due diligence. Find out who these people are."

"If you like. But they're on the New York Stock Exchange and made a profit the last seven quarters in a row."

"Let me be sure I understand the terms you're expecting." Lee readjusted his stance and rubbed his palms together. "First, you want to sell the company, including its major asset, which is the new program you've developed for tracking sales according to shopper patterns, product placement in stores, and web presence."

"That's right." Somewhere in Annie's brain, a giant clock ticked.

"Second, you want Barrett to receive a substantial offer to return and run the company, especially the sales and marketing he's so good at."

"Right."

"And you want everyone on staff to have guaranteed employment for at least two years with a bonus if they sign an agreement to stay for that period of time."

"Right again." Annie glanced toward the door. Lee had heard this all three times. She wasn't going to change her mind.

"The profits from the sale are to be placed in a trust that even you can't undo."

Annie took a deep breath. "Yes, that's right. We can talk more later. Right now, I really have to go."

"As your attorney, I have to say—"

"Later, Lee." Annie left the suite.

It was 2:23. She still had seven minutes to get to the corner where Ruth would be waiting by 2:30.

At 2:29, Annie pulled to the curb just shy of the corner and put the car in PARK. The clock in her dash clicked to 2:30 then 2:31 and 2:32.

At 2:38 Annie started to worry.

Ruth wasn't used to the daytime shift. Everything seemed to go wrong. She passed off charts to the wrong charge nurse and missed getting vitals on patients in a block of six rooms. She was still in the middle of helping residents dress when she was supposed to be helping them to their seats in the wing's dining area. And now she faced a mess of chocolate pudding and apple juice splattered across the tile because Mr. Green wanted butterscotch pudding and grape juice. With one sweep of his arm, he made sure no one could expect him to eat the substitution.

The clock at the nurses' station, large enough to see from yards away, said 2:37. Panic welled in Ruth. In the hall, she found a housekeeping cart.

"Mind if I take a couple towels?" she asked Tara, who pushed the cart. "I've got a small mess in here."

"Help yourself."

And then she saw him—a man who looked like Tom Reynolds. But what would Tom be doing here?

Familiar shoulders, the jeans and plaid shirt. He had just passed the nurses' station, striding toward the exit where automatic doors would wheeze open.

"Do you know that man?" Ruth tried to sound casual.

Tara glanced down the hall, two towels between her hands. "Sure. He comes a couple of times a month to see his mother, Mrs. Renaldi. But I think he changed his name."

"Reynolds." Ruth felt the blood drain from her face.

"Yeah, that's it. Know him?"

His name lodged in her throat as she saw the doors close behind him. For the first time, she noticed the red truck parked in the space nearest the door.

"Tara, do me a huge favor? Clean up the pudding mess in Mr. Green's room? I'm already late clocking out, and I have an appointment." Ruth put on her best pleading face.

Tara grimaced at the mess. "I guess so."

Ruth flew down the corridor. The doors opened slowly, with a hesitancy she found aggravating even on a good day. By the time she stepped outside, she saw only the back end of Tom's truck leaving the parking lot.

Groaning, Ruth ran back to the staff lounge to clock out and grab her purse. On her way out of the building, the clock at the nurses' station announced 2:44. He had a seven-minute head start. If he got there first, all her hoping would be for nothing.

Rufus sat in the office in the back of the Amish furniture store.

David, who ran the store, was flipping through pages of hand-written notes on a small yellow pad.

"I don't know why I write down half the stuff I do." David turned another page. "I'm afraid I'll forget something important. Then I can't remember what I thought was so important that I had to write it down."

Rufus attempted a laugh.

David riffled more pages. "I know I've got that special order in here somewhere. The lady was very specific about wanting matching end tables, and she doesn't want any shortcuts. Of course I thought you were perfect for the job."

"I'll be glad to take it on," Rufus said. *If you ever find your notes.* The little battery clock on David's desk said the time was 2:45. Now that Rufus had agreed to see his sister, every minute bonged in his head, a reminder of lost time. He imagined Ruth sitting in the passenger seat of Annie's car, the two of them pulling onto a busy street, stopping at a light, searching store signs.

Her packet of letters was safe in his bedroom, each one read at least three times.

"Oh, here it is." David tapped the page. "Yes, she admired the one on display. She'd like two, but slightly larger. She gave me measurements. Oh yes, she also wants a hope chest that matches."

"That sounds fine," Rufus said.

"How long do you think it will take? She was anxious to know."

"We'd better say six weeks."

"She'll want to hear four."

Rufus shook his head. "I can't promise that. We'd better stick with six."

"All right, six. I'll remind her that if she wants the best work, it takes time." David fished around in a desk drawer. "Let me write up the order on an official form with the measurements she gave me."

In the silence of David's concentration, the clock turned to 2:51.

Annie turned on the ignition as Ruth threw herself into the car.

"Sorry," Ruth said. "I just couldn't get away. I had no idea what the day shift was like."

"It should only be about twelve minutes." Annie put her foot to the accelerator. "We should be fine."

"I saw Tom Reynolds," Ruth said.

Annie scanned the view ahead, rapidly evaluating which route would be quickest. "Really? Tom was at the nursing home?"

"I didn't know, but his mother is there recovering from a fall. I guess he usually comes to see her during the day before my shift starts. He left before I did."

"Uh-oh. Maybe he had another errand."

They came to a major intersection, and Annie turned right onto the six-lane grid. Almost immediately she slammed on the brakes. Traffic in front of them was at a standstill. Two police cars crossed the lanes, barricading the northbound traffic.

"An accident." Annie leaned to the left to try to look around the congestion. Behind them an ambulance screamed at a searing pitch. The Prius shuddered as the emergency vehicle weaved past them at high speed.

Ruth moaned. "Can we go another way?"

Annie glanced in the mirrors. In a matter of seconds, vehicles sucked up any space to maneuver. "We're stuck."

Rufus gave David a price for the three pieces of furniture, knowing David would add another 15 percent to the number he reported to the customer. They agreed on some other pieces Rufus could make for David's showroom. Rufus would stop by again in two weeks with two cedar chests he was nearly finished with.

It was after three now. Rufus wandered through the shop one last time and then out the front door. A simple backless bench ran along the stone wall beneath the display window. Rufus took a seat and fixed his eyes in the direction he believed Annalise would come from, though he could not be sure. Across the parking lot, traffic flowed past in six lanes, knotting and unknotting with the rhythm of the well-timed traffic lights.

He wondered if Ruth had grown thin, how she supported herself, if she was sorry, if she was happy. He squinted as if he might find the answers in afternoon sunlight.

Rufus watched three cycles of the lights before the red pickup maneuvered into the parking lot and rattled Rufus to attention. Tom was back.

Tom opened the cab door, got out, and raised an eyebrow at Rufus. "Ready?"

"I guess I was daydreaming." Rufus stood up and glanced around the parking lot again, wondering if he should say something to Tom.

"Then let's get going," Tom said. "There's a parents' meeting at Carter's school. I promised Tricia I would be home for dinner so we could go together."

"Of course." The last thing Rufus wanted to do was inconvenience Tom or cause distress in his family.

The clock in Tom's truck said 3:17. They probably were not coming anyway, he decided. Annalise would not have waited until the last minute. Ruth must have backed out.

"I got lucky," Tom said, "and just missed a big accident on my way up. I heard it hit behind me. The southbound lanes should be fine, but I think I'll find another way out of town just in case."

"Whatever you think best." Rufus pulled the seat belt over his shoulder and snapped it into place. *God's will.*

They had moved barely twenty feet in ten minutes, but Annie had her eye on the entrance to a shopping center. If she could just make that turn, they could snake through connecting parking lots and come out north of the jam.

By the time they reached the entrance and Annie made the turn, Ruth burst into tears. The Prius was nimble and responded well to the frequent turns as Annie drilled through back alleys behind restaurants and box stores at a speed for which she deserved to be stopped by flashing lights.

They pulled into the furniture store parking lot at 3:24. Ruth jumped out of the car and ran inside without waiting for a full stop.

Annie parked properly and wondered if she should go in. She did not want to intrude on the moment of reunion between brother and sister, but her own pulse was rapid with the expectation of seeing Rufus. Just as Annie decided it was too hot to wait in the car, Ruth yanked open the passenger door and tumbled in.

"We're too late." She used the backs of both hands to wipe tears. "He didn't wait."

"He said three thirty!"

"Five more minutes?" Ruth said. "What difference could that make on a two-hour trip back to Westcliffe? He didn't want to see me."

"You don't know that for sure," Annie said. But she banged a hand against the steering wheel nevertheless. "We'll try again in two weeks. He comes every two weeks."

"Is this God's will?" Ruth swallowed hard and wiped tears from both eyes. "Maybe I'm not meant to see him."

"I don't know." What else could Annie say?

Ruth fished for a tissue in her purse and blew her nose. "Can you take me back to my room? I have a lot of studying to do."

Annie nodded and started the car.

Two weeks might as well have been eternity.

Thirty-Five

Annie's instinct was to call Rufus's cell phone. If it had been anyone else, she would have. Find out what happened. Make a new plan. That was why everyone had phones. The rules were different with Rufus, though. If Ruth wouldn't call, then Annie shouldn't.

She sat on her frustration for a week.

Then came the date for closing on the house in Westcliffe. Annie boxed up a few kitchen items, packed several changes of clothes, grabbed a blanket, and stopped by a housewares store on the way out of town for a decent inflatable mattress so she would have a place to sleep that night. The closing was scheduled at the bank at the edge of Westcliffe.

Annie knew the way now. She had been back and forth in daylight and remembered the changes from one state highway to another. She recognized the sequence of small towns—each clinging to its moment of history—that culminated in Silver Cliff and released into Westcliffe at the foot of the mountains. She would sleep that night in a house she owned outright in a town she had not known existed a few weeks ago.

She did the final walk-through with the real estate agent. Happily, the house was no more dilapidated than the day she bought it. Next came the closing, where she signed her name until her fingers cramped. At last the agent dropped the keys to the front door in Annie's hands. The key to the back door had been lost years ago, the owner claimed. If Annie wanted to lock that door, the locksmith in Silver Cliff would be happy to help.

Annie drove the few blocks from the bank to the house. She parked in the driveway and carried her suitcase in through the back door.

Sitting cross-legged on the floor of the empty living room, she opened her laptop and used her phone to give herself an Internet connection. With a few keyboard strokes, she was logged into her company's server and looking at everything she would have seen if she had been in her office in Colorado Springs. She could ensure no funny business happened before the business deal closed. Her cell phone signal was strong. Annie turned on the speaker, pressed Jamie's speed dial number, and set the phone on the floor.

"Did you really do it?" Jamie asked.

"I did." Even with no one there to see her, Annie could not help smiling.

"It sounds empty."

"I've got some serious shopping to do." Annie looked around, visualizing furniture.

"How long are you going to stay?"

"Just a night or two. Or three. I'm not sure."

"Mr. Solano called three times."

"I'll call him," Annie said.

"He sounded agitated. Is everything all right?"

"I'm doing my best to make sure it is." Annie looked around the room in satisfaction. "I'll check in again tomorrow."

She called Lee next.

"The papers are almost to the final draft stage," he said. "Are you ready to review them?"

"Anytime." Annie untangled herself to stand up and begin pacing through the house. "Are they pressing back on anything?"

"They're asking questions about why Barrett left, considering the nature of the offer you want them to extend."

"Make it work, Lee," Annie said simply. "It's a deal breaker."

"Really? Of everything that's on the table, hiring the guy who tried to rip you off is a deal breaker?"

"Yep."

"I've only known you a few weeks," Lee spoke through a sigh. "But I have to say, this is not where I thought we would end up when you first came to me."

"Things change. People change."

"You could ask for more money, you know. They would ante up."

"The offer is fine." She wasn't going to use the money anyway. "When everything is final, I want to be the one to talk to Barrett."

"You drive a hard bargain."

"Make it so."

Annie ended the call and leaned against the living room wall in the silence. Then she bent over to close her laptop and silence her phone. She did not even leave it set to vibrate or alarm. "Silent"—as close as she ever came to "off." Her eyes scanned the room and found nothing to land on. No electronic green lights glowing with reassurance of the steady flow of power. No cords dredging life from outlets toward convenience. No gizmos beeping urgent summons. No stacks of books and magazines she never got around to reading. Slowly, she lowered herself to sit again on the bare floor. Beneath her, oak planks pushed against her with their stories. Annie spread her hands on the wooden floor on either side of her and closed her eyes, letting her fingers trace slight ridges her feet would not have noticed. A vague coating of dust stuck to the crevices of her palm, and in the mustiness that stirred, she inhaled questions of past and future.

When she opened her eyes, she saw the inch-long weak raised wallpaper seam on one wall. Yellow paint did not quite seal the history behind it. Annie got up and walked toward the spot then scraped at it gently with a fingernail and looked closely. She could discern four—no, five—distinct stubborn layers of wallpaper that had resisted efforts to smooth the seam over the decades. Even Annie, with all her domestic challenges, had seen enough home decorating television shows to know the right thing was to remove wallpaper rather than add layers of paint or paper. She had a hazy notion that the process involved steam. But at the moment, she was grateful for the painted wallpaper. The stories of the house were still there, not whitewashed into oblivion. She was strangely curious to know what they were.

The house was nearly a hundred years old—but young compared to the stories rattling around Annie's brain. Jakob Byler and Elizabeth Kallen were an unlikely pair, as unlikely as Rufus Beiler and Annalise Friesen. Yet somehow they found a life together. *Were they happy?* she wondered. *Were they certain they made the right choice?*

In silence, Annie wandered through the rooms. In the kitchen, the stove and refrigerator were at least thirty years old, one mustard yellow and the other avocado green. Make that forty years. The real estate agent said they worked, but it was difficult to believe they were efficient. Annie leaned against the refrigerator and pushed, moving it just far enough from the wall to find the power cord and plug it in. The prompt reward for her effort came in the whir of a motor.

The dining room asked for a narrow table to be settled under the window, leaving space to walk through and access the stairs. Under the stairs, the wall was made of dark paneling, and Annie realized a door opened to storage space.

Over the next hour, Annie carried loads from her car and inflated her mattress. She arranged a few dishes on shelves in the kitchen, swept the wood floors, satisfied herself that the refrigerator was indeed becoming cold, however slowly, and hung towels in the bathroom. Her mind's eye saw furniture and window coverings and new kitchen cabinets.

She knew just who she would hire to build them. Surely Rufus would be willing. She would be a paying customer, after all, and she could pay him well.

Rufus. Ruth would hang like a curtain between them now. She couldn't just ask Rufus to build cabinets without first asking, *Why didn't you stay to see your sister?*

It was a good thing he did not have Annalise's phone number, Rufus decided, because he would be tempted to call it. Since the reason was neither business nor an emergency, it would be wrong. He had Ruth's number, but he never called it. If something happened to *Mamm* or *Daed*, he would use it. A mix-up about a meeting time was not an emergency that justified using a phone.

The remodeling work in the motel lobby was finished, including installing the replacement face panels and a new desktop. Rufus was now working on custom cabinetry for two homes in the new subdivision. The deadline was far enough off that he could spend time teaching his employees some of his craft, giving them a chance to create cabinetry and woodwork, not simply install it. He had just sent his crew home for the day and was getting ready to work on the tables for David's customer in Colorado Springs.

Rufus looked forward to times alone of careful, slow sanding, sensing the exquisite plane of pressure that would break open the beauty in the hardwood. Even a side table could reveal the artistry of the Creator through the grain of the wood. With each passing of sandpaper over the surface, Rufus breathed a prayer of thanksgiving for the blessing of work.

The workshop door opened and Jacob appeared. "*Mamm* says to ask you a favor."

"What would that be?" Rufus's hands hesitated to leave the rectangle of wood that would become the tabletop.

"She promised to take preserves to Mrs. Weichert's shop. She wants to know if you have time to do it."

Rufus carefully set aside the tabletop. It was a long way to town just to deliver preserves. But if his mother asked him to do an errand, she had a good reason. "Are the preserves ready to go?"

Jacob nodded. "Two dozen jars of peach preserves. I hope she saved some for us."

Rufus smiled. "She always does. Go tell *Mamm* I can do it right now. I need to go to the new job site anyway."

"I was planning to stay a few nights," Annie said into her phone. "I already made sure I can access the server from here. I don't need to come in."

Sighing, she listened to the plea from one of her software writers and regretted checking her messages. The project was due to the client in two days, and he was stuck.

"All right," she finally said. "I'll drive back tonight and be there first thing in the morning."

Before she left, she took some measurements of windows and room sizes. When she grew hungry, she reluctantly carried her denim bag out to the car and backed out of her driveway. She could stop somewhere for food on the way back to the condo.

Pulling onto Main Street, she saw Rufus's horse and buggy outside Mrs. Weichert's antiques shop. The buggies all looked alike to her, but Annie recognized the horse. When she saw the shadow in the door frame, she almost stopped.

Rufus looked at the passing Prius as it moved away from him. The car was unmistakable. Annalise had come to town and not tried to see him. Disappointment twisted into him.

But why should she see him? It was better that she didn't. He would write to Ruth and explain what happened. He hefted the box of preserves and took it inside the store.

In the buggy a few minutes later, Rufus nudged Dolly into the street and toward the gleaming mountains that still made him draw a deep breath every day, even after five years of daily greetings. At the edge of town, he turned north and drove past the sign that announced Kramer Construction and into the next cul-de-sac. Rufus had been careful to make sure his new customers were using another builder and not Karl Kramer. It was the end of the day even for the construction crews that labored long into the evening, and he saw workers collecting tools, readying to leave the site for the night.

Rufus tucked Dolly's reins in a crevice in the midst of a convenient pile of lumber. He crossed the dirt that might one day be a lawn or, given the climate, a Xeriscaped garden of rock and mulch and uncut natural grasses. Inside the front entrance, the stairs were roughed in and the downstairs space portioned by unfinished walls. Rufus had blueprints with specific measurements. Still, he liked to stand in a room and sense the life that might someday exist there.

"Hello, Rufus." The site foreman emerged from the would-be kitchen. "Is Tom hauling something here for you?"

Rufus shook his head. "No. I just need to get a feel for the place. I'm doing wall-to-walls in the family room and the master bedroom."

The foreman nodded. "Okay, then. You may be the last one out."

"I'll only be a few minutes. I promise."

Rufus heard the grind of engines outside as the crew started their cars.

He was glad the others were gone. It would be easier to feel the place, to stand where the windows would be and judge the light falling into the room. In the silence, he would hear the rustle of clothes against furniture, the scuff of slippers against the floor. He would see hands reaching for the cabinet knobs he was yet to create, fingers closing around them in a habit of a thousand repetitions. Rufus slowly paced the family room, standing still and silent several times.

Then he moved up the stairs to the master bedroom. One

wall opened out to a deck with a view of the mountains. Large windows on the opposite wall would no doubt reflect the vista. His cabinets would fill the far connecting wall. Rufus faced the wall now, his eyes closed.

A second too late, he realized he was not alone. He turned in time to see a pair of black work boots before he slumped into gooey murk.

Thirty-Six

July 1739

Christian Byler loved the fields. The smell of wet earth, the rustle of eager corn in July, the sweeping bow of wheat in the wind—it was as if he felt the farm coming to life as his own bones and ligaments stretched. He was sure he would never forget putting crops in for the first time. His father sometimes fretted over what might go wrong—not enough rain, too much rain, hungry insects—but Christian savored each turn of dirt, every furrow, the mystery of seed covered in darkness springing to light.

Holding his straw hat in place, he ran now through the shortcut in the cornfield to where he knew his father would be judging whether the plants were of sufficient height for their stage of growth. He found his *daed* sliding off his horse at the far end of the field.

"How are the vegetables looking?" Jakob squatted and slid his hand under a cornstalk.

"Anna promises fresh beans for supper," Christian answered, "as much as we want." He leaned in to look over his father's shoulder, inspecting for insects boring through.

"Is Maria still sitting in her patch waiting for the beets to grow?"

Christian nodded. "She sings to them. She says it makes them happy."

"Seems to me they should be happy enough to harvest."

"Elizabeth knows how to make ink from beet juice. She promised to show us. Even Anna wants to learn."

Jakob moved to another plant and rubbed a leaf between his thumb and forefinger. "Elizabeth likes to try out everything she reads about. She's very creative."

"I wonder if the new baby will be creative." Christian hunched over to inspect a stalk for himself.

"Lisbetli will have to get used to not being the baby." Jakob paused to wipe sweat from his forehead.

"As long as Lisbetli can be with Elizabeth, she's happy," Christian said. "I still hope that someday Elizabeth will join the church—when we have a bishop."

"You could be waiting a long time for a bishop to come from Europe."

They moved another few feet to inspect plants, and Christian knew the conversation was over. His father had less and less to say about the church. The Amish families were cautious around Elizabeth—anyone could see that—but without a bishop to pronounce discipline, no one fully shunned Jakob for his choice to marry an outsider. The families needed each other too much.

Christian heard the flapping steps of someone running through the corn. He abruptly stood up straight.

"What is it, Anna?"

The girl breathed heavily and tried to speak between gulps of air. "Bar-bar says you must come. Right now!"

"Elizabeth?"

Anna nodded. "Her pains started only a few hours ago, but Bar-bar is already worried. She's afraid to be alone with Elizabeth when the baby comes."

Jakob stepped back to where he had left the horse and grabbed the bridle. "Both of you, quickly, get on." He picked up Anna, though she tended toward lanky at thirteen, and lifted her to the horse. Christian saw his father squat slightly with intertwined fingers and knew he was meant to step into the makeshift stirrup and swing himself behind his sister. "Tell Mrs. Zimmerman it's time." Jakob slapped the horse's rump as Anna took the reins.

As the horse began to trot, Christian looked over his shoulder at his father. He had never seen Jakob move as swiftly as he did now in the direction of the cabin.

"I want Elizabeth," Lisbetli said quite distinctly and adamantly.

"I told you," Jakob said, "the baby is coming. Elizabeth can't play with you right now."

"But I need her," Lisbetli whined and went limp as a rag doll across his lap.

"She can't play with you now." Jakob sighed heavily. He was on the cabin's small front porch with Anna, Christian, Maria, and Lisbetli. Barbara was inside with Mrs. Zimmerman. Bar-bar was sixteen now, old enough to learn something about birthing. How much longer would it be before she married and started birthing her own children? Several of the families had sons who must have noticed Barbara's industrious nature. Perhaps one of them would soon show interest.

Christian sat on the bottom step scratching in the dirt with a stick. Jakob never had to remind him to work on his sums, because he was constantly recalculating the number of acres they planted and the expenses that had gone into the effort so far.

Maria stood up. "It's too hard to do nothing. I'm going to talk to my beets. Call me when the baby gets here."

Jakob let her stomp off. Her garden patch was within sight of the porch. His eyes moved to Anna, who looked blanched and withered. When the next scream came from inside the cabin, he and Anna flinched at the same time.

"Take Lisbetli and go feed the chickens." Jakob gently dumped

Lisbetli out of his lap and then shoved open the door and went inside.

Mrs. Zimmerman appeared from behind the curtain that separated Jakob and Elizabeth's bed from the main living space of the cabin. She wiped her hands on a rag and shook her head slightly.

"What is it?" Jakob whispered.

"I don't think the baby is turned right." Mrs. Zimmerman kept her voice low. "It will take a long time to birth."

"Is Elizabeth in danger?" Jakob's heart pounded at the thought.

"They both are. You know that."

"You must do something."

"It is in God's hands, Jakob."

"You have been helping to birth babies for years," Jakob said. "You must know something you can try."

She shook her head. "I tried to turn a baby once."

"Then do that."

"It didn't help, Jakob, and the poor woman. . ."

Jakob forced himself to breathe. "Birthing was so easy for Verona. It was always a time of joy. Now this."

"Elizabeth is quite old to be having a baby for the first time." Mrs. Zimmerman shook her head again. "You must trust God."

"I cannot lose Elizabeth."

"You must trust. It's up to God."

Jakob pushed past his old friend and neighbor, past the curtain, past Barbara. Elizabeth lifted her eyes to his and held out one arm. He grasped her hand and fell to his knees at the side of the bed.

"Jakob, the pain! Something's wrong."

"Rest." He gripped her pallid hand in both of his as if in prayer. "Save your strength."

"I love you, Jakob Byler. I want you to know that before—"

He cut her off. "Before nothing. The baby will turn. The baby will come. We will have many years together."

She clenched his hand, her fingernails digging into him, and screamed.

A second scream, higher pitched, echoed—coming from behind Jakob. He turned to see Anna's whitened face.

"Anna, what are you doing here?" Jakob scolded. "I told all of you to go feed the chickens."

"This is all my fault!" Anna wailed and ran from the scene.

"Go to her, Jakob." Elizabeth gasped and waited for the height of the pain to pass. "She is such a confused child."

"I don't want to leave you."

They heard the cabin door creak open and slam shut.

"Go," Elizabeth said again. "Mrs. Zimmerman is here, and Barbara. I am not alone."

"No, I cannot."

"You must." Elizabeth untangled her hand from his.

Jakob looked at Mrs. Zimmerman, who only shrugged. Finally, he strode across the cabin and out the door. Fortunately, Anna had not gone far. He found her huddled under the front porch.

He squatted. "Anna, come out of there. I'm too old to crawl under porches."

At first he heard nothing, and then she scuffled across the dirt and into the light, hanging her tear-streaked, pale face.

"What is wrong, Anna? What is this nonsense about it being your fault?"

"It is. I did not want Elizabeth to come, and then I was so mean to her. And I did not want the new baby. I thought maybe she would leave if she did not have a baby."

Jakob took a controlled breath. "You are old enough to remember when Maria and Lisbetli were born."

She nodded.

"And neighbors have had new babies." Jakob leaned forward and grabbed Anna by the elbows to pull her out and into his embrace. "Sometimes birthing is harder than other times. It's not anybody's fault."

"But I thought such mean things!" Anna buried her face in his chest. "Before. . .before. . .I do not want Elizabeth to go away now because of me."

Jakob stroked her head. "It's not anybody's fault. Why would God punish Elizabeth for your thoughts?"

"Is it in God's hands?"

Jakob hesitated only slightly. "Yes it is."

"*Maam* used to say everything was in God's hands. But if that's true, why did *Maam* die? She loved God."

"You ask deep questions, Anna Byler. Perhaps it is not for us to understand God's ways."

Elizabeth screamed again, hideously. Anna gripped her father's neck. Suddenly she felt to him as small as Lisbetli.

The cabin door opened.

"*Daed*!" Barbara called.

"I'm here." Jakob stood so she could see him, pulling Anna to her feet as well.

"Mrs. Zimmerman is trying to turn the baby. It's awful. I can't stand it."

"Stay here with Anna." Jakob nudged Anna toward Barbara. "Let me go in."

"I never want to have a baby," Barbara said.

The shrieking stopped only long enough for Elizabeth to gulp and again gash the air with unearthly vehemence.

Christian took his younger sisters further from the house. He remembered when Lisbetli was born, and it did not sound like this.

And then came the aching silence during which anything could happen. Taking turns kicking a stone, Christian, Maria, and Lisbetli worked a jagged route back toward the cabin. At the porch, Christian caught Barbara's eye, but she said nothing. The five Byler children huddled on the narrow front steps ascending the porch.

And then the baby cried.

Anna was the first on her feet and pushing the door open. They tumbled into the cabin in a rolling mass, stopping just short of the curtain.

Their father came around the curtain and grinned at them. "It's a boy!"

"Can I hold him?" Anna, again, was the first.

"In due time," Jakob said. "Elizabeth has been through an ordeal."

Jakob returned to Elizabeth and drew a clean damp rag across her face, pausing to cradle one cheek. Mrs. Zimmerman wiped off the baby, wrapped him in a towel, and laid him in Elizabeth's arms before bundling up bloody rags in a sheet and moving away from the bed. Jakob straightened the bedding then pushed the curtain open to reveal Elizabeth propped up with the baby, swaddled in a small quilt, on her chest.

Anna took the first steps then halted.

"Come on, Anna," Elizabeth said, "come and meet your baby brother." She held out one arm.

Anna settled on the bed in the crook of Elizabeth's arm, and Elizabeth transferred the bundle of red squall to the girl's grasp.

"What's his name?" Anna asked.

Elizabeth looked up at her husband. "I'd like to call him Jacob."

Anna giggled. "It will be fun to have a little Jacobli in the house."

Christian watched as Anna cooed at the baby and tentatively explored his features with one gentle finger. It wasn't long before the other girls gathered around the bed as well, all of them anxious to meet their brother. Even Lisbetli climbed up on the bed and touched the baby's wrinkled wrist.

A boy. A brother.

Christian was used to having sisters—four of them. But a brother. He had been the only son. He was the one who worked beside his father in the fields, who kept the supply lists, who knew the trees that marked the corners of their land.

This new baby was not even Amish, yet he bore their father's name.

Thirty-Seven

Jamie never interrupted a meeting for anything less than urgent. Annie raised her eyes in question when Jamie slipped quietly into her office.

"Excuse me." Annie nodded to the group gathered around her conference table.

Jamie whispered into Annie's ear. "A Ruth Beiler is on the phone, and she says it's an emergency. I tried to tell her you would return the call later, but she insists. She sounds like she's been crying."

"I'll take it at your desk." Annie stepped out of her office. She picked up Jamie's phone and punched the flashing button. "Hello, Ruth?"

"I'm sorry to call," Ruth said, "but it's Rufus."

"What happened?"

"Sophie sent a letter. No one has ever written, so I knew it had to be bad."

"Ruth, tell me what happened."

"Rufus was attacked. Three days ago. They took him to the hospital in Cañon City. Sophie said it was awful."

"We'll go to Cañon City." Annie was the one who had to be

calm. She knew that. "You and me. Can you get away?"

"I'm not working until day after tomorrow."

"Good. I'm coming straight over."

A pall settled on them in the car thirty minutes later.

"Will he even want to see me?" Ruth asked.

Or me? Annie thought. She said, "You should be there."

"My mother might not think so."

"I know your mother," Annie said, "and whatever happened between you, I believe she loves you."

"That doesn't mean she'll be glad to see me. You have to be Amish to understand." Ruth looked down at her long brown skirt. "She'll hate what I'm wearing. And Sophie will be in trouble for writing to me."

"Surely under the circumstances they would all want you to know what happened."

"You might think so."

They didn't speak for a long time after that. Annie followed the directions displayed by the navigation system in her dash. *You have to be Amish to understand.* The simple sentence tolled in Annie's head. She was fond of the whole Beiler family and curious about her own family roots. But no, she was not Amish.

Finally, the hospital was in sight. Annie found street parking close to the main entrance.

"You're coming in, aren't you?" Ruth asked. "Rufus will want to see you, won't he?"

Annie shrugged. "Not sure."

"I need someone." Ruth pleaded with those violet eyes that were just like Rufus's. "Please come in."

They walked through the sliding doors together and stopped at the information desk. Rufus was still listed as a patient on the floor just above them.

"Get off the elevator and turn right." The woman wearing a pink smock pointed. "There's a nice waiting room on the wing. They just redecorated."

When the elevator doors opened on the second floor, Franey Beiler stopped her pacing down the center of the hall. Ruth stared into her mother's sallow face. Everything in her heaved, and she barely avoided falling into a stagger. Annie hung back a little, moving just far enough to let the doors close behind her.

"You've come," Franey said simply in Pennsylvania Dutch.

Ruth stared at her mother's crossed arms, aching for them to open. She straightened her skirt and tugged at the sleeves of her pullover shirt as mother and daughter considered each other. She searched for a hint of forgiveness or understanding. Even a simple welcome would give her something to hold on to.

"He will be glad to see you." Franey's voice sounded haggard. Ruth wished her mother would reach out and hold her. Then she would know it was all right to reach back. If only she had thought to wear a prayer *kapp*. At least her hair was braided and pinned up.

Annie moved a little closer. "May I ask what happened?"

Franey pushed out her breath and moved her fingers to her temples. She switched to English. "Somebody hit him from behind then apparently pushed him down a flight of stairs. Tom found him, by God's grace. We're not sure how long he was there. Rufus doesn't remember much. Yesterday they took out his spleen. Several ribs are broken and he has a concussion. He's resting right now."

Ruth opened her mouth to speak, but the knot in her throat refused the passage of air. She forced herself to swallow and found her voice. "*Mamm*, this is so much for you to bear."

"If I hadn't asked him to take preserves to town, he might not have been there at all." Franey's voice cracked.

"It's not your fault, *Mamm*."

"God's will," Franey muttered. She gestured into the waiting room. "It's comfortable in here. Your father is sitting with Rufus now. We take turns."

In the waiting room, a little boy in a straw hat looked up from a book. His face split into a grin. Jacob hurtled himself into Ruth's arms, and she spun him around once. He was so much bigger than the last time she saw him. She soaked up the weight of him straddling her hip, the feel of his limber form fitting against her torso, the smell of his hair under her neck carrying the scent of home.

"I'm happy to see you, too, Annalise," Jacob said, "but I haven't seen Ruth in a really long time."

Annie smiled. "I understand."

"Did you bring her in your car?"

"Yes I did."

"*Danke.*" He nestled his head under Ruth's chin, knocking his hat off.

Ruth squeezed him and avoided her mother's glance. If *Mamm* disapproved of Jacob's enthusiasm, Ruth did not want to know.

Annie picked up the hat and reached for Jacob. "Why don't we go look at your book together so your mom and sister can talk?"

Jacob let Annie take him out of Ruth's arms and set him on the floor. She took his hand and led him to the far end of the waiting room. Ruth watched as they settled into a wide, stuffed chair together. Her cheeks burned, knowing her mother was looking at her. Finally, she turned to Franey.

"It's good to see you, *Mamm*," Ruth said in the easy language of her childhood.

"*Dochder*," Franey answered. Daughter.

A simple word that might have reassured Ruth instead stung. She was a daughter who disappointed her mother deeply. Ruth doubted her mother meant anything but that simple truth.

A reminder of the choice she did not make. Could not make.

Franey chose a chair, and Ruth sat beside her. "Elijah Capp has spent many hours here waiting with us for news," Franey said.

Elijah? Here? Another sting.

"He had doubts, too, you know."

"I do know." Ruth could hardly get the words out.

"But he was baptized that day."

Ruth had always supposed Elijah went through with his baptism. Even knowing his doubt and what it would mean that she did not follow, she let him do it. She had sealed both their fates that day.

They retreated into flaccid silence. Ruth sucked back her tears.

"Would you like me to take Jacob home?" Annie approached Ruth and Franey a few minutes later. She was no mother, or even a babysitter, but she could see the boy was getting wiggly.

"The girls are busy with the animals and canning." Franey rotated her slumped shoulders. "Joel is in the fields. They have no time to look after him."

"I'll stay with him."

Franey tilted her head and considered the offer. "He has some lessons he should be working on."

"I can do that."

"I don't know when I'll be home." Franey clutched a used tissue in one hand. "It's a long way to be going back and forth."

"Take your time."

Franey turned to her son. "You mind Annalise."

Jacob nodded. "They won't let me see Rufus. At least at home I can see Dolly."

"Do your chores."

He nodded again.

"Thank you, Annalise," Franey said.

"I'd like to see Rufus," Ruth said.

"I'll take you now." Franey stood to lead the way.

Annie caught Ruth's eyes and hoped her smile spoke reassurance. If Ruth's nervous state during the drive down was an indication, Rufus was not the most daunting mountain Ruth faced.

At the main doors on the first floor, Annie hesitated and

swallowed hard. Her stomach burned. She was leaving the hospital without seeing Rufus for herself. She'd been in enough hospitals to picture what it must be like for Rufus. He was the man so many depended on, and now he was lying in a hospital bed minus a spleen.

This did not have to happen. If Rufus had fought back even a little bit when Karl Kramer had been slashing tires, this might never have happened.

Annie settled Jacob in the backseat and made sure his seat belt was fastened. In the driver's seat, she adjusted the rearview mirror slightly so she could see him. "Have I ever told you that you have a great name?"

"Jacob Beiler is a great name?"

"Yep. Some very good men have had your name."

"*Daed* says it's a family name."

"You can be proud of your family."

"No I can't."

"You can't?"

"That would be *hochmut*. Pride is against *Ordnung*," Jacob said simply. "I think I'm going to like riding in your car. We can't have a car. That's against *Ordnung*, too."

Annie started the ignition.

At the Beiler house, Annie found the schoolwork Franey wanted Jacob to do, got him settled on the porch where she could keep him in sight, then stepped off the porch to use her phone. Somehow it seemed sacrilegious to use it in the house. Her eyes gazed at Rufus's workshop as she tracked down the number she needed.

"Tom Reynolds."

"Tom, this is Annie Friesen. I just heard about Rufus today."

Tom sighed. "He's in bad shape. I want to get over to the hospital to see him again."

"Tell me the police are involved now."

"Of course. I called 911 when I found him."

"And?"

"And not much. Because it's a work site, the place is crawling with footprints, so nothing stands out. So far they haven't found anybody who saw anything out of the ordinary. It's not like there's a neighborhood watch looking out for a bunch of half-built houses. But they're still talking to people who might not realize they saw something that mattered."

"Are they talking to Karl Kramer?" Annie paced in fury. "It's been three days. They should have arrested him by now."

"Nobody would like that more than I would," Tom said. "They just don't have any evidence."

"Somebody must have heard Karl threaten Rufus at some point."

"Maybe. But that doesn't mean Karl actually did anything."

"I'm going to talk to my lawyer," Annie said.

"Rufus would rather you didn't, I'm sure."

"Probably," Annie said, "but look where that's gotten him so far."

"Annie, leave it alone. The police are involved whether Rufus likes it or not. Give them a chance."

"Even if they press charges, he'll refuse to testify in an *English* court. We need evidence that doesn't depend on Rufus."

"We have to respect his wishes," Tom said. "I don't think he'd want you fishing around."

Thirty-Eight

Ten days later, Annie slowly pushed open the door to Rufus's room at the Beiler home.

"It's all right. I'm awake."

His voice, though weak, poured relief through her. "Your *mamm* said I could come up for your lunch dishes."

"Yes, I'm finished." Rufus was propped up in bed, but at least one of the pillows had escaped.

Annie moved to the side of the bed and gently pressed the pillow back into place. Rufus had eaten little from the tray. "Would you like something different to eat?"

"No thank you. I'm not very hungry. They keep bringing me food."

Annie smiled. "They want to help." *Just like I do.*

"How is the new house?"

"I have a long way to go with it," she said, "but I have no regrets."

"So this means we will see you. . .often."

"I believe so."

"*Gut.*"

"Ya. *Gut.*"

Rufus started to chuckle but winced.

293

He struck her as surprisingly well, considering what he had gone through barely two weeks ago.

"Lydia tells me you plan to attend church tomorrow," Annie said.

"She tells you the truth. They won't let me help with the benches, though."

"Your mother made me promise not to disturb your rest." Annie picked up the tray.

"I admit I'm ready for a nap. Thank you for coming. And for bringing Ruth."

Annie would have liked to pull up a chair and watch Rufus sleep, or if he stayed awake to be helpful so he would not have to move. But Franey's instructions had been strict.

Thank You, God. Thank You.

Downstairs in the kitchen, breads, cheeses, garden vegetables, and *schnitz* pies lined up in anticipation of the next day's congregational meal. Annie set the tray on the table. "Rufus is frustrated he can't help with the benches for church tomorrow."

"He's only been home a week." Ruth's hands were busy in the sink. "I tried to tell *Mamm* and *Daed* that they should let someone else take their turn to have church. But Rufus is determined to attend the service."

"Then I guess it's better it's here. All he has to do is come downstairs."

Ruth shook water off her hands and reached for a dish towel. "Thank you for bringing me home again."

"Your *mamm* seems glad to have your help caring for Rufus."

"He won't stay down much longer. He's threatening to go out to his workshop on Monday. The men who work for him have already been asking."

Annie carried Rufus's dishes to the sink and began to wash them. "What about you, Ruth? Are you going to church tomorrow?"

Before Ruth could answer, Eli Beiler entered the kitchen.

"The benches are almost set. Perhaps we could offer the men a cold drink."

"Of course, *Daed*." Ruth opened a cupboard and began taking down glasses.

Annie helped Ruth fill them with cold water and put them on the tray to carry into the wide rooms cleared of the family's furniture and filled with wooden benches. In her very *English* jeans and T-shirt, Annie stayed in the kitchen and let Ruth serve the men. But the door was open, and with fingers playing with the gold chain at her neck, she watched the way several men gathered to speak in hushed tones. The words that wafted toward her were Pennsylvania Dutch. As Ruth approached them, they straightened up and put on smiles. Even in another language, Annie recognized someone changing the subject of conversation.

"What were they talking about?" she wanted to know as soon as Ruth returned to the kitchen.

Ruth set down the empty tray. "I didn't hear everything, but I think it's about Rufus's medical expenses. Mrs. Troyer is having cancer treatments, so the fund is stretched."

"What does that mean?"

Ruth lifted one shoulder and let it drop. "They may ask families to contribute more."

"I hope everything works out." Annie tossed a dish towel on the counter. "I'd better go. I have an errand to run, and there's a lot to do at my house."

"Are you coming in the morning?" Ruth asked. "Please?"

"I'll be here."

Annie picked up her denim bag and went out the back door. She strode around the house to her car. With a little luck, she could get to the hospital before it closed. And with a little more luck, the business office would be open on Saturday.

Ruth sat in the back with Annie on Sunday morning. Both wore solid-colored, long skirts and high-necked blouses with no buttons, but still they stood out among the river of blues and purples and blacks. Ruth glanced at Annie to make sure she had remembered to tuck her chain under her blouse.

Worshipers stared not only at Annie, the visitor. Ruth felt the stares of families she had not seen in eighteen months, the last time she gathered with them for worship. For the most part, she avoided their eyes. This was not the time to explain to anyone why she left.

When the opening hymn began, Ruth's throat thickened too much to sing. How long it had been since she heard the timbre of unaccompanied voices slowly pondering the beauty of the High German words of worship. *Kommt her zu mir, spricht Gottes Sohn.* "Come to me," says God's Son, "all you who are burdened." Ruth let the hymn flow richly around her, adding her voice when she could gather enough air to sing a few words. The first stanza faded, and the second began. Ruth closed her eyes, wanting to believe the words that rose from the rows of benches. "I will help each person to carry what is difficult; with my health and strength He will win the kingdom of heaven."

Ruth held the hymnal open for Annie, who did her best to keep up with the German words printed in elaborate script without knowing the tune. Most hymns had ten stanzas or more. Hymn followed hymn for an hour's time. In between, the men whispered, "You sing," as they encouraged each other to begin a new song. In the custom that swarmed Ruth with familiarity, men humbly deferred to each other until someone at last intoned a long note. Ruth knew most of the hymns by heart, and as she sang them, she tried to forget she had been gone these long months.

But she had been gone. And she would be gone again. Ahead of her, sitting with the unmarried men and next to Rufus, Ruth saw Elijah Capp. He had to know she was here. How long would he wait before he approached her about the night that changed their lives? For the moment, Ruth wanted only to lose herself in the music and its assurances of God's help and presence.

The sermons followed. Ruth's body still remembered how to sit perfectly still for hours on the wooden bench. Next to her, Annie crossed and uncrossed her legs. Even Jacob, sitting a few rows ahead with their mother, was keeping still with more success than Annie.

Following worship, the men turned the benches into tables with practiced ease, and the women soon had the food laid out. The men of the church migrated to Rufus so that he could hardly get a bite in before receiving the well wishes of a representative of every family present.

Among the women, Annie seemed to mix in surprisingly well, a welcome visitor. She seemed more at home than Ruth felt. Even the minister and his wife called Annie away from the group for a private word on the porch, and Annie went without hesitation—even with a smile.

The smile faded, and Ruth saw Annie wander away from the gathering. Ruth followed her off the porch and across the yard toward the barn. Though Annie quickened her steps, Ruth caught up with her.

"What's wrong?" Ruth grabbed Annie's wrist to slow her pace.

Annie shook her head. Ruth could see the water in her eyes.

"Tell me," Ruth urged.

"The minister spoke to me—the one who gave the second sermon. I thought perhaps he wanted to welcome me. But what he was really doing was scolding me."

"For what? We've always welcomed visitors."

Annie sagged against the side of the barn. "I'm not just a visitor. I'm the *English* woman who paid Rufus's hospital bill yesterday."

Ruth's eyes widened. "The whole bill?"

Annie nodded. "Apparently it was a bad idea."

"The Amish care for each other," Ruth said softly. "When someone has large medical bills, the community takes care of them. Granted, it may be difficult because we don't have as many families as districts in Pennsylvania or Ohio, but we still are responsible."

" 'We'?" Annie asked. "You still see yourself as one of them. And I keep blundering on the outside. Why do the Amish say no to so many things?"

"Our life is not so much about saying no, but about saying yes and meaning it."

"But I have money. Plenty of it. Why shouldn't I use it to help?"

"Perhaps *because* it costs you so little," Ruth said gently. "Money does not answer every question."

Annie exhaled and looked at Ruth. "You understand the secret unwritten code better than I do, but you don't fit here any more than I do."

Ruth sucked in her lips before speaking. "No, probably not. But they are my family. My people. I have to figure it out."

"Well, so do I," Annie said, "just for different reasons."

Ruth nodded, not speaking.

"I think I'll go to my house." Annie dug the heels of her hands into her eye sockets. "I'm worn out from trying to be somebody I'm apparently not."

"Only you know." Ruth floundered for words of comfort.

"I'll pick you up in the morning to go back to town."

"I'll be ready."

Annie stood at the corner of the barn and looked back at the families eating lunch, still separated by gender. She watched Rufus. He sat up straight as he spoke and laughed with the other men, eating heartily among friends. This was his world.

Now he lifted his eyes to her across the yard. The quizzical look on his face sharply tempted her to go speak to him, but of course he was eating with the men. She would just make things worse by approaching him. She offered a weak wave and walked around the back of the barn to find her car.

She slowly maneuvered around the line of buggies with their black boxlike bodies. The horses were all in the pasture, Dolly's territory. She pulled out onto the highway feeling like a city girl through and through. Why had she ever thought she was meant to buy a house in Westcliffe?

Annie had managed to have some basic furniture delivered to the new house. She had a sofa to sit on in the living room with an ottoman to prop her feet on while she worked on her laptop. Mrs. Weichert's antiques store yielded a brushed brass floor lamp and a small oval oak dining table with four mismatched chairs. Both front and back doors had new locks. She let herself in the back door, dumped her bag on the table, and slouched into the couch with her laptop. On autopilot, Annie checked her e-mail, scanned through Facebook posts, rolled through Twitter, and clicked through a few blogs.

Nothing interested her. Her brain absorbed few of the words that reeled past her eyes. She opened up iTunes and played several favorite selections while she flipped through three of the unread magazines she had brought from her condo. Nothing made the jiggling in her knees stop.

Only one thing would help.

Annie went upstairs to the bedroom, where she still slept on an inflatable mattress while she shopped for a bed to suit the room, and pulled a pair of tennis shoes out of a box. She changed quickly into shorts with a sweatshirt and the shoes. The cul-de-sac was only a mile and a half away. An easy run. She hooked her house keys to her waistband and slipped one other item into a back pocket.

She was there in under twenty minutes. The crime scene tape was long gone from the house where Rufus had been attacked, a fact that infuriated Annie. She paused to stretch and catch her breath in front of the house, glancing around while she did so. On a Sunday afternoon, no crews were at work. Fairly sure she was unseen, Annie circled around to the back, seeking an unobtrusive way in.

The credit card in her back pocket came out and quickly earned its annual fee by slipping the back lock open. She was in the kitchen then walked through the hall to the stairs. The floor was tiled with large brown ceramic squares, and the stairs newly carpeted in a muddy beige. By the smell of it—she sneezed twice—Annie speculated that it had been installed only two days ago. There was no telling how many signs of Karl Kramer's presence the construction crew had covered. She opened a couple of closets and wished she had thought to bring a flashlight. Slowly Annie walked up the stairs, picking at the edges of the carpet. They were firmly tacked in place. Upstairs she easily found the master bedroom, where the attack happened. Her heart thudded in her chest when she saw that the padding was down, but the carpet was still in a roll at one end of the long room. She knelt and fished along the seams of the padding, determined to find something in the afternoon light. Inch by inch, she moved down the seams and along the edges of the room looking for loose spots.

On the third wall she found it. Something. A triangle of paper, barely an inch wide, was trapped between the wall and the carpet pad. With a gentle touch, Annie scraped one finger down the wall to get a grip on the paper and dislodge it. She groaned when she felt the edge rip away from a larger paper that was probably nailed down. But she had something. Holding it in her hand, she leaned back on her haunches. Handwritten letters—*ner*.

Or maybe half of an *m—mer*.

Written in black ink on a line. A signature.

Annie sensed a shadow cross hers. She jumped to her feet and moved toward the hall. "Who's there?"

She saw no one but in the stillness heard shifting weight, the creak of a step on subfloor in an uncarpeted room.

Thirty-Nine

Annie clenched the scrap of paper and stepped cautiously into the upstairs hall. Hardly breathing herself, she heard panting to her right. She stepped to the left and found the top of the stairs.

"What are you doing here?" a man's voice said.

Annie tapped down three steps rapidly then couldn't resist the urge to turn and look. The man she saw was dark, with black hair that needed cutting and a ragged mustache. He was older than the man her mother had spotted at the motel. Annie had always imagined Karl Kramer would look more businesslike.

"You're Karl Kramer, aren't you?" Annie surprised herself with the words and her own intuition. She moved down three more stair steps. "What are *you* doing here?"

"You should not be here."

He crept toward her with just enough persistence to drive her down another two steps.

"I could report you," Annie said.

"And have to explain yourself? I don't think so." He took the first step off the landing. "This is a small town. Everybody knows you bought that old house."

Two more steps and she was on the first floor, just as he took his second step down the stairs.

"The front door's unlocked," he said. "Get out of here."

Annie opened it, stood in the door frame with her hand on the doorknob, and turned toward the stairs. "If you hurt Rufus, I will find a way to prove it."

She slammed the door hard and ran even harder. It was still daylight. Anyone watching would see a young woman out for a Sunday afternoon run in the late August mountain sun. At the back of her house, Annie fumbled with her keys, breathless, and heaved herself into her kitchen. Inside, she leaned against the refrigerator and unclenched her fist. The scrap of paper was scrunched into the size and shape of a spitball, but she carefully unfolded every crease and pressed it flat.

Yes, she was sure now. It was *mer*, and it was a signature. Now all she had to do was find a sample of Karl Kramer's signature. Her laptop sat open on the ottoman, and she went to it to search for images of his contractor's license or title to a house or any kind of legal document that would bear his signature.

She came up with nothing. Her dreams that night shuffled documents and television crime show scenes together. She woke exhausted. But she had to pick up Ruth at six so they could be back to their lives in Colorado Springs before nine. At a staff meeting at ten, Annie would explain to her team what had been going on with the recent series of covert meetings.

Craving coffee, Annie pulled into the Beiler driveway. Rufus sat in a chair on the covered front porch. She had planned to simply wait for Ruth in the car without disturbing the rest of the family, but because Rufus was outside, Annie got out of the car and approached the steps.

"I didn't expect to see you out here so early." She leaned on the railing at the bottom of the steps.

"*Gut mariye* to you also," he said.

"Sorry. Good morning. But why aren't you still in bed, resting?" She moved up toward the porch.

"I have rested for two weeks. I want to work today."

"Aren't you pushing it?" Annie sat in a chair next to him and felt the warmth coming off his skin. She resisted the urge to put a hand to his forehead to see if the warmth was feverish. Outside, in the fresh air, he smelled more like himself instead of an arsenal of medicine.

"Work is a gift from God," Rufus said. "I simply want to receive His gift."

Annie decided not to argue the point. "I found something last night. I think it proves Karl Kramer was in that house. I just need to find a sample of his signature to compare and be sure." She told him about the scrap of paper.

Rufus turned slowly to look at Annie full on. "You went to that house?"

She met his violet-blue gaze and willed her thudding heart to slow. "The police aren't getting anywhere. I thought maybe some fresh eyes would see something they missed."

"You were foolish. You could have been hurt."

"I was investigating."

"You were trespassing."

"I didn't hurt anything."

"Didn't you?" His eyes turned back to the mountains.

"No. Besides, I wasn't the only one there. I've never met Karl Kramer, so I can't be sure, but I would bet my company that he was the man I saw in that house. Talk about trespassing. It's not his building project. The fact that he came back suggests he's up to no good."

"That logic is not exactly flawless."

"You know what I mean." Annie was not giving up easily. "What was he doing creeping around a house he is not even building?"

"I suppose you think he was looking for the paper you found."

"Could be. Most of it is still under the carpet pad."

"It's not your business, Annalise."

She reached across the chairs and put a hand on his forearm.

303

The muscles under her fingers tensed. "I care about what happens to you, Rufus. The sooner the police nail Karl Kramer, the sooner you can get your peaceful life back—without all these complications."

"I do want a peaceful life," Rufus said, "but you confound me more than anything else."

He withdrew his arm from her touch. His words silenced her, and a flush rose in her cheeks against her best effort to subdue it. Why was it so hard for him to see that she was trying to help?

"You must let it go, Annalise." Rufus sighed and leaned forward in his chair. "You can't control everything. You have to stop trying to win. You certainly do not have to win anything for me. That is a way of life from your world, not mine."

"I just want justice. God likes justice, doesn't He?"

"God *is* justice," Rufus said. "You don't understand that. You have been in our home. You have been in our church, among our people. You have even used your technology to study us. Still you do not understand. Just when I think you begin to grasp our ways, you take things into your own hands again."

"I'm just trying to help."

"I don't expect you to be Amish, Annalise, but I do hope you can respect our ways."

"I *do*."

He shook his head. "Our life is grounded in submission, and yours seeks control. You can't have both."

Glassenheit. Ruth had used that word. Annie Friesen had never been very good at submission.

The front door opened, and Ruth emerged. Annie stood up.

"I hope you feel better soon. I've got some things to go control." Annie's dry tone sounded hollow even to her.

Rufus looked up at Ruth. "Did you say good-bye to *Mamm*?" he said, still speaking English.

She shook her head, and Annie realized how pale Ruth looked.

"She's staying in bed late. I don't think she wants to talk to me."

"Neither of you is willing to talk about the one thing that

matters. You started something when you left," Rufus said, "and you are picking at a sore when you visit."

"I came back for *you*," Ruth said. "You could have died."

"And I thank you. But you came back again."

"To see how you are healing."

"You are training to be a healer. You will have to heal this thing between you and *Mamm*." Rufus leaned back and closed his eyes. The conversation was over.

Annie and Ruth got in the car and buckled their seat belts.

"Does Rufus always do this?" Annie asked.

"Do what?"

"Dump a pithy impossible challenge on people instead of just saying good-bye."

"He's hardest on people he cares about most."

Annie waited in the upscale downtown bistro for her mother. Once a month they met here for lunch. Generally they both pretended to review the menu, hunting for something new to try, and then both ordered the corned beef on rye they loved. It came with coleslaw they dissected, trying to discover the secret ingredient that made them want to buy a container to go—which they invariably did. In the fairer months, they ate outside at a small sidewalk table sequestered from passing pedestrian traffic by a iron fence. Annie had chosen a table in the shade.

When Myra arrived this time, Annie set her menu aside. "Let's just get the corned beef."

"Seems like the efficient thing to do." Myra had been shopping. She kissed Annie's forehead, and then she set a boutique bag on the sidewalk under the table. "Summer sweaters are 40 percent off."

Annie smiled. Myra loved to shop, but even more, she salivated over bargains. Annie's closet was full of bargains Myra had picked up over the years. Most of them Annie never wore.

The food came quickly. Annie suspected the waitress, who

served them every month, had put the order in to the kitchen before her mother arrived. She made a mental note to leave a huge tip.

"So you've been to the Amish place again." Myra corralled meat between bread slices.

"It's not the 'Amish place,' Mom. It's a quaint, historic small town with a few Amish families in the area."

"When do I get to see the house you bought?"

Annie swallowed a bite. "Let me get it fixed up first."

"I can't imagine what the kitchen must be like in a house that old."

Annie shrugged. "I don't do much in the kitchen anyway."

"I should have taught you better."

"You taught plenty, Mom. Penny learned, after all. She has food on the brain. I just thought other things were important."

"It's not too late to learn to cook."

"I suppose not."

"I could sew curtains for your new windows."

"I might take you up on that one," Annie said, "but you have to teach me. Did you know the Amish women make all the clothes for the family?"

"That's a little extreme, don't you think?" Myra sucked coleslaw off her fork, her eyes rolling in pleasure.

"I don't know. Maybe. But there's something appealing about the way the Beilers live—well, all the Amish, I suppose."

"What do you mean?"

"When I'm there, I hear sounds I don't hear in town. Instead of televisions and stereos, dishes clink around the table and milk makes that *whoosh* when it comes out of the cow. And I smell things I've always been in too much of a rush to notice. They have a reason for how they live. They hear the voice of God. They choose life instead of letting it happen to them."

"We all choose our lives," Myra said. "You chose to go to college. You chose to start a business. You chose your condo."

"Did I? The whole system is so competitive. Of course I started a business. That's what winners do."

"Annie, what are you talking about?" Myra put her fork down, laid her hands in her lap, and stared at her daughter.

"I wonder what it would be like, that's all."

"Living without television? Without electricity? Without that computer you use like an appendage?"

Annie spread coleslaw around her plate with a fork. "The trade-off might be worth it."

"You need a vacation. Let's go somewhere that has a beach."

"Mom. A vacation is not the answer. I've had a lucrative offer for the business. I think I'm going to take it. I could sell the condo. This may be the time to rethink my life." Annie shrugged. "And yes, the Amish may help me do that. They already have."

"Didn't you tell me that your friend Ruth left the Amish way after growing up in it?"

"She's still trying to figure it out. She's choosing something. Answering a call. It's very spiritual for her, even if it does come at a price."

"If you want to be more spiritual, maybe you should just go to church a little more often." Myra resumed eating. "We always went when you were little. We all got out of the habit. But when your dad and I go now, people still ask after you."

Annie nodded. "I might try that. But I might want more."

Myra's eyes narrowed. "You mean, like join the Amish?"

Annie pinched a piece of bread off the sandwich she had not eaten. "I don't know if I would make a very good Amish woman, but I wonder about it. I'm at least going to get serious about faith again and find out where it takes me." In her mind's eye, she saw herself standing in the purple dress in the barn. Rufus's scent filled her nostrils even now.

"Annalise Friesen, buying a weekend house near the mountains is one thing, but I've seen that look on your face before. You're seriously considering joining the Amish."

"I don't even know if they would have me, but what if I did?"

"Think about your family, Annie. Everything would change."

"Not everything."

"This is about that man, isn't it?" Myra said sharply. "He's got your brain scrambled."

"I admit Rufus—well, he's not like any man I've ever known. But I wouldn't do this just for him. I would do it for me. For my relationship with God to change."

Myra pushed her chair back and stood up. "I've lost my appetite." She tossed her napkin onto the table and picked up her shopping bag. "I believe it's your turn to get the check."

Annie's mouth hung open as she watched her mother walk away without looking back. *Great. Someone else fed up with me. Okay, God, what am I supposed to do with that?*

Forty

October 1747

Elizabeth flung open the green shutters and breathed in the view of the Byler farm from the kitchen window. Fall air snapped through on the breeze.

After Jacobli was born in the cabin, Jakob drew up plans for a house. When John arrived the next year, and Christian started sleeping in the barn because the cabin was so crowded, Jakob began stacking stones and smearing mortar. By the time Sarah arrived a year after John, the home was nearly finished. Joseph and David, Elizabeth was glad to say, were born in the bedroom upstairs.

The home was simple and functional, but compared to the cabin, it was spacious beyond Elizabeth's dreams. She enjoyed the roomy kitchen and the broad table large enough for the family to gather. Whether for meals, lessons, or conversation, the table was in constant use. The kitchen had a small hearth for cooking, but Elizabeth's favorite wall was in the main room. In the evenings, Jakob tended the fire in the wide wall made of stone harvested from the fields during the clearing years and matching the outside of the house. The black oak mantel seemed to give him particular pleasure. A rank of upstairs bedrooms sheltered all the children with no more than two to a bed even when all ten of them lived at home. Now when Barbara's husband traveled overnight, there was plenty of room for Barbara and her toddler and infant sons to stay a few days.

Barbara married Christian Yoder, and Anna was engaged to his brother. Anna was already staying at Barbara's house most of the time because it was closer to the man she was engaged to—and whose family was planning her wedding.

Yoders. They arrived from Europe five years after Jakob. Already they were becoming a dominant family among the Amish settlers. The fact that their mother had been a distantly related Yoder made it easy for the Byler girls to gravitate toward Yoder sons.

Neither of the older girls even once wavered about remaining in the Amish faith. When an Amish bishop visited from another district, Barbara, Anna, and Christian were baptized. When he came again, Barbara married. The girls made their peace that Elizabeth would never join them and that their own father would be out of place in an Amish gathering. Christian, of course, held out hope that his father would return to the fold.

Elizabeth's only regret was that Jakob felt out of place at his daughters' weddings and chose not to attend. And someone else would host the celebrating families when Anna and Lisbetli married.

And Maria. What about Maria? At fifteen, she seemed in no hurry to join the Amish church, but Elizabeth did not want the teenager to make such a choice because of her.

At least there was Sarah. Perhaps by the time she was old enough to marry, there would be a proper church for her to marry in. Elizabeth did not even care if it were Lutheran or Presbyterian. Jakob would be there to see their daughter married.

Elizabeth smiled at what she saw from the window. Coming in from the vegetable garden, Lisbetli had Joseph by one hand and David by the other. Behind her, John and Sarah carried a basket of vegetables between them—most likely squash, Elizabeth thought. Not much was left in the garden at this point in the season. The cellar was well stocked for the winter.

"*Mamm*, I'm hungry!" David called out as soon as he spotted his mother in the window.

"You're always hungry," John responded.

It was true. At age four, David could keep up with Jakob or Christian at meals.

Elizabeth turned around and ran a rag over the table, wiping up the last evidence of lunch just before the children burst through the back door with their supper bounty. John and Sarah quickly disappeared into the other room, no doubt intending to be out of sight when Elizabeth vocalized the next chore.

"I thought Bar-bar would be here by now," Lisbetli said. The little boys freed themselves of her hands and clambered on Elizabeth, who dropped into a chair for support against their weight.

"I'm sure she'll come any minute." Elizabeth snuggled her little boys.

"Where's Maria?"

"Upstairs. She needed to put on a fresh apron."

"Are you sure you don't mind if I go?" Lisbetli asked. "The boys will be underfoot while you're cooking if I'm not here."

Elizabeth kissed both boys' foreheads and nudged them off her lap. "Lisbetli, the question is whether you want to go to the quilting bee. You're so helpful to me with the younger children, but you won't be a child yourself much longer. What do you want to do?"

"I don't want to hurt anybody's feelings." Lisbetli moved her fingers nervously across the back of a chair her father had made.

"Lisbetli," Elizabeth said softly. "You don't have to worry that you'll hurt my feelings if you decide to join the Amish church. Your father sacrificed something when he married me, but you are free to make your own choice."

"What if Maria decides to be baptized when the bishop comes

311

for Anna's wedding?" Lisbetli said. "If I don't join the church, I'll be the only one."

The only one of her mother's children not to stay true. Lisbetli did not have to speak aloud. Elizabeth knew—had always known—that the toddler she loved, now becoming a woman, would face the question.

"You are twelve years old, and today is only a quilting bee." Elizabeth pulled herself to her feet and examined the bounty the children had carried in. "You only have to decide what you'd like to do today."

"I do love to quilt," Lisbetli admitted. "I'm good enough that they'll let me do more than thread needles now. I'd like to make a baby quilt all on my own."

"A baby quilt?"

"For Anna. She's getting married in a few weeks. Maybe she'll need the baby quilt next year."

"That's a lovely thought. I have some scraps I can give you."

"Thank you." Lisbetli hesitated. "They have to be. . ."

"I know. Plain. They're left over from the dresses I used to make for you and Maria." As she spoke, Elizabeth adjusted the skirt of her own blue, flowered calico dress. Six-year-old Sarah was the only daughter she could dress in the prints and patterns she enjoyed. "I'm sure Anna would love to wrap a baby in a quilt made by Aunt Lisbetli."

"I've been thinking that maybe I should just be Lisbet now," the girl said. "It sounds more grown-up."

Elizabeth nodded. "I'll try to remember." She had to look harder and harder to glimpse the toddler who captured her heart.

"It's okay if you forget sometimes."

"Bar-bar's here!" John's enthusiasm rang from the other room.

Elizabeth heard the clatter of the buggy and went into the main room to look out the front door. Barbara wrapped the reins around a post and waved. A moment later she came through the door.

"Hello, everyone."

"Where are the babies?" David wanted to know.

"Anna is looking after them." Barbara looked at Lisbet. "She'll meet us at the bee."

Since Barbara hadn't brought the babies, David lost interest and wandered away.

"Where's Maria?" Barbara asked.

Clomping on the stairs answered the question. Maria appeared in a dark blue dress covered by a black apron that crisscrossed her back. She arranged her prayer *kapp* on her head.

"Where is your *kapp*, Lisbetli?" Barbara asked.

Lisbet's hand went to her head. "It must be on my bed."

"Then go get it. You can't go out with a bare head."

Lisbet dashed up the stairs.

The door swung open again, and Jakob came in with Christian.

"I thought the two of you went back to the wheat field after lunch." Elizabeth raised her cheek, knowing Jakob would brush his hand across it.

"Not yet. We had some work to do in the barn." Jakob obliged his wife with the gesture of affection. "One of the milk cows is acting strangely. If we're not careful, she'll dry up."

Christian lifted his hat a couple of inches and wiped his hand across his forehead casually. "Are the Yoders coming to the bee?"

Elizabeth suppressed a smile, but Maria was less discreet.

"Christian is *en lieb* with Lizzie Yoder." Maria grinned at her brother.

"Hush, Maria!" Jakob said sharply. But Elizabeth saw the twinkle in his eye. Anyone could see how Christian felt about Lizzie Yoder.

"It was an innocent question," Christian said.

"I do believe the Yoder girls plan to be there," Barbara said. "Perhaps I'll have opportunity to speak to Lizzie."

Lisbet thumped down the stairs, her black *kapp* askew on her head.

When his sisters were gone, Christian turned to his father. "*Daed*, on Sunday next week a visiting preacher is coming. We

313

don't get to have church very often."

Jakob nodded. "I'll make sure you're free to spend the day."

"Thank you." Christian looked from Jakob to Elizabeth. "I would like to take Jacobli with me."

In the fracture of silence, Elizabeth felt the eyes of her four youngest children lift and settle on their father. "John and Sarah," she said to her two eldest, "please take the little ones to the table and help them learn to write their names." She looked at them in that way that forbade argument, and they quietly complied.

Jakob took a log from the stack beside the fireplace and methodically adjusted its angle before returning it to the pile. "Jacobli would feel out of place in Amish worship."

"He's only eight," Christian countered. "No one would hold your choice against one of your sons."

Elizabeth was on her feet. "You seem to forget that Jacobli is my son as well. He will *not* go to church with you."

"*Daed*, you've always said that all your children were free to make their own choices, each one according to his conscience."

"That's right."

"How can Jacobli choose something he has not experienced? Would it really hurt him to go to church with his own sisters and brother?"

Elizabeth stepped across the room and positioned herself between father and son. "Jacobli is too young. Your father and I will decide when he is old enough to visit the Amish."

"But there aren't any other churches around here." Christian gestured widely. "Isn't it better that he go to church somewhere?"

"I include religious instruction as a regular part of schooling my children." Elizabeth hated the feeling of heat creeping up her neck. "He is learning everything he needs to know about the love and mercy of God."

"*Daed*," Christian said, "this is your decision. You're the man of this house."

Jakob did not hesitate. "Elizabeth is right."

"But *Daed*—"

"I have made my decision, Christian. Will you check on the cow again in about two hours?"

Elizabeth let out her breath. Jakob had made his choice nine years ago. Never once had he disappointed her when Christian pushed him. And the older Christian got, though, the harder he pushed. If he wanted Jacobli this year, would he want John next year? Would he put Sarah in a *kapp* and apron the year after that? Elizabeth did not require an elaborate life, but neither did she think a church rule book should dictate what color her dress could be or how long her husband's hair must be. While she would never openly oppose them—for Jakob's sake—it seemed to Elizabeth the Amish went to unnecessary extremes.

Christian pressed his lips together and sat in the rocker Jakob had crafted when Sarah was a baby.

The door opened yet again, and Jacobli entered. He looked around. "Why is it so quiet in here?"

"No reason." Elizabeth turned to greet him by smoothing his dark red hair. "We were just having a discussion. Why is your face so sticky?"

He grinned. "I ran all the way up from the tannery. I have great news, *Daed*. Mr. Hochstetler and his boys have been out hunting. They got three deer and a bear, and they want to sell you the hides."

Jakob nodded with pleasure. "Soft deerskin will bring a good price."

"He's going to bring them in a few days," Jacobli said, "as soon as they get the meat off. Can I help you put them in the vats?"

"We'll see."

Elizabeth caught Jakob's eye. He knew how she felt about having Jacobli so close to the lime solution. How could something that could take the hair off a hide be good for a little boy? Nevertheless, Elizabeth loved seeing the pleasure in Jakob's eyes when their son grew excited.

"I think we should add some bark to the pit, *Daed*. But first we should take out the cattle hides from the Siebers. They've been in there three months already."

"You might be right about that." Jakob nodded.

Christian stood up and straightened his hat on his head. "Jacobli, you seem to know a great deal about tanning for an eight-year-old."

"I'm going to be a tanner when I grow up."

"It's messy business," Christian said. "Smelly and dangerous. Wouldn't you rather be in the fresh air?"

Jacobli shook his head emphatically. "The tannery is the place for me."

Christian sighed. "Give me the farm any day."

Jakob smiled. "Christian, you were just like Jacobli at his age. Have you forgotten your maps and charts and planting schedules?"

"Farming is the way of our people, *Daed*."

Jakob readjusted the same log again.

Elizabeth nudged Jacobli toward the kitchen. "Come on. I'll help you clean up."

Forty-One

Ruth loaded her backpack strategically. She did not want to lose valuable time shuttling back and forth between her dorm room and the library because of overlooked items. She had booked six hours of computer time. Her class schedule allowed her to work three eight-hour days back-to-back and have three days in a row to devote to her studies and still enjoy a Sabbath.

In the four days since Ruth left Rufus sitting on the front porch, tears spurted at unpredictable intervals. Mrs. Watson asked Ruth to read, but she had avoided the task because she was uncertain the lump in her throat would allow the formation of spoken words. She completely forgot the shower she promised to give Mrs. Bragg, and she mixed up dinner trays for several residents. Seeing Mrs. Renaldi on the wing reminded her of Tom Reynolds, which made her think of Rufus, and then her mother and the rest of the family.

Ruth braced herself for the weight of the backpack bulging with textbooks and notebooks for four courses. She had her hand on the doorknob when she thought to make a phone call. Lowering one shoulder, she slung her burden down long enough to find her cell phone tucked into the pocket of the strap.

"You sure you want to do this?" Lee Solano asked.

Annie exhaled and rolled her eyes. "You ask me that every time we speak to each other." They stood together outside the doors to a downtown bank. Walking through them would take her to the meeting at which she would sign papers that meant she was letting go.

"I have to ask," Lee said. "I've never had a client express such extreme wishes. I wake up in the night thinking I must have heard you wrong."

"You heard me right. This life is not for me anymore."

"Maybe someday you'll do another start-up."

Annie shook her head. "I've done it twice. That's enough."

"You're only twenty-seven," Lee said. "Don't paint yourself into a corner you can't get out of."

"You're in cahoots with my mother."

"Never met the lady," Lee said, "but it sounds like she has the smarts you used to have."

"Let's just do this." Annie pushed open the bank door.

Lee did not have to understand her choices. He was being paid handsomely for arranging the legalities. Beyond that, Annie was not trying to persuade anyone of anything. She wanted only to make a choice and see it through.

Lee pushed the elevator button, and they rode to the third floor without speaking. From there it seemed as if she were watching someone else's motions. Annie wore a blue silk suit and four-inch navy heels, the tried-and-true choices she relied on for business meetings of this caliber. Though young, female, and casual in an old boy's world, she was not some sort of teenybopper with a ponytail and chewing gum. But even as she shook hands and took her seat and tugged the bottom of her jacket straight, the weight of the purple dress in the barn draped off her shoulders, and it was soft cotton that she adjusted around her waist. She picked up a pen to sign documents with elevator music playing in the background and phones ringing and lights blinking, but she was sitting on the sofa in a hundred-year-old house, listening to sounds hidden in silence. Bearers of modern success surrounded her in a sleek conference room while outrageous numeric figures popped off the printed pages for something she could not hold in her hands, but she was on the Beiler front porch, sitting next to Rufus in the fragrance of a garden that proved where food came from.

Finally, the others left, with handshakes and claps on the back for a deal well done, and Annie was alone with Lee, holding in her hands a manila folder of legalese.

Lee picked up his briefcase from the floor and set it on the table to open it.

"Okay," he said, "now for stage two." He slapped a stack of papers on the table. "You can still back out of this part."

"I'm not backing out of anything." Annie picked up the pen again. "Where do I sign?"

"That's a pile of money in your hands," he said. "If you sign these, you're not leaving yourself much to live off of."

"I don't plan to need much. And there's still the condo. I told the real estate agent to lower the asking price by 15 percent."

He groaned. "Annie, please."

"I want it to sell quickly."

"The market is soft on high-end stuff like your place. You'll take a loss."

Deadpan, she looked at him.

"All right, I get it. You're not worried about money."

"In my recent experience, it's been more trouble than it's worth."

Annie paused only briefly over the signature line. The bulk of her assets would go into a holding account that could never revert directly to her. She needed more time to sort out just where it would go eventually. She couldn't just leave it without a purpose, like a forgotten trinket in a box. But it would never be hers for personal use.

Annie signed.

"You've been a great help in all of this, Lee. Thank you."

"You're welcome." He picked up the document and returned it to his briefcase. "The money should be transferred before the end of the day."

"You know where to find me if you have questions."

They exited the conference room, descended in the elevator, and stepped into the blinding Colorado sun. Annie squinted at her car parked across the street. Above the sounds of traffic, she recognized the vibration of her cell phone in the small purse she carried when she dressed up. Lifting the flap of the purse, she saw that the caller was Ruth.

"Hello, Ruth."

"Hi," came a diminished voice. "Do you think. . .could I . . . maybe see you today?"

"Yes, of course." Annie was eager to see how Ruth was. "I have one other meeting to go to right now. Should I pick you up later?"

"I can get a ride to your place," Ruth said. "I thought I could bring what I need to make dinner for you."

Annie smiled. "Yes. Absolutely. About six?" She dropped the phone back in the purse.

Now to talk to Barrett.

Sated with chicken stew and shoofly pie, Annie picked up a box of books and added it to the stack in the entryway.

"Are you really giving all this away?" Ruth followed with a second box.

"I didn't need most of this stuff living here," Annie answered. "I'm sure not going to need it in Westcliffe. I've tagged some furniture to take, with some bedding and practical items. But a lot of my things will find better homes elsewhere."

"I admire how ruthless you're being in packing things up."

"I've got time now." Annie grinned. "No job."

Ruth laughed. "How soon will you move?"

"I couldn't arrange for the furniture movers before next week, but I'll take some things this weekend by car."

"Oh good. I mean, that sounds like a good plan."

Annie paused, a roll of packaging tape in one hand and a permanent marker in the other. "Would you like to come with me, Ruth?"

Ruth straightened the top box in the stack then turned hesitantly toward Annie. "I can't leave things the way they are with my mother. Rufus is right about that."

The ashen face of her friend twisted Annie's heart. "Then we'll go together."

Annie padded down the hall in her bare feet to the bedroom. Ruth followed. The twin doors to the walk-in closet were wide open, though most of the closet's contents were strewn in piles around the room. In one corner a supply of flattened boxes awaited new lives of service. Annie picked one up, popped it open, and sealed the bottom with tape.

Ruth wandered to the bed and momentarily hung a soft pink cashmere sweater from her fingers. She folded it neatly then reached for a starched white shirt with a delicate string of blue and green flowers hand-embroidered down the front. "You have some very nice things."

"You know, you can have anything you want." Annie scribbled a label on a box. "If you need some clothes. Sweaters. A coat. Or a radio or a lamp or anything you see. A TV."

Ruth picked up a linen blouse, sat on the bed, and folded the blouse in her lap. "Thank you, but I would never be comfortable. I am still Plain at heart."

Annie put down her packing tape and sat next to Ruth on the end of the bed. She leaned into Ruth's shoulder. "I think your mother would be glad to hear you say that."

"Perhaps. But I have a lot to ask forgiveness for. And being Plain at heart will never be the same as joining the church."

"Perhaps if your family understood more about what you're doing, they would soften. You're doing something noble, in my opinion."

"Noble is too close to proud, *hochmut*. Is it humble? That is always the question. *Demut*. Am I submitting?"

"Well, how do you answer those questions?"

Ruth fingered the collar of the linen blouse. "If I submit to God, I can't be anything but what I am. If God created me to care for people, perhaps He also means for me to have the education to know how to do it."

"Rufus would be dead without people who knew how to care for him in a crisis," Annie said. "Surely your parents can appreciate that fact."

"I was not baptized." Ruth's voice was barely above a whisper. "So my choice to leave is not the greatest wound to my mother. It is the way I left that stabs her."

Annie wasn't sure she knew what Ruth meant, but the moment quivered too fragile for questions. She put an arm around Ruth's shoulder and leaned her head against Ruth's. "Talk to her."

In the silence, her advice echoed in her own mind. Perhaps it was true that her own choice to leave her life in Colorado Springs would not be her mother's greatest wound if she too did not leave well.

Ruth was the one to rupture the stillness. She stood and began folding vigorously. "We're going to need a lot of boxes."

"I can always buy more." Annie pulled a box closer to the bed and dropped in the linen blouse then a whole stack of shirts from the bed.

"Make sure you keep enough warm things for the winter. Westcliffe gets cold."

"I will."

"Does Rufus know you're doing all this?"

Annie grimaced. "He knows about the house but not that I sold my business and put my condo on the market."

"When do you plan to tell him?"

"I'm not sure it matters."

"Of course it matters."

"I don't want Rufus to think I'm doing any of this because of him." Annie expertly laid another strip of tape across a box.

"Are you sure you're not?" Ruth challenged.

"I'm not expecting anything from your brother, if that's what you mean."

"But you have feelings for him, *ya*?"

Annie dropped a trio of sweaters into a box. "It's hard not to," she admitted softly, "but that does not mean anything. He already said he does not expect me to be Amish. I am *English*. So what can happen?"

"He would not ask it of you, that is true," Ruth said. "But if you were to choose?"

"I don't know if I'm ready to choose to be Amish. And I don't think he believes I ever could. Besides, it would be wrong to make Rufus the reason."

"That is true."

"I've seen a different picture of life, and I wonder if it's meant for me. A life that does not ignore God." Annie taped a box shut and labeled it. "You and I are not so different. I never really asked what God wants of me before. Now I will."

Ruth laid a pair of wool trousers in the new box. "I wonder about our ancestor Jakob Byler. Growing up in the church, I heard stories about his son Christian, who is my ancestor. But now you discovered Jakob had a second family—your family. What made him choose as he did?"

"I'm sure it wasn't easy." Annie went into the closet and came back with a load of dresses on hangers. "I believe he arrived in Philadelphia an Amish man with a wife and five children. Then his wife died. There he was, in a new land—not even a country yet—with five children and a plan to homestead with a few other Amish families. It had to be tough. We have to put ourselves in his place and imagine the rest."

"And choose the best we can, just the way Jakob did."

Annie nodded. "I think so."

They folded clothes without speaking for a few minutes and filled two more boxes.

"So when are you going to talk to your mother?" Ruth asked.

Annie looked up and caught Ruth's eye. "Tomorrow. And then we'll go to the valley, and you'll talk to yours."

Forty-Two

December 1750

"One more day," Christian said to Lizzie Yoder, "and you'll be stuck with me forever."

"I don't want to be stuck with anyone else." Lizzie shivered under her shawl.

They sat in separate straight-back chairs next to each other on the Yoders' front porch. Early December sun looked brighter than it felt to Christian. It was probably selfish to keep Lizzie out in the cold, but it was the only place they could have a private moment. They were in plain view, but members of the large Yoder family thoughtfully managed to be occupied elsewhere.

"What a blessing to be ready to marry just when Bishop Hertzner has come to stay." Christian set his jaw in satisfaction. "Our children will grow up going to church every other Sunday, and not just when a visiting minister comes through."

"Christian, do you hope that God gives us a baby right away?" Lizzie looked at him shyly out of the sides of her eyes.

He reached over and patted her hand briefly. "We will be grateful for whatever God gives us. His will is certain."

Lizzie nodded. "Ours is the last wedding. All the fuss of the last few weeks will be over."

"I'm sorry we couldn't be first instead of the last of five," Christian said. "If only I had spoken to the bishop when he first arrived."

"It would have been prideful to insist on being first. Besides, what difference does a few weeks make when we have our whole lives before us?"

Christian twisted his hands together. "I wish I had finished our house. I didn't know we would have such difficulty getting the harvest in this year." He brightened. "But now we have our own land just a few miles away. Next year we'll have our own harvest."

"Do you really think so? Can we get enough acres cleared by spring?"

"I will chop down trees in the middle of a blizzard if I have to."

"I keep telling you I can help."

Christian shook his head. "You will be busy visiting and gathering the things we need for the house. We will spend a few weeks here with your family, then with the Kauffmanns and the Troyers and the Zooks. Before you know it, we'll be in our own home."

"I cannot wait."

Christian considered his bride-to-be. He had no doubt she was the prettiest of the Yoder sisters, but her devotion to the church had won his heart.

A wagon rattled into view and hurtled toward the house.

"Why is he driving so fast?" Lizzie rose abruptly, clutching her shawl against the wind, and moved to the edge of the porch. "My uncle! Something must be wrong—it may be my aunt."

She stepped to the front door, pushed it open, and screamed for her family. The answer came in a thunder of footsteps from every direction. When the wagon came to a halt only a few feet from the porch, Christian was there to grab the reins and steady the horses. Yoders swarmed around the wagon.

"Miriam!" Lizzie's mother pushed past and clambered into the wagon. Her sister looked nearly unconscious. "Adam, how long has she been like this?"

"Three days." Adam jumped from his seat into the back of the wagon. "She cannot hold anything down, Martha. She was determined to be well enough for the wedding tomorrow, but I am worried today. I could not wait any longer."

"Is she with child again?"

"She did not tell me," Adam answered. "But she must be. It is the only time she gets like this."

"Take her in the house. The room at the top of the stairs is ready."

Christian caught Lizzie's eyes. The room at the top of the stairs had been readied for them. He had not yet seen the preparations for where they would begin married life.

A tangle of arms lifted Miriam's limp form, cradling her as they transported her into the house. Stair-stepped small children climbed out of the pit of the wagon and raced each other around the house, oblivious to their mother's plight.

Christian was left holding the reins and stroking the horse's neck. Lizzie was frozen in place.

"I suppose I should put the horses in the barn." Christian found the horses' lead. "I'm sure they'll stay the night for the wedding tomorrow."

"Christian," Lizzie said, her face blanched, "they will stay far longer than that."

"Your aunt seems quite ill, but with your mother's care—"

Lizzie was shaking her head, her lips pressed together. "You don't understand. Miriam is with child. This happens to her every time. It lasts until she is at least four months along. With the twins, it was even worse. She'll be in bed for weeks. My mother will have to spoon-feed her. My uncle will have a terrible time keeping up with the cousins, so the little ones will stay here, too."

Christian considered these facts. "You mean, she will be in bed *here* for weeks?"

Lizzie nodded.

"She will be in. . .our bed. . .for weeks."

Lizzie nodded again. "Christian, where will we live after our wedding?"

Elizabeth used a long, thin washing bat to lift Jakob's shirts out of the barrel where she had left them in lye to soak out the stains. One at a time she plopped four identical white cotton shirts into a basket then bundled up assorted children's clothing and tossed them on top of the load. Lisbet was fourteen now, more than old enough to look after the children while Elizabeth sought creekside refuge. Elizabeth took her warmest cloak off the hook in the kitchen and arranged it around her shoulders.

"But it is cold out there." Sarah, nine, poked at the load with one finger. "Why are you washing clothes in January? Why not wait for spring?"

"Your *daed*'s shirts are dirty now." Elizabeth hefted her basket.

"Is Lizzie going with you?"

"No. This is Lizzie's baking day." Elizabeth's answer was quick. Lizzie was the reason she had decided to do laundry in the middle of January in the first place. Lizzie's second batch of buckwheat loaves sat on the table, rising in the warmth from the oven.

Outside, the slap of brisk air was welcome. Elizabeth started down the path to the creek. The water had frozen solid a couple of weeks earlier, but temperatures had risen again, and the creek yielded a sluggish flow.

A sluggish creek was good enough for Elizabeth.

It was not that Elizabeth disliked Lizzie. She was a perfectly lovely girl and well suited in temperament to Christian. Elizabeth was genuinely happy for the young couple. But Lizzie had been sheltered all her life from anyone who was not Amish and didn't seem to know what to do with Elizabeth, or Jakob, or Christian's half siblings. Over the years, Elizabeth certainly did not intentionally offend her neighbors. Most of them would speak to her in friendly ways. Mrs. Zimmerman helped her birth five babies, and Mrs. Stehley enjoyed borrowing Elizabeth's books. Elizabeth had learned to sew clothing for her Amish stepchildren, and mothers with younger children happily accepted her garments as serviceable hand-me-downs. Though Jakob repeatedly offered to bring her whatever she wanted from Philadelphia, in many ways Elizabeth lived as plain as her neighbors.

Lizzie did not say most of what she thought—Elizabeth was certain of that. It was Jakob whom Lizzie wordlessly condemned. Elizabeth was merely an unenlightened outsider. Jakob was the one who left the church when he married her. He was the one who put his children in the difficult position of choosing between him and the church. *How does he bear it?* Elizabeth sometimes wondered.

Christian was the third of the Byler children to marry into the extended Yoder family. The truth that their mother had been a Yoder was never far from Elizabeth's mind, nor, she suspected, from theirs. Newly married, Christian and Lizzie lived as separately as they could while sleeping under the same roof with Jakob and Elizabeth.

And now the bishop was here to stay. For the first time, the Amish families of Northkill and Irish Creek had an authority living among them permanently. Jakob seemed unconcerned, but Elizabeth wondered if the presence of a bishop would disturb the careful balance of their life together. Only a few hours ago, Elizabeth overheard Lizzie murmuring to Christian that the bishop should talk to Jakob. It would be best for everyone, Lizzie had said, if Jakob came back to the church and brought his family with him. If he repented publicly, no one would withhold forgiveness. It would be against *Ordnung* not to forgive.

At that moment, Elizabeth had knocked a pot against the table with particular swiftness, announcing her presence. She was *not* something to be repented of.

Elizabeth reached the creek and set down the basket. Closer to the water, the air was even more biting, but she did not care. Below a thin layer of ice, the water was moving. Elizabeth gripped her washing bat and broke the ice in one strike, creating an opening where she could rinse the clothes. One at a time, she swirled shirts and dresses and trousers in the frigid water and watched the dirt break free and flow downstream.

If only life were that simple, she thought. She picked up a shirt and wrenched the excess creek water from it.

By the time Elizabeth returned to the house, her hands were red and raw, but her nerves were settled. The aroma of Lizzie's baking efforts filled the kitchen, though the room was unoccupied. The trouble with Lizzie using the kitchen all day to bake was that Elizabeth could not feed her family more than cold meat and cellar fruit. Her own bread shelf did not offer much at the moment. Tomorrow would be her turn to beat and knead her bread dough and slide the loaves into an oven that took three hours to heat sufficiently.

For now, Elizabeth picked up the limp end of a rope and attached it to the nail on the opposite wall. If she left her laundry on the bushes outside, it would freeze before it would dry, so she hung it in front of the kitchen fire. Then she went in search of her children, wanting nothing more than to fill her arms with them while she dried off and warmed up.

As she passed the broad table, Elizabeth saw the mound wrapped in a dish towel. Laying her hand on top of it, she absorbed the rising warmth. She sensed someone was watching her and looked up. Lizzie leaned against the door frame leading to the main room.

"I thought you might enjoy some bread with your supper," Lizzie said. "I made plenty."

Elizabeth's breath caught. She was so cold, and she craved the heat of the fresh bread, even just a bite. "Thank you, Lizzie. It smells delicious."

"Mrs. Byler, I feel convicted that I have made you feel unwelcome in your own home. I hope you can forgive me."

Elizabeth hardly knew what to say. "Thank you, Lizzie."

"I promise to be more mindful of my actions," Lizzie said. "I do not want to appear ungrateful for your hospitality."

"You are Christian's wife. Of course you are welcome in his family home."

"The Kauffmanns will soon be ready for us. Christian says we are to move in three days."

Elizabeth shivered, and not entirely from the cold. Relief would come soon.

"Jacobli has built a wonderful fire in the other room," Lizzie said. "Come and warm up away from the wet clothes."

"Yes, I shall do that."

Lizzie moved out of the way, and Elizabeth stepped into the main room. The beauty of what she saw swelled and lodged in her throat. Lisbetli sat on a large rag rug with Joseph on one side and David on the other, the three of them with their heads bent together over a book Rachel Treadway had sent from Philadelphia. Sarah sat on her favorite window seat and stared out, just as Anna often had done in the cabin ten years ago. John and Jacobli were on their knees in front of the fire, poking at it with sticks and laughing about things that only brothers shared. The moment was worth every hardship they had endured.

"*Mamm*, come and get warm." Jacobli waved her over with a hand.

Elizabeth suddenly noticed how tall his form had become. Even folded up before the fire, his height announced itself. He was eleven, but she saw the man he would be soon enough. She perched on a low footstool in front of the fire, close enough to stroke Jacobli's head, and welcomed the flickering heat.

"*Mamm*," Jacobli said. "I think I want to meet the new bishop."

Her hand rested at the base of his neck now, trembling. "Have you spoken to your father?"

"Not yet. I wanted to tell you first. Lizzie says I would like him. He is very friendly, she says."

Lizzie. Of course she would be in league with Christian over the children's faith.

"We have always told you that when you were old enough, you could choose for yourself, according to your own conscience."

"Am I old enough?"

"What do you think?" Her heart pounded.

"I think I want to meet the bishop." Jacobli stabbed the fire with his stick.

He might as well have stabbed his mother's heart.

Forty-Three

"Can we park down here?" Ruth asked when Annie turned the car into the long Beiler driveway. "I'd like to walk up. She's probably in the garden."

Annie pulled to one side of the lane and turned off the car. "I'll give you a head start then see if you need anything."

"Okay. Thanks."

Ruth got out of the car and glanced back at Annie, the only friend who knew her in both worlds and felt the pull of both for herself. Then she drew a deep breath, puffed her cheeks in an exhale, and turned her steps toward the garden. Her mother was there, just as she had thought. Lydia and Sophie were supposed to look after the vegetables, but Ruth knew her mother did not regard the patch as a chore but as a place of solace. The Beiler children had learned long ago not to disturb Franey when she knelt there. She was as likely to be praying as weeding. On her knees now in the far end, Franey was picking out bits of growth that did not belong in the ordered rows and tossing them in an old basket. Remembering when that basket was new, so long ago, Ruth watched her mother for a few minutes.

"*Mamm?*" Ruth finally said.

Franey shifted her weight, putting one hand down on the ground to support the turn, and raised her face to her daughter. "Your brother is doing well. There's no need for you to go to all this trouble to check on him."

"That's not why I came." Ruth stepped forward. "I came for you."

"What does that mean, Ruth?" Franey stood now and brushed her hands together. Loose crumbs of black dirt tumbled to the ground, not back to where they came from, but to the new place where they belonged now.

"You're my *mudder*. I need you in my life."

Franey stooped to pick up her basket and the hand shovel she had used as long as Ruth could remember. She simply waited.

"I want to explain." Ruth moved closer, her toes at the edge of the garden now. "It might not change anything, but at least you will know."

She wished her mother would suggest sharing tea or sitting on the porch, but Franey was planted in the earth with her basket of weeds in one hand and her shovel in the other. Franey had done nothing wrong that day. Ruth was the one to deceive and disappoint.

Annie waited a few minutes before starting up the lane on foot. Instead of following to the garden, though, Annie took the path that forked toward Rufus's woodworking shop. The gray, brooding sky almost certainly held a torrent to unleash on the valley.

Annie pulled open the shop door and breathed a sigh of relief. "You're here."

Rufus looked up from his bench, where he was working on a hinge. "Why is it you never say good afternoon?"

"Sorry. Good afternoon."

"Good afternoon. I'm surprised to see you." He raised his eyes to her and straightened the front of his shirt.

Annie stepped closer to the workbench. "Actually, I'm moving

334

into the house in town."

"Will you be coming down every weekend, then?" Rufus blew the dust off a hinge. He gripped a screwdriver in one hand, his eyes on her.

"I'm going to live here full-time." It wasn't the color of his eyes that transfixed her now, but the grasping that swirled in them.

"That sounds like a rash decision." Rufus set down the screwdriver and unrolled one sleeve toward his wrist, then the other.

"You're not the only one who thinks I've gone around the bend, but I'm sure it's what I am supposed to do." Annie put both hands on the workbench and leaned in.

"I suppose your technology allows you to run your business from here. You've been doing that already." Rufus gently lifted one cabinet and moved it to the end of the bench then put a new one, still looking raw, in the space in front of him.

"I sold it."

He looked at her. "The business?"

She had his attention now. "I sold it, and I'm not keeping the money."

Rufus stilled. "How will you support yourself?"

"I can live simply." Saying it, she believed it.

"And why are you doing this?"

"I know you don't believe me, but I want a different life."

"I did not say I don't believe you."

"You don't think I can do it, do you?"

"That is not for me to say." He put his hands in pockets of the tool belt around his waist and fished out another hinge. "I hope you can live simply enough to simply leave Karl Kramer alone."

"God's will, as you always say."

He shook his head. "Do not say that lightly, Annalise."

"I don't. I'm really, really trying to let go of managing everything my way."

Rufus picked up the screwdriver again, saying nothing. Annie saw several identical cabinets lined up on the floor awaiting hinges and front doors. This was work his crew could perform easily, yet clearly he intended to do it himself. Did he even have a crew anymore, or had his hospitalization and recuperation forced them to look elsewhere for employment? He looked tired—tired in body and tired in spirit. She wanted to sit with him and put her arms around him, draw his head down against her. She would stroke his brown hair, his clean-shaven cheek, his muscled arm, and he would close his eyes and rest.

But it could not be.

"I brought Ruth," she said abruptly.

He looked up at her again.

"To talk to your mother." She met his gaze. "To try to remove whatever it is between them. She thinks you are right about that."

Rufus set down the hinge and screwdriver then picked up a rag and wiped his hands free of the dusty evidence of his task. He repeated the motion more than necessary.

"You're thinking of going to find them, aren't you?" Annie crossed her arms over her chest.

Rufus tossed the rag onto the bench. "I am not sure how *Mamm* will respond."

"Who is trying to control things now?"

Rufus turned up one corner of his mouth. "Not control. Just be there."

"Can you imagine what I thought when I found you hiding in that outbuilding?" Franey did not take a single step out of the garden.

"I know," Ruth said. "It was wrong."

"Elijah Capp was in love with you."

Franey's voicing of simple fact stirred in accusation.

"I know," Ruth said. "I was not fair to him."

"He told his parents—our good friends—that he loved you, but he was not sure about being baptized." Franey's eyes fixed on Ruth.

"I told him he should not be baptized for me." Ruth slipped off her shoes. She felt the ground soften under her toes as she edged into the garden plot. "It had to be the decision of his own heart."

"But he thought you were going to be baptized. We all did. You took the instruction. You met with the bishop. I made you a new dress for the day. The church voted to receive you as a member—and Elijah, too. It was all set. Elijah loved you enough to put his doubts aside."

"I never asked him to do that." Ruth heard the breaking in her own voice.

"You didn't try to stop him," Franey said. "You knew what he was going to do, and you let him do it even as you planned your own escape."

"It was not an escape, *Mamm*." Ruth took several steps toward her mother down a loam-layered row. She had not felt the give of earth beneath bare feet for a year and a half.

"It certainly looked that way. You knelt with the baptismal candidates when we bowed for prayer so the bishop could ask God's blessing on all of you. And when we opened our eyes, you were gone."

A sob rattled up through Ruth, forcing its way through her throat with a gasp.

"When they saw you were gone, no one would disturb the solemn occasion for the other candidates." Franey barely opened her mouth to speak now. "Certainly not Elijah. He was the first. The bishop came to him and poured the water on his head. Elijah made his promises, but you were gone. He sacrificed everything for you, and you spit on his sacrifice!"

"It was not that way."

"Wasn't it?"

"Elijah knew I had doubts. He knew I believed the Bible and trusted God, but he also knew I wanted to be a nurse. I couldn't choose!"

"But you did choose." Franey threw her shovel down and pointed at Ruth. "Afterwards, when we should have been rejoicing in your baptism and celebrating that you joined the church, we were tearing up the farm looking for you. Your father and I had no words for anyone. I'll never forget the way Mrs. Capp stared at me. What could I say? I could barely congratulate Elijah. He looked for you, too, you know."

Ruth swallowed hard. "No, I didn't know. I'm sorry I put you all through that. I should have just told you what I was doing. I corresponded with the university for months about how I could meet their requirements without a high school diploma. I didn't run on a moment's whim."

"I know it was no whim, because you arranged a ride with that *English* man who takes people to Pueblo."

"I knew I could get a bus in Pueblo."

"You were hiding in that shed. You had a suitcase. He knew exactly where to pick you up. The only thing you didn't plan was for your *mudder* to find you first."

Ruth felt a hand on her shoulder. She leaned back against the solid form of her brother. She knew then she could finish this conversation. Annie was beside her when the rain started in earnest.

"I didn't know until the last minute that I would really go." Tears flowed with rain down Ruth's face. "I didn't know what to say to you or Elijah or anyone."

"So you said nothing." Franey's voice barely rose above the patter from the sky.

"I would choose differently now," Ruth said. "I would tell you. I want to tell you now."

"Others have left, you know. You were not baptized. People would have understood. You would not have been shunned."

Rufus squeezed Ruth's shoulders, and Annie slipped a hand into Ruth's.

"*Mamm*," Rufus said, "I think Ruth is saying she's sorry."

"I want you to forgive me," Ruth pleaded, "for the way I left."

"Are you repenting?" Franey's question had an edge to it.

"I was thinking of myself, and that was wrong. I do repent of my selfishness."

"But not for leaving."

"Leaving was the right choice for me. I truly believe God wants me to be a trained nurse. I want to obey God's will."

"God's will." Franey gripped her basket with both hands now. "It's hard to argue when someone claims to know God's will in the matter."

The rain cast a shiver through Ruth. She squeezed Annie's hand.

"*Mamm,*" Rufus said, "It's raining. Let's go inside and talk."

Lightning cracked the sky just as they reached the shelter of the porch, but they were drenched already. Inside, Franey said nothing to anyone. She handed them towels, disappeared for a few minutes, then sent everyone upstairs for dry clothing.

Annie opened Ruth's bedroom door and stared at two simple dresses lying across the Tumbling Blocks quilt, one blue and one purple.

With a nervous smile, she turned to Ruth, who was right behind her. "Your mother did this."

Ruth let her breath out hard. "I'm not sure what she means."

"I've had that purple dress on before, you know." Annie picked up the dress.

"It looks like you're going to wear it again," Ruth said. "You won't find any dry jeans hiding around here."

"You can help me do it right this time." Annie held the dress against herself. "How about you? Will it feel strange to wear one of your old dresses?"

Ruth picked up the blue dress and held it in front of her at arm's length. "It's just until we can get our clothes dry. Perhaps it will reassure *Mamm* that I have not turned my heart away from God."

"And this one will tell Rufus I can make changes that take me closer to God."

Forty-Four

September 1757

Elizabeth wrapped both hands around her cup of steaming coffee and shared a corner of the table with Lisbet. Jakob and David were out milking cows. She had called once already for the others to come down to breakfast, but she relished the thought of a few moments alone with Lisbet, so she was not disappointed at their sluggish response.

"Tell me everything." Elizabeth leaned forward on her elbows. "It was the middle of the night when you and Jacobli got home."

"I've been going to apple *schnitzing* bees at the Hochstetlers' for years," Lisbet said, "but this was the most fun."

"Was Quick Jake Kauffmann there?"

Lisbet nodded, her eyes glowing. "Can I tell you a secret?"

Elizabeth smiled and set her coffee down.

"We're going to announce our engagement as soon as the harvest is in." Lisbet reached across the table and gripped Elizabeth's hand. "I really want you to be at my wedding in November. I can't get married without you, and I want to have my wedding in my own home."

Elizabeth unsuccessfully tried to swallow the knot in her throat. "I'll try, Lisbetli. I'll talk to *Daed*." Jakob did business with the neighbors and gave assistance when he could. But he had not been to a church event in all the years of their marriage, not even the weddings of his own children.

"I want *all* of my family there," Lisbet emphasized. "I wish. . ."

"You're thinking of Maria, aren't you?"

Lisbet nodded, tears springing to her eyes. "She should have been next, after Christian. Now we don't even know where she is."

"I'm sure she thinks of you often."

"If she didn't want to be baptized, she didn't have to. . ." Lisbet set her mug down hard. "Why did she think she had to run off like that?"

Elizabeth shook her head. She had no answer.

Lisbet swallowed her sorrow and forced a smile. "And Jacobli had better behave himself at my wedding."

Elizabeth rolled her eyes. "What did he do last night?"

"He was supposed to be peeling apples, but he gave Mrs. Hochstetler conniption fits by cutting faces into the apples and giving them names. Once they had names and faces, no one wanted to cut them up or crush them for cider."

"That sounds like my Jacobli."

"Then the Hochstetler boys started doing it. Mrs. Hochstetler took away their knives and sent them all outside."

Elizabeth gestured to the generous basket of apples and peaches gracing her table. "Are there any faces in this bunch you brought home?"

Lisbet laughed. "Mrs. Hochstetler threw the faces in the cider press herself before they could turn brown."

"How many bushels did you put out for drying?"

Lisbet shrugged. "I lost count. They just kept coming, so we kept peeling and paring. Their peaches are ripe, too, so that will be the next harvest. Jacobli is already scheming about what he can do with peaches."

Elizabeth tried to picture her eldest son frolicking with the Amish young adults. He was eighteen and attended their church services frequently, though not regularly. John had been a few times also but seemed less interested. Or perhaps the difference was that Jacobli could get along with just about anyone and John was more particular. So far, to Elizabeth's relief, Jacobli had said nothing about being baptized and joining the Amish church—though Christian and Lizzie raised the question frequently. He simply seemed to enjoy friendship with the neighbors. Jacobli's recent habit of wearing Amish clothing unsettled her, however. He hardly took off his straw hat anymore, as if he were trying on a choice.

Lisbet giggled again. "Mrs. Hochstetler kept making jokes about how many *schnitz* pies she would have to eat over the winter to keep her weight up."

"She's fatter than any woman in the valley!" Elizabeth said.

"Because she makes the best *schnitzboi* in the valley, too."

"The next time you see her, thank her for the basket she sent home with you. We'll have a feast for breakfast today." Elizabeth stood up and headed for the stairs. "I'd better get those sleepy heads up once and for all."

She stood at the base of the stairs and called her children's names one by one.

A deep, hoarse voice joined her with more urgency. "Jacobli! John! Joseph! Come down immediately."

"Jakob, what's wrong?" Elizabeth spun to face her husband who was standing in the door. David was right behind him.

"Where are the boys? Jacob! John! Now! David, bolt the door." The bolt thudded into place almost immediately.

"Jakob!" Elizabeth said again. She could count on one hand the number of times she had heard her husband raise his voice in the last nineteen years.

The weight of boys in men's bodies tested the stairs as Jacob, John, and Joseph thundered down in a gangly knot of arms and legs.

"Make sure you bring Sarah," Jakob boomed, and the girl

appeared at the top of the stairs.

Jakob was at the mantel now, pulling rifles off racks and stuffing them with gunpowder. He slapped one Brown Bess musket into Jacobli's hand and the next one into John's.

"Jakob!" Elizabeth put a hand on his arm. "I must insist you tell me what is going on. Why has it become so urgent to go hunting before breakfast?"

"We're not going hunting," Jakob said, putting a gun into Joseph's hands.

"But—"

"They shot John Miller in the hand," Jakob said rapidly, "while he was swinging an ax like he does every morning. Like we all do every day. Just chopping wood."

"Who would want to hurt John Miller?"

"We've lived in this valley for twenty years, most of them peaceful," Jakob said. "The Indians never bothered us until this ridiculous war between the French and the British. First the British build a fort in Northkill, and now the French have the Lenni Lenape shooting at us."

"But surely, Jakob—"

"Lisbet," Jakob snapped, "what time did you and Jacob leave the Hochstetlers' last night?"

"Late. After midnight. Once we finished with the apples, most of us stayed around talking or singing."

"*Daed*," Jacobli said, "what does that have to do with why you are handing out guns?"

"Or John Miller's hand?" Elizabeth added.

"The Indians took advantage of the moonless night." Jakob stood a rifle on its heel, gripped the steel shaft with both hands, and looked around the room. "You're all old enough to hear this. They attacked the Hochstetlers. I suspect it was not long after everyone left. By God's grace, you were gone already. The Indians set fire to the house. By the time neighbors saw the flames and got over there, it was too late to save anything—or anybody. The

Hochstetlers crawled out through a cellar window, but nobody could get close enough to help, not even when Mrs. Hochstetler was stuck in the window."

Elizabeth and Lisbet exchanged glances, regretting the banter about Mrs. Hochstetler's size.

"The Indians found them trying to hide. Mrs. Hochstetler was stabbed to death and scalped. One boy and the girl were tomahawked. Hochstetler and the other boys are missing. The neighbors saw the Indians ride off with them—after they torched every building on the land. Even their married son had to watch from across the field and could do nothing."

Elizabeth sank into the nearest chair. Sarah threw herself into her mother's arms. "What are you planning to do, Jakob?"

"I plan to assure myself that my children and grandchildren are safe. I'll ride all day if I have to. Jacobli and John, you're coming with me. Joseph and David, you're staying here. I know you're all good shots."

"Jakob, what are you saying?" Elizabeth could not believe her ears.

"We've never shot at anything we did not intend to eat," Joseph said.

"They are still boys." Elizabeth's pitch rose. "You cannot ask them to do this."

Jakob laid his hands on Joseph's shoulders and looked him square in the eye. "You're fifteen. We've raised you to follow your conscience. I hope you don't have to do anything at all, but if you do, I know it will be right." He turned to David, a year younger. "That goes for you, too."

Elizabeth rose. "I've heard rumors that Mrs. Hochstetler was not always kind to the Indians who came to her looking for food. Perhaps they chose her in particular. Perhaps the danger is past."

"I want to know my children are safe," Jakob said. "Christian and the girls' husbands—they would do what I suspect Hochstetler did. That man had guns in his house, and he knew how to use them. Why is his family slaughtered as if they did not have the means to defend themselves?" Jakob picked up his own rifle and stuffed his pockets with gunpowder packets and lead. "Bolt the door and stay away from the windows. If there's any danger, go out through the tunnel from the cellar. And take the guns."

Jakob and two of his sons rode their horses hard. He allowed himself a moment of relief when Christian's house came into view and appeared unharmed but pressed on to see for himself that Christian, Lizzie, and their three small children were alive.

He swung off his horse just as Christian swung open the door to his home.

"I see you've heard the news." Christian's eyes went to his father's gun. "You don't seriously think that using a rifle is going to solve anything."

"Is your family safe?" Jakob asked.

"We are unharmed, if that is what you mean."

Lizzie appeared behind her husband, baby Magdalena in her arms and Christli and Veronica clutching her skirts. The sight of his grandchildren slowed Jakob's heart rate.

"What if it had been your farm, Christian?" Jacobli asked.

"But it was not," Christian retorted.

"What if it were?"

"Our lives are in God's hands," Christian answered.

"I imagine that is what Hochstetler said to his screaming wife and children," Jakob said.

"They would not have been screaming," Christian answered calmly. "They knew they were in God's hands as well."

"I'm not certain this is God's way."

"*Daed*, in all these years, I have never heard you sound so *English*," Christian said. "In your heart, you are Amish. You cannot possibly be thinking of doing this."

"Don't tell me what is in my heart, Christian."

"If you shoot a man, will you have it in your heart to repent and ask forgiveness?"

Jakob ignored the question. "Please tell me you have prepared a place to hide. In the thicket perhaps, a dense place well away from the house where you could keep the children quiet."

Christian nodded. "Lizzie and I have talked about this, especially if something happens when I am away. We would never raise arms against another human being, but of course we would do all we could to avoid harm to ourselves."

Jacobli shifted in his saddle. "That's not true, Christian. You would not do all you could. Would you rather see your children toma—"

"Jacobli!" Jakob spoke sharply then lowered his voice. "Do you not see the children standing right there?"

Christian murmured to Lizzie. She took the children and withdrew into the house. Christian closed the door and strode over to the horses.

"You have been to our worship services," Christian said to Jacobli. "You have many friends among our people. You know our ways. I hoped that perhaps you would be ready soon to join the church yourself."

Jacobli shook his head. "I've hunted with the Hochstetler boys. Their rifles were right next to the door when I was in their home a few hours ago. Only their father would have forbidden them to defend themselves. If I had a wife and children, if I were in the place Mr. Hochstetler was in, I believe I would make a different choice."

"Your conscience would be forever smeared," Christian said.

"Perhaps," Jacobli said, "but my children would be alive."

"When everything is calm again, you will reconsider."

Jacobli reached for his straw hat. "I don't believe so. May God give you grace, Christian, but I am no Amishman." He tossed his hat on the ground. "*Daed*, we must find out if the Yoders are safe."

Forty-Five

Ruth removed the plain glass chimney of Annie's new lamp, turned the wick up slightly, and struck a match. The wick caught, and she replaced the glass.

"It's that easy," she said.

Annie nodded. "I guess even a techno-addict like me can learn to do that."

"This knob," Ruth said, demonstrating, "controls the flame size."

"Got it."

"It's a pretty lamp. You've found some real treasures in Mrs. Weichert's store."

"Her store seems perfect for a hundred-year-old house. I find myself wondering what the house was like when it was built. Maybe electricity had not even come this far out from the main cities. Maybe I'm not the first owner to light a kerosene lamp in this room."

"Maybe not."

Annie had added a cozy deep red armchair and a couple of end tables to the living room. The dining table shone with Ruth's labor of the last hour. Upstairs a new bed suited the proportions of Annie's bedroom. In the second bedroom, Annie had a small desk and a bookcase, but the main feature was a chair that folded out to a guest bed.

Ruth settled into the armchair. "I suppose soon you won't have reason to run back and forth so much. I want to be sure to thank you now for helping me reconnect with my family."

"It was my privilege." Annie toyed with the kerosene flame. "You'll be back, somehow. Remember, you promised to show me what to do with my floors."

"It's hard work to do yourself."

"Hey, I'm all about hard work."

Ruth saw the hesitation in Annie's face. "It's all right to talk about it, you know."

"Talk about what?"

"*Mamm* and me. We talked for a long time. I'm not sure she will ever accept that I am not going to be baptized into the Amish church, but she has managed to get past her hurt at how I left. I am grateful to you for that."

"And Rufus?" Annie asked.

Ruth tilted her head and twisted her lips. "I'm never quite sure what you're asking about Rufus."

"Is he well?"

"You know he is."

"And happy?"

"He's happy when you're around."

"That's nonsense." Annie fluffed a pillow on the sofa. "I have nothing to do with your brother's happiness."

Ruth shifted out of her chair and put a hand on Annie's arm. "You've been avoiding him. It's all right to talk to him."

Annie wriggled free of Ruth's grip to straighten papers on the coffee table. "There's nothing to say."

"I don't believe that."

Now Annie looked at Ruth. "It's impossible. He's Amish to the core. And I'm. . .well, not."

"But you're living more simply now."

"You know that's not the same as being Amish. Baptized Amish is what matters. Rufus says there's no such thing as accidentally Amish."

"Maybe you should think about it," Ruth said. "Not for Rufus. I don't mean that. But for yourself."

"Wow. Coming from someone who. . ."

"Ran out on her baptism," Ruth supplied. "You can say it. We both know I did it."

"Well yes," Annie said. "It seems ironic that you would suggest I think about becoming Amish."

"It wasn't right for me. It might be right for you."

"I have to take one step at a time," Annie said. "I have so much to learn. Being around Rufus confuses me."

"He's a good, good man."

Annie put her knees up under her chin and wrapped her arms around them. "Ruth, why has Rufus never married? He's quite old, isn't he?"

"I suppose so, in the Amish way."

"Has he had his heart broken?"

Ruth shook her head. "I don't think he's ever let it open far enough to break. Not until you."

Annie's feet thudded to the floor. "Now you're being ridiculous."

"Why not find out? Hire Rufus to build some cabinets for you."

"I plan to."

"After he finishes the cabinets, ask him to build you a table for a propane lamp. It hides the canister underneath. The kerosene lamp suits your house, but no one really uses them anymore."

"I'll keep that in mind."

"Then Rufus can help you with the soft spot in the kitchen floor."

"You're full of ideas." Annie tossed a pillow at Ruth. "Don't you have homework to do?"

"I suppose so." Ruth caught the pillow and rolled her eyes. "What time are we going back to town?"

"Why? Do you need some computer time?"

"It would help."

"Use mine. I think it might need charging, though." Annie moved into the dining room, picked up her laptop from the table, and pulled the cord out of her denim bag. "Whenever this place was wired, it was not for the Internet age. I only have two outlets in the living room."

"Maybe you can add more."

Annie reached behind the sofa and plugged in the laptop's cord. "I have a feeling that would lead to having the whole place rewired. I'm leaning in the other direction."

"What do you mean?"

"Other sources of energy."

"That sounds very Amish-like." Ruth still held the throw pillow to her chest, which warmed with an image of Annie and Rufus in this room together.

"I called a local company," Annie said. "They're sending someone out to have a look around and make some suggestions. After that we can head back to the Springs."

"That sounds fine."

Annie put the computer in Ruth's lap. "I'd like you to have this."

"Thanks for letting me use it." Ruth set the pillow aside and adjusted the computer on her lap. She would have to get used to how it felt, but the convenience of it sparked something in her.

"No, I mean *have* it." Annie lowered herself to the floor next to Ruth's knees. "I've been looking for the right time to give it to you."

Ruth's eyes widened. "You really are getting serious about changing."

Annie nodded, her fingers twisting in the gold chain in absentminded habit.

"But your computer! That's like giving me your arm."

"Not anymore," Annie said. "I've cleared all my old business files off. It's a good computer and not very old. You should get good use out of it until you finish school."

"I'm already grateful to you for so much, and now this!" Ruth's hand moved over the sleek casing.

"You made a hard choice that came at a cost," Annie said. "You should at least have the tools to do what you set out to do."

Ruth raised the lid of the laptop, her hand trembling with the thought that it was hers.

Annie pointed to a file icon against the blue background of the screen. "I did save some of the genealogy information. I thought you might be interested."

Ruth clicked open the file and scanned the documents Annie had gathered. "Do you still think about Jakob and Elizabeth? And the choices they made?"

"All the time! I imagine what their life must have been like. I'm used to everything being comfortable and convenient. They challenge me to learn that right choices come at a cost. You help me see that, too, you know."

"Me? All I did was hurt people I love."

"You followed God's call. And you're working on fixing the relationships. You remind me that perhaps I can avoid that mistake if I choose well."

A knock on the front door diverted the moment. Annie scrambled to her feet to pull the door open.

"Hello," a young Amish man said. "I'm answering your inquiry for an estimate on some gas lines and a generator."

"Yes, come in," Annie said. "This is my friend Ruth."

Ruth was on her feet, the color gone from her face.

"Hello, Ruth," the man said quietly.

"Hello, Elijah."

Forty-Six

June 1765

Elizabeth held her first flesh-and-blood grandson in her arms. Jacobli's *boppli*. They called him Jacob Franklin Byler. Chubby cheeks defined the shape of his face, fresh and red and squalling. She stroked the downy softness of his head. It had been a long time since she held a child only a day after birth. David, the last baby born in this house, was twenty-two.

"I think his hair will be dark red," she said to Jacobli, "the way yours was before it turned brown." One of the baby's eyes opened to a murky slit. An arm flailed loose from the swaddling. "How is Katie?"

"Resting." Jacobli closed the tiny fist in his own hand. "It was awful to see her in so much pain. The thought of losing her—"

Tears welled in Elizabeth's eyes, but she refused to release them. Instead, she focused on adjusting the baby's bundling.

"You're thinking of Lisbet, aren't you?" Jacobli asked.

Wordless, Elizabeth nodded.

"So am I," her son said quietly.

Somehow three years had crawled by since the day Lisbet labored. After four years of childless marriage, she was bursting with joy in the life she carried within her. The child slid easily into waiting arms, but the bleeding was too rapid, and Lisbet died without ever holding her baby. Quick Jake insisted on calling the baby Veronica, after the mother Lisbet did not remember. He did not let Elizabeth see the girl often. Before her second birthday, Veronica caught croup and stopped breathing.

Elizabeth's being fractured that day.

Now Lisbet and her child lay in the earth beside Verona, and Elizabeth's own mother-heart was a constant seeping wound. Perhaps this child, a grandson who was truly hers, would stem the flow and lead her to the future once more.

"I'm so glad to have you and Katie here," Elizabeth said. And she meant it. Jacobli was a grown man, married. He could have gone anywhere.

"We wouldn't think of leaving you."

The tannery, which had been a second source of income for Jakob, was Jacobli's territory now. Over the years, he had expanded the lime vats and bark pits and learned to craft the raw leather into an array of useful items. Residents of the Northkill and Irish Creek settlements knew Jacob Byler's leather was unmatched even in Philadelphia. They were eager to sell him their hides then buy them back in the forms of saddles and reins and satchels and shoe leather and overcoats.

Jakob shuffled in from the kitchen. Every day, Elizabeth thought, he moved a little more slowly. She could hardly blame him. At sixty, she was slowing down herself, and he was seventy-eight. Only recently had he left the work of the farm to Joseph and David. He still presided, white haired, over the midday meal with detailed questions about the farm's operations and was always ready with advice, but he left the physical work to his sons.

"Can an old man hold his grandson?" Jakob asked.

Jakob settled in next to Elizabeth, and she gently laid the child in arms long accustomed to holding the bundled shape of a baby. Pleasure crinkled his weathered face, and Elizabeth felt herself go soft at the center, just as she had all those years ago when Lisbetli clung to her father's neck and he patiently waited for her to be ready to let go. Now it was Elizabeth's turn to cling. Aware that she was fortunate to have her husband still with her at his age, she did not want to think of letting go. She leaned into him, laying one hand at the center of his back and scratching in that place he liked so well.

"Christian and Lizzie are coming soon," Jakob said. "I suppose the others will be along before much time passes, too."

By suppertime, Elizabeth was exhausted. Her joints did not move as nimbly as they used to. None of Jakob's Amish children ever stayed long when they visited On this occasion, Anna was the first to come, and before she had been gone half an hour, Barbara arrived to inspect the new baby. Elizabeth welcomed them with platters of food and cool water drawn only that morning from the creek. John stayed a good part of the afternoon. Joseph and David peeked in between chores and availed themselves of the food. Sarah was the only one absent. She had planned months ago to come from Philadelphia when the baby was a month or so old. Katie remained secluded in her bedroom, only appearing at intervals to wonder what had become of her baby during these visits.

As it turned out, Christian was the last to come, and to Elizabeth's surprise, he came alone. Jakob was resting on their bed while Christian and Jacobli stood at the wide window gazing out on the farm as Elizabeth came and went from the kitchen, tidying up after the wave of visits.

"I am thinking of moving to Conestoga, or perhaps Lancaster," Christian said, staring out as he spoke. "My land is worth a good deal more than I paid for it, and I can easily get new land down there."

"But you've done so much work on your land," Jacobli said.

"That's why it is worth so much."

"You'll start over, then?"

Christian nodded. "It won't be as hard the second time. I'll have some capital to begin with. Still, it would be easier with help. You and Katie could come with us."

Jacobli laughed softly. "You never give up, do you, Christian?"

Elizabeth stacked plates left from the afternoon round of pie and carried them into the kitchen.

"It's good land," Christian said, "richer soil."

"I'm a tanner, Christian, not a farmer. What you mean is it's Amish land," Jacobli said. "I've seen the number of families that moved out after the French-Indian War and what happened at the Hochstetlers. Conestoga is farther from the frontier. Farther from the Indians. Further from the question of bearing arms on your own land."

"That has nothing to do with it." Christian put his hands on his waist, the stance he always assumed when he was about to be intractable. "If you saw the offers I have received on my land, you would understand why it is in my family's best interest to consider them seriously."

"You can't run away." Jacobli turned from the window to look his brother in the eye. "War is coming. The Stamp Act. The sugar tax. This nonsense about quartering British soldiers in private homes. Those things will still be true in Conestoga."

"I am not running away from anything." Now Christian crossed his arms on his chest.

"Does it not try your patience at all to think that the Crown expects the Colonies to absorb the debt of England's war with France?"

"The Amish have nothing to do with any war."

"War will follow you," Jacobli said. "And there *will* be another war."

"You cannot be certain of that."

Jacobli laughed aloud. "Perhaps living apart has insulated you too much. No one from the Colonies seems to be able to reason with Parliament. Even Benjamin Franklin got nowhere. The burden of taxes is growing too fast."

"We pay the same taxes anyone pays when we buy goods or file documents," Christian said. "We have no quarrel with that."

Elizabeth leaned against the door frame between the kitchen and main room, listening and wanting to believe Jacobli was wrong about a coming war.

"The time will come when the question will be far more complex," Jacobli said. "Sam Adams has organized the Sons of Liberty in Boston, and other cities are following suit. What if the Colonies go to war against Britain? What will you do then?"

Christian sighed heavily. "Do you ask these questions specifically to exasperate me?"

"Everyone in the Colonies must ask these questions. Do any of us know what we will do in the event of war?"

"The Amish will not fight. You know that. Our only concern is our own community."

"When the time comes, it won't be that simple," Jacobli said.

Christian uncrossed his arms and put one hand out to lean against the window frame. "So you have no interest in moving? Having your own land?"

"The tannery is a thriving business," Jacobli said. "And I won't go anywhere as long as *Mamm* and *Daed* are here."

Elizabeth caught Jacobli's eye and smiled. Her other sons were less predictable. Jacobli was the steady one.

"Conestoga is not as far as all that," Christian said.

Jacobli shook his head. "I am not Amish, Christian. You're my brother, and I love you, but we've made different choices." He raised his eyes again to the rolling land outside the window. "Katie likes the idea of something entirely new. Someday I might like to see North Carolina. I hear a man can build a good life for his family there."

Forty-Seven

February 1771

"He is gone." Elizabeth emerged from the bedroom, from the reek of death that had taken so long to come, and told Jakob's gathered children.

Earlier she had shooed them all from the room, wanting only to be alone with him, to feel the thickness of his hair grown long in the cold months, to put her hand in his and hold their intimacy between them, to press her lips on his. And she had not wanted spectators for any of that, especially not the whispering kind.

They all came, except Maria, who had never returned, and Lisbet, who awaited her father in the burial plot.

They came and they brought their children. Barbara and Anna even had grandchildren. They rotated in and out of the bedroom saying their good-byes. The number became too great for Elizabeth, and when it seemed to her that some were returning for a third good-bye, she banished them all to the outer room. The end was breaths away. In the final moments, she heard their murmuring hum from the corners of the house and ignored it, listening only for the air going in and out of Jakob's lungs. Elizabeth held his hand.

And then the ragged rhythm stilled and the hum became thunderous.

When she could no longer resist the creeping weight of his lifeless hand, their clasp fell off the side of the bed. She laid her head on his chest and listened to the emptiness.

Jakob was gone.

Only when Elizabeth was sure she could speak did she gather her skirts and walk into the main room. She spoke three simple words. Then without even a shawl around her shoulders, she walked straight through the house, out the front door, and into the February wind. Snow gave way beneath shoes made from her son's leather, while voices on the porch called to her to come out of the cold. She paced from the house to the barn, then to the smokehouse, then through the garden, brown and crunchy. "Maria's beet patch," the square of land at the far end of the garden, had long ago grown over but never lost its moniker.

Shivering and out of breath at last, she leaned against the stable, breathing in the hay that fed and warmed the horses. She and Jakob had built this together. It would never be the same. He was gone.

They assembled the next month for the onerous reading of the will, which Jakob had written just weeks after Jacobli's first son was born. Perhaps with Jacob Franklin's birth, his mind had moved to the next generation. Elizabeth imagined the conversations between father and son about looking after her. Christian had become surprisingly wealthy buying and selling land, which seemed to increase in value every month. It should have been no trouble for him to provide for her. But ultimately, Christian was not her son. She was not Amish, so Christian and Lizzie would never take her into their home. Not that she wanted to go there. She did not. Nor to Barbara or Anna or even her own John. Jacobli was the eldest of the children Jakob and Elizabeth shared, and it was his concern to do what he knew his father wanted.

A widow's seat, the will said. She would have the house and the stable and the garden. To continue an income, she would have the three cherry trees near the house and a meadow behind the barn, which the next owner—Jacobli—was obliged to plow for her.

Two rows of trees in the orchard.

Ten bushels of wheat and five bushels of rye each year.

The right to keep a cow and a hog in the field.

Jacobli was the only child mentioned with a particular grant in the will. All the children received a few pounds, but Jacobli was permitted to clear ten acres around the tanyard and build a house of his own. Katie would like that, Elizabeth knew.

Jakob had thought this through. He so clearly expected the land to be sold to settle his estate. But he also expected that Jacobli would be the buyer. Elizabeth would be comfortably cared for in the years without Jakob.

If she married again, she would lose it all.

Marry again?

No, she was not tempted, and Jakob had made sure she would not need to. Even if she were twenty years younger than her sixty-six years, she could not imagine another life with another man. She would see out her days in her widow's seat, surrounded by land she no longer owned but upon which they had built their life together.

He was gone.

Forty-Eight

Two weeks later, Elijah Capp turned the wrench on the last bolt behind the refrigerator. "That does it. This house would pass *Ordnung*."

"I'm glad to hear that," Ruth Beiler said. "I'll probably still have to teach Annie how everything works."

"I used propane and bottled gas whenever I could," Elijah said. "Seemed like the simplest thing."

"Thank you. I know Annie is so pleased." Ruth was determined to smile at him, despite the knot in her stomach that came with being in his presence. His familiar shrug. The way he was hinged at the shoulders and elbows and knees. The faint smell of oil perpetually sunken into his pores. The arms that had held her when no one was looking.

"We'll get through this, Ruth." Elijah turned to pick up his toolbox.

"I know it's been awkward," she said. "I wasn't expecting to see you when you first came to the house any more than you were expecting to see me."

"I'm glad Amos sent me out on that call," Elijah said. "I knew you were back in the valley sometimes, but I didn't know how to approach you."

"I can never tell you enough how sorry I am." Ruth found the nerve to look him in the eye. "We should have both said we wanted to wait another year for baptism. We might have figured out our doubts."

"I'm not giving up," Elijah said.

"On us?"

"That's right."

"But I'm not baptized into the church, Elijah, and I'm not going to be."

"I know."

The weight of contradiction hung between them. Ruth remembered what it felt like to have Elijah at her side—the security, the certainty of love. She shrugged off the sensation. "I won't be the reason you leave the church."

"You won't be."

"No Elijah, don't talk like this."

"You're the only one who ever understood me, Ruth. We can go back to that."

She shook her head. "No."

"Yes."

"I'm going back to school," Ruth insisted.

"I know. You should."

Ruth swallowed. "You were the only one who understood me, too."

"Then don't say no. We'll keep talking."

She looked at him a long time before she nodded.

They both jumped at the knock at the front door. Ruth moved swiftly to answer it, expecting to see the face of her brother. She was not disappointed.

Rufus smiled with half his mouth. "What are you up to, Ruth?"

"I thought you might like a tour." She pushed open the screen door and pulled him into the room. "This is the living room. Tell me what you see."

Ruth glanced through the house to the kitchen. The back screen door closed. Elijah was gone.

Annie saw Dolly and the buggy in the street and retreated into the dimness of the garage. She smiled to herself as she pictured what was happening in the house while she waited in the narrow, listing structure. Ruth would make Rufus look at every room—the living room, the dining room, the kitchen, then up the narrow stairs to the bedrooms and bathroom. The basement would be last. Rufus would look behind and under everything. What he saw would tell him more than any words she could muster.

Elijah Capp had been busy during the last two weeks. After walking through the house with him and hearing his observations about what changes were needed, Annie gave him a key and left the adaptations in his hands while she returned to Colorado Springs for final preparations.

Now Annie did not plan to return to her condo. Following her real estate agent's advice, she left enough furnishings for a potential buyer to imagine the place as a home. When the unit sold, the agent would sell or give away the furnishings. As a concession to her mother, Annie agreed to store the Prius at her parents' house rather than sell it at this point in time.

Curious, Jamie drove Annie and Ruth down, saw the house, poked around town, and continued on to weekend plans at the nearby Great Sand Dunes. On Sunday evening, she would return to ferry Ruth back to school. Sadness trickled through Annie in the shadows of her garage. She had not written a personal letter in years, but she expected to discover the virtues of the postal system very soon. She would miss Ruth too much not to write. Annie would keep a cell phone but planned to use it as minimally as possible. A second concession to her mother was a weekly phone conversation, but otherwise Annie would follow Amish practices about using phones only for business and emergencies. And at the moment, she had no business.

When Annie and Ruth saw what Elijah had done, they nearly

giggled. He was thorough, modifying everything from the heating system to the water heater to the aged major appliances. Nothing in the house ran on public electricity.

Annie smoothed her skirt for the fiftieth time and once again straightened the shoulders of the dress. Through the small window, she saw that Ruth was now leading Rufus down the three steps from the small back porch and following broken cement blocks toward the garage. Annie stood straight and got ready to smile.

Dear God, this seems crazy and right all at the same time. Be here, please.

A moment later, the garage door creaked open and a square of daylight framed Ruth and Rufus. Annie stepped forward.

"Annalise, what have you done?" Rufus said.

For a flash, she thought he was angry. Then she saw the smile twitching in his jaw.

"You're wearing the dress," he said.

Annie caught Ruth's eye as Ruth stepped out of the garage. "Ruth says I can keep it. It's the only one I have." She pulled up handfuls of purple cotton skirt. "But I'm going to find someone to teach me how to sew, and I'll make more."

Rufus laughed more heartily than Annie had ever heard him do.

"You don't think I can learn to sew?"

He grinned and wagged his head. "I believe you can do anything you decide you're going to do. I suppose you're going to learn to cook, too."

"Yes I am," she said. "And next spring I'll plant a garden."

"Where is your car?" he asked.

"In storage."

"How will you get around?"

She turned around and pulled a bicycle away from the wall, another thrift-store find.

Rufus stepped over to the bike and took it by the handlebars. "It looks like a sturdy bike. Simple, practical. Useful baskets. Good tires."

"Of course. Did you think I would buy something fancy? Simplicity. Thrift. Humility. When I can't bike, I'll arrange an Amish taxi, just like you do." Out of long habit, Annie's fingers went to her neck, where she found only the simple curve of the dress.

Rufus's eyes followed her fingers. "Where is your chain?"

"I gave it away. It was a trophy of my old life. I don't need it anymore."

"Annalise," he said, his voice low, "I'm not sure what you want me to say."

"Say what you want to say." Annie put a hand on top of his on the handlebars.

"You must know I'm fond of you."

"You've never said so."

He paused. "I'm saying so now. But. . ."

"But there's no such thing as accidentally Amish." Annie finished his sentence. "I'm not playing dress up, Rufus. I don't know where this journey will lead me, but I know I have to take it."

"You really want to live as we do?"

"I want the faith I see in you. I want to understand what you value, how you make choices that bring meaning to your life."

"When I see you in that dress, I'm inclined to believe you." He leaned toward her slightly.

"Maybe you knew something that morning after I stole away in Tom's truck, when you first brought the dress to me."

He laid a tremulous hand against her cheek. "I knew you were beautiful sleeping in the hay. I knew I admired your spirit, even if you didn't know what you stumbled into. I knew I thought about you all night."

"Rufus." Annie wrapped her fingers around the hand at her cheek. "Let's figure out what this is."

"You are still *English*," he murmured.

She took a deep breath and let it out slowly. "I know."

"In the *English* world, this is where the kiss comes, *ya*?"

"*Ya.*"

"In the Amish world, too."

She stood expectant yet hardly daring to hope.

"Perhaps being certain is not necessary at every moment," Rufus said.

He bent to meet her, and she tasted his first sweet, lingering, freely given kiss.

Author's Note

This particular project brings me joy, because through it I have been able to explore my own family history. I am a descendant of Jakob Beyeler through the first son of his marriage to Elizabeth Kallen. The research process yielded certain historical hooks on which to hang a story, such as the passenger manifest of the *Charming Nancy*, the oath Jakob had to take in order to step onto a new continent, the property description of black oak that defined Jakob's property, the slaughter of the nearby Hochstetler family, Jakob's will describing his wishes for his surviving wife with particular detail. From there I imagined much of the story—what might have happened with my own ancestors and the choices they made that determined future generations. As I researched, I became mindful of the power of choice, and the contemporary story took form around that theme. Three hundred years after my ancestors arrived in Pennsylvania, the choices that shape our lives come in updated packaging, but they are essentially the same. We have the ability to say yes to what brings meaning and joy to our lives. May you embrace that choice on a daily basis.

olivia@olivianewport.com
www.olivianewport.com
@olivianewport on Twitter
www.facebook.com/OliviaNewport
Olivia Newport
c/o Author Relations
Barbour Publishing
1810 Barbour Drive
Uhrichsville, OH 44683

Olivia Newport's novels twist through time to find where faith and passions meet. Her husband and two twentysomething children provide welcome distraction from the people stomping through her head on their way into her books. She chases joy in stunning Colorado at the foot of the Rockies, where daylilies grow as tall as she is.